ENTHRALL ME

UNDERBELLY CHRONICLES BOOK FOUR

TAMARA HOGAN

DEDICATION

With heartfelt thanks to friends old and new.

As always, countless thanks to Mark—for holding down the fort, for herding the cats, and for the gift of time.

THE UNDERBELLY CHRONICLES

TASTE ME
CHASE ME
TOUCH ME
TEMPT ME
ENTHRALL ME
INTOXICATE ME

THE UNDERWORLD COUNCIL

Incubus:	Elliott Sebastiani *
Second:	Antonia Sebastiani
Siren:	Claudette Fontaine
Second:	Scarlett Fontaine
Were:	Krispin Woolf
Second:	Jacoby Woolf
Vampire:	Valerian
Second:	Wyland
Valkyrie:	Alka Schlessinger
Second:	Lorin Schlessinger
Humanity:	(vacant)
Emeritus:	REDACTED
Sec/Tech:	Lukas Sebastiani
Second:	Jack Kirkland

* President

CHAPTER ONE

Tia Quinn peered over Bailey Brown's shoulder, glaring at the computer screen. "Are you finding anything?"

"It's what I'm *not* finding that's interesting." Bailey's fingers jabbed at the keyboard with machine-gun bursts. "Someone's working pretty hard to cover their tracks." The desk chair creaked as she shifted her meager weight. "Have you seen anything like this before?"

"No." The comment someone had posted to *In Like Quinn*, her humble contribution to independent investigative journalism, had alarmed her so much that she'd immediately called her friend, Underworld Council member Scarlett Fontaine, for advice. Two hours later, Bailey Brown, one of the world's foremost cyber-security experts, had knocked on her front door. "I'm not imagining things, am I?" Despite moving from Minneapolis to bucolic, sleepy Stillwater a couple of months ago, she still felt a perpetual itch between her shoulder blades.

"'Sebastiani Labs' so-called board of directors must be called to account for their illegal acts, and for abandoning the old ways,'" Bailey read aloud. "'If you don't expose them, I will.'" She tapped her finger against the screen. "The comment was posted in

ILQ's financial news section, which makes it look vaguely on-topic, but…"

Their gazes locked. Sebastiani Labs was a privately held, wildly successful technology behemoth that had its fingers in many, many pies. The company didn't trade stock, didn't seek contracts, didn't advertise its wares, and…its board of directors secretly doubled as the governing body of Earth's non-human species.

"Should we delete the comment?" she asked. Tia had strong feelings about freedom of speech and freedom of the press, but the fact that humanity had shared Earth with extra-planetary beings for thousands of years was a closely guarded secret—a secret humanity was nowhere near ready to learn.

"Deleting it might start an online shit-storm and draw even more attention," Bailey said. "This isn't your garden-variety troll harassing a woman for having an opinion on the Internet. Let's call Lukas."

Tia glanced at the clock. Scarlett was nearing the end of a perfectly normal pregnancy, but her bondmate, Lukas Sebastiani, was a wreck. Right now, they both needed all the sleep they could get. "This can wait until morning."

Bailey shook her head. "He'll be pissed if we don't call." She plucked an unusual-looking phone from the side pocket of the heavy computer bag she'd brought with her—one of the whispered-about, super-secure Sebastiani Labs prototypes?—and pressed a button. Being Bailey worked for Lukas at Sebastiani Security, and did some consulting for both Sebastiani Labs and the Underworld Council, it was probably safe to take her word for it, but…

"Hey, Lukas. I'm at Tia Quinn's place." There was a long pause while Bailey listened to Lukas's reply.

He was probably grilling Bailey about why she was at Tia's house in the first place. Lukas had serious reservations about Scarlett's friendship with an investigative journalist, someone whose very occupation required that she expose information the powerful would prefer stay hidden. But damn it, Lukas should know by now that she'd never publish anything that would put their culture's most precious secrets at risk.

"Someone posted a comment at *In Like Quinn* earlier today that feels a little off." Bailey listened again, and then read the comment aloud. "Yeah, Tia saw it and called me." Bailey neglected to mention that Scarlett had served as the middleman. "I haven't been able to track the comment back yet—I don't have the right tools with me—but once I get back to the office, I can… Oh, you're at Valerian's? You're practically down the street."

Bailey planned on driving back to Sebastiani Security yet tonight? Talk about working vampire's hours. Didn't the little human ever sleep? And speaking of not sleeping, why was Lukas Sebastiani, the Underworld Council's Security and Technology First, meeting with Valerian, the elderly Vampire First, after midnight on a weeknight?

Very interesting.

Bailey covered the mouthpiece of the phone with her hand. "Lukas wants us to meet him at Valerian's place."

She nodded her agreement, trying to hide her excitement. Valerian lived less than fifteen miles away, in an old mansion perched high upon the rocky ledges of the St. Croix River. He'd been fighting illness for nearly a year, and very little information

3

had been released about the true state of his health. She'd tried to squeeze some information out of his Second, Wyland, at Rafe Sebastiani's gallery show last winter, but the chilly, tight-assed vamp had shut her down cold.

"Let me close things down here," Bailey said to Lukas, already capturing screen shots. "We'll see you soon." The exquisite fire opal ring Rafe had given Bailey flashed in the light as she ended the call. Bailey and Rafe had just returned from an extended honeymoon. No *way* would Tia have thought that driving a tricked-out RV from Minneapolis to Alaska, then camping out for a couple of months, would have interested either of them. But then again, being newbonds, they probably hadn't left the RV very often.

"Ready?" Stuffing away the last of her equipment, Bailey zipped up her computer bag.

"Yeah. I'll follow in my car." They walked to the front door. As Tia grabbed her purse and keys, the house's ancient air conditioner gave a mighty wheeze. The thing was on its last legs—one more thing to replace in this money pit she'd bought in haste, but had come to love.

They stepped outside. "Damn, it's hot." Bailey swiped at her temple with the inside of her wrist.

Tia surreptitiously scanned her surroundings. She didn't see anyone, but...

"You okay?"

She pasted a smile on her face. "You and Rafe came home to one of the hottest Augusts on record." The sun had set hours ago, but it was still a muggy, miserable eighty degrees outside.

Bailey pointed a key fob at Rafe's Jeep. Headlights

flashed and the doors unlocked with a *ka-thunk*. "We didn't want to miss Coco's birth, and there's always so much work to do."

Bailey's tiny smile made every journalistic instinct stand at attention. "Coco?" she asked. Lukas and Scarlett had named their daughter *in utero*? What a scoop. Too bad she couldn't publish it.

"Scarlett's had massive hot chocolate cravings throughout her pregnancy, and she and Lukas started calling the baby "Cocoa Bean" as a joke." Bailey opened the Jeep's driver's door. "Once they found out the baby was a girl, the name kinda stuck."

Tia yanked the detached garage door open. "Cute." And it was something she should already have known. Too much time had passed since she'd talked to Scarlett.

"Do you know how to get to Valerian's?"

"Yeah." She'd never been inside Vamp Central, which was only fifteen miles away, but her mother's lavish descriptions made the place sound more like a museum than a private home. With her luck, she'd probably spill something on a centuries-old rug or carpet. "Go ahead." She waved Bailey on. "I'll be right behind you."

As Bailey pulled out of the driveway, Tia got into her own car. As she backed out, she absently reached to the sun visor for an automatic garage door opener that wasn't there. "Crap." Braking to a stop, she slammed the car into Park, turned it off, pulled the keys from the ignition, got out of the car, and managed to close and lock the garage door before the Civic's automatic headlights dimmed. The automatic garage door opener and motion lights she'd bought at Home Depot last week were still in her trunk.

Though perfectly capable of installing them herself, she'd probably end up hiring the job out.

Her new neighbors already thought she was odd for mowing her lawn after the sun went down.

She had human neighbors. A lawn to mow. Appliances to replace, a house to maintain…activities she'd never envisioned mere months ago, before… "Shit," she whispered, scoping out the surroundings yet again. Sparing a final, wistful thought to the anonymous, maintenance-free condo she'd been forced to leave, she backed out of the driveway and followed Bailey's tail lights.

✸

"Wyland, please. I'm fine." With a final, skeleton-rattling cough, Valerian waved him away. "Sit down. Enjoy your wine."

Wyland glanced at Lukas, who'd risen from the oversized chair by the fireplace when Valerian's violent coughing jag started. Lukas looked as concerned as he felt.

"Both of you. Sit." Valerian twitched his mohair wrap closer to his neck. "I survived The Black Death. A nagging respiratory ailment won't finish me off."

Wyland wasn't so sure. Was Val even aware of how long he'd been sick? When a man was over nine hundred years old, months probably passed like finger snaps, but he, who'd watched Val cough, wheeze, and struggle for breath, had felt each day pass with acute, painful precision. No treatment he'd tried, no medication he'd prescribed, had helped very much.

Thankfully, the old standby—copious amounts of rich, healing blood—still provided Val with some relief.

While Lukas talked to Valerian, Wyland went to the glossy bar transplanted from one of Valerian's favorite English pubs, pulled a plastic bag of blood from the small refrigerator, and set it in the warmer. Studying the wine rack, he selected a robust merlot, removed its cork, and poured a measure into a glass the size of a small goldfish bowl.

"Lukas, you look tired," Valerian said. "When was the last time you slept?"

Lukas sipped from his bottle of Summit Pale Ale. "I'm fine, Val."

Wyland assessed Lukas with a professional eye. Sympathetic morning sickness had plagued Lukas throughout Scarlett's pregnancy. He had dark circles under his eyes, he'd probably lost the thirty pounds his bondmate had gained, and despite it being high summer, he looked pale and drawn. Worrying about Scarlett on top of his crushing workload was going to put Lukas in the hospital. Thankfully, she was due to deliver within a week or two.

"Bailey should be here in a couple of minutes," Lukas said around a jaw-cracking yawn. "Thanks for letting us meet here tonight."

It was too much to hope that Lukas might consent to a quick exam before Bailey arrived.

"As for the reason you drove here in the first place," Valerian said, "do you need to speak with me privately?"

Wyland blinked. "I'll give you a moment." Between his physician's duties, legal work, and serving as the Underworld Council's Vampire Second, there was very little information he wasn't privy to, but—

"No, I need to speak with both of you—or rather, I need to show you something." Lukas glanced at him. "Valerian, you're the repository of our culture's tribal knowledge, and Wyland's familiar with the materials in our archives."

Intriguing.

"And as long as she's on her way, I'd like to get Bailey's take, as well," Lukas continued. "She...notices things. Connects some odd dots."

Yes, she did, and etiquette be damned. During the long hours he and Bailey had worked together on the massive effort to digitize their archives, Rafe's little hacker bondmate had certainly connected *his* dots, coming up with some uncomfortably accurate conclusions. The little human probably knew more about him, and his past, than anyone save Valerian.

When the warmer chimed, he plucked the bag of blood from the water bath. After drying it with a tea towel, he punctured the bag with a plastic spout, poured the warm blood into the wineglass, and swirled. He hadn't seen Bailey since she and Rafe came back from Alaska. He should try to talk her into an exam as well. Was her perforated ulcer healing as expected?

Stepping out from behind the bar, he delivered the wine to Valerian. He was a fine one to lecture Lukas and Bailey about job stress. Between hospital rounds, office hours, legal consulting, time spent working with the archives, Underworld Council business, and the vicious commute between Marine on St. Croix and downtown Minneapolis, he hardly had time to eat or sleep.

The majestic doorbell rang. "I've got it, Thane," he

called toward the closed kitchen door. Though Thane considered hospitality his purview, there was no need to interrupt him when Wyland was standing right there. He crossed the foyer, disengaged the locks, and opened the thick wooden door. "Bailey, right on schedule—oh." Tia Quinn? Why had Bailey brought an investigative journalist to their home?

Why *this* investigative journalist?

"Hi, Wyland." Bailey kissed both his cheeks and cheerfully popped him on the arm with her tiny fist. "How's it hangin'?"

Before he could take her to task for her grammar-impaired reference to his genitalia, she'd brushed past him to greet Valerian. His smile lit up the room like a Saturnalia tree.

"Hello, Sir," Tia said, hesitating slightly before extending her hand. "I don't know if you remember me. We had a short conversation at Rafe Sebastiani's gallery show last winter."

He remembered. Her hair and lips had been the color of ripe eggplants, and her curvy body adorned entirely in black, as it was tonight. During their short conversation, as she'd subtly tried to pump him for information about Valerian's health, he'd felt a distinct sexual stirring—something that hadn't happened in well over a century. Tonight, her hair was auburn, the color of mulled wine, with unnatural green tips.

Why had his dormant sex drive awakened for a wild child who changed her hair color on a whim? Maybe he was having a mid-life crisis.

"Sir?" she repeated.

Hearing the word 'sir' from her lips was…withering. With a little mental shake, he took her black-nailed hand. To not acknowledge another vampire, someone whose interests he represented on the Underworld Council, would be unspeakably rude. "Of course I remember you, Ms. Quinn." In the tradition of younger vampires more thoroughly assimilated into human culture, Tia Quinn's parents had given their daughter more than one name.

Tia Quinn's *parents* were younger than he was.

She wrinkled her nose at his formality and smiled up at him with eyes the color of roasted coffee beans. He hadn't imagined the rings of vivid leaf green surrounding both pupils. "Please, call me Tia," she said.

"And I'm Wyland."

She looked at him strangely. "Of course you are."

And now she thought him addled. He sighed. What was she, thirty to his three hundred plus? Apparently his dusty libido didn't find her youth a serious impediment, because the fantasies he'd had about her after their last conversation were absolutely debauched. He withdrew his hand from hers. "Why are you here, Ms. Quinn?"

"Wyland, don't be rude to our guest." Valerian was on his feet, supported by Bailey on one side and Lukas on the other. "Tia." He extended both wrinkled hands. "How nice to see you, my dear."

Leaving him standing by the door without a backwards glance, Tia crossed to Valerian, took his hands, and gently kissed both papery cheeks. Wyland watched her take mental notes, her sharp reporter's gaze recording every detail of Valerian's appearance: his ruddy skin tone, the luxurious mane of silver hair, his satin smoking jacket, the shawl, and the wool-lined leather slippers he wore even in the summer heat. Yes, Valerian was having a good night. Having guests—young guests—obviously agreed with him.

As Wyland closed the heavy door and re-engaged the security system, he watched Tia treat Lukas to a thorough physical assessment before they, too, kissed each other's cheeks—the traditional greeting *he* apparently hadn't rated. Well, it was better all the way around if she kept her distance, because Tia Quinn had a bad habit of sticking her nose in where it didn't belong. Like Bailey, she saw too much. As an investigative journalist, it was her *job* to see too much—a fact that both Valerian and Lukas seemed to have forgotten.

After offering them a libation—Diet Coke for Bailey, merlot for Tia—he rejoined the group. By some trick of fate, the only open seat was on the settee next to Tia. "Your wine," he said, extending the glass.

"Thank you." As she accepted it, the heavy ring she wore on her left middle finger clicked against the crystal stem. Hammered gold, with strands encasing a green stone, the ring managed to look simultaneously ancient and modern. She glanced at his hips, and then at the open space on the firm cushion next to her. "There's not a lot of room here, is there?"

His teeth started to tingle. If she looked at his groin again, he'd embarrass them both. "We'll make it work."

Her sudden off-kilter grin lit the room. "Do you watch *Project Runway*?"

"No."

"Oh."

As he sat, his pressed khakis brushed against disintegrating black denim. The high, curved back of

11

the antique Adams settee embraced them, pressing them together from shoulder to knee.

She smelled like VampScreen and lilacs.

Tia looked around with amazement. "This room is…" Her voice trailed off as something on the nearby bookshelves caught her eye.

It was a common reaction. Their home, with its hodge-podge decor spanning centuries, frequently left visitors speechless. Georgian tables supported Art Deco lamps, Beaux Arts cozied up to Eames, and Moroccan tassels brushed against Windsor chairs and Federation hutches. Several pieces of current-era furniture, like the oversized shabby chic chair where Lukas sat, were recent additions. Not long ago, he'd finally convinced Valerian that the furniture pre-dating the Reformation, along with many of the rare books and manuscripts stacked haphazardly on the floor-to-ceiling bookshelves, should be moved to the Archives for preservation and protection. On the night he and Val had selected which tchotchkes and *objets d'art* would remain on display, memories and stories had poured out of his mentor like an uncorked cask of wine, especially when they'd sorted through Valerian's precious collection of tintypes, cameos, daguerreotypes, and photographs. People he'd known, people he'd loved and lost.

So many people loved and lost.

Tia's eyes widened. "Is that a Fabergé egg?"

"Yes." The Tsar had given him the priceless, bejeweled object as thanks for his counsel—not that Nicholas had followed his advice.

She looked, wide-eyed, around the room. "There's so much history here."

To one so young, it was history, but to him and

Valerian? It was simply their life. He and Val had first sat side-by-side on this very settee almost three hundred years ago, at Valerian's London residence. Wyland had spent years—decades—studying medicine, law, business, and history by candlelight, reading until his eyes stung with fatigue. He'd become Valerian's apprentice. When the American Civil War broke out, Val named him the Vampire Second, and then moved to America, trusting him to serve as the Council's European liaison. Wyland glanced at a particular photograph on the bookshelf, then quickly looked away.

Look how well *that* had worked out.

When Lukas murmured something that made Val laugh out loud, something pinched in his chest. Time had a way of passing, regardless of one's wishes. He no longer had centuries, or even decades, before he'd have to take Val's place.

"Wyland?"

There was such care in Tia's voice, even after he'd been rude to her. He cleared his throat. No more reverie; it was time to start this impromptu meeting. Time to get Tia Quinn out of his thoughts, out of his house, and out of his life.

Lukas beat him to it. "What's up?" he asked Bailey.

"Tia asked me to look into a comment someone posted at *In Like Quinn* earlier today." Reaching into the side pocket of her computer bag, Bailey pulled out several pieces of paper and passed them around.

In Like Quinn had a financial news section? The last time he'd glanced at Tia's website, the front page had featured a picture of a young pop star's latest unfortunate tattoo.

As the last piece of paper reached them, Tia

passed it to him without comment. He glanced at the story's headline—something about Wall Street corruption—and then at the comment Bailey had printed. "'Sebastiani Labs' so-called board of directors must be called to account for their illegal acts, and for abandoning the old ways,'" he read aloud. "'If you don't expose them, I will.'" He looked at Bailey. "Do you know this person's identity?"

"Not yet. Looks like whoever it is used a burner account." Bailey's eyes snapped with annoyance. "I'll do more digging once I get back to the office, but someone's working harder than the average bear to disguise their identity."

While Bailey and Lukas launched into a detailed technology discussion, he picked apart the message. 'Sebastiani Labs' was self-explanatory. 'So-called board of directors' could indicate either generic disgust with the board's decisions, or very specific knowledge about the board's true nature. 'Called to account for their illegal acts?' Which illegal acts? According to whose laws? Called to account how? By whom? What did the commenter expect Tia to investigate? And did the commenter mean 'old ways' in a general way, or The Old Ways? In their culture, the second phrase had a specific, shameful, meaning.

Tia took a sip of wine. "I feel stupid bothering you about this, but the comment felt...off."

"Yeah," Lukas said. "We need to look into this."

Bailey shot Tia a look. "I told you so."

"Okay, but I don't get it." Tia's husky alto voice vibrated into him where their arms and thighs touched. "My regular readers know that financial reporting isn't my beat. The financial stuff, the celebrity news, the political stories, are aggregated from other sources. I have content-sharing arrangements in place with dozens of other writers and journalists."

If he remembered correctly, music used to be her beat. She'd gotten her start writing reviews for music magazines like *Rolling Stone* before shifting her focus to investigative journalism.

"There's no way the person who commented could be sure I'd even see what he or she wrote," Tia continued.

"What are you working on right now?" Bailey asked.

"I just finished a series on data privacy—thanks for the sources, by the way," she said to Bailey. "Now, I'm researching human trafficking, with a regional slant. I'm interviewing a young woman who recently escaped a sex trafficker who forced her to work in the Bakken oil fields in North Dakota. After so many arrests at hotels and motels here in the Twin Cities, a lot of procurers are now doing business from private homes."

He and Lukas exchanged a glance. Stephen, the incubus who'd nearly killed Lukas and Scarlett several years ago, had murdered a man at just such a location as his need for death energy had escalated. Stephen had somehow escaped their most secure psychiatric facility and was still at large. Somewhere along the line, Tia would probably contact their police commander for information, but when she did, she'd hit a brick wall. Gideon Lupinsky couldn't— wouldn't—comment on an open case.

He'd call Gideon himself to ensure it.

"Are you taking safety precautions?" Lukas asked Tia.

"I know how to take care of myself."

"That doesn't answer my question."

No, it didn't. Despite its squeaky-clean reputation, the Twin Cities had the same problems as any large metropolitan area. In addition to the residential sex clubs, gangs had staked out turf in north Minneapolis. There were areas of the city where no law-abiding person wandered after dark.

Tia Quinn probably considered those areas her workplace.

"What do you carry?" Lukas asked.

Not '*do* you carry,' but '*what* do you carry'—an interesting assumption on Lukas's part. Wyland skimmed Tia's body. Where in the world would she carry a weapon where no one could see it? Her Vlad Drac T-shirt clung to bountiful breasts, and faded black denims hugged her dangerous curves. She wore a pair of those hideous rubber flip flops—black, with her toenails painted to match—so she couldn't hide a weapon in her footwear.

She gestured to the battered leather purse sitting on the floor next to the settee. "Stun gun."

He reluctantly approved. The defensive weapon would temporarily incapacitate only the assailant, and not cause irreparable or fatal harm, but...why did she have to put herself in danger in the first place?

"I'll have Jack give you a call," Lukas said. "He teaches self-defense."

She raised a brow. "I'm well-trained."

"It never hurts to practice. When Scarlett and her band were still touring, she worked out with Jack all the time."

His eyes narrowed. Too many women found Jack Kirkland, Sebastiani Security's big, blond managing partner, appealing—and damn it, now Lukas was staring at him. There was no hiding one's emotional state from any incubus or succubus, much less one of Lukas's skill. Lukas plucked emotional energy out of the air, absorbed it for sustenance like humans digested food or vampires drank blood.

Why did the prospect of Tia physically grappling with Jack annoy him so much?

Her big toe brushed his pant leg. Nerve endings, dormant for years, sat up and blinked. When blood rushed to his penis, he choked back a groan at the barely-remembered sensation. Setting the piece of paper on his lap to disguise his condition, Wyland tried to ignore Tia's wine-wet lips as Lukas asked her questions about her website. His jaw throbbed, but he kept his fangs from shooting down through sheer force of will.

"Speaking of The Old Ways..." Lukas reached into the battered messenger bag sitting near his feet, extracting a piece of paper stored flat in a clear plastic bag. "This...screed arrived with the latest batch of Scarlett's fan mail."

Though Scarlett hadn't performed in public since the night Stephen killed her sister Annika, she still had a rabid fan base—and unfortunately, with it, all the security problems that accompanied fame in this era. When Lukas handed him the bag, he saw an adhesive tag affixed to the corner. The item had been logged as evidence.

When he read, he understood why. The word-processed document, two paragraphs long, invoked The Old Ways against Scarlett and Lukas's "unborn half-breed abomination."

Glancing at Tia, he passed the packet to Valerian.

"We shouldn't discuss this matter with a reporter present."

Valerian waved a regal hand. "Tia knows what 'off the record' means."

One, no one had actually said it yet, and two, he wasn't so sure. A threat made against the unborn child of two Underworld Council members was a pretty big scoop. "Ms. Quinn, this conversation is off the record."

Her gaze gored him like a bull at Pamplona. "Ya think?"

"Wyland, take a chill pill," Bailey said.

Lukas speared a weary hand through his hair. "He's just doing his job."

Yes, he was—and no matter how alluring he might find Tia Quinn, the protocol was clear. The safety of their people depended on him remembering his responsibilities. "Ms. Quinn, this conversation is off the record. Do you understand?"

Her fingers skimmed her inner forearm, where a phrase he couldn't quite read was tattooed onto her pale skin. "All topics having to do with our culture have been, and ever shall be, off the record," she said. Each word was precisely spoken, sliced with a razor-sharp knife. "Do you require a signed affidavit?"

"Your words have been witnessed by three sitting Underworld Council members. That won't be necessary."

She angled her body away from him, the tilt of her chin reminding him of royalty displeased. He was certain she hadn't meant to expose her neck to him quite so alluringly, but she had, and it was. The sexual charge that zinged through his system was completely and utterly inappropriate.

Tia seemed startled when Valerian handed her the evidence bag. After reading the message, she flipped the packet and looked at the envelope, also stored in the bag—something he hadn't done. "U.S. Postal Service, downtown Minneapolis zip code and postmark."

Lukas nodded. "Adhesive stamp, so no saliva, but we're testing it for prints. There are no fingerprints on the paper itself. The paper and ink are disgustingly generic. That leaves us analyzing content, which is why I came here."

"I'm sorry for barging in," Tia said.

"No worries."

Speak for yourself, Lukas.

"The fact that you and Scarlett are having a baby has been well-publicized, even in the human press, but this mention of The Old Ways? The mention at *ILQ*?" When Tia tapped her pursed lips with her index finger, her ring caught the light. "That's us. That's Underworld."

Wyland's brows rose. "I wouldn't have thought someone your age would be aware of the phrase."

"I *am* an investigative journalist, and reasonably well-informed."

If looks could kill, he'd be dead on the floor.

"Hey." Bailey waved her arms in the air. "Human here. What are The Old Ways?"

How could he explain their ancestors' practice of euthanizing newborns who exhibited severe physical abnormalities? Marooned on an inhospitable planet with no hope of rescue, with little medicine and even fewer options, their ancient ancestors had made unspeakably painful decisions for the good of the tribe. He knew better than to judge an ancient culture by contemporary standards.

But he did.

"So much waste. So many lives forever changed," Valerian murmured. He looked at Bailey. "You're familiar with our culture's origin story?"

She nodded. "Your ancestors' spaceship crashed in northern Minnesota several millennia ago, marooning the passengers, forcing the surviving incubi, succubi, vampires, Valkyrie, were-shifters, sirens, and faeries to fight for survival in the dead of winter."

Wyland half-listened as Valerian told Bailey of their history, the story passed from generation to generation unchanged—until last summer, when Lorin Schlessinger had made the archaeological discovery that had thrown their oral histories' timeline into complete disarray. The otherworldly lockbox Lorin had found at the Isabella site had yielded a big surprise: extra-planetary technology lying next to three-thousand-year-old native wild rice. It boggled the mind.

"When I was young and I'd misbehaved," Tia said, "my parents joked that if only The Old Ways were still in vogue, they could wring my neck with impunity."

"Wrung necks and smothering were the preferred methods of dispatch," Valerian said matter-of-factly, "but rarely did one's own family perform the grisly task. My predecessor, Sigurd..."

Wyland stilled. There was exactly one reference to Sigurd in their entire Archives: his death announcement. Valerian never spoke of him. He'd assumed this was because Val had few, if any, memories of the man.

Clearly this was not the case.

As Tia took Valerian's gnarled hand, offering comfort, he observed Val from a great mental distance, and through the long lens of time. Why *hadn't* Val ever spoken of Sigurd? Why were there no artifacts, no written records, and no mention of Sigurd's life and accomplishments, in their Archives?

Damn it, he'd been so focused on the documents *present* in the Archives that he'd never questioned why some materials might be *absent*. Val had some explaining to do.

Tia gestured to the letter. "But the baby is healthy, right?" Worry was etched on her face. "It's been too long since I talked to Scarlett."

"She's fine. They're both fine." After a pause, Lukas added, "I'm sure she'd love to see you."

The invitation sounded reluctant, rusty. She quirked Lukas a crooked smile Wyland couldn't interpret.

A red stain crept up Lukas's neck.

Well. Wasn't *that* interesting.

"So, back to the letter," Bailey said, looking at it. "The writer is suggesting that Lukas and Scarlett kill their 'unborn half-breed abomination' because Scarlett is a siren and Lukas is an incubus? That's really fucked up."

Lukas took another swig from his beer bottle. "As if most of us don't have mixed ancestry to begin with. At this point, species designations are almost beside the point."

"Don't let Krispin Woolf hear you say that," Bailey muttered. "He'd demand your resignation."

Lukas snorted. "Let him try."

Underworld Council representation was species-based and tended to run along powerful family lines, but little Coco Fontaine, the daughter of two sitting Council members representing different species, was a game-changer. Never before had two family dynasties merged in such an overt manner. He'd spent countless hours poring over Council records, bylaws, and succession planning documents to assess her precise status.

The child wasn't even born yet, and she'd already given him his first silver hair.

"It sounds like whoever sent this letter might share the Alpha's opinion," Tia mused. "Have you been able to connect Krispin Woolf to the Genetic Purity League yet?"

Shock rocketed through his system. "What do you know about the Genetic Purity League?" Or about Krispin Woolf's suspected leadership of the organization?

"I know that a couple of years ago the GPL petitioned the Council to demand that the law be changed to require bondmates to register their relationships. Krispin Woolf's preference for wolf/wolf pairings is well known." She looked at Valerian, and then, reluctantly, at him. "Thank you for voting that one down."

"Who is your source?" Lukas snapped.

Individual members' votes were supposed to be confidential.

"I'm not about to reveal who my source is, dude."

Lukas might be wearing jeans and drinking a beer, but one of *his* subjects had just called a sitting Underworld Council member 'dude.' It was completely unacceptable, regardless of how well Tia and Lukas knew each other.

Just how well *did* they know each other?

Lukas set his beer bottle down. "Tia, if we have a security breach within the Council—"

"You don't. This information didn't come from the Council."

"So it came from the League itself?" Lukas pressed.

Tia paused, considering her words. "My source read a draft of the proposal several months before you received it—and before you ask, no. I will not reveal the person's identity."

There weren't too many civilians Lukas couldn't bully into submission through sheer size and attitude. Apparently Tia Quinn was one of them. She didn't seem the least bit intimidated by Lukas's pissed-off glare.

"I don't remember seeing any reference to The Old Ways in the Archive material I've worked with," Bailey said, diffusing the tension.

"It was so very long ago," Valerian said softly.

And as he'd heard Valerian say many times before, winners wrote history. Valerian, the world's oldest living vampire, defined the word 'winner.' For centuries, he'd been the sole arbiter of which information was stored in their Archives, and which information was omitted.

Anger rose like the tide. What information had Val omitted, and why? Damn it, could he trust any of it?

"Wyland, how much Archive work did you get done while Rafe and I were in Alaska?" Bailey asked. "God, I have so much work to catch up on."

"We've transcribed the written artifacts back to about 1400 AD," he answered, watching Valerian carefully. They were processing the written archive materials in reverse chronological order, working with the newer, less fragile documents first. The next batch of documents would bring them closer to those dark days Val had mentioned.

"I don't know how much I'll be able to help." Bailey glanced at Lukas. "I'll be working on the tech unit with Sebastiani Labs' quantum computing folks."

Wyland blinked. "You were successful?"

Bailey shot him a satisfied grin. "I figured out how to turn it on and off, and how to separate it into components, but I don't know what the hell to make of the chip."

"Your idea worked." Several days after its discovery at the archaeological site where their ancestors' spaceship had crashed, the otherworldly device had somehow managed to access Sebastiani Labs' secure computer network despite having been buried in a box for a couple thousand years. At that point, Bailey had insisted that any additional work take place far beyond the reach of ambient technology. She and Rafe had driven to the wilds of Alaska, where they'd worked and played while enjoying several months of precious newbond privacy. "Congratulations. Where's the RV right now?" He shot Val a look. "The Airstream deserves a place in the Archives."

"It's parked in Sebastiani Labs' lower level loading dock," Bailey answered.

He nodded, satisfied. The vehicle was stored in as safe a place as he could think of at the moment.

"Can I help?" Tia suddenly asked. "With the archiving work?"

He shot her a surprised look.

"Despite the danger you seem to think I court on a regular basis, I'm a research specialist. If Bailey has other priorities—which I hope you appreciate I'm dying to ask about but am *not*—I can give you a few hours here and there."

The two of them, working together? His fangs throbbed at the thought. "Thank you for offering, but—"

"Excellent." Valerian smiled in benediction. "Wyland could use the help."

He could, but—

"Great idea," Bailey seconded. Amusement danced in her eyes. "I'm sure Lukas can clear Tia for Archive access fairly quickly."

"Allow a journalist access to our Archives? Are you bloody delusional?"

Bailey raised clasped hands to her heart as if swooning. "Ah, there it is."

"What?"

"Your gutter English. I missed it while I was gone."

And no one drove him to it faster, damn it—unless it was Lukas's sister, Antonia.

Tia unabashedly listened, studying him with narrowed feline eyes. As if she suddenly found him…interesting.

Ignoring his body's blunt response, he looked at Lukas. Though Bailey's opinion was obvious, she wasn't a Council member. Valerian had weighed in, but Lukas, the Security/Technology First, would surely put a stop to this madness.

"Bailey needs time to work with that tech unit," Lukas mused, studying Tia. "Maybe we shouldn't look a gift horse in the mouth."

Damn it, her mouth was part of the problem.

Lukas detailed the background check process,

outlining what Tia's well-intentioned offer would cost in terms of privacy. As she listened, Tia looked like she'd swallowed one of the crickets chirping in the tall grass outside—or maybe she was starting to realize that she'd be spending time, lots of time, alone with *him*.

"Do you want to proceed?" Lukas asked Tia.

Tia took a deep breath he could see, hear, and feel. "Yeah. Let's do it."

Bollocks.

As Lukas started gathering preliminary information, he tongued a stinging incisor. Maybe drinking some blood would help.

Rising from the settee, he went to the bar, withdrew a bag of blood from the refrigerator, and poured it over ice cubes. As he drank, he could almost feel Bram's gaze mock him from across the room, where the old photograph sat on the bookshelf. Could almost feel the weight of Bram's arm slung over his shoulder, and the curve of Deirdre's soft hip, as the three of them smiled for the camera.

He turned his back. This time, he'd keep his hands, and his fangs, to himself.

Even if it killed him.

As Tia's husky laughter stroked him from across the room, he thought it very well might.

CHAPTER TWO

Turning his back on the noisy group behind him, Dominic Reese hunkered down at the bar, nodding his thanks to the woman who'd delivered his beer.

What a colossal waste of time. In the absence of an agenda, or any concrete marching orders, GPL members under age twenty-five no longer even pretended their monthly meeting was anything but a party, or a way to hook up. Tonight, they'd met at The Ivy, a swanky hotel in downtown Minneapolis. There were hundreds of rooms, hundreds of beds, right upstairs—not that he'd waste his money renting one just to have sex. Nope. If he rented a hotel room, he'd want the place all to himself. He'd order some food someone else had cooked, get some uninterrupted sleep, and then take a long, hot shower without his sister knocking on the bathroom door, yelling at him to hurry up.

But with his father flat on his back in a hospital bed, unable to move, Dom's personal wants and needs were *way* down on the priority list.

A loud bray of laughter assaulted his eardrums. He'd only come to tonight's event because his father, a Genetic Purity League elder, had insisted. "It's important our family is represented," he'd said, glaring at the nurses who'd come in to adjust his orthopedic bed, flipping his body face-up and face-down on a strict schedule to reduce bedsores.

Dom bit back a frustrated sigh. Three more years would have to pass before he'd be allowed to attend the adult GPL meeting, where the real work occurred. But earlier that day, his dad had surprised him, revealing his life's work: maintaining a secret genealogy database that spanned their culture, and went back generations. His father had described it as being *Debrett's Peerage* for paranormals—whatever the hell *that* was—and then had given him the access codes.

"Dad, GPL meetings are such a waste of time," he'd said. He was itching to log on, to explore the database.

"Dom, get away from the hospital for a night. Have a beer, kiss a pretty girl." A pause. "And wait for further instructions."

"Instructions for what?"

His father hadn't responded. The hopeless expression he'd tried to hide as Dom left his hospital room was a kick to the gut.

He lifted the glass of dark ale and took two large swallows. Nearby, someone laughed too loudly. The clink of beer bottles and wine glasses, the posturing, the flirty hair flipping, the cloying scent of too many people in too small a space wearing too much cologne... He didn't belong here anymore. Tomorrow night he'd be able to tell his father that he'd attended the meeting. That he'd had a beer. But that he'd enjoyed himself? Not so much.

He rubbed his tired eyes. Maybe an age exception could be made. Maybe he could take his father's place at the Elder's meeting, just until he recovered.

If he recovered.

Dom shoved the insidious thought aside. He felt like he'd aged a decade in the last month, and if he felt that way, his mother surely felt worse. Since his father's accident, she'd pretty much spent every waking hour at the hospital. Dom had finally returned to work—his mother had insisted—but Mom needed his support, and Hannah, no matter how big a pain in his ass, needed to be fed, needed help with homework, needed rides to school and to soccer practice. The house had to be cleaned, the lawn mowed, and they needed groceries and clean clothes. A rogue yawn escaped.

Damn Tia Quinn for moving so damn far away.

"Dominic?"

"Hi, Mila." Mila Stanton, only child of purebred vampires Lyudmila and Stanton, was an odd duck— pretty enough, but odd. Her father was a GPL Elder, but Dom had no clue whether Mila shared the organization's political goals. She came to meetings, but didn't flirt, drink alcohol, or troll for sex. Instead, she worked the room like a very efficient butterfly, chatting and laughing as she flitted from group to group. She usually attended meetings on her way to her job at the hospital, and if her clothes were anything to go by, the same was true tonight. The gray dress pants, flat black shoes, white blouse, and long-sleeved black sweater were hardly hook-up bait. The purple scarf wrapped around her neck provided the only flash of color.

A sweater, in this heat? Yeah, she was odd.

They kissed each other's cheeks in the traditional greeting, then she sat on the bar stool next to his without asking whether he wanted company. "How are you?" she asked.

"Fine." One thing he'd learned since his dad's accident was that very few who asked that question actually wanted a truthful answer. "Are you on your way to work?" Given how rich her family was, he was impressed that she did—work, that is. Mila Stanton's family could buy this hotel hundreds of times over.

"Yes, I'm going to work from here." A pause. "How is your father doing?"

Concern shone from her eyes, which were a deep, thundercloud gray. Maybe Mila was one of the exceptions.

"I saw a picture of the car after the accident," she added. "It's amazing he survived. C4 spinal injury, right?"

He nodded. So many lives forever changed because another driver thought he could thumb through his email and drive a car simultaneously. "He's…" How could he explain? His father could have a lucid conversation, could breathe without assistance, but he couldn't move his limbs, couldn't control his bladder and bowels, and couldn't digest food. Despite the family's initial high hopes, he wasn't getting better. Dom swallowed, hard. What could he say about his father's condition that would preserve what little dignity he had left?

Mila touched his bare forearm. "I'm glad he's stable enough that you could be here," she said softly. "Please give him and your mother my best."

"Thanks. Damn, your fingers are like icicles." Without thinking, he covered her chilly hand with his. Her eyes widened in surprise—her gaze flew to his— but she didn't move her hand away.

What the hell…?

Noise receded into the background as they considered each other. He couldn't mistake the spark of attraction she felt—he could smell it, thanks to his werewolf nose—but she was clearly wondering what, if anything, to do about it.

Despite the nondescript clothes, she really *was* beautiful—willowy, with shoulder-length black hair, imperious eyebrows, and plush pink lips against the whitest skin he'd ever seen in the middle of summer. She reminded him of the actress Rooney Mara, or a prima ballerina. The Queen of Snows, reigning over her subjects with intelligence, care, and concern. When she flexed her fingers, he felt the touch below his belt. He shifted against the barstool, levering his body toward hers.

Why hadn't he noticed her before?

She quickly withdrew her hand, sat up straight, and turned to face the bar. "I really should get going."

"Already?" He gestured to the almost empty glass she'd brought with her. "Can I get you another drink?"

She glanced at her watch, then back at him.

What could he say to keep her there? "I'd really appreciate the company."

"Okay, a quick Diet Coke," she finally said. "I'm due at work soon."

He gestured to the bartender, ordering them both fresh drinks. "You work at the hospital, right?"

She nodded. "I'm a systems analyst."

"Huh?"

Her self-deprecating laugh twinkled over him. "I work with patient data at Memorial Hospital. Utterly invisible and boring, until there's a problem with either storing it, or accessing it. And you work at

Woolf Den Fitness?" She gave his body an approving up-and-down glance. "You look like you work out."

"Yes to both." She'd noticed his body. "I'm the assistant manager—one of them, anyway. Free use of the facilities is one of the job perks." Not that he'd had time to work out lately.

She looked around. Bit her lip. "Can I admit something horrible?"

Curiosity thrummed through him. "Of course." He brought his head a couple of inches closer to hers. Lowered his voice. "Your secrets are safe with me." She smelled like a rainforest, humid and exotic. He wanted to breathe her in for hours. Open his mouth to the sky and drink her.

Their eyes met again.

"I hate to work out. Absolutely loathe it."

He laughed. "That's your deep, dark secret?"

She grinned back, exposing very white teeth. One incisor was slightly crooked, not quite perfect. Somehow, it made her more attractive rather than less. "What did you think I was going to say?"

The bartender delivered their drinks. Dom nodded his thanks, and took a quick sip of Moose Drool. "You strike me as a...very complex woman," he replied. "I was prepared for anything."

A shadow passed over her eyes, there then gone, and she reached for her Diet Coke. Before she could take a drink, a loud beep shrilled from the depths of her purse. "I'm on call," she muttered. "I have to take this."

"Sure."

She reached into her purse and pulled out her phone. As she swiped and read, The Count from *Sesame Street* flashed his fangs at him from her phone case.

Brains, body, *and* a sense of humor. Why had he never talked to her before? Why weren't other men swarming? As she tapped and read, he considered her businesslike behavior, how she methodically worked the room during these events. Maybe Mila was as frustrated about how little GPL business got done here as he was.

Maybe he had an ally, at last.

Dropping the phone into her purse, Mila rose from the stool. "I have to go."

Damn. "Can't someone else fix whatever the problem is?"

"No. I'm the one who's on call."

"When can I see you again?" he blurted. Hell, why would *she* want to see *him* again? Though his family connections and pristine genetic panel ensured his GPL membership, he was under no illusions about his looks. Though his family was comfortable enough financially, her parents were loaded.

She was digging in her purse again. When her hand came out, she was holding a key ring. "How about coffee?" she suggested.

Relief sluiced through his system. "Perfect. When?"

"You work days, right?"

"Some days, some nights."

"I work nights—vampire's hours," she said. "How about we sync up after checking our schedules?"

"Great." He was busy as hell, but he'd make time to see her. After they exchanged phone numbers, he reluctantly rose. "I look forward to it, Mila." They kissed each other's cheeks again. This time, he let his lips linger. Her surprised exhale brushed against his stubble, soft as a breeze.

Clearing her throat, she finally stepped away. "See you soon."

"'Bye." As she walked toward the door, he watched her high, tight butt shift under the businesslike gray fabric. Imagined how it would feel, shifting beneath his hands.

He was suddenly hard as a barbell.

Time to get out of here. The sooner he got to Stillwater and back, the sooner he could check out the genealogy database, then get to bed. Scaring the shit out of Tia Quinn had been so much easier before she'd moved to the freaking Wisconsin border.

Dropping a tip on the bar, he nodded his thanks to the bartender and left with new energy. Beer, check. Pretty girl, check.

Coming to the meeting hadn't been an epic waste of time after all.

✳

When Wyland finally called, Tia almost told him to shove it up his autocratic ass. Three things held her back: she was curious about the Archives, he *was* her Second, and he sounded utterly exhausted. These reasons, plus a host of others she didn't want to examine too closely, had her agreeing to meet him at a long-term storage facility just down the road from Vamp Central instead of dancing with friends at First Avenue as she'd planned.

Her headlights sliced through the dark as she turned into the parking lot of the building she'd barely noticed the other night. Despite a newish sign that said "River City Storage," the battered building had seen better days. Hers was the only car in the lot.

She'd rushed through her own work to help Wyland with his, and now he wasn't even here to meet her? "Figures," she grumbled, pulling up to the door illuminated by a single, stingy bulb. The building and the gravel lot were surrounded by tall trees and overgrown grass, and she couldn't see a hint of Valerian's house just down the road.

The place was seriously creepy. What possible business could Wyland have here? "Not that there's any sign of him," she muttered.

As she plucked her phone from her purse to call him, a light flicked on inside the building. Snagging the purse from the passenger seat, she scanned the lot, got out of her car, and locked the doors. As she approached the entrance, gravel crunched under her feet. Crickets chirped, the trees swayed in the breeze, and she could smell the St. Croix River from here. "Antonia?" Yes, that was Antonia Sebastiani trotting toward the door from the inside. Antonia was reputed to be a diabolical genius—probably the reason her father selected her to serve as the Incubus Second after Lukas abdicated the seat, choosing to focus on the security and technology risks that might reveal their existence to humanity.

Just how many Underworld Council members were working on this archiving project?

Antonia opened the door. "Hey," she said around a wad of pink gum. "Tia, right? Nice to meet you. We appreciate the help."

When something howled nearby, Tia scurried into the empty beige foyer. The dim light didn't disguise the fact that the walls needed a fresh coat of paint. "I'm glad to be here." *Inside, rather than out there.*

Antonia started walking down the hallway, her flip-flops snapping and her long black braid swishing back and forth across her cut-off jean shorts. "Come on, I'll bring you down to Wyland."

Down?

Antonia chattered about the heat and the traffic, probably trying to put her at ease. It was a characteristic most of the Council members she'd met seemed to share. Even Wyland had tried the other night, serving her a civilized glass of wine though he clearly hadn't wanted her there. When he sat down beside her on that too-small settee, she'd been hyper-aware of his body heat. His crisp, clean scent. Every shift of his weight. She hadn't been able to shake the unsettling sensitivity since.

"How did you know I was here?" she asked.

"Security cameras. We saw you drive into the lot."

When the hallway dead-ended at a heavy door, Antonia slapped her hand against a small screen mounted at its side. It scanned her hand from top to bottom, and after a couple-second pause, a tiny light changed from red to green, accompanied by a near-silent click. Antonia gave the metal door a full-body yank, revealing an identical door straight ahead, more security cameras, and a stairwell leading down.

Her body hair prickled. What was this place?

Antonia gestured to the other security door. "Parking is through there. Wyland will give you a garage door opener."

Indoor parking. So *that* was the reason she hadn't seen any cars in the lot. "That's convenient," she said, following Antonia down the stairs. With cars parked

36

inside and the foyer light turned off, passers-by would have no idea anyone was here.

Which was probably the point.

They stopped one flight down, at another security door guarded by cameras and biometrics. The stairwell descended at least one more floor that she could see. Curiosity simmered as Antonia repeated the access sequence she'd performed at the top of the stairs, yanking on the heavy door.

"Come on in."

She followed Antonia from the dingy stairwell into a huge, white, blindingly-bright room that, depending on which area caught your attention, looked like a high-tech computer lab, Dumbledore's office at Hogwarts, or an artifact storage facility like the one she'd seen in a documentary about The Smithsonian Institution. "Wow."

"Sorry," Antonia said. "I should have warned you about the lights."

The back half of the huge room was filled with floor-to-ceiling shelving units, cleverly floor-mounted on a track system that allowed the shelves to be moved when a document or artifact was needed, then pushed together to maximize the storage space. Right now, the units were positioned so they created a long center aisle, except for one shelf that jutted into the empty space. Closer to the entrance and off to the right was a bank of computers, scanners, and monitors. Bailey slouched at one of the computers, headset on, bobbing and typing to a song only she could hear. On the long table to the left sat an ancient leather-bound book, a pair of white gloves, and an open pack of Bubble Yum. In the corner behind the table was an open doorway leading to what looked like a kitchenette. Given the antiseptic cleanliness of the work area, the scent of coffee was startling.

"Hey, Wyland!" Antonia shouted.

Bailey's chair whipped around. "Christ on a freaking cracker, Antonia—oh, Tia. Hi." She removed her headset and glanced up at the bank of security monitors reflecting nearly a dozen different views of the building and its surroundings. Sure enough, two screens displayed the entrance, and her car. "I didn't realize you'd arrived."

"Wyland asked me to keep an eye out for her. Where is he?" Antonia peered down the center aisle. "Wyland, Tia's here!"

Wyland's head and upper body suddenly appeared from behind the jutting shelf. "One moment," he called back.

"Hurry up, dude. We're late!" She turned toward Tia. "Bailey and I were supposed to be at Dad and Claudette's house over an hour ago, and it's going to take us almost that long to drive there."

There was a mechanical hum as the shelves moved back into tidy alignment, and then Wyland was walking toward them, dress shoes clicking against the hard floor, wearing trim black pants and a sky blue button-down shirt that did amazing things for his icy Nordic coloring. His pale hair was slicked back into a low ponytail, showcasing his haughty cheekbones.

He reminded her of a runway model—lanky, striking, and…hungry. Yes, his killer cheekbones were even more prominent today. "Do you have any blood here?" she asked.

"Yes." Antonia glanced at Wyland and swore. "Why does such a smart man wait until he's practically starving before he feeds? Be right back."

Wyland reached her as Antonia disappeared into the kitchen. "Tia."

"Wyland. Sir."

After the slightest hesitation, he bent to kiss her cheeks. His subtle body scent snarled her thoughts, and the slight scratch of stubble sent lust streaking down her spine. His lips were surprisingly warm, and so much softer than they looked.

Stepping back, she cleared her throat.

He shoved his hands into his pants pockets, then removed them again with a faint scowl. His eyebrows, several shades darker than his hair, framed pale blue eyes the color of faded jeans, or a glacial lake. "Thank you for offering to help, and please don't call me 'Sir,'" he said with a sigh. "It makes me feel positively ancient."

Sweeping his tall, lean frame with a head-to-toe glance, she snorted a laugh. "Yeah, right." Sensuality, tightly leashed, simmered off him in waves. *Stop mooning. Back to business.* "What am I helping with tonight?" She looked around in amazement. "What *is* this place?"

"It's our Archives—the primary site, at any rate." His face was etched with exhaustion. She could tell by the subtle movement of his mouth that he was tonguing his left incisor. "Let me show you around."

"First things first." Antonia carried an oversized plastic cup emblazoned with a purple and gold Minnesota Vikings helmet. "It's snack time."

"You're a fine one to lecture people about taking care of themselves," Bailey scolded. "Thankfully Tia noticed you look about ready to drop."

He shot her a look she couldn't read, but accepted the glass from Antonia. The rim of the Big Gulpsized glass was so large it covered the lower half of his face, but as he drank, she could see the double grooves carved between his eyebrows smooth out slightly.

"Thank you," he said, lowering the glass. "I'd lost track of time."

There wasn't the slightest hint of blood staining his lips, not even in the corners of his mouth. A sudden urge to muss him up, to drive her hands into that slicked-back hair and lick blood from his lips, almost clobbered her sideways.

Did he look so neat and clean after drinking from the vein?

Antonia glanced at her, then at Wyland, her nostrils delicately flaring. Yeah, there was no way to hide knee-knocking lust from the young succubus— not when her species absorbed emotional energy for sustenance. "Why don't you show Tia around, Wyland?" Antonia suggested. "Bailey and I have to get going."

Wyland's gaze found hers. "Are you comfortable being here without a chaperone?"

Comfortable? Hardly. "This is hardly Regency England," she replied, not hiding her amusement. "No chaperones required—not on my end, anyway."

His black pupils dilated, shoving the icy blue out of the way.

Okay, that came out a *lot* more suggestively than she'd planned.

He cleared his throat. "I'd be pleased to give you a tour."

Oh yeah, he felt it, too. Anticipation bubbled like champagne.

"All righty then." Bailey tugged on Antonia's arm.

"We'll just…leave you to it."

Despite what she'd said to Wyland, Tia watched Bailey and Antonia gather their belongings with more than a little concern. What the hell was she thinking, flirting with the Vampire Second? Wyland wasn't a casual hook-up, someone with whom she could share a simple night of pleasure and then move on. There would be no 'simple' about it, not with him.

"'Bye," Bailey called from the security door.

"If you see Scarlett, tell her I'll call soon," she called back.

"Will do."

The women disappeared, the heavy steel door slamming behind them.

Leaving her and Wyland all alone.

＊

As the door closed with a dungeon-like clang, Wyland cursed his testosterone-addled stupidity. Tia's words had been a challenge, a silky sexual gauntlet thrown right at his feet. He should have left it lying there, ignored and unheeded, but he hadn't—and he couldn't blame it on the fresh blood surging through his system, or on a monumental lack of sleep.

He hadn't made such a critical error in a very long time.

He barely stopped himself from rubbing his burning eyes. Between emergencies at the hospital and his Council responsibilities, he hadn't slept deeply in nearly two days. But did she think he was asexual? Neutered? That it was safe to tease him, given his

TAMARA HOGAN

advanced years? He ached to show her, in the most direct, primitive way, that he was no Regency fop bound by the rules of the *ton*.

"Could we start the tour back there, in the kitchenette?" Tia asked. Her voice stroked like velvet. "I could use something to drink."

"Certainly." He gestured for her to precede him. He'd offer her basic hospitality, give her the tour she'd requested, and assign her a task so monumentally tedious that she'd never come back again. Then he'd go home, seek the oblivion of his featherbed, and try to get a couple hours' sleep before the next emergency call. Unfortunately, blood diseases didn't operate on a predictable timetable— and to vampires, blood was life.

As they passed the long table on their way to the kitchenette, he dragged his gaze from Tia's swaying, heart-shaped bottom, looking at the ancient leather-bound book Antonia hadn't put away before leaving. One of the oldest artifacts in their collection and not scheduled for preservation for months, he'd asked Antonia to look—to *very carefully* look—for references to a youthful Valerian, to Sigurd, or to The Old Ways. Though she'd worked diligently, popping annoying bubbles, she hadn't bothered to disguise her yawns.

It was a perfect assignment for Tia. And speaking of perfect…her curvy rear end, covered in tight, black denim. Clothing styles had changed dozens times or more since he'd last thought about undressing a woman, and the fashions of this era left very little mystery about a woman's physical contours. Back in turn-of-the-century England, it had taken long, long minutes for Deirdre's ladies' maids to remove corsets, chemises, petticoats, silk stockings, and whisper-thin

42

shifts while he watched from a nearby chaise. Deirdre's gowns, made by top French *modistes*, had been exquisite pieces of art, requiring, as she'd said, "a delicate touch" to remove. Watching the slow, careful disrobing had been foreplay in itself, but Tia's denims looked like they'd stand up to rougher handling—

"Wyland?" Tia glanced over her shoulder. "How long has all this—" she gestured to the roof and to the floor with a wave of her arm "—been here?"

He fought to get his thoughts back on track. "We acquired the building and property about five years ago," he said as they reached the small kitchen, "and we excavated the underground facility soon afterward." Up until that time, most of their culture's fragile artifacts and documents had been stored in the catacombs under Valerian's house—not that everything had been moved yet. There was still one room to deal with, at the far end of the tunnel. There never seemed to be enough time. "Right now, we're focused on document preservation work, and digitizing the written materials." The project was moving at a snail's pace, but there were only so many people he trusted to work with these materials. According to Lukas's background check, Tia Quinn was one of them. Lukas had reassured him that Tia had never—not once—reported anything that would put their culture at risk. For a journalist, she'd somehow managed to walk on the right side of a mighty fine line.

She looked at the speckled linoleum floor. "How many floors down?"

"Three floors underground, all climate controlled, with the garage up top." He put the plastic cup in the sink and turned on the water. "What would you like to drink?"

"Some blood, I think. It's been a long day." Not waiting for him, she went to the refrigerator, opened it, and peered inside. She pulled a plastic bag of blood off the top shelf, raised it to her mouth, and drove her sharp, tiny fangs into it with a soft pop.

Lust zinged. "May I offer you a glass?" he strangled out.

"No, thanks," she said around the bag. "This is fine."

His eyes locked onto her lips as she suckled, onto her throat as she swallowed the life-giving blood. He imagined her hands, cradling his cock like she did that bag. Her lips, greedily suckling on his—

Bugger. With a quick pivot, he turned back to the sink, washing the cup with more attention than the task required.

"Mmm." Her low moan slithered down his spine.

He had to look.

She pulled the bag away from her mouth and licked her lips. "This is good."

His heart pounded in time with the pulse he could see fluttering at the base of her neck. His penis stiffened. Reaching into the refrigerator himself, he snatched another bag from the shelf and drove his fangs into the flexible plastic.

It was either that, or her neck.

She threw away her empty bag and explored the kitchen, opening cabinets and drawers, oblivious to his bloodlust.

Scowling, he drank faster.

"There you go," she said approvingly. "You really shouldn't let so much time go between feedings."

Her maternal tone irked him. He was Wyland, the

Vampire Second. He'd been feeding himself three hundred years longer than she'd been walking the Earth.

It irked him even more that she was right.

He drained the bag, then dropped it in the garbage can. The top closed with a metallic clang. Nourishment surged through his system, but the blood didn't do anything to counteract his desire for her. Time to get out of here. "Are you done snooping?"

She closed the door of the cabinet under the sink, the slightest hint of pink staining her cheeks. "Sorry. Occupational hazard."

"Let me give you a quick tour of the rest of the place, and then we can get to work."

"Okay."

Despite her agreement, there was nothing quick about the tour. An hour later, he was still showing her their treasures, and if pressed, he'd have admitted he enjoyed it. She had a quick mind, and asked clever, probing questions. She seemed especially interested in how their worldwide information network had evolved over time.

"So vampires scattered throughout the world have sent reports to the Archives for hundreds of years?" she marveled. "That's a lot of material."

He nodded, gesturing to the rows and rows of shelves with a wide swing of his arm. "That said, much of what you see here is the work of a single person. Valerian started recording information about our culture, and its intersection with humanity, when he was a very young man. Much of our history was literally written by his hand."

Tia appeared awed, as well as she should.

"Remember that before the printing press was invented, the ability to read and write was largely the purview of clergy. Valerian masqueraded as such for many, many years."

"He's older than the printing press," Tia murmured.

"Its invention was a quantum leap for our people as well as for humanity," he said. "As Val encountered other literate vampires during his travels, he asked them to record their observations, and send them to the Archives."

"I'm aware of his great age, of course, but I've never given much thought to things elderly vampires have seen over their life spans." She looked at him. "I understand you started studying with Valerian in England, in the late 1600s?"

"Early 1700s." Bloody hell, why bother correcting her? Either date meant he was old as graveyard dirt.

"You met Valerian back when you were in medical school?"

Met him? Valerian had sought him out, and probably saved his life. Wyland's passionate interest in blood transfusion had bordered on heretical, and Valerian had provided the means for him to explore the properties of the rich, red nectar that provided sustenance to their kind away from prying human eyes.

"And you became the Second less than a hundred years later?"

Her warm alto voice, and the way she framed her questions, invited one to confide. He couldn't forget he was being interviewed, and by an expert. "When the Civil War broke out, Valerian felt he was needed in the Colonies. I remained in Europe, and expanded our network." Until Bram had published that damn novel. Who'd have thought that, after toiling away with pen and paper for years, his friend would find literary fame with a vampire story?

Bram's subject matter couldn't be a coincidence.

He turned his attention back to Tia. "Modern communication methods both simplify this effort, and make it more complex."

She grinned as she glanced at the computers. "You're buried in email?"

"Yes. Encrypted email has become our primary collection tool—very efficient—but I occasionally remind our gatherers that images and objects tell important stories, too. Let me show you something." He guided her into the aisle with a courteous touch at the small of her back, brushing the slice of warm, bare skin above her low-slung belt. Clenching his jaw, he manipulated the shelves on their tracks, exposed the rack he wanted, and opened one of the dozens of shallow, flat storage drawers.

She looked at the scrap of wrinkled, soot-covered parchment under treated glass, and read the shakily-written words aloud: "They are burning us as witches." She looked up at him. "This is from The Burning Times."

"Yes." When he'd placed the artifact under the translucent glass, he swore he could still smell smoke.

"I knew we'd lost some of our people during that time, but—" she traced her finger over the clear glass "—it's another matter to see hard proof."

Were those tears in her eyes? "I didn't mean to make you sad."

She straightened, blinking furiously. "My feelings pale next to those who suffered. Or who've seen what you and Valerian have."

He busied himself closing the drawer, and moving the shelves back into place. She saw too damn much.

"So, you were our European liaison for over two hundred years?"

He nodded. "I moved to America in the early nineteen hundreds. Valerian needed me here." And he'd needed to get away from England—away from Deirdre's scheming, and from his growing suspicious about where Bram had gotten the idea for his story.

He hadn't been careful enough, and his people had paid the price.

His phone vibrated in a distinctive SOS rhythm. "It's the hospital. Excuse me."

Nodding, she wandered over to the table where Antonia had been working to give him some privacy. She leaned over the ancient book, hands behind her back, peering at its yellowed pages without touching them.

Very good.

He scrolled through the patient intake report. Mila Stanton had passed out at work again, and the nasty gash at the back of her head definitely needed stitches. The delicate young vampire had autoimmune hemolytic anemia, and she didn't always comply with her treatment plan. She refused to share her diagnosis with her parents, so they couldn't help. With a couple of taps, he instructed the resident to handle the wound and to start transfusing. With a mental apology to the very capable resident, he added that he was en route. Now would be a good time to deliver a strongly worded lecture, reminding Mila that she *had* to drink more blood. He hit 'Send' and slipped the phone back into the leather holder clipped to his belt.

"Unfortunately, our work will have to wait for another time." A time when he was better prepared to deal with her.

"You're going to Memorial?" She glanced at her watch. "Now? Are you okay to drive? Do you need a ride?" She paused. "You looked so tired earlier."

"The blood rejuvenated me."

"Do you have a place you can rest? At the hospital, or a place in town? What about the sun?"

"Tia." He put his hand over her mouth. It seemed to be the only way he'd get a word in edgewise. "I'm fine. I'll catch a nap at the hospital before I drive home, but thank you for your concern."

She pulled his hand away. Her fingers felt warm against his skin, an intimate brand. "Make sure you do."

She sounded…worried about him. It had been a long time since a woman had worried about him.

She abruptly dropped his hand. A delicate blush washed over her cheeks, turning her skin a delightful shade of pink. "Do you suppose Valerian is awake?"

He nodded. "I think he and Thane planned to watch *Downton Abbey* tonight."

"I love that show! Do you watch it?"

"No." He grabbed his suit coat off the back of Bailey's chair and handed Tia her purse. The drive to the hospital, on the nearly-empty night highway, would give him almost an hour to get his unruly body under control again.

He *had* to get himself under control again.

"When will we work together next?" Tia asked. "We didn't get anything accomplished tonight."

He started walking toward the stairwell. "I'll let you know." He'd find some diplomatic way to decline any future offers of assistance.

She didn't follow. Instead, she lifted her chin in challenge.

"I'll call. I promise." The words were out of his mouth before he knew he was going to say them, and he felt a trickle of admiration for her chutzpah. No one had questioned his actions, or as Bailey would say, called him on his shit, in a very long time. He flipped the light switches next to the door, dousing the clinical, bright light. Several dim security lights illuminated the space well enough to navigate. "I'll escort you to your car."

"No need."

It wasn't worth discussing. "Come on." After a quick glance at the security screens, he led her through the heavy metal door and up the stairs. When they reached the entrance, he scanned the parking lot again, and opened the door. "Drive safely."

"Here's your hat, what's your hurry?" she murmured, amusement in her eyes. But she didn't move. Mosquitoes buzzed and crickets chirped. Finally, she put her hands on his shoulders for balance, rose onto her tiptoes, and softly kissed both of his cheeks.

She smelled luscious, like blood and lilacs. It was all he could do keep his tongue in his mouth.

Tia studied him for several seconds, her gaze flicking down to his lips momentarily before her own quirked into a smile. "Take care." She hit a button on the key fob in her hand, and her car's headlights flashed, spotlighting them. She about-faced, walked to her car, got in, buckled up, then drove away.

He watched until her tail lights disappeared, pondering her words. "Take care." A huff of self-mocking laughter escaped. Take care? That's what he did. That was *all* he did.

And damn it, it wasn't enough anymore.

CHAPTER THREE

"Hello, Miss Lyudmila."

Hansen, Mila's family's black-suited butler, stood at the kitchen door—the one she'd hoped to sneak into. "Hello, Hansen." She really shouldn't have expected anything different. Very little happened in her parent's palatial Lake Minnetonka home that Hansen wasn't aware of. He was probably the only person in the household who'd noticed she hadn't slept at home for over a day.

"Sorry I didn't call." She set her backpack on the floor, just inside the door. "My shift at work went longer than I expected. The sun came up, so I decided to sleep at the hospital until it set again." Strictly speaking, she wasn't lying. Ever since her diagnosis, she'd become *way* too adept at such conversational shades of gray. The tiny staples hidden in her hairline stung and throbbed—she couldn't believe she'd fainted at work—but at least the wound had stopped bleeding.

"Your parents are just about to break their fast."

Her aristocratic parents ran their household on strict vampire time, sleeping during the day and waking at sunset. No new-fangled VampScreen or UV-treated windows for them, thank you very much; they had no need to be out and about during the daylight hours. At sunset, they woke up, bathed, then dressed to meet the day. You could set a watch by them. Hansen likely did.

"Will you be dining with your parents this evening?"

"Yes." She felt like a bloated tick after being transfused at the ER, but it was best for everyone that she join her parents and eat what Hansen served. She looked down at her shirt and pants. Her work clothes would annoy her mother, but at least she hadn't bled all over them when she fell. She tugged at her sweater sleeve, making sure it hid the bandage and cotton ball at the crook of her elbow—which she really should have removed before coming home, damn it. She sighed as she walked to the formal dining room. There was no help for it now. If her parents smelled the blood and asked questions, she'd just tell them she had her period.

Though the glossy mahogany table could comfortably seat twenty, her parents sat adjacent to each other at one end. Hansen had set the table with the everyday Lenox, with pale green cloth napkins providing a shot of color. A lead crystal vase of chrysanthemums served as the centerpiece. The flowers' coral heads were as large as the bread plates.

"Hello, Lyudmila."

"Hello, Mother." Leaning down, Mila kissed both taut cheeks, and quickly backed away. Her mother's heavy floral scent made her feel woozy. "Are the chrysanthemums yours?" Her mother excelled as a hostess, and grew flowers year-round in a greenhouse on the property.

"Yes. Aren't they beautiful?"

As she started talking about how she'd trained the

flowers, Mila looked at her mother's face, a surgically smooth canvas where no age line dared tread. No one looking at the chic vampire Lyudmila would ever guess she had a daughter Mila's age—which was probably the point of all those nips and tucks. Mila had been a late-in-life baby, conceived at the outer boundaries of her mother's fertile years—but five years after Mila had been born, there'd been one more pregnancy, one more birth.

Did her mother mourn Katarina? Did she even remember her?

Her father dropped his *Wall Street Journal.* "Hello, dear. How was the League meeting?"

It cracked her up how the Elders shortened the Genetic Purity League's name to something so...philanthropic-sounding, as if by leaving off the first two words they could disavow all knowledge of why the organization had been formed in the first place. Its original mission, to preserve the pure bloodlines of the Ancients who'd survived the crash, might have been well-intentioned at one time, but damn it, they knew better now.

"It was fine." She kissed her father's cheek as she passed him.

Most younger members knew that the GPL's mission was ignorant and ass-backwards—their species' robustness lay not in genetic purity, but in genetic diversity—but the group continued to meet anyway. And why not? It was a way to socialize. The booze flowed free and freely, and people hooked up with abandon. Not her, not anymore; she'd quickly learned that having sex for entertainment's sake wasn't for her. These days, she attended the meetings as a personal challenge, as a way to force herself to interact with people her own age.

She plopped into her chair, ignoring her mother's disapproving frown. Approaching Dominic Reese had been one of the most difficult things she'd ever done, but she'd made herself do it, and—she disguised a shiver of delight—he'd actually asked her out. She'd been so distracted by his low, rumbly voice, and by the silky, cinnamon-colored hair on his muscular forearms, that she'd had a hard time concentrating on the questions he'd asked about her job, her family, and her life.

Hansen entered the dining room with a click of hard-soled shoes against the parquet floor. Ice cubes clinked as he set a glass before her: cream soda, barely tinged with blood. "Thanks, Hansen." Wyland had told her to increase her blood intake—and she would—but she wasn't going to stop drinking her favorite breakfast beverage.

"Lyudmila, you're a grown woman," her mother said as Hansen went back to the kitchen. "Why do you insist on drinking soda pop for breakfast?"

If I'm a grown woman, why do you insist I live with you? The angry words went unsaid. Over the years, Mila had learned to choose her rebellions very, very carefully. She took a sip—a small, safe rebellion—and felt the bubbly chill effervesce on her tongue. "Because I like it."

"And those unattractive work clothes." Her mother picked up a goblet of dark red blood that glistened in the chandelier's prismatic light. "Must you wear such drab colors?"

Mila eyed her mother's black silk blouse, but didn't say a word. Her clothes weren't the problem; the work was. Her mother didn't understand Mila's need to do something useful with her education. To work outside the home, to earn a paycheck that didn't have Daddy's signature on it.

"Well, we'll take care of the drab when we see the dressmaker about your gown," her mother said. "The calligrapher needs the names and addresses of your League friends for the party invitations."

"Huh?"

Her mother sighed. "Must you use such coarse language?"

Mila set the glass down on the tablecloth and mentally counted to three. "To which party are you referring, Mother?"

"I can't believe you've forgotten." Hansen entered the room again, pushing a rolling cart holding three plates covered by shiny silver domes. He served her mother first, then her, and then her father, before leaving again. "Lyudmila," her exasperated mother continued, "it's time for you to take your rightful place in our community. It's been far too long since we offered hospitality to Valerian and Wyland."

Wyland, here? The last thing she wanted to do was socialize with her doctor—the doctor her parents didn't realize she was seeing. She looked down at her plate. The small steak, swimming in bloody *au jus*, suddenly looked nauseating instead of appetizing. "Why invite them to the party?"

"Are you daft? They're our leaders. They represent us on the Underworld Council. They're the most powerful vampires on the planet." Her mother picked up a silver-plated knife and fork. "Lyudmila, social and political networks don't just…happen. Like flowers, they require constant cultivation and care."

"I saw Wyland at Sebastiani Labs a couple of

weeks ago," her father volunteered from behind his newspaper. "We exchanged a few words. He asked after your well-being, Mila."

Her stomach bottomed out. Had Wyland told them—

"It's high time Wyland took a mate." Her mother sliced into her steak. "He's a very attractive man, don't you think? Barely three hundred years old, and his parents were purebloods."

Attractive? Wyland? Surely her mother wasn't suggesting—

"You're nearly twenty-five, Lyudmila. It's time you thought about the continuity of our family line."

Apparently she was.

"Wyland is the perfect choice for you," her mother bulldozed on. "The only choice, really."

Mila picked up her fork and mutinously stabbed a strawberry. What if she didn't want a bondmate? What if she wasn't interested in having children? Ever? The very thought would put a stake in her mother's heart. "I'm sure Wyland's far too busy to socialize, Mother—especially with Valerian being in such poor health."

"Lyudmila." Her mother's knife clanked against the china. "Wyland asked after your well-being. We must strike while the iron's hot." She picked up her goblet again, considering her with more than a hint of calculation in her eyes. "Do you ever see Wyland at the hospital?" A pause. "Maybe taking that job wasn't such a horrible decision after all."

If her parents knew how often she saw Wyland, and why, they'd shit a gold-plated brick. It was time to nip her mother's delusions in the bud. "Mother, Wyland's not interested in me, not that way. He's simply being polite." She gave a light laugh. "And he's over three hundred years old. If he wanted a bondmate, don't you think he'd already have one?"

Her father eyed her over the top of his newspaper. "Perhaps you can change his mind."

The words hit like a depth charge. Apparently her parents weren't above pimping out their only daughter for political and social gain.

As she tried to catch her breath, her mother chattered on about menus, guest lists, gowns, and seating plans, not at all concerned about Mila's reaction. Not bothering to assess her daughter for damage.

What else was new?

A shriek of frustration threatened to leap from her throat, but she shoved it back, shoved it down—and that, she admitted with a sigh, was part of the problem. Given her past behavior, why *wouldn't* her parents think she'd simply fall in line with their plans? They were so certain she'd obey that they hadn't even bothered to thrall her to ensure her compliance.

Little Mila, meek and mild.

Not anymore. Damn it, she *was* nearly twenty-five years old, an adult vampire with full rights and autonomy. She had a good job, friends, her own money…it was high time she took control of her own life, stood on her own two feet. Either she needed protection, or she was old enough to take a bondmate, run her own household, and continue the family line.

Her mother couldn't have it both ways.

She picked up her glass and took a slow sip. So, her parents thought they could offer their perfect, pristine daughter to the Vampire Second on a silver platter? *Ha.* What would they do if they discovered she wasn't so perfect? Wasn't so pristine? That a hot guy like Dominic Reese was interested in her, and that she was interested right back?

What then?

She lowered the glass with a hand that shook. She might have been perfectly healthy at birth, but she was far from healthy now. And little Katarina's snuffed-out life was proof that, in her parents' minds, imperfections were simply not acceptable.

*

Ignore it. Just ignore it. Don't look at the screen.

"Easier said than done," Tia muttered, scrawling her name on the bottom of the check. After posting some new content to *ILQ*, she'd caught up on email, returned a few phone calls, and had done some long-overdue filing. Now, truly desperate, she was paying bills—something, anything, to avoid clicking on the icon that mocked her from her laptop screen.

Ever since Bailey had given her access to the Archives, she'd hit the database as often as a crack addict hit their pipe. And was it any wonder? What marvelous things she'd read; what amazing facts she'd learned.

Sighing in defeat, she swung her chair toward the laptop sitting on the other side of her home office's L-shaped desk. After clicking on the icon and logging on, she opened the files she'd started to build on Sigurd, Valerian, The Old Ways, the Genetic Purity League, and Wyland—who hadn't called her as he'd promised.

She shook off the thought. She had plenty to keep
her busy, other stories to work on, even if
Commander Gideon Lupinsky hadn't returned her
phone calls yet. While she waited for the Archives'
login sequence to finish, she glanced out the window,
where a floodlight illuminated her neglected back
yard. If she didn't mow her lawn soon, she'd need to
scare up some goats... Ah, there. The main screen
was finally up.

Bailey had warned her that the Archives were still a
hot mess—a hodgepodge of scanned original
manuscripts, documents, images, and electronic files,
all crying out for organization and deeper indexing—
but the biographies were solid, and rudimentary
search capabilities were up and running. Though Tia
hadn't found any information on The Genetic Purity
League or The Old Ways, she'd been amused to find
her own small biographical entry, probably due to her
parents, who were noted philanthropists. Bailey had
formatted the biographical materials in a manner
anyone familiar with Wikipedia could navigate.

She pulled up Wyland's biography, clicked on one
of the first links, and watched Valerian's distinctive,
slanted handwriting fill the screen. Against the cream-
colored parchment, the ink was still surprisingly
legible, and the scan was so pristine that she could see
places where his incisive downstrokes had caused the
nib of his pen to cut through the paper. She took
notes as she read, tapping pertinent facts into the
word processing document she'd created for Wyland.

Thanks to Valerian, Wyland had a well-
documented life. Born to aristocratic vampire parents
in England in 1702, he'd been studying medicine

when he'd come to Valerian's attention. His primary research interest? Blood, of course. Wyland had become Valerian's apprentice soon afterward, continuing his medical research, studying law, and familiarizing himself with their culture's history via their fledgling Archives. As Wyland had previously told her, Valerian had designated Wyland as his Second in the mid-1700s. He'd remained in England while Valerian traveled back and forth between Europe and the ascendant American colonies.

But damn, the things Wyland *hadn't* told her. According to these materials, he was quite the political mover and shaker, advising royalty and military alike. His research into blood, particularly transfusion, had resulted in some of 'humanity's' earliest hematology advances.

As for his personal life... She pulled up an enlargement of the scanned photograph that she'd quickly glanced at the previous night. *Lyceum Theatre - Opening Night - July 1896*. Wearing a beautiful Victorian tailcoat, a crisp white shirt and tie, and smiling for the camera, a marginally younger-looking Wyland stood in front of the theatre with another man, and with his arm wrapped around the nipped-in waist of an absolutely stunning redhead. Actress? Mistress? Paramour? Whoever the woman was, Tia would bet her trust fund that she and Wyland had just rolled out of bed. She leaned toward the photo, and read the names written in faded ink along the picture's border. "Who are you, Deirdre d'Amour?" she murmured to the lushly curved woman. She didn't want to think about what the other woman had done to put that relaxed, sex-soaked smile on Wyland's face.

The other man, Abraham Stoker, was similarly dressed, wearing a black Victorian tailcoat, and— "What?" Abraham Stoker? *Bram* Stoker? Wyland knew the man who'd written *Dracula*? "Awesome."

Her phone rang. She considered letting it go to voice mail, but put it on speaker when she saw it was Bailey.

"Are you at your computer?" Bailey said. "I'm going to send you a link."

She'd spent so much time on the phone with Bailey over the last couple of days that the other woman's lack of phone etiquette didn't faze her anymore. Obtaining access to the Archives had taken more time and effort than she'd anticipated. "Did you know Wyland knew Bram Stoker?" she asked. "The guy who wrote *Dracula*?"

"Whatever. Incoming."

A soft chime announced the arrival of the link in her chat window. She recognized the base URL. Why was Bailey sending her a link to a comment at *In Like Quinn*? "The story about crappy handicapped access in public buildings?"

"Read it."

She clicked on the comment. "'Jacoby Woolf's father should put him down like the damaged mongrel he is.'" A sick feeling washed over her. Like the previous comment, this one was marginally on-topic, but... "Someone's using my website to make threats against the Council."

"It seems that way," Bailey said. "After the first comment about Coco was posted, I wrote a script to find and flag comments made about Council members and their families, but I never expected anyone to be stupid enough to actually mention a

Council member by their full name. I'm trying to track it back, but, like the other comment, it's anonymized pretty damn well."

"Isn't that hard to do?"

"Not nearly as hard as it used to be."

Hmm. "'Put him down?' What kind of prehistoric throwback says something like that?"

"It's classic Genetic Purity League."

"And it's batshit insane."

Bailey didn't disagree. "Does *In Like Quinn* have a moderation policy? Standards of behavior, terms of use and such?"

"Yes." Freedom of speech didn't mean freedom from consequences, and this person had crossed her line. With a couple of clicks, she put the comment into Moderation state, making its offensive text invisible to readers. "Done," she said. "Feel free to moderate other messages if you feel it's necessary."

There was a long pause. "Okay."

Bailey, with her hacker pedigree, was no doubt looking at the same admin screen she was, password be damned.

"Have you seen Wyland recently?" Bailey asked. "He's not answering his phone."

She almost laughed at Bailey's grumpy tone. Tethered to gadgets 24/7, Bailey clearly couldn't conceive of someone making a different choice. "We worked together at the Archives a couple of nights ago, but I haven't heard from him since." So much for his promise. "Valerian and I have a movie date in a couple of hours." She and Valerian had enjoyed themselves so much watching *Downton Abbey* together the other night that he'd asked her to visit again, and to bring a movie from her vast collection. Tonight's feature would be *The Hunger*, with Bowie, Sarandon, and Deneuve. "If I see Wyland, I can let him know you'd like to speak with him."

"Please do," Bailey said. "Talk to you soon."

"'Bye."

What was Wyland's deal? For a man so hung up on etiquette, he sure was rude. She picked up the pen, tapping it against the top of her desk. She wasn't due at Valerian's for a couple of hours yet, but he'd issued an open invitation, telling her to come over any time.

She logged out of *ILQ*, saved her research files, logged out of the Archives, and powered down. As she stalked upstairs to take a shower, she spared another thought to her overlong grass. Maybe she'd have to call in those goats after all, because right now, instead of mowing, she was going to give the Vampire Second a giant piece of her mind.

＊

Sitting on the edge of the mattress in Valerian's bedroom, Wyland studied his patient, lying in bed with his upper body propped up by pillows. Val had passed a comfortable day's sleep. He was alert, his color was good, and his lungs were clearer tonight than they'd been yesterday. The antibiotics were finally starting to work.

"Why do you insist on doing this? We both know what the problem is. I'm old." Valerian pushed away the stethoscope and buttoned his flannel pajama top. "Write that on my tombstone, Wyland. 'He was old.'"

"Tombstone? I thought you wanted a Viking

funeral." Over the last twenty years, the funeral plans Valerian had considered included entombment in an unmarked Scottish cairn, floating away in a flaming pyre on the Ganges, classic Egyptian mummification, and having his ashes compressed into a diamond.

"Gene Roddenberry's cremains were launched into space," Valerian mused. "Now there's a mighty fine send-off."

Wyland put the stethoscope in the black bag sitting at his feet, trying to hide his exhaustion. Sebastiani Labs had an aerospace division. A similar celebration could definitely be arranged when the time came.

Whenever the time came, it would be too soon.

With a contented sigh, Valerian relaxed against the pillows, pushing aside the nasal cannula. They'd exchanged some harsh words about the oxygen tank standing next to the mahogany four-poster, an argument Wyland had won. But what good was winning the argument if Val wouldn't use the thing?

"Sometimes I think Sigurd had the right idea."

Wyland stilled, waiting for him to say more, but Val moved on to another topic. These days, having a conversation with Valerian was like skipping rocks, with Val jumping from subject to subject until he sank back into sleep, or into private reverie. And now he'd stopped speaking, lost in thought, looking into the middle distance with unfocused eyes. What did Val see? What did he remember?

He'd probably never know. "Would you like to feed?" Without waiting for an answer, Wyland walked to the other side of the bed, climbed onto the mattress, and lay down, cradling Valerian's frail body in a gentle embrace.

"Have you finished emptying out the catacombs

yet?" Valerian suddenly asked.

"Not yet." During the last few days, he'd barely had time to breathe, much less empty the last dank alcove at the far end of the catacombs tunneled under the house. He'd spent hours at a Sebastiani Labs manufacturing facility, overseeing the final testing of a bagged blood formulation Sebastiani Labs had developed. And then there'd been Lukas's request. Little Coco Fontaine, not yet born but already causing trouble—not that he could blame Lukas and Scarlett for asking him to confirm their daughter's precise status. After many eye-blurring hours of research, he'd discovered nothing in their Council charter that would prohibit the mixed-species offspring of two sitting Council members from representing either species—or both species simultaneously, for that matter.

And he hadn't had time to call Tia Quinn, but perhaps that was for the best.

"Maybe Thane can help with the catacombs." Valerian settled more comfortably into Wyland's arms. "Sigurd's trunk is back there."

Sigurd's trunk? In the catacombs? His pulse kicked as he surreptitiously checked Val's.

"Stop that."

Or perhaps not so surreptitiously.

"Wyland, I'm not going to die today."

"Not if I have anything to say about it." And no matter how much he wanted Valerian to reveal more information about Sigurd—a trunk in the catacombs?—Val needed to feed. He extended his right wrist to his First.

"You honor me," Val murmured.

He and Valerian, the two most powerful vampires

in the world, had exchanged blood for centuries, but the words still moved him.

"And I worry about you," Val added.

"What? Why?"

"It's been months since you've taken my vein. Who feeds you?"

"Thane. Or I drink bagged blood." Drinking from the vein was the ultimate act of trust, bestowing healing, strength, and the ability to discern one's emotional state to the drinker. Each pleasurable tug and pull created a connection, an echo in the blood, which could not be broken except by death. Deirdre been dead for years, but sometimes he swore he still felt her, throbbing in his head.

He'd learned the hard way that vulnerability was the price one paid for intimacy and pleasure.

"Bah," Valerian scoffed. "Bagged blood contains all the nutrients you need, but where's the warmth? Where's the connection?" Valerian suckled at his wrist, preparing his cephalic vein for his bite. "And when was the last time you enjoyed a woman? Don't think I haven't noticed how you act around young Tia."

"Young is right," he said grimly.

"Wyland, she's fully of age." Another swirl of Valerian's tongue. "I'm surprised at your historical relativism. Less than two hundred years ago, it was quite common for a young woman half her age to be married and have a half-dozen children."

"Less than two hundred years ago, she wouldn't have had much choice in the matter." Such behavior persisted even into this time, with powerful men inflicting their attentions on beautiful young women who didn't think they could refuse. He said as much to Valerian.

"Wyland, you're not creeping on Tia."

He blinked. "Creeping?"

"Sexually pursuing her in a stalker-like, inappropriate manner. You know, creeping."

How easily current era slang slipped from Valerian's lips. It always had. "You watch too much reality television, Val."

"It's a fine source of cultural information," Valerian said against his wrist. "As far as I can tell, you're not pursuing her at all, sexually or otherwise— which is a damn shame."

"She's barely out of the schoolroom."

"She's thirty years old, Wyland. She's a homeowner, a businesswoman, and serves on the board of her parents' charitable foundation." Valerian paused. "I think she's interested in you, too."

"No, she's not." He could still feel her soft, pouty lips against his cheek, but that was his problem, not hers.

"You're wrong. If you don't believe me, ask Lukas."

"I will not ask Lukas," he said testily. The last thing he needed was an incubus playing matchmaker. "I don't know that she's interested in me as much as she's...curious. She *is* a journalist, after all—a journalist who just got carte blanche access to our Archives. Against my recommendation, I might add."

"I tell you, she's interested in you. Sexually."

His fangs tingled at Valerian's frank words. "That doesn't mean I have to do anything about it."

"Why ever not?" Valerian asked, exasperated. "You want her. She wants you. She's of age—she's older than Deirdre was when you first met her—and you're a vampire in his prime." Valerian pointed a long, bony finger at him. "Don't scowl at me. It's long past time I said this aloud. Deirdre was a glorious creature who used her sexuality like a bludgeon. You fell in love with her, and—" Val gave a pragmatic shrug "—she didn't reciprocate. It happens."

He kept his face expressionless, lifting his mental drawbridge with exquisite subtlety. Over the years, he'd succeeded in keeping his suspicions about Deirdre's deception from Valerian.

"Damn, boy, you haven't had a relationship in over a century. Times have changed. There's nothing stopping you from hooking up with Tia."

A chuckle escaped at Val's language. Hook up, have sexual congress with, fornicate, copulate, have coitus with, roger, tup, play hide the salami, fuck, make love with… However it was said, in whatever era, he wanted her. Sexually. In this, Valerian could read him like an open book.

"You're too alone, Wyland. I worry about you." With that, Val drove his fangs into Wyland's wrist. The sting quickly subsided, and as Val suckled with a familiar pull and tug, Wyland relaxed back against the pillows, relaxed into the silence. It was very poor form to hold a one-sided conversation with someone who couldn't respond.

And this was one conversation he didn't want to continue.

CHAPTER FOUR

As she strode up the sidewalk leading to Vamp Central, a raindrop spat on her arm. Climbing the steps, she shifted the cardboard box of movies she carried to the other arm, then rang the doorbell. The eight-note Westminster chime clanged inside the house. One of the gargoyles lurking above the door had a glowing red eye, and she waved to whoever might be observing her from a security screen somewhere inside.

The locks disengaged with a series of clicks, and the door opened in a welcoming wedge of light. "Miss Tia." Thane, Valerian's majordomo, wore a flour-dusted apron that said *Kiss the Cook*. "Please, come in. Let me take that."

She'd interrupted his work. "I'm so sorry," she murmured, handing him the box. "I'm early for my movie date with Valerian." And she'd been so intent on chewing out Wyland that she hadn't given a thought to how her early arrival might impact other members of the household.

"Please, please. Come in." Thane gestured for her to enter the foyer, closing the door behind them. "Valerian's so excited."

Seven hundred years old, yet appearing a fit human seventy, Thane had graying red hair, a bruiser's build, and a hint of a Scottish brogue. The vampire had served Valerian for as long as anyone could remember. Though he surely had a kilt and sporran in his closet, tonight, under the apron, he wore pressed blue jeans, a pale blue polo shirt, and brown leather sandals.

"I'm preparing Valerian's breakfast tray. He'll eat in his bedroom today, but Wyland should be down soon," Thane said. "Let me set another place."

She hadn't anticipated chewing Wyland out over a cozy breakfast for two. "Nothing for me, thanks."

"He'll appreciate the company."

No, he wouldn't. He'd tolerate it—maybe—but appreciate it? She'd never met a man more comfortable with solitude, but apparently Thane wasn't going to take no for an answer. She followed him into the great room, her gaze skittering past the settee she'd shared with Wyland the other night. At odd moments, she swore she could still feel his muscled thigh against hers.

Thane set her box down on the bar, where a large silver urn towered over bone china cups and saucers so delicate she could almost see through them. Champagne flutes, wine goblets, and chunky highball and lowball glasses sat next to icy-cold pitchers of orange and tomato juice. Bloody Mary makings stood at the ready.

Breakfast at Vamp Central was a bit more of a production than it was at her place.

"Coffee? Some warm or chilled blood?"

"No, thank you. Please, go ahead and serve Valerian."

He nodded. "Make yourself at home. Join me if you wish." When he opened the heavy wood door leading to the kitchen, the scent of frying bacon wafted into the room.

Ignoring her growling stomach, she wandered over to the bookcase. There was the Fabergé egg she'd admired the other night. White and pale blue enamel, encrusted with diamonds, topped by lions and an elephant and poised on a delicate tripod stand, it had to be worth a king's ransom. It shared shelf space with a well-thumbed paperback set of Anne Rice's *Vampire Chronicles*, a fist-sized agate, and a framed, matted photograph of…what *was* that? It looked as though someone had carved a rough map into a slab of solid rock. Forest to the left, waves carved into a huge void on the right. The land mass had a distinctive arrowhead shape.

She leaned closer, squinting. Was that a rocket, sailing over the trees?

The petroglyph cave. This had to be the petroglyph cave she'd heard about, one of the first discoveries at the northern Minnesota archaeological site theorized to be the location where their ancestors' spaceship had crashed. The land mass was unmistakably northeastern Minnesota. The wavy void had to be Lake Superior.

"Amazing." Now that she had access to the Archives, she could research all the discoveries they'd made at the site—not that she'd be able to do anything with the information other than satisfy her curiosity, but sometimes that was enough.

Wandering the length of the shelves, she admired Valerian's treasures, wondering about the untold stories behind each item, in such a reverie that suddenly seeing so many pictures of Wyland on the last shelf startled her. Positioned on the center of the shelf was a framed and matted sketch of him as a young man, head bent over a thick book, his hair tucked behind his ear. Scattered around the sketch were other framed photographs, some yellowed with time and with swoopy, decorative edges, and others of more recent vintage. Several pictures were labeled with dates and locations, written in ink along the borders. Going by the dates and the fashions, the pictures spanned the late 1800s to current day, but in each, Wyland looked much the same, wearing a dark suit, with his pale hair lashed back in a low ponytail, ruthlessly exposing those knife-blade cheekbones. She peered at one picture, grinning. Even the Vampire Second hadn't managed to side-step the seventies' leisure suit craze. And there, tucked into the corner, was a copy of the picture she'd seen in Wyland's Archive bio, of Wyland and Bram Stoker, with the beautiful Deirdre d'Amour cropped out of the picture.

Interesting.

She wandered back to the bar, where condensed water dripped down the glass pitcher of orange juice. Suddenly, her bladder felt ready to burst. She scanned the room, looking for hallways or doorways that might indicate a nearby bathroom. There was a bathroom off Valerian's decadent sitting room upstairs; she'd used it when they'd watched *Downton Abbey* a couple of nights ago.

Valerian's open invitation probably didn't include walking without escort to the private areas of his home, but the last thing she wanted was for Thane to see her holding herself as she searched for a place to pee.

As she climbed the gently curving stairwell leading

to the second floor, the carpeting, a faded cranberry with gold *fleurs-de-lis*, muffled her footfalls. At the top of the stairway, she turned left and walked down the hall, past sconces and graceful framed landscapes, past Wyland's closed bedroom door. As she slipped into Valerian's dark sitting room, she couldn't help but wonder what Wyland's private rooms looked like. What would they reveal, if anything, of the man?

She quickly used the restroom and washed her hands, noticing as she had the previous night that there were two toothbrushes in the stand next to the soap. With a mental shrug, she returned to the sitting room. On the far side of the dark, yawning space, Valerian's bedroom door was ajar, with a soft, inviting light illuminating the gap. Before she knew it, her feet were moving. She paused when she reached the threshold—*what the hell are you doing?*—but her curiosity got the better of her.

She peeked inside.

The sumptuous décor and the medical supplies barely registered. Instead, her gaze was riveted on the two men lying together on the huge antique bed. Wyland, wearing loose cotton sweatpants and a white T-shirt, held Valerian in a gentle embrace, his eyes closed, and his hair loose over the pillow. The older vampire suckled contentedly from Wyland's wrist.

Her fangs tingled, then shoved down into her mouth. A rogue wave of desire nearly knocked her to her knees.

Wyland's eyes suddenly opened. His ice-storm gaze seethed with heat.

"Sorry," she mouthed, backing out of the room and closing the door behind her. Leaning against it, she waited for her legs to steady beneath her. She'd interrupted something precious and private, but she'd already received her punishment.

The sight of Wyland, casually sprawled on that bed, would haunt her for a long time to come.

✸

Wyland shot his cuffs, adjusted his already-tight tie, and then left his rooms. Across the hall, water ran; Valerian's personal care assistant was helping him get ready to meet the day.

He strode down the hall and took the stairs at a controlled clip. Valerian apparently had a movie date with Tia Quinn. No one had informed him of this fact.

What on earth had Thane been thinking? Guests were not permitted to wander their home without escort. *This* guest had interrupted the First as he fed, an unconscionable breach of etiquette. It simply did not happen—or hadn't happened before Tia Quinn had crashed into their lives.

Damn it, he'd think of her the next time he fed Valerian, as if thoughts of her weren't elbowing into his mind at the most inopportune times as it was. Was he to have no respite from her, even in his own home?

On the other hand, who was he to berate her for an etiquette breach? The way her fangs had dropped, and the dazed look on her face, had driven him from flaccid to firm in a heartbeat. In Valerian's *bed*. "Bugger." He had to stop thinking about her lust-glazed expression, because it was happening again.

He and Ms. Quinn were going to have a very serious conversation.

He stalked to the kitchen, stumbling to a stop just inside the door. The table where he and Thane bolted down a quick breakfast together most evenings was set with the Royal Worcester instead of their usual casual crockery. Thane had added a lemon-yellow tablecloth and matching napkins, and nestled between the salt and pepper shakers was a tiny crystal vase holding a sprig of rosemary. Tia sat in Thane's usual place, turned sideways in the chair with her bare legs exposed, listening to Thane as he flipped pancakes. Her hand moved toward the platter of bacon sitting next to her on the table. She selected a slice, brought it to her mouth, and nibbled.

"So Wyland swooped in—on horseback, mind you—and snatched me away from the rabbling mob. The sun was about to rise, and they'd already started the fire!"

Bloody Christ, why tell Tia this particular story? Two hundred years later, even thinking about Thane's imprisonment and near-execution made his stomach turn. It had taken Thane months to recover from the torture inflicted by human hands.

They didn't even know he was there. "Ahem."

Thane turned away from his griddle. "There you are. Just in time for pancakes. Let me get you two squared away, and then I'll bring Valerian his tray."

A cozy breakfast for two? With Tia Quinn? *I think not.* "Thank you, but I'm expected at the hospital. I'll make do with some blood and a muffin."

Thane slipped a final pancake onto the stack. "Ms. Quinn has some questions about the Archives— questions I think only you or Valerian can answer."

Framing Tia's issue in such a manner made it impossible for him to leave, and Thane knew it.

Thane set the platter of pancakes on the table next to the bacon. His amusement shimmered through their blood bond.

Tia looked back and forth between them. "You two have entire conversations without saying a word, don't you?"

It was unusual that a vampire so young could perceive the throb of mental shorthand that he, Thane, and Valerian, strong vampires who'd shared blood for centuries, shared with each other. How…interesting. With reluctance, he took the chair across the table from Tia. "You'll have to make do with me answering your questions today. Valerian is still preparing for his day."

At his pointed words, Tia's cheeks turned a satisfying shade of pink.

She murmured a soft 'thank you' to Thane as he placed two pancakes on her plate, then turned her attention to him. "I spoke with Bailey earlier. She said you hadn't returned her phone call, and I volunteered to pass along a message if I saw you."

He nudged the butter crock, and the small pitcher holding warmed syrup, closer to her plate. "What is the message?"

"To return her phone call." Her overly-sweet smile called him an ingrate.

Over at the hissing espresso machine, Thane cleared his throat, as if trying not to laugh.

Tia slathered her pancakes with butter, poured a river of maple syrup on top, and dug in. The pleasure on her face as she tasted the first bite was too painful to watch. He dropped his gaze to his plate, to the artist's delicate rendering of sage.

Suddenly Thane was at his side with his espresso. It was thick as thieves, with a small dollop of blood for added kick. "Have you fed this evening?" Thane murmured.

Wyland sighed. As if Tia couldn't hear him perfectly well, sitting three feet away. "Yes, Mother."

"Are the pancakes to your liking, Miss Tia?"

"Please, it's just Tia—and they're fabulous." Her pink tongue swiped away a glistening drop of syrup from her lower lip. "I don't think Toaster Strudel is going to cut it anymore."

Thane shook his head. "You and Wyland, eating on the run. He wouldn't sit down and eat breakfast if I didn't make it for him."

Wyland scowled. The comment was true on its face—he usually ate a muffin or a bagel in the car during his commute to Minneapolis—but Thane made it sound as though he was used to being served, or couldn't fend for himself. Neither was true.

"Are you two set for now? Tia, are you sure you won't have some coffee? An espresso?"

"No, thanks," she said. "The bloody Mimosa is great."

"We're fine, Thane," he said pointedly. "Please, see to Valerian."

Thane slid two pancakes and three pieces of bacon onto a plate, and set it on a tray next to Valerian's "chocolate milk." The clinical-strength nutritional beverage was almost a meal in itself, high in calories, lipids, electrolytes, vitamins, and protein. Thankfully Valerian could tolerate its flavor—a fact they'd discovered after Wyland had threatened to insert a central line if Val didn't start eating on his own.

As Thane left the kitchen, he glanced back at Wyland. "Be polite," he mouthed behind Tia's back.

Wyland ignored him.

Tia abruptly set down her fork. "I feel silly eating when you aren't."

"I don't have much of an appetite upon waking." Not that he'd actually slept. He'd spent the daylight hours at his desk, looking for references to Sigurd and The Old Ways, until his eyes had gone blurry. "Please, enjoy the food. I'll catch something at the hospital after rounds."

"Drive to the hospital on an empty stomach when you just fed Valerian? Eat out of a vending machine when Thane made this delicious meal?" She aimed a scornful glance his way. "And here I thought you were an intelligent man."

"Tia, I'm a doctor. I'm well able to assess my nutritional needs."

"Well, apparently you're not very good at it, because your cheekbones look sharp enough to cut a bitch, and the dark circles under your eyes are the size of black holes," she said. "You need food and blood. Nourishment, not caffeine." Rising from the chair, she went to the stainless steel refrigerator, opened it, and removed two bags of blood. After opening several cabinets, she found a glass, poured, and returned to his side of the table. "Here." She thrust the glass at him. "Drink."

Rather than going back to her seat, she stood there, glaring down at him.

He looked up. She smelled like lilacs and VampScreen again, and her black and white-plaid Bermuda shorts and Viper Room T-shirt skimmed her luscious curves. Her green-tipped auburn hair spilled to her shoulders, and as far as he could tell, she wasn't wearing a lick of makeup. The bright kitchen lights accentuated the green in her eyes, making the ring and spires spark. "I've never seen central heterochromia in that precise color or pattern before," he murmured.

"Hmm?"

"Your iris has two distinct colors—in your case, green and brown—with one of the colors ringing your pupil."

She handed him the glass of blood. Her nails were gunmetal gray tonight. "Central heterochromia. I didn't know it had an actual name."

"Most things do."

"You know what I mean." She slugged his bicep. "Drink up. I'd like to finish my pancakes before they get cold."

When was the last time a female vampire had touched him so casually? Bemused, he obeyed. Energy and strength surged as he drank. Damn it, she was right. Again.

"This kitchen is a chef's dream," she said. "All this hickory and stainless steel? Every appliance known to man? Chadden would love this place."

He turned sideways in the chair to face her. "You know Chadden?"

"Yes."

He tried not to read too much into her answer. The vampire Chadden, owner of the eponymous Chadden's restaurant in Loring Park, was extremely talented and utterly debauched. "We modernized the kitchen about five years ago," he explained. "Chadden consulted with Thane on the design."

"Thane's a treasure." She eyed her plate and

sighed. "If I ate like this every day, you'd have to put a Wide Load sign on my ass."

"Your ass is fine." The words escaped without his permission. He had no business noticing her anatomy, much less making comments about it.

"You think so?" Instead of looking offended, she wore a Mona Lisa smile.

He couldn't think of a prudent response, so he drank more blood. And she watched, staring at his mouth. Never had he been so conscious of every sip and swallow. She stood less than an arm's length away, close enough that he could hear her gentle breaths, see her breasts rise and fall as the air expanded her lungs.

Close enough to touch.

"I'm sorry I interrupted you earlier," she blurted. "While you were feeding Valerian."

He noticed she didn't apologize for being in Valerian's bedroom in the first place. Still, he nodded, accepting her apology.

She shifted her weight, cocking a curvy hip. "I came here to yell at you, and now I can't."

He couldn't remember the last time someone raised their voice in his presence. "Why did you want to yell at me? And why can't you now?"

"You said you'd call me about working at the Archives, and you didn't. But I can't call you on it because I was rude to you and Valerian. Reciprocal rudeness. We cancel each other out."

"Etiquette math," he murmured.

"So the score's even for now."

She thought to keep score? Against him? Fascinating. "I apologize for not contacting you." Without thinking, he rubbed the back of his neck, trying to work out a lingering kink. "I haven't had a chance to think about the Archives, much less work there." But he'd thought about *her*—during rounds, reading legal briefs, working at Sebastiani Labs, and during the long drive between work and home.

She stepped closer, assessing him. "You're still too pale. Do you need a vein?"

His cells surged at her offer. "I'm fine," he gritted out, trying not to look at her pulse throbbing at the base of her neck.

Trying and failing.

"Patients, legal clients, Valerian, the Council, the Archives…" With one more step, she made room for herself between his knees, her bare legs brushing against his suit pants. In this position, there was no disguising the rude bulge below his waist. "You take care of everything and everyone," she murmured, cupping his face in her hands. "But who takes care of you?"

Her gaze was molten, and her hands were so warm. There was nothing maternal about her touch, but he felt the care in it nonetheless. An odd pressure tightened his throat, and he clutched the glass like a lifeline. Her gaze flicked over his face and body, a matchstick leaving sparks in its wake, but he held himself still through sheer force of will. He yearned to touch her—would die to touch her—but the first move had to be hers. He would not abuse his power.

With a whispered curse, she lowered her lips to his.

The first sexual touch he'd allowed in over a century rolled over him like a fireball, searing him with long-forgotten sensations. Tia gripped his head with surprising strength, exploring his mouth with hers, learning its shape, texture, and taste. Her lips were so pink, so plush, so hot… He held himself still, not responding in kind, letting her seek and rove at will. *His* will had no place here, because he wanted to sweep the plates to the floor, spread her out on the kitchen table, and lap her up like the most decadent dessert in creation.

Hot, damp, ravenous…she was eating him alive. Burning his honorable intentions to a crisp.

She licked the corner of his mouth, sipping traces of the blood she'd served him. Her purr of pleasure grabbed him by the balls, and he pressed his mouth more firmly against hers. With a low hum of approval, she threaded her fingers into his hair, trying to pull him even closer. Her fang grazed his inner lip, drawing blood.

His fangs descended. He shoved to his feet and grabbed her by the waist. The glass of blood fell to the floor, unheeded.

The full-body contact crashed into him as if he'd been defibrillated. He absorbed the shock, savored it, then plunged his tongue into her mouth. She met him halfway, their tongues twining in an intimate tango. She tasted like maple syrup and orange juice—sweet and tart, like her personality, a complex flavor he'd never tire of—

No. Get a bloody grip. He was no young girl who had to spin romantic, happily-ever-after dreams to justify having a sexual experience—not that Tia seemed to be having that problem, either. Her body was plastered against his from chest to knee. She writhed against his erection, and clutched at his hair with abandon, her mouth demanding and hungry against his. Her tongue was an adventuress, discovering his every weakness—

"Wyland's in the kitchen, Nick." Thane's voice, from the other side of the kitchen door.

They sprang apart. Tia sauntered to the other side of the table and sat down again, as if nothing out of the ordinary had happened. For some reason, her calm reaction stung.

"I'll let him know you're looking for him." By the time Thane shouldered through the door carrying an empty tray, Wyland had taken his seat, too. "Okay, who's ready for more pancakes—Miss Tia? Are you hurt?"

"What? No."

Thane set the tray on the table and crouched down. "There's blood on your leg."

Wyland peered under the table. Sure enough, her bare calf was stained with blood. He yearned to lick it from her skin, one taste at a time.

"It's just splash-back from the glass," she said. "Wyland dropped his glass on the floor."

Thane glanced over at the glass, lying on its side next to the refrigerator, then back to Tia, who sat a good eight feet away. There was no way a blood splash could have reached her sitting in that chair, and Thane damn well knew it.

But Thane said nothing, just prepared a warm, wet washcloth for Tia with his typical no-fuss efficiency. "Wyland, Nick needs to speak with you before you leave for the hospital." Thane handed Tia the cloth. "And Tia, Valerian is ready to start watching the movie anytime you are."

She scrubbed her leg with the cloth, then handed it back. "I'll go up then." She stood, kissing Thane on both cheeks. "Thank you so much for the delicious breakfast." Finally, she looked at him with an expression he couldn't quite read. "We'll talk soon."

About what? Working at the Archives? The argument they hadn't had? The incendiary kiss they'd just shared?

She didn't wait for him to answer. Nodding, she left.

He and Thane watched the kitchen door swing back and forth until it stilled. Her departure created an odd vacuum in the room, as if she'd taken all the oxygen with her.

Thane turned toward him, his eyes dancing.

"I don't want to hear it," he muttered. "Where's Nick?"

"In his office, but you might want to change before you see him."

"Why?"

Thane gestured to his lower legs. "You have blood on your pants."

Sure enough, there was blood splashed on the summer weight wool—and though Thane was too polite to mention it, he was still half hard. "Bloody hell."

"Indeed."

Ignoring Thane's poor joke, he left the kitchen with as much dignity as he could muster.

"You might want to check your hair while you're at it," Thane called after him.

He stalked to the stairwell and checked his reflection in the ornately framed mirror hanging at its foot. His hair was noticeably mussed, his queue hanging askew. His lips were swollen, and his cheeks were ruddy with arousal. Never mind Thane's overdeveloped powers of observation; any teenager with dancing hormones would know exactly what he and Tia had been doing in the kitchen.

The evidence of his weakness was there, for anyone to see.

Embarrassment belly-crawled, but he stiffened against it. Pushed through it. Allowed the self-preservation instincts that had served him so well for three centuries to shove to the forefront. Yes, he'd been weak, but thankfully only Thane had witnessed his hormone-addled folly.

It wouldn't—couldn't—happen again.

Good luck with that, boy.

Ignoring Thane's snarky mental comment, he stalked upstairs to change.

CHAPTER FIVE

As Dominic plopped down on Crackhouse Coffee's leather loveseat, he swiped a bead of sweat away from his temple and surreptitiously sniffed his armpit. The sun had gone down over an hour ago, but it was still hotter than a mofo outside. The Pathfinder's AC had crapped out on the way back from Stillwater—one more thing he had to find time to take care of—but thankfully his anti-perspirant was holding.

At least one thing was going right today.

The Twins game had just ended, and the place was a madhouse. Every table was full, but Mila hadn't arrived yet. He had a couple of minutes to check *In Like Quinn*. Had anyone responded to his comment about Jacoby Woolf? He flicked at his phone and squinted at the screen.

This comment has been moderated.

She'd modded him? What the…?

With a few more pokes and swipes, he went to the financial section, to the comment he'd left about Sebastiani Labs' corrupt board of directors. That one was gone, too—whitewashed, scrubbed away. His father had warned him that Tia Quinn was more concerned about preserving access rather than speaking truth to power, and here was proof. She'd failed the test—not surprising, given her tainted blood.

When he'd first started digging into her background, he'd been curious how she earned a living, because *ILQ* didn't accept advertising. He hadn't been surprised to find old family money and a massive trust fund—nothing unique there; even the most clueless vampire could amass a fortune when investments had hundreds of years to appreciate in value—but the genealogy database had revealed a nasty surprise: her fraternal grandmother was a faerie.

Faeries were empathic. Some could gauge complete strangers' emotional states with pinpoint accuracy, and those with off-the-chart skills could influence others' feelings telepathically.

She'd probably sensed him following her from the start. Hell, he was probably the reason she'd moved away from the city in the first place.

Thankfully, Tia was an infant in vampire years, so at least he didn't have to worry about her thralling or glamouring him, but…a vamp/faerie cross? How did each species' innate abilities combine in Tia Quinn? She was a wild card, an unknown quantity.

Someone tapped on the plate-glass window. There was Mila, smiling at him from the other side. He smiled back. With a tiny wave, she pivoted and strode toward the entrance, eating up the sidewalk with long, confident strides.

All thoughts of Tia Quinn vanished.

He'd known Mila was pretty, but in casual clothes she was a knockout. She wore skin-tight, low-riding jeans that showcased long legs and a first-class ass, and a brown leather belt clung for its life at her hips. A thin, long-sleeved white T-shirt covered her arms down to the wrists, but exposed a slice of belly just above the belt. Her dark hair was pulled up in a loose bun. A colorful scarf hung from her neck, and she carried a bright blue jacket.

He inhaled slowly, felt his chest expand. He hadn't mistaken the attraction he'd felt at the GPL meeting, and...it really complicated things. He'd asked her out so he could pick her brain about her job—having access to patient information could really help the GPL's cause—but his body had an agenda of its own.

When Mila entered the coffee shop, she stepped out of the traffic pattern and slipped the jacket on, covering her graceful arms and small, high breasts with fabric encrusted with beading. Strappy leather sandals exposed her feet, and her scorching red toenails screamed sex. He stood as she approached, suddenly conscious of his plain T-shirt and no-name jeans.

She looked him up and down with an approving smile. "Hello."

The hair on his arms stood at attention. "Hey." After a slight hesitation, he leaned down and kissed her cheeks. Her scent, a combination of a light, citrusy perfume, fabric softener, and musk, swirled in his head. "Please, sit down."

"Thanks." She set the purse on the floor and curled into the corner of the loveseat, her feet hanging over the edge so she didn't transfer dirt from her sandals. "I haven't had my first cup of coffee yet."

Vampire, he reminded himself as he sat. She'd probably just woken up. "I could use a cup myself."

"Long day?"

"Yeah." And it wasn't going to end once he got home. The clothes he'd worn delivering Tia's surprise earlier that day were stuffed in a duffel bag in the back of the Pathfinder. He had to wash them before his mother and sister picked up the unusual scent.

"With your father in the hospital, I imagine you have a lot on your plate right now." Mila's porcelain skin glowed in the light of the nearby floor lamp. "Just let me know when you need to leave."

He nodded.

"Hi, there." A waiter with flame tattoos climbing his arms suddenly appeared on the other side of the coffee table. "What can I get for you tonight?"

"I'll have a red cappuccino, please," Mila said. "Caffeinated."

His first week working at the health club had started with a rotation through the snack bar. Though he'd learned to disguise his revulsion, blood drinks still squicked him out. "A tall Crackhouse Blend, please." A big cup of the coffee house's namesake beverage should do the trick. "Caffeinated, no cream or sugar." If Mila was surprised that he'd ordered a caffeinated drink at 10:00 p.m. on a weeknight, she didn't show it. "Can you drop in a couple of ice cubes?" The sooner he could mainline the kicky brew, the more alert he'd be.

The waiter nodded. "Be right back."

Silence as he walked away.

"I'm nervous," Mila blurted.

He laughed in relief. "Me, too."

She leaned the slightest bit closer. "Somehow meeting here by ourselves seems a lot more…loaded than it did when we talked at The Ivy."

She probably hadn't intended the movement to be flirtatious, but his body sure interpreted that way. The air suddenly seemed heavy and viscous.

They shared some small talk—the hideous traffic delays caused by summertime road construction, the weather, the Minnesota Twins' winning streak—while they waited for their coffee. The conversation flowed smoothly from subject to subject as they got to know each other better. The longer they talked, the more Mila seemed to relax, her face bright and animated, curving her body toward his. She listened as if she was genuinely interested in what he said.

Where had he gotten the impression that she was snooty and stuck up?

The waiter came back with their coffee, setting it on the low table in front of the couch before leaving. Mila picked up the bowl-shaped mug in both hands and took several dainty sips, closing her eyes and humming in appreciation. When she came up for air, a dollop of pink-tinged foam clung to her upper lip. She swiped it away with her tongue.

Jesus. He took a quick gulp of his own life-saving brew. Thankfully, the ice cubes had done their job.

"So, tell me about your job at the health club. I worked at a hotel one summer, back when I was in school." Mila's eyes rolled in self-deprecating amusement. "Let's just say I learned more about human nature than any teenager should."

Once he talked about his work, he could ask about hers. "I'm one of the club's assistant managers." He described his day-to-day responsibilities—facilities management, administration, reams of paperwork—certain he was boring her stiff. "I started working there after I graduated from the U in May." Had graduation only been three months ago? With what had happened to his dad, the big party his parents had thrown for him had faded from his memory. "I'm learning the ropes from Andi Woolf. She manages the place."

"The Alpha's daughter, right?" She sidled closer. "Does Krispin Woolf ever show up at the club?"

"Not that I've seen." Actually, the last place he'd seen the Alpha had been at Memorial Hospital, just a couple of nights ago. Flanked by bodyguards, he'd arrived just as Dominic was leaving.

"Andi seems nice," Mila said. "I've seen her at Underbelly a couple of times."

He tried to hide his surprise. Mila Stanton was the *last* person he could envision drinking, dancing, and cutting loose at the raucous nightclub next door—but then again, she'd proven several of his assumptions wrong already. There was obviously more to her than met the eye, not that what met the eye wasn't very, very fine. "How about you?" He took another sip from the tall black mug. "It must be interesting working in a hospital."

She shrugged one thin shoulder. "It doesn't seem like a hospital to me. I park in the ramp, badge into the IT department, and then sit in a cube. Sometimes, for an exciting change of scenery, I go downstairs to the server room. It's warmer there."

"Are you warm enough now?" He gestured to her jacket. "The AC is jacked in here."

"I'm fine, thanks. I'm always cold, no matter what the season." A shadow seemed to cross her face, but it quickly disappeared. "Thin blood, I guess."

"So, what is it you actually do at the hospital? When we talked the other night, I was a little surprised you seemed to know so much about my dad's condition."

Color flooded her cheeks. "I'm so sorry. I wasn't

thinking. It was a complete invasion of his privacy—"

"No." He laid his hand on her forearm. "I'm not upset. I just wondered how you—" he casually shrugged "—knew. Aren't there policies and procedures about that?"

"There are, definitely, even though we're not bound by human law. But policies and procedures don't really account for someone whose job requires them to analyze huge volumes of data, and—" she lowered her voice and slanted a guilty glance his way "—who has a photographic memory."

"You remember everything you see? Everything you read? How awesome!" And how potentially useful. He shot her a teasing glance. "I bet that came in really handy in school, studying for exams."

She seemed to relax at his reaction, tucking a tendril of dark hair behind her ear. "Sure, but it can suck, too. Intake records at the ER? Surgical reports?" A shudder wracked her slim frame. "Just one glimpse of some of my test data makes me want to reach for the brain bleach."

"I can imagine." If she could read the data, it wasn't encrypted. Could she query medical records without setting off red flags? Questions buzzed like bees in a hive. She had a treasure trove of information stored in her head.

She suddenly seemed spooked about what she'd just revealed, because she shrank back against the loveseat, focusing on her cappuccino like it held the secrets of the universe. "So, I have to ask. Do you find GPL meetings as big a waste of time as I do?"

"Thank you! I thought it was just me."

"Nope."

"I don't know why I even bother to go anymore."

They both knew why; their parents expected it. The odd sense of communion he'd felt with her deepened. "It's just one big party," he said, sighing. "We haven't had a concrete mission for ages. And talk about hypocrisy."

"What do you mean?"

"Jacoby Woolf, and his...what's his health problem called again?"

"He has a motor neuron disease, like ALS or Lou Gehrig's disease in humans."

She'd answered his question without batting an eyelash. What other data did she have available at her fingertips? *Go slow.* "All I can say is, it must be nice to have power and connections."

"What do you mean?"

He shrugged. "If Jacoby Woolf was anyone else's son...?" He drew his finger across his throat in a slashing motion.

"The Old Ways?" She looked aghast. "You can*not* be serious." He could smell her anger, and an odd, inexplicable panic. "Jacoby Woolf was perfectly healthy at birth. His condition wasn't diagnosed until a couple of years ago, when he started having mobility issues, and he'd been the Beta for years by that point." She looked at him like he had the intelligence of an amoeba. "Seriously, what do you expect the Alpha to do?"

"Put him out of his misery, like any good father would."

She recoiled. A wave of cappuccino sloshed onto her jacket.

"Oh, hell. I'm sorry."

Setting the cup down with a click, she snatched up some napkins from the pile on the coffee table and started blotting the spill. Somehow, she managed to look down her nose at him—a fine trick, being she was a foot shorter than he was.

He'd obviously upset her, but...hell. Could Jacoby Woolf run? Follow a scent trail through the woods? Enjoy a lover? Could he even shift anymore? "Why would anyone want to live such a stunted life?"

"His brain works just fine. He serves his people well."

"Easy for you to say," he scoffed. "These days, he votes with the majority more often than with his father."

"And from what I hear, he's right to do so."

"Oh, come on," he said scathingly. "Do you really think we receive accurate information about what's going on at Council meetings? It's a nest of nepotism. The information we receive is carefully crafted to keep powerful families in power." Just look how dominant the Sebastiani family had become in such a short period of time. "It's all propaganda."

Her chin rose. "Wyland keeps the vampires quite well-informed."

"So you think."

"So I *know*."

The silence hung.

"I didn't mean for us to get into an argument," he said. She obviously had no clue how big the Council's propaganda machine was. "My question is, why are there different rules for those in power than there are for everyone else?"

"Exactly which rules—" she made an air quote gesture with two fingers of her free hand—"are you talking about?"

He couldn't believe she was going to make him say

it. "You know what I mean."

"I do, and I think The Old Ways are retrograde, ignorant crap." A sudden sadness flitted across her face as she gestured to the street, and to the other patrons in the restaurant. "Look around, Dominic. Times have changed." She shifted another inch closer, lowering her voice to a soft murmur. "Consider your own species. We all know about the genetic mutations so prevalent in the wolves—the sensory damage, the limb abnormalities. If The Old Ways were still followed as frequently now as they were in the past, people with these conditions wouldn't be here for us to see."

It was because The Old Ways *were* practiced that people didn't see even *more* damaged werewolves. He held his tongue. Punishment for revealing such information would be swift and severe.

"Look at the Lupinsky family," she continued. "Gabe Lupinsky has macular degeneration. His mother and sister have missing limbs, and his other sister is deaf. Yet just last year, Gabe not only made an important discovery about the possible origins of our culture, he became a Council member's bondmate. Where's the hypocrisy there?"

If the rumors were true, it was the Alpha's childhood friendship with Gabe Lupinsky's father that had brought the family special dispensation. Proximity to power, and to the Council, meant rules could be made or broken. He suddenly frowned. "What discovery?"

"Oh, I'm sorry." Her eyes widened angelically. "Did the Alpha not inform you?"

Direct hit. Surprise grew as Mila described what Gabe Lupinsky and Lorin Schlessinger had found at the northern Minnesota archaeological dig last summer. Otherworldly metal fragments? A capsule containing ancient organic material?

"Dominic, these 'rules' you're talking about… They're archaic and barbaric. Outdated. Medicine has advanced to the point where serious health conditions can be treated or managed. We *know* better now. We know better." She looked out the window, but not quickly enough to hide the sheen of tears.

What the hell—?

"Hi, there." Sasha Sebastiani stood on the other side of the coffee table holding a damp cloth. "Let me help with that spill."

Being succubi plucked emotions out of thin air, her attention had probably been snagged by more than spilled cappuccino.

Hell. This date was *not* going as he'd planned.

When Mila turned away from the window, she'd blinked away the wetness. "Oh, thank you," she said, accepting the cloth Sasha offered. She gestured to the little white paper balls clinging to her jacket. "The napkins gave me dingleberries."

Sasha laughed, but she eyed him with more than a hint of suspicion. "Well, we wouldn't want dingleberries on such a beautiful vintage jacket."

"It's my mother's."

As Mila and Sasha talked about the jacket—made in Paris by someone named Madame Grès—he took a quick glance at his cell phone and smothered a yawn. He'd spent too much time playing with the genealogy database last night, and his sleep had definitely suffered.

"We're boring him to bits," Sasha said to Mila, then looked at him. "I apologize for my rudeness, just barging over here and chattering away without introducing myself first." She extended her hand, sending a bundle of bracelets jangling. "Sasha Sebastiani."

He rose to his feet and shook it. "Dominic Reese. Nice to meet you."

He had to give her credit for humility; everyone in their world knew who Sasha Sebastiani was. The daughter of Council President Elliott Sebastiani, sister of Council members Lukas and Antonia, she managed the Sebastiani family's entertainment holdings, including Underbelly and Crackhouse Coffee. Even dressed like all the other workers, in jeans, a black T-shirt, and black apron, she was the one you noticed. She positively crackled with charisma. Her short black and fuchsia hair stood on end, as if her tiny body couldn't contain her energy.

Sasha gestured to their cups. "Let me get you some refills."

"Thanks, but none for me," Mila said, rising to her feet. "I think Dominic could use one to go."

Apparently their date was over. Hell, if he was Mila, he'd cut the evening short, too.

Sasha glanced at his cup. "Tall black Crack?" He nodded. "Be back in a minute."

They both watched Sasha as she made her way back to the counter, checking in on tables along the way. The deadly silence grew. "I'm sorry this was such a disaster," he blurted.

She smiled enigmatically. "Oh, I wouldn't say that."

"It's my fault you spilled on your jacket. Please let me get it cleaned for you."

"No need."

Silence made panic churn in his stomach. She didn't want to see him again, and he couldn't blame her—

"Would you like to go to Underbelly with me sometime? Some night when we're both free?"

Surprise rocked him back on his heels. "Um, I'd love to. But...why?"

"Hmm?"

"Over half a cup of coffee, I've started a political argument, made you cry, and ruined a vintage jacket." Her tiny grin of acknowledgment enchanted him. "Why would you subject yourself to this again?"

"You're nice to look at, and I found our discussion...interesting."

He blinked. "Really?"

"Do you only have conversations with people who agree with you?"

"No, but..." Taking a chance, he took her hands in his. Even after holding a hot coffee mug, they were as chilly as refrigerator air. "What did I say that made you cry?"

There was that sadness again. "Why don't we save that for another time?"

Before he could press, Sasha came back with a tall to-go cup. He pulled out his wallet, but she waved him off. "It's on the house tonight."

"It's not your fault I spilled all over my jacket," Mila said.

"Nope. It's mine." He held out his hand. "Please let me get it cleaned for you."

She hesitated.

"Please."

She finally nodded. "I guess I won't need it next door."

"Going to Underbelly from here?" Sasha asked, handing him the to-go cup.

Mila nodded. "I'm meeting some friends."

Friends that aren't me. For vampires, the night was still young, and he couldn't join them anyway. Not that she'd asked.

"Nice to meet you, Dominic," Sasha said. "Have fun, Mila." She walked away, leaving them alone.

There was another uncomfortable silence, then Mila shrugged out of the jacket and handed it to him. "I'll text you the name of the place my mother uses for her dry cleaning."

"Thanks." Even if she was blowing smoke up his ass about going to Underbelly together sometime, he'd see her at least once more—to return the jacket, which he suddenly suspected cost more than his truck.

Another pause. "Well, thanks for the coffee and conversation, Dominic."

"Thank *you.*"

Rising up on her toes, she kissed him on both cheeks. Her subtle scent tangled around him, and it was all he could do to keep his hands at his sides. She'd honored him with the traditional greeting of respect, but interest glittered in her eyes—a sexual interest she didn't try to hide.

As they stared at each other, the space between them throbbed—with anticipation, with possibility. Maybe the date hadn't been such a disaster after all.

She cleared her throat and took a step back. "Well, I'll see you soon. Please give my best to your parents." Picking up her purse, she shot him a cheeky wink and swung away, waving at Sasha as she strode toward the door that led to the nightclub on the other side of the building.

His heart and brain and cock fought a silent battle. He liked her. He wanted her. And...he was going to use her.

Sasha Sebastiani eyed him from behind the counter. *Time to go.* The sooner he started his laundry, the sooner he could tumble into bed and lose himself in hot, mindless dreams.

When he'd left Stillwater earlier that evening, Tia Quinn had been sleeping, too—but thanks to him, her dreams would be anything but sweet.

✳

The slinky touch tickled Tia's shoulder, then meandered up to her neck, then over to her cheek. Something flicked against her earlobe, followed by a soft nibble. Wakefulness tapped her on the shoulder—the sun had set long, long ago—but she ignored it. Shoving the sheet aside, she turned onto her stomach, hugged her pillow, and willed herself back into the delicious dream.

Time drifted by as she wallowed in sensation...a languid stroke on her ankle, a lazy touch on her knee...long, blond hair drifting over her upper thighs—

Blond? Her usual fantasy men were tall, dark, handsome, and hung, but this dream lover was pale and lean, with a patrician profile, a soft waterfall of hair, and a wickedly talented tongue.

Hung? Oh, yeah.

Rolling onto her back, she threw her arm over her

eyes. "Damn it." She couldn't be blamed for the R-rated movies her unconscious enjoyed while she slept, could she? No, she could not. Little wonder her dreams had taken an erotic turn after the fiery, edgy kiss she and Wyland had shared in his kitchen.

She'd thought him cold? *Wrong*. Steam lurked under his placid surface, just searching for a convenient vent.

She stretched her other arm overhead, then lowered them in a slow, snow-angel arc. What would have happened if Thane hadn't interrupted them? It was probably better that he had—

She froze as her arm bumped into something…warm.

Moving slowly, she reached for the reading lamp on her bedside table, turning it on with a soft snick. When light flooded the room, shock kicked her in the stomach.

A snake. There was a snake on her bed—coiled, brown with bright green accents, and with a flicking tongue.

There was a snake on her pillow, too. "Jesus." She leaped off the bed, but jumped right back on again.

The floor was…moving.

Snakes, dozens and dozens of them—on the hardwood floor, on her new throw rug, and crawling under the jamb of her closet door. The floor positively writhed. Several snakes were climbing the bed frame to join their pals on the pillow.

A violent shudder quaked through her body.

"Okay," she breathed. "Okay. They're just snakes. Suck it up." Garter snakes were perfectly harmless little animals that had their place in the food chain—not that this was a natural occurrence. Hundreds of snakes didn't suddenly decide that a second floor bedroom was a great place to party.

Someone had put them there. Someone had broken into her house—and her stun gun was downstairs, in her purse. "That's fucking helpful," she muttered, slowly and carefully climbing off the bed again, wincing as the bedsprings squeaked. The snakes were scattered all over the floor, shades of brown, beige, and green writhing against the dark wood. Avoiding the snakes, she tip-toed to her bedroom door, the one she'd left yawning wide open when she'd gone to bed. It was half-closed now.

Yes, someone had broken in.

Her breathing sounded unnaturally loud as she closed the door and locked herself inside. She made her way back to the bed, snatched the phone off the bedside table, hurried to the en suite bathroom, and twisted the lock.

After a quick look around—no snakes—she snatched one of the bright purple bath towels off the wall rack and jammed it against the gap where the door met the floor. Sinking down to the fuzzy rug, she dialed.

One ring. Two. On three, he finally picked up. "This is Wyland."

Even scared to bits, her body responded to his rough voice, to the intimate stir of bedsheets. Her blood heated as she visualized him rumpled in sleep, shoving long, blond hair out of his eyes as he reached for the phone. "I'm—I'm sorry to bother you."

"Tia? Is something wrong?"

"Snakes," she said through suddenly chattering teeth.

"What?"

"Snakes. In my bedroom. Hundreds of them."

"Were you bitten?"

Of course he'd ask about medical emergencies first. "No, they're garter snakes. I'm okay, but—"

"Are you safe?"

"Yes."

"Tell me what happened."

Somehow, his imperious command steadied her, helped her gather her thoughts. She explained what she'd woken to—how startled she'd been by the snakes, and her suspicion that someone had broken in and put them in her bedroom while she slept. "I've locked myself in the bathroom."

"Good." Something rustled in the background. "Did you hear anyone downstairs?"

"No. I think whoever did this is long gone." Like most young vampires, she'd slept like a corpse during daylight hours. If the person who'd broken in had wanted to kill her, she'd already be dead.

No, this person wanted to scare her.

Mission fucking accomplished.

"Do you have a security system?"

"Not yet."

More rustling. "You'll have one tomorrow."

Okay, his imperiousness was getting out of hand. "I can take care of it myself—"

"You can, but you haven't."

She bit back a sarcastic response. He was right. Damn it, he was right. The air conditioning came on with a mighty whoosh, pebbling her bare arms and legs with gooseflesh.

There were more rustles, louder this time. "What's that noise?" she muttered.

"You're on speaker. I'm getting dressed."

Oh my.

On the other side of the line, he muttered a curse. "I'm calling Lukas and Jack. Stay in the bathroom until I get there."

"Okay." She didn't fancy shivering on the cold tile floor wearing nothing but a camisole and men's boxer shorts for the next twenty minutes, but she'd do it. "Be careful."

"I will. Hang tight." The phone clicked as he hung up.

She grabbed another bath towel from the rod, wrapped it around herself like a blanket, and settled in to wait. Had the same creep she'd felt watching her for months stepped up his game, or was this someone new?

"Hell." She dropped her head onto her upraised knees.

It was probably time to ask for some help.

✻

Twelve frantic minutes later, Wyland whipped into Tia's driveway—and just his luck, her next door neighbor was sitting on his front porch. What in the world had possessed Tia to move into a family neighborhood, teeming with nosy humans?

"Hello," the burly guy called as Wyland got out of the car. "Nice ride."

"Thanks." The man's bare chest was covered in tattoos, and his knee-length basketball shorts exposed a prosthetic limb.

The man sipped from a red aluminum can. "You

must be Tia's boyfriend."

Did Tia have a lover, one that spent time at her house? How could she not?

"I can see why you're in a hurry." The man pursed his lips in a good-natured whistle. "She's a hottie."

His fangs shot down. Before he could take a step, a sleepy-looking brunette poked her head out the front door. "I still can't get the baby down," she murmured. "I think she wants her daddy."

The man smiled at the woman, stood, and drained what was left of his soda. "Duty calls," he said, sketching a salute. "Nice to meet you." He dropped the empty can in a recycling bin sitting on the porch. "I didn't catch your name."

Wyland gave the man a mild mental push. "Good night."

With a baffled expression, Tia's neighbor went into the house, closing the door behind him. "And stay there," Wyland muttered, then crossed the driveway and climbed the steps leading to Tia's front door. She might not have a security system, but she'd installed heavy steel shutters on the windows—manual crank, and tightly closed against the morning sun whose rise was still hours off. The door and door jamb were still intact. The doorknob, functional but flimsy, was undisturbed. Whoever had broken into Tia's house hadn't come in through the front door.

Unless he'd used a key. How many people had keys to Tia's house?

He shoved the thought away with a snarl. Lukas would find out during his investigation of the break-in. With a glance at the porch next door—still empty—he picked the flimsy lock, entered the house, and closed the door behind him.

Other than a very dim light coming from the kitchen, darkness dominated. A clock ticked nearby, punctuating the silence. He made himself stand still for thirty long seconds, until he was satisfied he didn't sense anything other than typical household noises. Tia was right; the person who'd broken in was long gone.

With the relief came more anger. As if her profession wasn't dangerous enough, Tia came from a philanthropic family. The Quinns had money, disposable income on a massive scale. What had she been thinking, moving into a house that didn't have a security system?

He crossed to the stairway, and patted the nearby walls. Finally, a light switch. He flicked it, wincing at the bright light, but quickly climbed the stairs. No snakes, and no damage that he could see. No visible footprints on the pristine carpet runner crawling up the hardwood stairs, no smudges on the walls. When he reached the top of the stairs, he saw a cardboard box lying askew, with small slits cut into it at regular intervals. Carefully skirting the box—it had likely been used to transport the snakes, and Lukas would collect it as evidence—he walked toward the door at the end of the hall.

"Yeah, yeah, I get it. You're a bad-ass." Tia's voice. She sounded amused, not frightened.

During the drive, he'd tortured himself with thoughts of exactly how much damage a man could wreak in fifteen uninterrupted minutes, and she had an overnight guest? A low growl rumbled in his chest. With fists and jaw clenched, he slipped into the room.

The bedroom lights blazed, spotlighting a beautiful—and empty—maple sleigh bed. Her duvet was eye-searing, purple and lime green, and several small garter snakes lazed on her tangled purple sheets. Her walls were painted a dusky lavender, and were covered with framed prints and photographs. On the floor, snakes slithered over hardwood, and dozens more curled on the abstract-patterned rug. Across the room, two wriggling tails disappeared under a door jamb.

"Bloody hell," he whispered. He did not like snakes, lampreys, or eels, and he never had. Deirdre had enjoyed eating jellied eels—they'd been all the rage in turn-of-the-century London—but he'd had to leave the room when she ate them. Across the room, the snake on Tia's pillow reared up, flashing its tiny fangs. He flashed his own, hissing for good measure.

"Oh, hey." Tia walked out of the bathroom carrying a purple pillowcase by the open edge.

Hey? That was all she had to say? He simply nodded, not trusting what would come out of his mouth. Who'd follow her out of the bathroom? Who would he have to maim for seeing her in such a skimpy get-up? She wore what looked like men's underwear, with a smiley face emblazoned on the arse. Her camisole was a ridiculous excuse for a garment, the knit so fine it was nearly translucent. Her taut nipples were tempting little points.

Outrageous—so outrageous that it took him several seconds to realize they were alone, that she was talking to the snake coiled around her wrist.

"I know, I know," she said, gently tugging. "I wouldn't want to go in that pillowcase, either, but we need to get you and your friends back outside." The snake finally loosened its grip. She dropped it into the pillowcase and gave him a deadpan look. "One down, a couple hundred to go."

He quickly assessed her—no obvious injuries or symptoms of shock—but she was covered in gooseflesh. "Do you have a bathrobe?"

She pointed to the door where the two snakes had just disappeared. "Sweatshirt and sweatpants are in there. Shelf on the left."

He swallowed, hard.

"Speaking of which…" She looked him up and down. "Look at you."

When she'd called, he'd thrown on whatever clothing had come to hand, shoving his bare feet into loafers on the run. What had come to hand was mismatched workout gear.

"Who'd have thought the Vampire Second had such great muscles?" she said with an impish smile.

Pleasure streaked through him.

"And your hair. It's loose."

"Your call woke me up." He started to comb it with his fingers, but she stopped him with a touch.

"It's beautiful," she whispered.

The room suddenly felt humid and warm, and the scent of lilacs swirled between them. They stared into each other's eyes— "Bugger!" he yelped, recoiling. He gave his foot a shake, and a snake went flying.

"Hey!" Tia picked it up just behind the head, gently cradling it in her hand. "The bad man didn't mean it," she crooned. "You startled him."

"He startled me first."

"And look at this. Someone stapled a note to the poor thing." Her hand hovered over a small piece of white paper, about two inches square, attached to the snake at mid-body.

"Don't touch it," he ordered. "It's evidence." Her

disapproving glance made him feel like an axe murder. "And the staples might be curled under its skin," he added. "We'll bring it to a vet."

"Okay." She peered at the piece of paper. "'Bitch, why aren't you doing your job?'" she read aloud. She shivered slightly, her first noticeable sign of unease since he'd arrived.

"Tia? Wyland?" Lukas's voice floated up from the lower level.

"We're in Tia's bedroom," Wyland called back.

"You're okay?"

"Yes. I haven't searched the house."

Tia turned toward him. "You actually called Lukas?"

"Yes." Steeling himself, he turned toward the closet door where he'd seen the wriggling tails disappear. "I'll get you your sweats." He'd have time to get Tia some clothes, and for her to dress, before anyone else saw so much pale, fragrant skin.

"I'll clear a path." Before he could protest, she set the stapled snake on the bed, then started picking up snakes from the floor and putting them in the pillowcase. He followed the trail of vertebrae down to her tempting, curvy arse. Imagined stepping close to her, grabbing her by the hips, and nestling his cock against that...that...ridiculous smiley face, with its lascivious tongue, mocking his helpless reaction.

Averting his eyes, he crossed to the closet and opened the door. Black clothing predominated, with the occasional flash of white or saturated color, and not a pastel in sight. Over on the left side was a floor-to-ceiling shelving unit holding folded jeans, T-shirts, workout clothes, and out-of-season sweaters near the top. He grabbed a pair of sweatpants in soft, black fleece, and reached down for what looked like a matching jacket—

A sudden, sharp pain. He jerked his hand to his mouth, sucking away a drop of blood. "Little bastard." Aiming a dirty look at the snake whose bed he'd disturbed, he snatched a zip-up jacket off the shelf, left the closet, and thrust the bundle at her. "Here."

She handed him the pillowcase, now bulging with the weight of the snakes she'd collected. "Thanks."

He froze. Surely he could hold this…writhing, jostling bag while she dressed.

She was dressing. Clearing his throat, he turned his back.

"Wyland, you're a doctor. Surely I don't have body parts you haven't seen before."

"There's a distinct difference between professional nudity and recreational nudity." Was that tight-assed voice his?

"You'd consider this situation recreational?"

"You're not my patient." Thankfully not, because he hadn't had such inappropriate thoughts about a patient in his life.

More rustling. "Since you're not my doctor… FYI, your ass looks amazing in those pants."

He ignored the spurt of masculine pride. He wasn't her doctor, but he *was* her Second. Apparently that fact wasn't enough to govern her tongue. "Are you dressed?"

A zipper whooshed. "Yes."

Thank the universe.

There were heavy footfalls on the stairs. "We're at the end of the hall," he called. When he turned toward Tia, she was reaching for another snake, wearing pants with the word "Juicy" emblazoned in a cursive arc across her buttocks.

Twenty-first century fashion was going to be the death of him.

Lukas and one of his senior lieutenants, Chico Perez, appeared at Tia's bedroom door. "I'm glad you got here so quickly," Lukas said, taking in the details of the room with an all-encompassing glance. He checked the bathroom and the closet. "Notice anything unusual? Other than the snakes?"

"I didn't check," he admitted. "I came right up to Tia when I arrived."

"How did you get in?"

"I picked the lock." A wave of relief washed over him as Lukas took the writhing pillowcase. "Be careful," he warned Lukas. "The little buggers bite."

"Were you bitten?" Tia passed the snake she'd just picked up to Lukas. "Let me see."

"I'm fine. It's just a little nip."

She took his hand. When she found the little bleeder on his index finger, she popped it into her mouth. Her soft, muscular tongue lashed over the pinpricks, sealing them with her saliva.

Chico cleared his throat. "I'll collect the rest of the snakes."

"I'll check in with Jack downstairs," Lukas said. "Join us when you're ready."

Tia abruptly released him, as if realizing what she'd done. "Chico, can you make sure you check the closet?"

"Sure thing, sweetness."

Wyland's eyebrow rose.

Chico disappeared into the closet.

"Let's go downstairs," he said to Tia. He watched

her hips sway, her weight shift, as he followed her down the hallway. She eyeballed the cardboard box as they passed.

Lukas was standing at the bottom of the stairway. "We'll take the box to the lab." He gave her a close look. "Are you okay?"

"Yeah," she said with a sigh. "I know garter snakes can't hurt me, but waking up to one licking my armpit really gave me the wiggins."

Jack came in from the kitchen. "I found an open basement window in the back."

Tia swore. "I haven't been in the basement since the day I moved in."

"There's no damage that I can see." Jack and Lukas exchanged a glance. "I think someone wanted to scare you. The only question is why."

Though their bodies weren't touching, Wyland felt Tia's deep breath as if it was his own. "Someone's been following me," she blurted out. "Since before I moved here."

"What?" This time, the teeth shoving down from his jaw had nothing to do with sexual attraction or jealousy. It was rage, blinding rage. His muscles twitched, tensing in readiness.

"Someone's been following me. Watching me," she said. "It's the reason I moved here."

"You've seen this person?" Lukas asked calmly. How the hell could he sound so calm?

"No." Tia rubbed her arms. "You know that funny feeling you get sometimes, where your body hair stands on end for no apparent reason? When something just feels...off?"

"Yes." That sense was ancient, primal, instinctive—and paying attention to it had saved his life on countless occasions. Tia had faerie blood in her lineage. With her empathic abilities, she'd notice something unusual in her surroundings earlier than most.

"I'm glad you trusted your gut," Lukas said, "but why haven't you—"

"Reported it to someone?" she said. "To you, or to Commander Lupinsky?"

"Or to me?" he asked, as calmly as he could manage. Because he was absolutely furious.

"I thought I'd drawn the attention of a neighborhood oddball," she said with a shrug. "It happens. I thought it would stop when I moved." She glanced at him, then upstairs. "But I guess not."

"This person—assuming it *is* the same person," Lukas said, "not only followed you to another town, but broke into your house and tried to scare the shit out of you." Lukas's gaze flicked to him, then back to Tia. "I'd like you to stay somewhere else until we figure out what's going on."

Finally, something he could do. "She can stay with me. With Valerian and me."

Lukas nodded. "I'm happier with the security at your place."

Tia was silent, then said, "Are you sure? I wouldn't want to put you out."

Putting him out was pretty much a given, but…that was his problem, not hers. One of his own was in danger, and it was his duty to offer safe refuge. "We'd be honored to have you as a guest."

Humor, and something hotter, danced in her eyes. "Okay, roomie. I'll pack a bag."

Was she laughing at him? At herself? At this situation, which had suddenly gotten completely out of hand?

They all watched as Tia trotted up the stairs. "What the hell have I gotten myself into?" he murmured.

"I don't know," Lukas said with a smile, "but if I were you, I'd strap in tight and enjoy the ride."

CHAPTER SIX

Several hours later, having abandoned all responsibility for settling Tia into their home to Thane, Wyland walked into the formal dining room. The space was dimly lit, with the chandelier tossing small, radiant prisms against the silver metallic Art Deco wallpaper. The windows were open, and the night breeze, lush with the scent of Thane's rose garden, gently ruffled the sheers.

Linen napkins, lead crystal, fine china, Georgian silver...

Damn it, Thane.

Not only had Thane put Tia in the bedroom next to his instead of in one of the perfectly lovely third-floor guest rooms, Thane had informed him that tonight, they were having their midnight meal in the dining room. "We have a guest," Thane had said, as if Wyland was a simpleton completely unaware of even the most basic points of hospitality. He glanced to the swinging door leading to the kitchen. Given what had happened the last time he and Tia had shared a meal, it was probably best they relocate. After that incendiary, ill-advised kiss, he could barely walk through the kitchen without getting aroused.

Thane shouldered through the door carrying a steaming bowl of green beans shimmering with butter. "There you are." He set the bowl on the table next to a platter holding crisp iceberg lettuce, ripe red tomatoes, pickles, and sliced onions. "I thought I might have to drag you away from your desk."

Thane knew him too well—he *had* considered working through the meal—but as Thane had scolded him earlier, they *did* have a guest. "Why is the table only set for three?" Thane usually joined them for meals. Frankly, he'd counted on Thane carrying the bulk of the conversation if Valerian tired.

"Tonight, I will serve."

He opened his mouth to argue, but a duet of laughter suddenly danced into the room. Stepping into the open doorway between the dining room and living room, he watched Valerian and Tia slowly walk arm in arm down the stairs.

Tia looked like a modern-day Audrey Hepburn in trim black pants, a crisp white blouse, and ballet flats, but Valerian, perhaps energized by the prospect of entertaining a guest, was resplendent in a garish purple 1940s-era zoot suit, complete with wide tie, suspenders, and decorative hanging chain. A ragged tricorn hat perched jauntily on his head, and he wore a pair of bright red Reeboks. Wyland barely blinked at the ensemble. The clothing in Valerian's closets spanned centuries, and he mixed and matched with impunity.

Tia canted her head toward Valerian and murmured something. Valerian tipped his head back and laughed.

Then he wobbled.

"Whoa." She quickly clutched Valerian's arm, steadying him. "Gravity surge." She didn't say anything else as she helped Valerian navigate the rest of the stairs.

"Hello, Wyland," Valerian greeted him.

"Hello. Hello, Tia." He managed to nod respectfully, all the while noticing the delicate veins exposed by her open-necked shirt and pulled-back hair. "Are you settling in?"

"Yes, thanks." She stood at the bottom of the stairs, supporting Valerian as he stepped down to the landing. "My room is beautiful, and that bathroom?" Her expression of ecstasy seared itself onto his retinas. "I could live in that soaking tub for days."

The subtle, humid scent of lilacs had wafted into his room earlier, so he suspected she'd already made use of it. "May I seat you?"

"Please." But she didn't let go of Valerian's elbow, leaving her walking between them. At her other side, Valerian looked strong and proud, like he was escorting her rather than the other way around. Tia hadn't been in the house more than a couple of hours, but the new spring in Valerian's step was unmistakable.

They walked into the dining room. "Oh, how beautiful," Tia breathed as she took in the table setting. Her glowing expression as they seated Valerian made him glad that Thane had made the effort.

Thane entered from the kitchen carrying another platter.

Of very rare hamburgers.

"Miss Tia's request," Thane murmured.

Of course it was. His mouth suddenly watered.

"Wyland." Thane tipped his head toward Tia, who stood by her chair—not waiting to be seated, but admiring the wallpaper. Before he could reach her, she slipped into her seat.

Bemused, he took the seat across from her.

The bemusement continued over the next hour, as they enjoyed what was essentially a picnic in the most formally decorated room in their home. As they ate loaded hamburgers and homemade French fries, conversation bounced from topic to topic. Valerian seemed delighted to talk about something other than Council business—had they really fallen into such a rut?—but Wyland had nothing to add to a conversation about the best television series finales in history. While Valerian made the case for *M*A*S*H* and *Six Feet Under*, Tia rhapsodized about *The Sopranos* and *Breaking Bad*.

Bloodthirsty little thing.

He took a sip of blood-mulled wine, watching her. She seemed fully recovered from her encounter with the snakes. Good for her, because he wasn't sure *he'd* recovered from the fear-spiked drive to her house. His uncharacteristic jealousy. Finding her unharmed, but surrounded by snakes. Waiting for her to pack a bag, then feeling her headlights stare at him as she followed his car from her house to his. All in all, it had been a discombobulating experience. He still hadn't quite regained his equilibrium.

That had to be the reason he kept staring at her rosy, unpainted lips as they smiled, ate, drank, and formed words.

Thane walked in with a beautiful raspberry cheesecake and coffee. As he served, Tia asked him to join them. "Could you fill me in on the household routine? I'd like to impact it as little as possible while I'm here."

One more small vampire wouldn't cause a ripple in

Thane's management of the household, but it was polite of her to ask about their routine, or lack thereof. Between Valerian's health issues, and him coming and going at all hours, there was no such thing as a typical day. While Thane and Tia talked, he watched Valerian enjoy his small slice of cheesecake. Half a hamburger, a dozen French fries, some green beans, and now dessert? He couldn't remember the last time Val had eaten so much food in a single sitting.

Across the table, Tia licked raspberry sauce off her fork with kittenish swipes of her tongue. Yes, her presence might help Valerian recover, but her effect on *him* was another matter entirely.

Tia set down her fork. "How is security handled during the daylight hours, when everyone's asleep?"

"Nick Solberg manages security for us," Thane answered.

"I thought Nick worked for Sebastiani Security."

She knew Nick well enough to call him by his first name?

"He does, and so do all the other guards." Reaching for the sugar bowl, Thane transferred a precise teaspoon to his coffee cup, and quietly stirred. "Being we're so remotely located, Lukas recommended that we have a full security team on site."

Tia nodded. "Makes sense. You're a fair distance out of the city."

Thane set the spoon on the rim of the saucer with nary a clink. "Nick and his team work out of a set of offices in the west wing. I'll tell him you're our guest at today's shift change. He'll probably want to speak with you in person," he added. "Don't take it personally if he's…taciturn."

She glanced at Wyland, amused. "I'm getting used to it."

"Indeed." Thane cleared his throat diplomatically. "We also have a rather large household staff—kitchen, housekeeping, lawn and gardens—all vetted by Sebastiani Security."

Perhaps in deference to Valerian, Thane hadn't mentioned Valerian's round-the-clock cadre of nurses and personal care attendants, whom they'd hired when Valerian became so ill with pneumonia last year. Even though Valerian seemed to be on the road to recovery, he and Thane had recently decided to keep them on as permanent staff. Knowing Valerian had dedicated care, and cheerful company, eased their minds immensely.

"So, tell me about your career," Thane said. "I understand you're an investigative journalist?"

Tia laughed. "Via a very roundabout route, yes."

Thane's smile invited confidences. "Sounds like there's a story there."

"You can't imagine."

Wyland listened as Tia told Thane some hair-raising stories about her early days as a music journalist, which, as far as he could tell, pretty much confirmed the 'sex, drugs, and rock and roll' stereotype. "I was on the road with an up-and-coming band, working on a story about how long it can take to become an overnight sensation—" she made air quotes with her fingers "—when I caught the stench of payola." She glanced at Valerian. "That's when—"

"Someone pays to get a song played on the radio," Valerian finished.

She nodded. "Pay for play. It can influence song

popularity, chart position, and ultimately sales. There's a lot of money on the line. So, I followed the money. *Rolling Stone* published my exposé, it became a series, and suddenly I was writing investigative pieces instead of music reviews. *Rolling Stone* couldn't publish them all, so I started *In Like Quinn*."

"Becoming your own publisher," Thane said.

"Yeah. I guess I did."

"An amazing thing."

She shrugged. "It's just a website."

Just a website? Did she have any idea what a bloody marvel it was to convey one's thoughts and ideas digitally, rather than laboring over pen and parchment by candlelight? To have one's words travel through the ether at the touch of a button or a click of a mouse, instead of hoping your messenger hadn't paid for the honor of delivering your words with his life?

No. She didn't. She'd never known a life without computers or air travel, much less electricity, antibiotics, or automobiles.

As she continued the conversation with Thane and Valerian, her eyes sparkled with verve, with life. Her impish grin conveyed such energy and delight.

Had he ever been so young?

"Right now, I'm working on a story about human trafficking," she said. "So many young people simply disappear, sold into sexual servitude. It's a bigger problem than most people realize."

His gaze whipped to Thane, whose flat expression camouflaged a hideous internal roar, a grief-stained rage that hadn't waned over the years. Thane's youngest sister had been stolen in a raid many years ago, never to be seen again.

Tia lowered her coffee cup, glancing at them warily. "Is everything okay?"

He and Valerian exchanged a quick glance. This wasn't the first time Tia seemed to perceive something...*more* going on between the vampires in her immediate vicinity without the benefit of a shared blood bond.

"Please," Thane said. "Continue. You're working on a human trafficking story?"

"It's slow going," she admitted. "There are so many angles to work—the man camps at the Bakken oil fields, the big sporting events, the suburban homes that are actually underground sex clubs..."

Wyland sat upright in the ladder-backed chair.

"Oh, cool your jets," she told him. "I'm backing off the Stephen/Annika angle—as you requested—but I've discovered that the house where Stephen killed his first victim is one of dozens of underground sex clubs based out of single-family homes in Twin Cities suburban neighborhoods," she said. "To me, this indicates organization, and a profit motive. Who owns the properties? Who's running the show? I'm following the money—or trying to, anyway."

"And what will you do once you find out?" Fear made his voice snap like a whip. "You agreed you'd drop the story."

"I did no such thing. I agreed to refine the subject. Which I do not have to clear through you."

Thane stilled. Valerian simply forked up a small bite of cheesecake.

The woman was going to drive him straight to Bedlam.

"Stephen's first victim was described as being found 'trussed up like a Thanksgiving turkey.' I'm

123

trying to find out if Commander Lupinsky worked the *shibari* angle—you know, the Japanese bondage art where a person is tied and suspended in a highly intricate arrangement of ropes? But he won't return my call," she said. "Skilled rope fetish practitioners are really quite rare, at least here in the Midwest."

Thane was gawping like a fish out of water.

Wyland leaned back in his chair and crossed his arms, as if her words hadn't shocked him, too. Maybe one small vampire *would* throw Thane for a loop.

"Did Stephen's victim know what he was getting into when he went to the sex club?" she continued. "Or was he simply in the wrong place, at the wrong time, with the wrong dom?" Raising her cup, Tia took another sip of her coffee. "I'm interviewing some people in the local BDSM, kink, and fetish communities to see how people consensually connect with others who share their interests." She shrugged one rounded shoulder. "It might be a dead end, but…"

But it might not be. If Lupinsky hadn't investigated the *shibari* angle, doing so now might give them a fresh avenue of investigation on a case grown too damn cold.

She was good, damn it.

"You might talk to Nick," Valerian suggested from the end of the table.

Her face lit. "Great idea. He'd know."

"He'd know what?" Lukas had fully vetted the man, but… "Tia." He held her gaze, pitching his voice low and languid. It would echo in her head, throb in her thoughts. "What connection does Nick Solberg have to your story?"

Her eyes went vague.

"Wyland, what are you doing?"

He ignored the censure in Valerian's voice. He had to get to the bottom of this. "Tia, what connection does Nick have with your story?"

"He's a dom," she slurred.

Nick, a dom? A sexual dominant? How could Tia possibly know such a thing? "For hire?"

"Of course not." Even in thrall, Tia's response was scathing.

Her answer was a relief, but there was another matter to resolve, once and for all. Pushing guilt aside, he threw every lick of his strength into his next words. "You need to drop this story."

"I need to drop this story?" Tia parroted.

"Yes."

"Wyland!" Valerian snapped. "Enough."

His head whipped to Val. "She's going to get herself killed."

Tia jerked in her chair, blinking rapidly. "Sorry." She lifted a hand to her temple. "I kind of zoned out there for a minute."

"Are you okay?" Valerian asked.

"I have a killer headache," she replied with a wince. "I think I'd better go lie down for a bit."

Good. He had to call Gideon, STAT.

Rising, she cleared her throat. "Thank you for your hospitality, for inviting me to be a guest in your home."

"We're pleased to have you," Thane said.

She rubbed her temple again. "Thane, thank you for the delicious meal. I think I'm going to go upstairs now."

"Our home is yours," Valerian said with a gentle smile. "Be at ease."

"Thank you." After kissing Val on both cheeks, she gave *him* a single, stingy look before leaving the room.

Both men stared at him. Thane's appalled expression spoke volumes, and Valerian looked as disappointed as he could remember.

Disappointed in *him*.

"Was that really necessary?" Valerian nearly whispered.

When Wyland rose from his seat, he felt creaky and infirm, as if he'd aged centuries in the last few minutes. "Yes. It was." And with as much dignity as he could manage, he left the men who'd raised him without another word of explanation.

✳

Dominic jolted awake, pricking his ears and lifting his snout to the breeze as he edged even further back into the tall ditch grass. The garage door was opening with a soft mechanical hum.

Finally, something was happening.

He couldn't believe he'd dozed off just down the road from Vamp Central.

Shifted.

Shit.

If humans saw him, they'd think someone's dog had made a break for it, but the few who knew better would recognize him for what he was: Werewolf.

Pushing slowly to his haunches, ignoring the stink of fear from a nearby rabbit, he watched as the door slowly rose. Two sets of feet. Two pairs of legs. A man and a woman—Wyland and Tia Quinn—together.

After leaving the snakes in her bedroom yesterday, he'd expected…well, in hindsight, he didn't know *what* he'd expected. To rattle her? Yes. To show her that her security was a fucking joke? Yeah. But if he thought she'd run out the door, squealing like a terrified little girl?

No, that hadn't happened.

What *had* happened was that Wyland, the freaking Vampire Second, had squealed wheels into her driveway not fifteen minutes after she'd discovered the snakes, with Lukas Sebastiani, Jack Kirkland, and Chico Perez arriving soon after. Kirkland, the human, didn't worry him that much, but Lukas Sebastiani damn well did, and Perez's werewolf nose was a serious threat. So he'd backed away from Tia's house, but not so far away that he couldn't see when everyone left. He'd followed Tia and Wyland to Vamp Central, where she'd pulled her car right into the garage under the watchful eye of a beefy security guard.

Three Council members—Sebastiani, Kirkland, and Wyland—at Quinn's beck and call. He could only imagine the services she provided in exchange for such dedicated attention.

The garage door was open now. He watched Wyland open the passenger door of his black Porsche, then guide Tia into the seat with a hand on the small of her back. His mother had once called Wyland a gentleman's gentleman— "Such beautiful, courtly manners" —but there was nothing courtly about the Second's fair-weather ride. The Targa had some serious horsepower under the hood.

Imagine being able to spend over a hundred grand on a car you couldn't even drive in the snow.

Wyland strode to the driver's side, slid behind the wheel, and started the car. Its soft purr rose to a growl as he backed out of the garage.

He had to follow.

Dom pushed to his feet and ran to where he'd parked the Pathfinder. A nervous squirrel dove into the underbrush as he passed, and an owl hooted nearby. Fireflies flickered in the distance. The air, damp as a sponge, smelled like fresh deer droppings, rotted leaves, and a hint of exhaust from Wyland's car.

There were no humans nearby.

He dropped to his haunches behind the Pathfinder. Taking a deep breath, he felt the pull of the new moon, hiding in the night sky. Felt the support of the ground beneath his belly. Then...his brain went on walkabout. Scents faded into the background as his snout receded. Fangs became teeth, claws became nails, and fur became flesh. Skin and bone shifted and popped as his body mass rearranged itself in a timeless rush.

Several seconds later, when he came to his senses, he was breathing hard and lying bare-ass naked in the itchy grass. Pushing to his feet, he reached into the open hatch for his jeans, T-shirt, and flip-flops, then quickly dressed.

The Targa's tail lights disappeared over the small rise to the south.

He followed with his headlights off, hanging well back. Reaching for the cup of gas station coffee sitting in the recessed holder, he sipped the cold, bitter brew. Next week, his dad's doctors wanted him to try to shift. "If I can't, you know what to do," his father had said.

Dominic rubbed his bleary eyes. Hadn't his dad ever seen *CSI*? How the fuck was he supposed to do his duty when the hospital had security up the wazoo? Even after his father moved home—gawd, his mother had already ordered a bed with a Stryker frame, and planned to put it in the formal dining room—how could he hasten his father's journey to the Pale without being charged with patricide? It wasn't as if he could just issue a Google search on how to kill someone and make it look like an accident.

Well, he could, but that would be really stupid.

How did the werewolves who followed The Old Ways get away with it? Or did they? Maybe going to prison was part of the deal.

He needed more information.

Brake lights glowed up ahead as Wyland pulled into the parking lot of a ratty-looking storage facility less than a half mile away from Vamp Central. What the hell...? Had Tia stored some of her belongings there when she moved? One of the big double doors was opening, creating a bright envelope of light as it rose. The Porsche idled in the gravel lot, waiting for the door to reach its apex. Once it did, Wyland pulled in.

They disappeared as the door closed behind them.

What the...

Dominic pulled off the road again, took another gulp of the cold coffee, and settled in to watch.

And wait.

*

An hour before dawn, Tia walked into Valerian's sitting room, rubbing her temples.

Valerian looked up from this week's *People* magazine. "Oh, hello, dear. I thought you were at the Archives with Wyland."

"I was, but then there was an emergency at the hospital." And it was probably just as well, because no matter how interesting she'd found the old books and manuscripts he'd asked her to read, her headache had dug in like a pickax. She'd downed two bags of blood at the Archives, but the throbbing was still vicious. "I told him I could walk back, but he insisted on dropping me off."

"As he should," Valerian said mildly, removing and folding his wire-rimmed reading glasses.

"It's just a short walk—"

"Down an unlit rural road in the middle of the night. Tia, you're a smart, capable woman. Why take unnecessary risks?"

Okay, that took the wind out of her sails.

Valerian smiled angelically.

Wily old vampire. As she bent down to kiss his cheek, pain lanced her temple. "Do you have any Tylenol?"

He waved to the bathroom. "Medicine cabinet. Help yourself."

"Thanks."

Opening the medicine cabinet, she grabbed the familiar red and white bottle, and shook out two capsules. After a pause, she added a third. What was the deal with the headaches? Maybe she was allergic to something in the house—mold, or a cleanser or something. Or maybe the stress was finally getting to her.

She had to find a way to shake it off, because she'd been utterly worthless working with Wyland tonight. They'd started out working side-by-side at the computers, with her searching the Archive, and him doing…whatever he'd been doing. She'd lost too much time staring at his elegant hands as he quietly typed, at the ferocious furrow of concentration that had wrinkled his brow. He'd taken quite a few phone calls while they'd been there—from the hospital, from legal clients, from Council members—and he'd given each call his undivided attention. No multi-tasking for Wyland, which made a lot of sense given lives could be at stake with each and every conversation.

Having been the recipient of a single, scorching kiss, she was dead certain he'd lavish the same focus, and exquisite attention to detail, upon his lovers.

She'd thought about the kiss too damn much.

"Tia? Are you finding what you need?"

"Yes," she called back, snapping the cover back on the pill bottle and returning it to the medicine cabinet. She tossed the pills into her mouth and swallowed them dry.

When she went back to the sitting room, Valerian was flipping through the box of movies she'd left. "A half-dozen versions of *Dracula. Nosferatu. Blackula, Dragula, Buffy the Vampire Slayer, Angel, True Blood…* Isn't it amazing the degree to which vampires have saturated human culture?"

She nodded. "It's an interest of mine. I'm pretty sure I have nearly every vampire film and TV series ever made—the good, the bad, and ugly."

Valerian picked up a luridly-colored DVD. "*Spermula.* How very interesting."

Interesting that vampire porn existed, or that she owned it? "Give me that," she muttered, snatching it out of his hand.

Out of the Vampire First's gnarled, arthritic hand. She closed her eyes, mortified. "I'm so sorry, Sir. Are you okay?"

"Certainly. And drop the sir, if you please."

"You make it way too easy to forget you're the most powerful vampire on the planet."

A smile lit his face. "What a beautiful compliment."

She set the movie back in the box. "Well, my mother would be ashamed of me." *My mother.* "Damn, I haven't told my parents where I am. I haven't told them anything."

"Is there anything they can do?" he asked with a shrug. "Maybe it's best they don't know."

Valerian was probably right. The fewer people who knew she was staying with Valerian and Wyland, the better. "I'll tell them to call my cell if they need to contact me."

"I think that's best for now. How's the headache?"

"Getting better, thanks." She eyed Valerian. His color was good, and his eyes snapped with energy. Maybe she could get some research done tonight, after all. "You said earlier that I could interview you for the Archives. Are you up for it right now?"

"Certainly."

She pulled a digital recorder out of her pocket and set it on the end table. "And maybe afterward, we could watch a movie." Rooting through the box, she grabbed *Love at First Bite*. Hopefully, Frank Langella's dark, smoldering sensuality would push Wyland's pale and broody version out of her mind for a while.

Valerian picked up the digital recorder, turning it over and examining it with careful hands. "Alka used a similar device when she recorded our dinner parties." He went on to describe the conversations he and Alka Schlessinger, the Valkyrie First, had enjoyed over a series of intimate dinners. "They think I'm going to die soon."

The matter-of-fact words snatched the breath from her lungs. "Who does?"

"Alka. Elliott. Wyland."

And Wyland was his doctor. "What do you think?"

He smiled cheerfully. "We're all dying. Every day we live brings us one step closer to the finish line."

She considered. "Can't disagree with that. How about some wine?"

"That would be lovely. Thane brought a lovely French merlot up from the catacombs yesterday."

She poured them each a glass of wine, noticing from the label that the vintage was older than her mother. Her first, testing sip positively melted on her tongue. "I'm going to get so spoiled while I'm here," she said, sitting in the closest chair. "I don't know much about wine beyond red, rosé, and white, but this tastes fantastic." After taking another sip, she set the glass down on the priceless antique table. "Shit," she muttered, quickly lifting the glass. "Do you have coasters?"

Valerian set his glass down on the ancient, polished wood. "Use it for its intended purpose, my dear. Treating it like it's fragile does it no honor."

Message received, loud and clear.

She spent the next hour interviewing him as

vigorously as she would anyone else, asking questions about his recent past, figuring she'd work back to his memories of Sigurd eventually. Valerian had other ideas. No matter what question she asked, or how specifically the question was phrased, he found a way to turn the topic to Wyland: His legal and medical work, past and present. His role as a political adviser. His cultural contributions. "He doesn't relax enough," he said with a sigh. "Work, work, work. Speaking of which, do you know if Elliott got ahold of him tonight? He called here right after you left."

Imagine being familiar enough with the Council president to call him by his first name. "I don't know. He took a lot of phone calls while we were there."

"Wyland's been researching how we might transition Council leadership from species-based representation to something a little more democratic."

She stared. Another scoop for the ages, another story she couldn't publish. "You probably shouldn't be telling me this."

He gestured to the recorder. "This interview is for the Archives, right? There's no need for secrecy."

He'd handed her the perfect opening, gift-wrapped and tied with a pretty bow. "If there's no place for secrets, why is there nothing in the Archives about your predecessor, Sigurd?"

When he finally answered, his voice was rough as sandpaper. "Because it hurts."

He suddenly looked every second of his nine hundred plus years. She couldn't press him, not now. "I'm sorry."

"So am I," he said, sighing. "I didn't mean to get so melancholy, but I'd like to save Sigurd for another time, if you don't mind." His sigh carried the weight of the centuries. He took a sip of wine, then suddenly smiled. "Let's talk about your attraction to Wyland."

"Um, I'm not..." The lie froze in her throat. "Okay, yeah," she said, brazening it out. "He's easy enough on the eyes."

His eyebrow cocked up with amusement.

"Okay, he's gorgeous," she admitted, "but he's so...solitary. So closed off, like he doesn't need anyone." Except for when they'd kissed. He'd needed her then.

No, not needed, *wanted*. Two entirely different things.

"There's a distinct spark between you."

Valerian's wise, rheumy eyes invited confidences. "Yeah, but most of the time he treats me like I'm a child."

"I can see where he might have some issues with your age," Valerian mused. "And with your profession. And with your independence, and—"

"Gee, let me take some notes."

"I was going to say, your feminine energy, your *joie de vivre*. We've lived in a staid bachelor household for many, many years. You must forgive us—you must forgive Wyland—if this shift takes us some time to get used to."

"I don't think I'll be staying here long enough for anyone to notice."

Valerian threw his head back and laughed.

"What?"

"Never mind." The remains of his smile lingered. "What else would you like to talk about?"

Hell, why not ask? "Does Wyland have a lover?"

"No. Why do you ask?"

"He seems so...alone."

"We, with our vampire longevity, love and lose, love and lose," he said softly. "It's a bittersweet experience, and some grow...remote...as a defense mechanism. In addition, making decisions which impact an entire species can be a very heavy load. It takes an extraordinary mate to stand at a Council member's side. Thankfully, many of my friends have found such partners."

She nodded. Lukas had Scarlett. Lorin Schlessinger, the Valkyrie Second, had Gabe Lupinsky. Bailey's relationship with Rafe definitely helped leaven her obsessive focus on work.

"Tell me about your tattoo," he suddenly asked. "Is that your own handwriting?"

She nodded again, bringing her bare forearm closer to his face.

"'The needs of the many outweigh the needs of the few. Or the one,'" he read aloud. "Ah! Mr. Spock. *The Wrath of Khan*."

"You're familiar with *Star Trek*?"

"Oh, yes." He shot her a glance. "Kirk or Picard?"

Which captain did she prefer? It was an age-old question between *Star Trek* fans. "What's the scenario?" Kirk solved problems with action and swagger. Picard was deliberate and cerebral. They'd both rock in the sack.

Valerian laughed again. "Yes, you're a wise one." He ran his crooked finger over the cursive letters etched into her skin. "This is beautiful work. Such crisp lines—and a good reminder for someone in your occupation, I would imagine."

He understood. "It reminds me that my personal needs and interests aren't always paramount."

"Let me show you mine."

Valerian had a tattoo?

He unzipped his Green Bay Packers warm-up jacket, spread the sides, and lifted his T-shirt hem up to his neck. Though the image was faded, blurred with time, Tia recognized it immediately: a Celtic Tree of Life. The upper portion of the tree was lush and leafy, broad enough to cover his entire chest, and narrowed into a twisted, gnarled trunk on his stomach. Thorny-looking roots spread wide at the base, disappearing below his sweatpants' elastic waistband. "Wow."

"When I was younger, I fell in with a group of pagans for a time. They thought me wise, called me a merlin." Smiling puckishly, he lowered his shirt, then patted the place next to him on the couch. "Come sit here. Let's work on that headache."

Rising, she obeyed. "Do you know a secret pagan massage technique?"

"No." Pulling up his sleeve, he exposed the veins in his wrist.

She recoiled. Did he mean for her to drink from him?

"Yes," he said, answering her unasked question.

"No. I couldn't," she blurted. "You're still recovering."

He smiled. "I'm as recovered as someone my age is going to get."

She couldn't drag her gaze away from his. "It's— it's too much. You're the freaking Vampire First." He was offering her the strongest vampire blood on the planet.

"Yes, I am." Such power in his voice. "And I want you to have some protection."

"From what?"

"From whatever might come your way," he said, exasperated. "Come. Come and drink."

His voice was like a whirlybird in her head, echoing and swirling. She felt her resistance draining away, like the water in the bath she'd taken earlier. "Are you sure?" So many questions embedded in those three simple words: Did he really want her to have access to his memories and emotions, and second-hand access to the memories and emotions of those whose blood he'd ingested? To Thane?

To Wyland?

That he'd offer her such a gift was utterly terrifying.

"Tia. Feed." He didn't sound ill or infirm now. It sounded like he'd given her an order.

After a hesitation, she sat beside him on the couch. "I've never done this before," she admitted. "As an adult, I mean." Her mom and dad had vein-fed her when she was young, of course, but bagged blood had been available for her entire life—convenient, always there, like humans carrying their bottles of water. The only time most vampires of her generation drank from the vein was with bondmates or long-term sexual partners.

Feeding during sex was supposed to result in stratospheric orgasms.

She believed it. Hell, she'd felt an erotic zing just watching Wyland feed someone else. What would it be like to feel his body, his fangs, plunging into her? To bite him back, to drink from him, as their bodies rocked and strained together?

Wyland. "Wyland wouldn't agree with this."

"Wyland has no choice in the matter."

"But he does—or should," she argued. "He's

chosen to share his emotions with you, not with me."

Approval gleamed in his eyes. "The second-hand effect will be negligible and short-term, but the fact that you're concerned about such a point makes me proud." He sighed. "Tia, I want you to have the strength of my blood. Drinking from me, from an older, stronger vampire, will provide you with some tools that might prove useful in the days to come."

"Such as?"

"It'll kick-start your ability to thrall, to glamour—and to detect and repel thralls in return."

The ability to thrall or glamour someone, to influence someone else's thoughts or actions with one's mind, was a skill a vampire her age could only dream of. Even the beginnings of that ability usually didn't manifest until a vampire reached the century mark. "You think I might need such a tool?"

"With all the strange goings-on, how could it hurt?" He glanced at her tattoo, then met her eyes again. "I trust you'll use your skills wisely."

He extended his wrist.

After a pause, she took it. And drank.

CHAPTER SEVEN

Wyland loosened his tie as he trudged from the attached garage to the kitchen, smelling the remnants of the *Beef Bourguignon* Thane must have served for Last Meal. If he looked in the refrigerator, he knew he'd find succulent leftovers, neatly packaged and ready to heat in the microwave, but he really didn't have the energy to deal with food. The hospital resident he'd been working with for long, long hours had said it best: What a complete and utter shit-show of a day.

A solar flare, unnoticed and of little concern to most humans, had sent dozens of vampires to the ER with UV burns. Then, Mila Stanton had wobbled into the ER, so anemic that she'd needed an immediate transfusion.

He rubbed his hand over the back of his neck. Mila's strain of vampire hemolytic anemia was a stubborn one, and the girl herself even more so. The stubbornness was a valuable trait—rather, it *would* be, once she started fighting with him rather than against him.

He went to the living room, stopping at the window overlooking the sprawling front lawn. It was freshly mowed, the pattern ballpark-sharp, and the gas-powered riding mower droned on the north side of the house. Out front, another gardener tended the hostas and spiky green *arborvitae*. Over near the tree line, one of the security guards did morning rounds.

He closed his eyes, savoring the sun as it beat through the UV-filtering windows. What astounding technology Elliott had invented. Maybe, at some point, the newness of the experience would wear off—he might even come to find the sun's heat annoying—but not yet. But on the negative side of the equation, their cars were fitted with the windows as well. He couldn't use the sun as an excuse to stay at the hospital instead of come home to their inconvenient houseguest.

Though he hadn't seen Tia for several days, her presence was unmistakable. He came across her possessions in unexpected places, heard her giggles floating through the walls. The scent of lilacs had taken up permanent residence upstairs. Her presence was a mischievous ghost, haunting him for the hell of it—and unfortunately, she wasn't leaving anytime soon. Chico had informed him that, so far, the lab had come up empty on the note Tia had found stapled to the snake. Printed in Times New Roman on a generic scrap of printer paper, the note was as untraceable as they came.

And speaking of Times New Roman…more work waited upstairs.

As he strode toward the stairway, he heard the distant twinkle of Tia's laughter. Valerian's lower-toned guffaw immediately followed. They were probably watching television again. He sighed, but couldn't begrudge Val the company. Val hadn't needed supplemental oxygen in days, and his appetite was improving. Thane reported that Val and Tia spent a lot of time camped out in Val's sitting room, immersing themselves in Tia's inexhaustible collection of movies and TV shows.

Another peal of laughter sailed down the stairs. What the hell were they watching?

Chirp chirp chirp.

And damn it, where was that where was that infernal noise coming from? Had a grasshopper somehow gotten into the house?

He skimmed the floor, the rugs, the pile of battered, brown leather lying on the credenza at the foot of the stairs.

Chirp chirp chirp.

Yes. The sound was coming from Tia's purse.

With a glance up the stairs, he went to the credenza and nudged the already-gaping purse open. It was a tumble of feminine detritus, with lipsticks, makeup, pens, and scraps of paper all elbowing for space. A black Moleskine notebook. A disposable lighter. A pocket-sized version of the human Bill of Rights. A small, plastic jar of a noxious-looking green paste, something called "Manic Panic." A tube of VampScreen lay next to her cell phone.

Ah, the phone. The face-up display was littered with text messages, including the one Chadden had just sent, asking if she wanted to meet him at Underbelly tonight.

Beneath the phone was a yellow plastic device. He carefully picked up the stun gun, felt its solid weight in his hand. The weapon was heavier than it looked, with a clever cartridge that propelled the hooks—

The cell phone suddenly rang, a raucous guitar and a man's rock and roll wail. The ring tone sounded like someone was squeezing the poor git's testicles in a vice.

"I'll be right back," he heard Tia say upstairs.

He dropped the stun gun back in her purse, closed the bag with a jerk, and moved away from the credenza. When Tia appeared at the top of the stairs, he was setting his briefcase on the bar, as if he'd just walked in.

"Oh, hey." Her breasts bounced as she trotted down the stairs. "I thought I heard my phone."

His heart nearly stopped at what she was—what she *wasn't*—wearing. Tia might call the camisole and boxer shorts pajamas, but he called them trouble. "Is that what that infernal racket is?" He winced as the phone—the man—shrieked again.

"Mr. Rose gets your attention, doesn't he?" she said with a grin. Pawing through the purse, she snatched up the phone and punched a button, cutting the man off in mid-wail. "Hello? Hello? Damn." Pulling the phone away from her ear, she scowled at the screen, then cursed under her breath. "No message. Very cagey, Commander Lupinsky, returning my call after the sun's up, when most vampires are asleep." She tossed the phone back into the purse, her disgust clear.

Why was Gideon calling her at all?

She stalked behind the bar and opened the refrigerator. When she stood upright again, she held a can of Diet Mountain Dew—an unnatural beverage that, thanks to Thane, was now stocked in every refrigerator in the house. "Do you know how much acid is in that can? Its pH level is off the charts."

"Yes, Dad. My dentist reminds me every time I sit in her chair." With that, she opened the can with a pneumatic hiss, and slurped with great relish.

His thoughts were anything but fatherly. He tried to keep his eyes off her mouth, but didn't know where he should focus instead. Her bare arms and shoulders? Her gloriously unbound breasts? Her curvy hips and long legs, with their obnoxious turquoise toenails? Why did everything seem so much more vivid when she walked into a room? He cleared his throat. "Speaking of daylight, I thought I'd find you and Valerian in bed already."

One eyebrow rose. "Together?"

"Of course not," he stammered. Heat rose from beneath his collar. "I meant asleep. In your own beds. Um, separately."

The little brat was grinning behind the can.

She made him feel like a foot-shuffling, pock-faced youth. "The sun came up hours ago," he said. "I thought you'd both be asleep."

"Valerian wanted to finish watching *El Vampiro*, but he's getting ready for bed now. I have a little bit of work to finish, and then I have a hot date with a bathtub."

El Vampiro? He wasn't even going to ask. He joined her behind the bar, pulling a bottle of Perrier and a bag of blood out of the refrigerator. It would hypocritical of him to advise her to get some sleep when he had no intention of sleeping himself. In this, they seemed to be kindred spirits.

Her gaze roved over his loosened tie and rolled-up shirtsleeves. "You look beat," she murmured. "How was your day?"

Something inside him jolted at the homey, ordinary question no woman had ever asked. "It was…busy."

"The solar flare?"

He nodded, wincing slightly as his neck muscles protested. "I spent more time in the ER than I'd planned."

She pointed to one of the tall leather barstools. "Why don't you take a load off?"

He was too tired to fight with her. So he sat, and watched, as she mixed and served him a bloody Perrier. "Thank you." He lifted the glass and took a sip. Cool bubbles danced on his tongue, and iron-rich hemoglobin hummed into his system. Somehow, she'd gauged his blood needs precisely. "This is perfect, thank you—Tia?" The space where she'd just been standing was empty.

"Relax," she murmured from behind him. Before he could prepare himself, her hands were on his shoulders, working his stiff muscles through the wilted fabric of his shirt. "Jeez, your neck is knottier than a tree trunk."

How was he supposed to relax when her hands were finally on him, stroking with such care and confidence? When she pressed her thumb where the trapezius joined with his deltoid, a groan of pain-laced pleasure escaped.

"This can't be helping." She pulled the black elastic band at the nape of his neck, spilling his hair over his shoulders.

The relief was immediate, as was the stirring below his belt. Something clicked against the bar—she'd taken off her ring—and then she really went to work, threading her fingers through his hair and massaging his scalp with the fingers of both hands. When she pressed her thumbs into the tense bundle of muscles at the base of his neck, he couldn't quite bite back a sigh. "You've had training," he noted.

"I like taking classes, learning new things."

That might explain her odd efficiency mixing his drink. "A very fine habit."

"I'm so glad you approve," she said dryly.

"You don't care whether I approve or not."

"See how well we're getting to know each other? Lean forward, rest your forehead on your arms," she murmured. Her soft breath fluttered against his hair, against his neck. "Just relax…"

Something in her voice made him obey. When was the last time he'd been touched like this? The last time he'd allowed it? Time drifted, her rhythmic touches and strokes lulling him into a pleasant haze…until she grazed his neck with her lips.

He shot upright in the chair as his fangs shoved down. "Enough." Maybe if he said it out loud, his body would get the message, because his body wanted blood—*her* blood—in the most elemental way. His teeth and cock throbbed with each beat of his heart.

"Wyland," she whispered. Just his name, slipping through her lips.

He twisted the chair around, thinking he'd stand, that he'd leave—which was a big mistake, because now that he faced her, he could see her beautiful breasts, see her hard, saucy nipples jutting from behind the fabric of her camisole. See the tips of her fangs pressed against her plump lower lip.

The air sizzled as they stared at each other. He slipped off the barstool, putting his feet on solid ground.

She looked down, to the stingy inches separating the tips of his dress shoes from her bare feet. Meeting his gaze again, she moved closer. Cocked her brow in challenge.

If he didn't want this, now was the time to move.

So, he moved—yanking their bodies together with a firm tug.

She *whoofed* in surprise, but recovered quickly. She looped her arms around his waist and tugged their hips together more firmly, pressing her soft curves against the mindless rod of flesh shoving so rudely against his zipper.

The pressure—too much, not enough—was absolutely maddening.

She learned forward, pressing her breasts against his chest, nuzzling his bare throat. She inhaled slowly, luxuriously. "Mmm."

She exhaled, sending a shiver through him. Her lips curved, then she kissed her way up his sternocleidomastoid muscle, her clever hands working at the knot of his already loose tie. "For future reference," she said, tugging the annoying strip of fabric out from under his shirt collar and tossing it onto the bar, "this is an excellent look for you."

"What is?"

"The loose tie? The rolled-up sleeves, the rumpled hair?" She nipped at his chin. "Sex on a stick. Absolutely panty-dropping."

A thrill shot through him. A chuckle escaped.

"What's so funny?"

"Have you shared those phrases with Valerian yet?" He slid his hand to the elastic waistband of her ridiculous boxer shorts, then cupped her right buttock with his palm. "You don't appear to be wearing any. Panties, that is."

Her answering smile was enigmatic, as if she enjoyed some private joke. Before he could ponder it too closely, she rose onto her tiptoes and laid a blistering line of kisses along his jawbone, finally nudging her lips up to his mouth.

He took control of the kiss, locking their lips into perfect alignment, then dove in to the dark oasis of her mouth like it was the only thing keeping him from dying of thirst. She gave as good as she got, their tongues thrusting and parrying, strong and slick as they tasted and tested each other. When her fang grazed his lip, the delicious sting zinged straight to his cock. Pulling away slightly, she licked at it, gathering a tiny drop of blood.

Tasting his most intimate, primal essence.

He watched as she sampled him, as she swirled the droplet in her mouth like a wine connoisseur judging this year's vintage. The mere seconds it took for her to murmur her approval and fuse their mouths back together stretched time to the snapping point.

The taste of his own blood on her tongue almost clubbed him to his knees. As she clutched at his hair, his mind flooded with deliciously carnal images: Tia, unzipping his pants and fellating him where they stood. Her, bent over the arm of the settee, him driving into her from behind. The two of them in her bed, his hair tickling her stomach as he bathed her slick inner folds with his tongue...

Her hands dropped to his belt.

"Wait." He took a shaky breath. Valerian was right upstairs. Gardeners, caretakers, household staff...the security office was right down the hall. "We can't," he muttered. "Not here."

She pulled at the leather and unfastened his belt buckle, the soft, metallic clank mocking his feeble protests. She reached for the tab of his zipper, drawing it down so slowly that he felt the gnash of each tooth.

His mind filled with hot, vivid visions: Moist, open lips. A blunt, hot weight, filling his mouth to capacity. Ravenous suckling.

His eyes narrowed slightly. Even at his most celibacy-addled, he'd never fantasized about dropping to his knees and sucking a man's—

Her thoughts, not his.

He shoved her out of his mind with a brutal mental blast, severing the connection she shouldn't have been able to make.

"Aaah!" She slapped her hands to her temples. He reached for her, but she stumbled away from him.

He should have noticed. He should have noticed the fragile new connection between them—weak, unschooled, but there.

Damn it, Valerian, what have you done?

When he reached for her again, she shied away. "Don't touch me." Anger had doused her desire dead. "It was you, wasn't it? That headache the other night." She rubbed her temples. "Damn, that hurts."

He wouldn't apologize for his self-preservation instincts, but he hadn't meant to hurt her. "I'm sorry you're in pain." Actually, with the strength of the shove he'd given her, she should have been lying on the floor, incapacitated. Instead, she looked ready to kick him with her tiny, turquoise-nailed foot.

"You thralled me that first night," she accused. "You abused your power."

"I use my power as I see fit." Her words carried an uncomfortable sting of truth, but damn it, *Val's* abuse of power was a far worse crime. Val had clearly shared his blood with Tia, transferring Wyland's blood at the same time, opening a fragile mental link between them. Though a vampire of his strength could easily thrall or glamour whomever he pleased, he'd need to drink from Tia, or drink from someone who'd drank from Tia, to create a reciprocal channel.

He zipped his pants and buckled his belt. He felt...hideously exposed. *They* were hideously exposed. How in the world had a baby vamp so quickly gained such intimate access to the Vampire First and Second?

Was this a honey trap? Was Tia a spy in their midst?

No. Lukas's deep background check had come back clean—and though she had the right physical attributes, she was temperamentally unsuited to be another Mata Hari. Every emotion she felt was displayed on her face, for anyone to read. Right now, despite her kiss-swollen lips and erect nipples, she looked like she wanted to wring his bloody neck.

Damn it. If Tia hadn't been a security risk before, she certainly was now. *Damn it, Val. What the hell were you thinking?*

No answer, but reassurance throbbed from upstairs.

"Don't blame Valerian," Tia snapped. "It wasn't his fault. He was trying to help ease my headache—a headache, it turns out, *you* caused."

"So you held Valerian down, and took his vein without asking?"

"Of course not—"

"Then I damn well do blame him." But there was plenty of blame to go around. Yes, he'd caused her headaches, but he'd also let her lick the blood from his mouth. He'd invited her to taste him, exalting in the desire that had dilated her pupils so much that her irises had been all but obscured. And that had been a mistake. "You're one of my subjects," he said in as remote a voice as he could manage. "I'm responsible for you. And now, I have to find time to train you."

"Don't strain yourself, Buckwheat."

He grasped her by her upper arms and gave her a little shake. "Do you realize what he's done? Do you realize that you can now be used as a tool against us?" When her eyes widened, he pressed the point home. "No one can learn of this. No one can know you've fed from Valerian."

She wrenched her arms out of his hands. "That's not the only reason you're angry."

He didn't answer; he didn't have to. Retrieving his tie from the bar where Tia had thrown it, he looped it around his neck. He buttoned his shirt and tied a Windsor knot, his hands on autopilot. "I'll talk to Thane. He and I will set up a schedule for your training."

"A schedule? Training?"

He snugged the tie up tight against his neck. Where it belonged. "You need to learn how to strengthen your mental barriers." And he needed to remember his own. Protecting his thoughts all the time, in his own damn house, was going to be utterly exhausting.

"Oh. That machine my parents have."

He nodded curtly. Recent vampire generations used a bio-feedback training device to learn how to protect their thoughts—and they'd use one with Tia to start—but he and Thane would have to teach her techniques most vampires never had reason to learn. "Drinking from Valerian transferred strengths to you, but it also created vulnerabilities for him, and everyone who feeds him."

"Meaning you," she said. "That's why you're so pissed off."

He didn't acknowledge her comment. "You now have mental access to me, to Thane, and to Valerian. You need to learn how to shield your thoughts, and shield them well." And someone needed to drink from Tia, to create a two-way bond, if only as a defensive measure.

The thought of Thane's teeth piercing Tia's skin, even platonically, made something inside him recoil.

Val, you wily old bastard.

"It's not that I can read your thoughts or anything," she muttered. "There's this vague sort of…throb. An emotional short-hand." She paused. "It was a lot stronger when we were kissing."

Because he'd dropped his guard—a mistake he wouldn't make again.

Her gaze lowered to the tie, then returned to his face again. "So we're really not going to talk about this?"

"About what?" The less he said, the sooner he could retreat to the safety of his bedroom.

"The fact that you put your tongue in my mouth, and that you liked it." She pointed to his necktie. "And the fact that you just put your goddamn armor back on."

The spicy scent of her arousal was going to drive him to his knees. "Why don't you go to bed?" He gave her a slight mental push.

She shoved back, hard, sending a spike of pain behind his eyes. "Stop it! Don't think you can send me to bed like a sleepy child." Her eyes dropped to the hard-on still bulging below his belt. "We both know you don't think of me as a child."

Her words hit the bulls-eye, and it took everything he had to hide the wince. The images she'd spilled into his head... "I'm going to bed." He didn't have the strength to argue with her anymore.

"Chickenshit."

"I see we've descended to name-calling."

With a growl of frustration, she brushed past him, snatched her purse, then stalked upstairs. He didn't need a blood bond to know she was angry. Confused. Feeling a raging sexual frustration that rivaled his own. And that she was disappointed.

Disappointed in him.

"Join the club," he muttered. Without thinking, he picked up Tia's can of Diet Mountain Dew and drank. Citrusy and oddly refreshing, the beverage tasted better than it should, given the information on the nutrition label. Hell, the caffeine content alone should be enough to keep him awake for hours—which was good, because he had plenty of work to do.

As he reached for his briefcase, a glint of gold caught his eye. Tia's ring. She'd left it on the bar. After a slight hesitation, he picked it up and put it in his front pants pocket. Carrying the can and his briefcase, he trudged upstairs. The hallway was dim, and Valerian's room dark, as he walked into his own room and closed the door behind him. In the quiet, he heard water running next door.

The bathtub.

Tia, naked in the bathtub.

Humming.

"Damn it." Setting the can and his briefcase on his desk, he went to the mini-fridge, grabbed a bag of blood, and popped it onto his teeth. He quickly drained the bag, grabbed another, then sat down. Since Tia had moved in, he'd been going through blood at a blistering pace, trying to keep bloodlust at bay. Thane had obviously noticed, but hadn't said anything.

As Tia sang something about pissing up a rope, he reached for the Stoker folder. Spreading its accordion pleats, he withdrew the letter he'd recently received from the software baron who now owned the original *Dracula* manuscript. His latest purchase offer had been very politely declined.

Again.

He wanted that manuscript, wanted to examine, touch, and smell the pages written in Bram's own hand. There had to be some clue he'd missed, some piece of information he could find, that would confirm, once and for all, whether his own carelessness and poor judgment had given Bram the idea for his book.

Exposing their people's existence.

Wyland's lips flattened. He'd back off, give it some time. Make another offer to the man's heirs after his inevitable death.

Time had a way of passing.

He slowly paged through the folder, studying his copies of Bram's research notes. Maybe he should go back to the Rosenbach and work with the original notes again… No. He couldn't leave home right now, couldn't even think about it until he was more confident about Valerian's physical recovery—and not until Tia gained better control over her thoughts.

Her inflammatory, deliciously wicked thoughts.

He straightened in the chair and dropped the now-empty plastic bag into the wastebasket. Between Tia's soda and the fresh blood thrumming through his veins, he'd be able to work for hours before he'd have to escape into sleep.

He closed the folder with a snap, pushed it aside, then reached for his reading glasses. After perching them on his nose, he picked up a thick sheaf of legal-sized paper from the top of the pile, and pushed thoughts of Tia, singing naked in the bathtub, firmly out of his mind.

✹

When Tia and Nick walked into Sebastiani Security later that afternoon, the last person she expected to see was Commander Gideon Lupinsky. *Gotcha.* "Commander," she greeted him. "What a surprise."

"Ms. Quinn," Lupinsky said. "Nick." He shook their hands.

The Commander wasn't as tall as Lukas, Jack, or even Wyland—werewolves tended toward average heights—but with his muscular build and dark, sharp-featured intelligence, you'd notice him. Though he never wore a uniform, tonight Lupinsky was dressed more casually than she'd ever seen, wearing faded jeans, a plain blue T-shirt, and a Twins baseball cap. He sported a definite five o'clock shadow, perfectly appropriate considering the time of day. "Going to the baseball game from here?" she asked.

He nodded. "Lukas told me about your break-in. I hope you don't mind if I join you at your meeting today."

"Not at all. I'd like to speak with you as well."

Lukas had asked her and Nick to come to Sebastiani Security to discuss her case. While it couldn't hurt to get the Commander's input, he sure as shit wasn't leaving without answering a few questions of her own. "We've been playing phone tag."

"Yes." Lupinsky didn't look at all sorry.

The stairwell door to the left suddenly opened, and Jack and Chico entered the lobby. There was a slightly discolored smudge on Jack's cheekbone, and they both had shower-damp hair. "Kicking the crap out of each other again?" The sparring cage in Sebastiani Security's basement was a favorite workout venue for its employees.

Jack threw Chico a dark glance. "Lucky shot."

"Yeah, my heel missed your pretty blue eye out of sheer dumb luck." Chico slapped his hand against the security pad mounted next to the heavy steel door separating the lobby from the work areas. After a soft beep and a click, he pulled it open, and gestured for them to enter.

"We're in the corner conference room," Jack said, pointing down the hall that ran the length of the building. He paused at the break room. "Can I get anyone something to drink?"

"Nothing for me, thanks." Since waking up a couple of hours ago, she'd pounded two diet Dews and a large cup of coffee. If she drank anything else, she'd float away.

They walked down the exposed brick hallway, past Lukas's cluttered office and Jack's neat one. Over in the main workspace, people talked and keyboards clacked. A raucous game of Nerf basketball was underway over in the far corner. They filed into the corner conference room, leaving the trash talk behind. Lukas was already there, sitting in one of the big leather chairs with his eyes closed.

Guilt swam. With everything else on his plate, the last thing Lukas should be worrying about was someone leaving snakes in her bedroom.

"Oh, hey," Lukas said, abruptly rising to his feet.

They kissed each other's cheeks. "Enjoying the silence?"

He smiled but didn't answer. "Please, have a seat." A dozen leather chairs surrounded the long, oval table. They gathered around one end, Lukas greeting everyone as Jack closed the door. Instead of taking a chair, Chico leaned against the wall.

"How's Valerian?" Jack asked her as everyone else settled in.

"He seems to be doing well." Valerian had still been asleep when she and Nick had left the house, with Nick behind the wheel of a muscular black SUV with UV-treated windows. Driving here in broad daylight, without needing to coat herself in nuclear-powered VampScreen, was an experience she wouldn't soon forget.

Wyland's parking spot had been empty.

Not that she cared.

Much.

Hell.

It pissed her off that she even noticed he was gone, that she wondered where he was. That she worried whether he'd gotten any sleep, even after he'd acted like a complete dick earlier that morning. She'd fallen asleep to Debussy's *Prelude to the Afternoon of a Faun*, with its haunting, evocative flute, leaching through their shared bedroom wall. With centuries of music at his disposal, why had Wyland chosen such an erotically charged piece?

"How's it going living at Vamp Central?" Lukas asked.

"Fine."

"Good, because I'd like you to stay there awhile longer."

"Why?"

Lukas narrowed his eyes. "You're not worried that we found trace evidence connecting your case to ours?"

"What trace evidence?"

Lukas explained that the lab had found some particles on both notes that merited further investigation.

"When did you discover this?"

"Earlier this morning," Lukas said. "Wyland didn't tell you?"

"He did not." Earlier this morning, Wyland's mouth had been otherwise occupied—and then he'd tried to send her to bed like a recalcitrant child. Had he known about the trace evidence then, or had he been notified after she'd gone to bed? It didn't matter. "Gentlemen, for future reference, any information pertaining to my case should be communicated directly to me."

"Certainly." Jack's voice was Scotch-smooth. "We found—"

"Wait a sec." Lupinsky's dark eyes were hard as flint. "You were threatened?"

Lukas told him about the letter he and Scarlett had received. "Someone also threatened the Council using comments at Tia's website, *In Like Quinn,* as the communication mechanism. Jacoby Woolf was specifically threatened."

"Folks." Lupinsky looked around the table, exasperated. "You really have to loop me in on this stuff."

"That's why we invited you here tonight." Lukas pushed a file folder toward the Commander. "Bailey's not having much luck tracking the comments."

Lupinsky lifted a brow, and Tia understood why. If Bailey couldn't figure out where the comments had come from, no one could.

Lupinsky quickly sifted through the papers. "These are in timeline order?"

"Yes."

"So, you and Scarlett receive a letter threatening your unborn child. Then two comments are made, a day apart, at *In Like Quinn*. And then, there's a break-in at Ms. Quinn's house—" Lupinsky flipped a page "—two nights ago."

It felt like she'd been sleeping next door to Wyland a lot longer than that.

"Ms. Quinn, you woke up just after midnight and discovered that someone had put dozens of snakes in your bedroom?"

She nodded.

"One hundred and sixty five snakes," Chico chimed in. "I counted the suckers."

Lupinsky skimmed another page, then eyed her. "And you think someone's been following you? Since before you moved to Stillwater?"

She hesitated. "I have no proof, no evidence. I've never seen anyone."

"Well, those snakes didn't get into your bedroom all by themselves."

He believes me.

"The good news is that the person left garter

snakes, not a toxic variety like rattlers, and that you weren't injured while you slept," he mused. "Fear seems to be the motive here. Why would someone want to scare you?"

"I have no idea," she responded, baffled.

"Are you currently in a romantic relationship? Did you recently end one? A pissed-off lover, perhaps?"

"No to all three." She hadn't had a lover in months, and it had been several years since her last serious relationship. Wyland's searing kiss had definitely been…an anomaly.

"Work?"

She shrugged. "*ILQ* aggregates and publishes content from dozens of sources, and hundreds of writers, besides me. I just published the last story in a series about inadequate handicapped access in public buildings. I've just started researching a series on human trafficking—which is the reason I've been trying to contact you—but very few people know it's a story I'm even working on."

Lupinsky picked up a pen. "Who knows?"

"What?"

"Who knows about your human trafficking story?"

"You," she answered. "Everyone sitting at this table. Bailey, Valerian, Thane. Wyland." Lupinsky scribbled quickly. Though her inner contrarian enjoyed the prospect of so many Council members finding themselves under the Commander's microscope, even temporarily, she just couldn't see a connection. "Do you really think—"

"What I think isn't as important as what I can prove." Lupinsky looked at Nick. "Anything unusual happening at Vamp Central?"

Nick shook his head. "No. We've been on

heightened alert since Tia's arrival."

"Seriously?" she said. Damn it, how many people were going to be inconvenienced by her problems? "When do you think I can return home?"

Lukas gave a noncommittal shrug. "There are many lines of investigation we need to pursue."

"I agree," Lupinsky said. "You're safer with Valerian and Wyland for the time being. Who's my coordination point here at SebSec?"

"Me," Jack answered. Lukas opened his mouth, probably to disagree, but Jack headed him off at the pass. "Lukas, Scarlett could go into labor any minute now."

Every lick of color drained from Lukas's face. Sweat popped on his forehead.

She touched his tense forearm. Lukas was a total bad-ass, but he turned into marshmallow fluff when it came to his family. "She'll be fine."

Lukas swallowed, hard. "I know."

Chico nudged a wastebasket closer to Lukas using his big, steel-toed boot.

Apparently the rumors about Lukas's sympathetic morning sickness were true.

"Ms. Quinn," Lupinsky said, "Wyland told me about a conversation the two of you had, about something called—" he flipped to another page in his small wire-bound notebook "—*shibari*, a form of erotic Japanese rope art."

Annoyance shimmered. "Wyland's been busy." He'd apparently found time to talk about her case, and her work, with everyone except her.

Sitting at her side, Nick was hyper-alert, and rightly so. This conversation wasn't about her human trafficking story—or if it was, the association was passing at best. The Commander wanted information. "You're referring to the homicide in Eden Prairie? The residence where Stephen is suspected of killing his first victim?" She waited for him to nod before continuing. "A source informed me that the victim was found alone, tied in an intricate arrangement of ropes. I wondered whether anyone had investigated a *shibari* angle." Time to ask a question of her own. "Is Stephen your only suspect?"

"The incubus Stephen is still at large," Lupinsky said evenly, "and he remains a person of interest in this case."

"'At large?' There's the understatement of the century." After killing Scarlett's sister Annika, attacking Scarlett, and nearly killing Lukas, Stephen had been captured, then transferred to a secure psychiatric lockdown. He'd somehow escaped, and no one had seen or heard from him since. "Commander, your case is so cold it's forming icicles."

"Which is why I'm talking to you. It didn't occur to any of our detectives that there might be something significant about the rope arrangement," Lupinsky admitted. "Mr. Solberg, I understand you have some familiarity with this subject. Would you mind looking at a few crime scene photos?"

"Not at all."

Picking up his phone from where it lay on the table—he also had one of the super-secure prototypes—Lupinsky retrieved the pictures, then passed the gadget to Nick.

Tia leaned over to look, then immediately wished she hadn't. Whoever had described the victim as being found 'trussed up like a Thanksgiving turkey' had a distinct gift for understatement. His nude body was curled up like a Butterball, with precisely placed red ropes lashing his arms and thighs tight against his chest. His penis had received…specific attention.

"*Shibari*, coupled with asphyxiation play," Nick said, his jaw tight. "He was found like this? Alone, and suspended from the ceiling?"

"Yes," Lupinsky said. "Do you recognize him?"

"No." Lips flattened into a thin line, Nick pointed to the ligature around the victim's neck. "Suspended in this position, his neck muscles would tire quickly. With no one to care for him, he'd black out, suffocate."

"Mr. Solberg, just how familiar are you with this kind of 'play'?"

Her stomach clenched in warning.

Jack held up a hand, indicating that Nick shouldn't speak. "Gideon, this conversation is a request for subject matter expertise, not an interrogation."

Lupinsky glared from beneath the brim of his baseball cap. "All I know is that I have a human body in the morgue, and a family who thinks he dropped off the face of the earth." He threw his pen onto the table with a tired-sounding sigh. "Too many questions, and no answers."

According to Tia's source, *their* police force had taken the initial call, from a terrified Valkyrie couple who'd arrived to use the facilities, only to find the unfortunate human victim. After processing the scene, a bio-hazard clean-up team had disinfected the place from attic to basement, scrubbing away the last evidence of Robert Johnson's existence. As far as his family was concerned, Robert Johnson *had* dropped off the face of the earth. Their media pleas had gone unanswered.

She felt a reluctant communion with Lupinsky. The line between human and Underworld law enforcement teams was like razor wire: very sharp, very thin, and very carefully trod. "Is it possible this was an accident?"

Lupinsky answer was a one-shouldered shrug. "We can place Stephen at the scene—his skin cells and semen were found on the rope used to bind Mr. Johnson—but we have no insight into his motivation. We have no idea why Stephen went to the Eden Prairie residence, whether he knew Mr. Johnson beforehand, whether he planned to meet Johnson there, or whether they met by chance." He gestured toward the picture. "We have no idea whether this 'play' was consensual or not, or whether the victim's death was intentional or accidental." He sighed. "So many questions, and so few answers."

Nick slid the phone back across the table, his expression grim. "All I know is, no dominant worth the name would leave their submissive alone during this kind of scene. It's simply too dangerous."

Speech didn't seem to be necessary; the swollen tongue protruding from the dead man's mouth spoke volumes. Finally, Lukas glanced at the ceiling. "Anything else tonight? I promised Scarlett I'd get the crib assembled."

He looked like he'd rather tangle with a tiger. "Would you like some help? Maybe I can keep Scarlett company." She didn't want to go back to Vamp Central yet.

"She's not home. She's visiting Dad and Claudette." He didn't sound happy about Scarlett not being under his own watchful eye. "Apparently Claudette has some baby things."

And Elliott Sebastiani and Scarlett's mother, Siren First Claudette Fontaine, had *beaucoup* security of their own. "Please tell her hello for me, and that I'll talk to her soon."

Nick rose. "Are you ready to go home, or do you have things you'd like to do here in town? I'm at your disposal."

She considered making a Target run, but then rejected the idea. Nick shouldn't have to pay because she didn't want to deal with Wyland. "Nope, let's go."

She'd use the hour-long commute to stew and plot. To figure out what she'd say to Wyland the next time she saw him. Something inside her revved into high gear. "Could we swing by Chipotle on the way home?"

Nick grinned. "Of course."

After eating a monster burrito, she'd be plenty fuelled up for the argument to come.

TAMARA HOGAN

CHAPTER EIGHT

"'Colton grabbed her with sawdust-covered arms, boosting her onto the butcher block countertop he'd just finished sanding, and moved between her legs,'" Tia read aloud. "'His heavy tool belt dragged at the waistband of his jeans, and a hammer and wrench bracketed the thick, hard cock that had taunted her all morning. Rough denim scraped her tender inner thighs.'"

She glanced at Valerian over the edge of the book. He lay under the bedcovers, propped up by a mound of pillows, his eyes closed and a slight smile curling his lips. He was breathing more comfortably now, thank the universe. When she'd arrived, carbo-loaded and ready to tear Wyland a new one, she'd found him arguing with Valerian about his oxygen. Listening to the men reminded her of two bucks clashing their antlers together, neither giving ground. She'd listened at the door for several minutes before entering the fray herself, offering Val a straight-up bribe: use the oxygen, just for a little while, and she'd read a chapter of the book they'd just started. Val accepted, and after placing the nasal cannula correctly, Wyland had left.

She hadn't heard a peep from him since.

Leaning toward Val from the upholstered chair she'd pulled next to the bed, she watched the reassuring rise and fall of his pajama-clad chest. Was he awake? Asleep? Remembering his own erotic adventures?

How much sex could someone have over a 900-year lifespan? The mind boggled.

Out in the hall, Wyland's bedroom door suddenly opened. The sound of his footfalls quickly faded away.

"He doesn't know what to do about you," Valerian murmured.

"Hmm?"

Valerian opened his eyes. "He wants you, but he's denying himself, denying you, out of a misplaced sense of duty."

"Duty is Wyland's middle name." Self-sacrifice seemed as essential to him as blood and bone. "You shouldn't give him such a hard time about the oxygen, Val."

"He thinks you're too young for him. That he'd be abusing his power if he acted on his attraction for you."

Tia's stomach gave a silky twist. Had Wyland told him this first-hand, or was the elderly sage simply guessing? She shot down the thought as soon as it formed. The two men had shared blood for centuries; they knew each other more intimately than most bondmates. She thought back to the explosive kiss she and Wyland had shared down by the bar. She knew lust when she felt it, when she tasted it. She knew Wyland felt it, too. Speaking of which… "Wyland wasn't happy that you shared your blood with me," she told Valerian. "We fought." After kissing the stuffing out of each other.

"So that's why he's in such a pissy mood."

She felt a squirt of satisfaction. It was only fair that Wyland feel as annoyed and out of sorts as she did. "Apparently I'm now a risk to all vampiredom." She explained Wyland's concern that she, with her untrained mental boundaries, could now be used as a tool against them.

"You also have strengths and insights you didn't have before," Valerian said, adjusting the thin tube draped over his left ear. "Life's a series of trade-offs, my dear. Risks and rewards, pros and cons. In the scheme of things, you drinking my blood is a net positive."

"Wyland doesn't think so." And it stung.

"Your boundaries will firm up quickly, just wait and see. I'll train you myself." Valerian shifted against the pillows. "Speaking of training, has anyone shown you the gym and lap pool? Down in the lower level?"

Why did Valerian always change the subject just when things were getting interesting? "You have an indoor pool?"

Valerian nodded. "It's where Wyland goes when he needs to escape his thoughts, to turn off his brain for a while. The door to the basement is down the hallway leading to Nick's office, right across from the powder room."

Rising from the chair, she handed Valerian the book. At some point during the last week, she'd apparently developed a serious masochistic streak, because, yeah, she was going downstairs. What she'd do once she actually found Wyland was anyone's guess—she was still really pissed off at him—but her body was already making its wishes known. Her teeth tingled in her jaw, and each beat of her heart sent pulses of blood through her body, stroking it from the inside. "Does he know you're such a schemer?"

"I have no idea what you're talking about." The twinkle in his eye contradicted his words.

"And you're a good friend."

"I hope you consider me one as well."

Sudden tears stung her eyes. "You honor me."

"Right back at ya."

She laughed, then kissed both papery cheeks. "Sleep well, my friend." As she left, he flicked the nasal cannula away as if its very existence offended him. He settled back into the pillows again, picked up the book, and started to read.

After exchanging a couple of words with Valerian's care attendant out in the sitting room, she went downstairs, walking toward the hallway Valerian had mentioned like a puppet pulled by unseen strings. There was the powder room to the left, its heavy wooden door standing ajar. Directly across the hall was another heavy door—this one firmly closed.

She studied its ornate oval knob. Did she really want to push this...this...*thing* between them? Knowing he wanted her, but that he was denying himself?

Ah, hell. How could she not? Twisting the knob, she walked through the door and closed it firmly behind her.

The narrow stairwell was well lit, and solidly and recently constructed, but she trailed her hands along the wall anyway. Humid, chlorine-scented air wafted over her as she descended; she could almost feel her skin sipping it in. When she reached the bottom stair, she took a ninety-degree turn. The room was larger than she'd thought it would be, and beautifully tiled in all the colors of the sea. There was a wrought-iron café table with seating for two, several padded chaise lounges, a massage table over in an alcove. Across the room was a rack of free weights, several Nautilus machines, and a stair stepper with a towel draped over it—serious equipment, but the place felt more like a spa than a gym.

A refuge, a private getaway.

The door across the room probably led to a changing area, but Wyland hadn't made use of it tonight. The tailored suit he'd been wearing earlier lay in an untidy mound on the bench set on the narrow edge of the lap pool, his hard-soled shoes and socks kicked haphazardly underneath.

She watched his body slice through the aquamarine water. Saw a flash of muscled white buttock.

Her fangs descended in a rush.

Blood humming, she sat on the bench next to his discarded clothes and watched. He was built like a channel swimmer, with long, lean muscles that cut swiftly and surely through the water. The taut globes of his ass shifted out of the water with each stroke of his arms, but his calves and feet barely broke the surface. He swam silently and efficiently, like a great white shark. She glanced down at the clothing mound. A shark who wore designer boxer briefs.

When she stopped ogling his underwear and looked back at the pool, he was standing upright in the waist-deep water, staring at her.

She stared right back. Men with his body type had always tripped her trigger, and damn it, Wyland's particular build would fuel years of future sexual fantasies. His hair was lashed back in its usual ponytail, the wet tail clinging to his shoulder. Drops of water glistened on his lashes, but his chilly blue eyes blazed. His arms and pecs were well-developed—he clearly used the weights across the room—and his tiny, tan nipples were visible through a delicious dusting of chest hair. Water dripped down his taut abdomen, bumping over a diagonal slash of a scar before reaching the silky trail of hair peeking above the water line. His lower body was a blur; the glimmering water hid too much.

The nasty-looking scar was a surprise.

"Is Valerian okay?" he asked.

"Yes, he's fine."

Silence hummed. "Pass me that towel, please," he finally said, gesturing to a neatly folded Caribbean-blue towel sitting on the other end of the bench.

Such high tea manners, even with his fangs descended. "Of course." She picked up the towel and took several steps toward the pool. Stopping well short of the lip, she extended her arm.

He'd have to get out of the pool to reach it.

His gaze flicked to the towel, then back to her face. His thoughts were well-guarded, locked down tight, but his gaze wandered over her breasts then dropped to her hips, hidden under the clingy yoga pants she'd put on before reading to Valerian. He muttered something under his breath—*brat?*—but then he took a deep breath. Moving slowly, he walked toward the pool's ladder. He met her eyes again as he grasped the silver rungs, pausing before he hauled his body out of the water with a whoosh and an impressive flex of muscle. Water sheeted off his body.

Valerian was right; Wyland wanted her. He was half hard, his cock jutting from a patch of water-darkened blond hair. Dragging her eyes away from his penis, she gave the rest of his body an admiring up-and-down, pursing her lips around a silent wolf-whistle. "Who knew the Vampire Second looked so great naked?"

His penis gave a kick as he padded toward her, leaving wet footprints in his wake. When he reached her, he didn't reach for the towel. No, instead he stood before her, wet and dripping, his eyes turbulent, looking like a vengeful sea god forced to come onto land. "Why."

She almost smiled. He'd asked so many impossible questions in a single, annoyed syllable. How many people ever noticed the volcano seething under his icy, placid surface? Despite the room's heat, she shivered. *All that pent-up steam, looking for a way to escape.*

She didn't answer, not with words. Instead, she slung the towel around his butt, grasped both ends, and yanked, bringing their bodies together. Opening her mouth, she showed him her fangs, her desire. Nicked her own lip, drawing a rich bead of blood.

And then she kissed him.

✳

Tia flicked her tongue over the tip of his fang, a silky caress that nearly unmanned him. Wrapping his arms around her, he opened his mouth and let her inside. The towel dropped unheeded to the floor.

Her blood. He closed his eyes at its ecstatic zing, groaning at the lush flavor. Her mouth was hot and hungry, eating him alive, and he ran his hands over her body, anywhere he could touch, palming and kneading her luscious frame. She was soft and curved, not whittled down to muscle and sinew like so many women of this era. Her hands were as busy as his, trailing heat over his water-chilled skin.

Tia was no shy miss who'd let a glimpse of a man's erect penis send her to a fainting couch. The ravenous way she'd looked at his body as he'd climbed out of the pool had been the final nail in the coffin of his control.

She pulled his hair out of its queue, wet strands slapping against his upper back. She speared her hands through it, tugging him closer, and he hissed as his cock pressed into her soft stomach. Her busy mouth dropped, trailing kisses along his jawline, down his neck and over his collarbones, sipping the dripping water. When she rubbed her nose and cheek against his chest hair, the gesture pierced his brain stem.

It was like she was marking herself with his scent.

She wants me as much as I want her. The thought brought both relief and torment. Valerian was right; Tia was an adult woman, fully capable of making her own decisions, and it appeared she'd decided on *him*—but she'd inevitably move on with her life, leaving him behind.

But he needed this moment, needed it with a wild, hot fury. Now was not the time to ask why, not when her clever hands were mapping his abdomen and slowly traveling south. He held his breath as she trailed her fingers down his body. A groan escaped when she threaded them through his pubic hair, combing with soft, diabolical tugs. He nearly whimpered when she removed her hands.

She met his gaze. "Are you sure you want this?"

A strangled laugh escaped. "How can you doubt it?" His cock, standing upright between them, was hard enough to drive spikes.

Tia acknowledged the point with a smile. "Your body does, but do *you*?"

He searched her eyes, her face. It suddenly hit him: consent. She was asking him to consent, to enter into this...this *experience*, with his brain as well as his body. To make a conscious decision, not just let his body carry him away.

What man with functioning brain cells wouldn't choose this? He might regret it later, but damn it, he *wanted*. He wanted her with a violence he barely recognized, barely remembered, and though her own motivations weren't entirely clear, her desire for him was. For some inexplicable reason, she wanted him, too. Just this once, he was going to take something for himself. "Yes." He cupped her face in his hands. "Yes, I want this."

I want you.

She covered his hands with hers, then stroked up his arms to his biceps. She gave them a testing squeeze, humming her approval. Suddenly, her fingernails bit in, hard enough to sting. "It took you long enough to decide."

Waves of weakness washed over him. "You're the one who asked me to think." He glanced down to where his penis bobbed between them. "It took some doing. My blood's pooled elsewhere."

"True." And with that, she took his cock in both hands.

He gritted his teeth and locked his knees, trying to steady himself against the barrage of forgotten sensations. Time whirled away as she stroked, cupped, and measured his need with a thoroughness he could better appreciate if it hadn't been over a century since a woman had touched his todge. When her fingers danced over the particularly sensitive patch of skin behind his bollocks, he bit back a curse and pulled away. "Any more of that and I'll spill where we stand."

She flicked her tongue against the corner of his mouth. "And why is that a problem?"

A frisson shot down his spine, snarling in his pelvis. "I appreciate your confidence in my recuperative powers, but that's not how I envisioned this."

"You've envisioned this? Us?"

Endlessly. Relentlessly. In his deepest death-sleep fantasies, he'd held her. Caressed her. Covered her body with his, losing himself in her wet, clinging heat for hours on end. Instead of answering, he captured her tongue, drew it into his mouth and suckled. The tiny, self-inflicted slice had almost healed, but the maddening taste of blood lingered. He delved into her mouth, exploring its contours, gathering as much of the dark essence as he could. His hands wandered down her back, over her waist, over her hips, finally making their way to her deliciously rounded arse. He palmed the voluptuous globes, flexing his fingers against her firm, resilient flesh. She was doing the same thing to him, her small hands roving his body with an explorer's gusto. When she scratched her nails over his buttocks, an involuntary grunt escaped. He couldn't stop his hips from rolling against the heat between her legs, still covered by the clingy fabric of her yoga pants.

She held him there, then grabbed his hands and

pressed them to her breasts.

He bit back a groan as their tender weight filled his hands, as her hard nipples pressed into his palms. He buried his face in her cleavage, absorbing her intoxicating scent. His knees weakened along with his resolve. "I need to see you." He reached for the hem of her camisole, but she stepped back and peeled it off before he could touch it.

He'd complain about that later, because such beautiful orbs deserved a slow and theatrical unveiling. They were a sumptuous feast for the eyes—art, really—with delicate, shadowy veins just visible under her pale, pale skin, and topped by saucy pinkish-tan nipples.

She put her thumbs under the elastic waistband of the clingy black pants and drew them down. When she bent over to remove them, his heart gave an extra kick. A slim strip of shiny black fabric disappeared in the crease between her buttocks, leaving the glorious globes completely bare.

Her pale, plump arse was the Eighth Bloody Wonder of the World.

She stripped off the garment, threw it on top of his suit pants, then drew herself upright, proud as a princess.

Oh, she had reason to be proud. Her frame had the classic hourglass shape that artists had celebrated for centuries, with full breasts, a narrow waist, and soft, rounded hips, and her skin was unmarked by any corset or attempt at restraint. She wore a birth control patch on her right hip, and had no tattoos beyond the one on her inner forearm. Her pubic lips were pink and bare, with only a small tuft of auburn hair adorning her mons.

Yes, he had much to learn about women of this era. It had been so long since he'd looked at a female body with anything but professional interest that he wondered whether he remembered how to bring her pleasure.

But her humid need called to him, prodding a dormant, voracious hunger awake. He took her in his arms, brought their bodies together, closing his eyes so he could better savor the sensation of her bare skin brushing against his. Angles to curves, concave to convex, male to female, fitting together like puzzle pieces. She scattered gentle kisses across his chest, but her hands clutched his shoulders with urgency. When she swirled her tongue over his nipple, he almost jumped out of his skin. Lust and need galloped through his body, finally running free.

As she suckled, his penis reared against her stomach, each soft tug pulling an invisible anatomical string. His bollocks drew up tight, and an unmistakable pressure snarled low in his pelvis. "I need to be inside you. Now."

Her eyes widened—had his blunt words surprised her?—but her answer was gift-wrapped in an approving, sensual smile. "Yes."

She squeaked when he swept her up in his arms, carrying her to the padded chaise lounge. When he laid her back against the cushions, they gave with a soft whoosh.

She parted her legs, making room for him to join her. Her pink folds glistened, beckoned. She was wet—for him—and unashamed of her desire.

She held out her arms. "Fuck me, Wyland."

The word he usually found coarse and vile took on an entirely different meaning when uttered with such breathy, feminine demand. He couldn't refuse her.

Couldn't refuse this.

He slowly lowered himself between her spread legs, groaning aloud when she wrapped them around his waist. She was so wet, so hot. So ready for him.

When she kissed his neck, scratching the tip of her fangs against a frantically pulsing vein, he pulled his head back. He couldn't allow her to drink from him, no matter how much his body throbbed for it. Instead, he locked his gaze on hers, and entered her—simply, directly, and inevitably.

He groaned as he pushed into her slick, lush heat. Her intimate muscles clutched and clung, stroking his violently aroused flesh. When he bottomed out in her body, he gritted his teeth against the urge to spill.

He'd bring her pleasure if it killed him.

Given the way his heart thundered in his chest, it very well might.

All too soon, her vaginal muscles gathered themselves, poised for the rhythmic clench of orgasm. She writhed, tossing her head back. "More. Faster. Now." Her heels and nails dug in, spurring him on. "Wyland. Now."

He plunged, riding them both into oblivion.

CHAPTER NINE

"Ow!" Mila slapped at the mosquito on her cheek, almost hitting Dominic. "Sorry," she said, giggling.

"I forgot to close the windows."

They'd been necking in the back seat for hours, and the SUV was swarming with the bloodthirsty little buggers.

She stretched her arms overhead. What had started out as a late dinner date had morphed into drinks, coffee, and conversation. They'd closed down the restaurant, talking about anything and everything, and when Dominic suggested going for a drive rather than taking her home, she'd quickly agreed. He'd headed west, toward the far side of Lake Minnetonka, leaving the windows open to the humid night air. She hadn't been able to stop staring at him, mesmerized by the way his Adam's apple shifted as he talked, at his capable hands on the steering wheel. At his leg muscles bunching and clenching as he worked the clutch. Finally, she couldn't take it anymore. When she laid her hand on his thigh, he covered it with his own. After a quick, hot glance, he'd pulled into what looked like a private boat landing.

So isolated. So quiet.

With a scramble of legs, he sat up.

"Where are you going?" She pressed her palm

against the bulge of flesh pushing against the front of his jeans. She wanted to see him, to touch what she'd only touched through his clothes.

"Look at the sky, Cinderella. I need to get you home."

A pinkish light glowed in the eastern sky. Sunrise was about half an hour off—plenty of time to make the drive home. On the other side of the seat, Dominic covered a yawn with the hand he'd just pulled out of her pants. He left the hand there longer than he needed to, inhaling deeply.

Her face flooded with self-conscious heat, but Dominic seemed to be in heaven. With his ginger hair mussed from her hands, his lips puffy from kissing her for hours, ignoring his own hard-on to savor her scent, Dominic was the hottest thing she'd ever seen. "When did you sleep last?" He'd mentioned earlier that he'd put in a full day at the health club, and he'd visited his father at the hospital before meeting her at the restaurant for their date.

He gave a half-shrug. "I'll catch up later this morning. I work the late shift today."

So they couldn't get together later, but that was probably for the best. She had some thinking to do, and she'd do a better job of it without being distracted by him. "I worry about you driving when you're so tired."

"I'm okay."

He certainly seemed that way. Despite the yawn, his eyes were clear and alert. He seemed so big, so sturdy and strong, sitting with his legs splayed wide, spilling onto her side of the seat. She zipped up her jeans, tugged the hem of her T-shirt back where it belonged, and scooted beside him. "Your hair's a mess." She smoothed it with her fingers, enjoying the springy texture that was so different from her own. When he leaned into her touch, her fangs throbbed with a fierce, unexpected possessiveness. "You can't keep going without sleep," she murmured. "And we need to find a private place, an indoor place. Without mosquitoes. And with condoms."

"I can take care of the condoms."

Where could they be together? Her house was out—it was never empty—but maybe they could steal an hour or two at his. They'd find a way. If she could bring the slightest pleasure or relaxation to Dominic's chaotic life, she would.

Sex. Maybe this time she'd finally understand what all the fuss was about. "Would you like to go to a party with me?" she blurted.

His brows lifted.

"My parents are having a thing next week."

Dominic laughed. "Mila, your parents have soirees. High teas. Cocktail parties, and full-on balls. They do not have things."

She nodded, acknowledging his point. "It's an evening gathering. Dressy." Her mouth was as dry as dust. "Would you go with me as my guest? As my date?" She really liked him, and he seemed to like her, too. If she arrived at the party with a date, someone her own age who would meet her parents' absurdly high standards, maybe they'd recognize just how squicky an alliance with Wyland would be. Yesterday, when he'd removed her staples, she'd barely been able to look him in the eye. She needed to nip her parents' ridiculous aspirations in the bud, and fast.

"I'd be honored to be your date."

"The honor is mine." She dropped a light kiss on

his lips, so similar, yet so exotically different, than her own. "We should get going," she said reluctantly, giving the horizon another look. The familiar, dragging tiredness—her body's instinctive demand for day-sleep—was a lot more noticeable now than it had been a couple of minutes ago. She probably shouldn't have declined the transfusion Wyland suggested yesterday. "Where are my shoes?" After finding them, she put them on, and they both climbed into the front seat. She pulled down the passenger seat visor and tried to restore some order to her hair. Her eyes were slumberous, her lips puffy, and her cheeks and neck were red from the scrape of his beard. "How's your father?"

"No change." Dominic turned the key, glancing at the eastern horizon as they pulled away from the boat landing. "Who will be at your parents' party?"

Okay, change of subject noted. She'd let him get away with it for now. "My parents' friends, members of the Council, people from GPL."

"Council members? Really?"

"My parents are always networking, always thinking about their position in society."

"At least they have a social position to preserve." He shot her a wry look. "My family? Not so much."

In her opinion, spending so much time and effort preserving that lofty social position was more trouble than it was worth. "Actually, you might already have received a party invitation. Mother asked me for a list of GPL members I'd like to invite." She flicked him a flirtatious glance. "You were the first name on the list."

He picked up her hand and kissed her knuckles. "It's been days since I checked the mail, but thanks so much for inviting me in person." He gave her knuckles a lick before setting her hand on his thigh.

They fell into a companionable silence, and after too short a time, he pulled into her parents' Deephaven driveway. "Damn, that's a big house. Nice."

Big, yes—but nice? Most of the time, it echoed with funereal silence. "Thank you for the ride. And the date. And the kisses."

His answering smile was both sweet and hungry. "The pleasure was all mine."

A thrill zinged through her. *Next time, it will be.* "Please get some sleep," she said. "Promise me."

"I will." With another glance at the house, then at the sky, he reached across the seat and opened her door. "You'd better get inside."

"I had a great time." *Screw whoever might be watching.* Leaning over, she kissed his cheek, grabbed her purse, then stepped out of the car. "'Bye."

"'Bye."

The sun broke over the horizon as he pulled away. She lifted her hand to her still-tingling lips.

"Miss Mila?" Hansen was at the door, holding it open.

Dominic's tail lights finally disappeared from view. "Coming," she called, trotting to the shadowed safety of the house.

"Will you be joining your parents in the dining room, Miss Mila?"

"Not today, Hansen. I think I'll just go straight up to bed."

Hansen eyed her. "That might be wise."

As Hansen closed the door behind them, she hid a private smile.

✳

Whoever had said that Minnesota had only two seasons, winter and road construction, was one hundred percent right. Just two blocks away, up Washington Avenue, Sebastiani Security's brightly lit windows taunted her. Tia had hoped to have a nice, long visit with Scarlett before attending the meeting Lukas had called, but at this rate, she and Scarlett would only have a stingy half hour before she'd have to go downstairs.

But maybe that was for the best. When she and Scarlett were both single, they'd talk about their lovers for hours—who was great in bed, who wasn't, and who was worth both time and effort. Once bonded with Lukas, Scarlett had clammed up tight, and Tia hadn't had any sexual dish to share in quite some time. Now that she did, she wasn't sure she wanted to.

She was *so* confused.

A horn blared behind her. She threw her hands up in exasperation, glaring at the tricked-out truck filling her rear-view mirror. "Dude, it's not like I can go anywhere!" It took forever to creep the final two blocks, but she finally hit her blinker and turned into Sebastiani Security's parking lot. As the F-250 passed, she saw a pair of those tacky truck testicles dangling from its trailer hitch.

"Why am I not surprised?"

Pulling her car into an open spot next to Bailey's MINI Cooper, she grabbed her purse, got out, and slammed her car door behind her. Hours after sunset, Sebastiani Security's parking lot was nearly full. The night was hot and humid, and smelled of road tar mixed with the muddy Mississippi. Across the street, Sex World was hopping, and the Warehouse District's sidewalks seethed with people. Humanity had no idea that real werewolves, and other so-called creatures of myth, lived, worked, and played right down the street from where the Timberwolves played basketball.

She glanced up to Sebastiani Security's top floor loft space, where Lukas and Scarlett lived. Behind bulletproof glass, the loft lights blazed.

Scarlett was still awake.

She entered the empty lobby and waved at the security camera. She'd barely lowered her arm when Chico poked his head around the security door separating the lobby from the working areas. "Hey, Tia. You're early, but come on back."

She jerked a thumb to the elevator. "Could you let me upstairs instead? I told Scarlett I'd say hi."

"Sure." He joined her at the elevator, his heavy work boots silent against the carpeted floor, and set his palm against the biometric pad. "Quite the party going on up there right now."

"What do you mean?" They got on the elevator. When the doors whooshed closed behind them, they both faced front.

"Sasha and Antonia got here about an hour ago, and Bailey just went up."

So an intimate chat with Scarlett was out.

"Lukas called his sisters and asked them to keep Scarlett company," Chico said. "He doesn't want Scarlett to be alone. And then Scarlett called me, asking me to make sure Lukas ate something. What is this, junior high school?" He looked harried. "I'll be so glad when she has that baby. Maybe then things can get back to normal around here."

"With a siren baby crying upstairs? Are you serious?" Who knew how much emotional energy the daughter of a legendary siren singer would shriek into the world with her little untrained vocal cords?

"Surely the loft is sound-proofed?"

When the elevator reached the top floor, the doors opened onto music she didn't recognize. Negative on the sound-proofing; the sound bled into the hallway from behind the loft's closed door. She got off the elevator and waved at Chico. "See you in a bit."

"Um, yeah. Right." The doors closed on his dazed expression. No doubt he'd begin vetting sound-proofing vendors the minute he reached his desk.

As she rang the doorbell, overhead cameras stared her down. After Scarlett and Lukas had nearly been killed here, by someone Scarlett knew and trusted, Lukas didn't bother hiding the surveillance equipment. She couldn't blame him.

The door opened. "Hey, Tia." Antonia Sebastiani had somehow managed to open the door holding Calamity, Scarlett's twenty-pound black cat. "Come on in."

"Hi," she said, carefully skirting the feline. The cat hated her—though, to be fair, Calamity hated almost everybody. "I didn't mean to interrupt your visit."

"No worries." Closing the door, Antonia gently lowered Calamity to the floor, then lowered her voice. "We're doing what we can to keep her occupied. Now that you're here, we don't have to listen to this music anymore."

Over in the loft's seating area, Sasha and Bailey

both leaned over Scarlett's shoulder, looking at the souped-up laptop teetering on Scarlett's rounded stomach. It was the source of the music she didn't recognize. "New band?"

Antonia nodded. "Scarlett's producing them."

Her reviewer's interest was piqued. "They're good."

"Not if you have to listen to the same eight bars over and over again."

"Tia!" Scarlett handed Bailey the laptop and started to lever herself out of the chair. Sasha quickly stepped in to help.

Her eyes widened. "Stay there. Geez." Scarlett's stomach was *huge*. How could she walk without toppling over?

Scarlett shoved against the arms of the chair, heaving to her feet with an assist from Sasha. "I need to move," she said grimly. "I might look and feel like a beached whale, but I refuse to act like one."

Despite her obvious discomfort, Tia thought Scarlett looked happy, excited, and well-loved. When they hugged, the baby nudged its way into their embrace. "Wow, she's really moving."

Scarlett scowled as she rubbed her stomach. "The kid's got some really sharp knees and elbows." She aimed a death-glare at Sasha. "I think she's going to be a dancer. Or a place kicker for the Vikings."

Sasha held up her hands in self-defense. "Don't blame me. I didn't knock you up."

"It's in the genes."

Now didn't seem to be a good time to mention that the kid's sense of rhythm could just as easily have come from her musical mother. Though Scarlett had disbanded Scarlett's Web several years ago and no longer performed in public, she still wrote, still recorded, and was an in-demand producer. Between her music career, representing the sirens on the Underworld Council, navigating a new bond relationship with Lukas Sebastiani, and a new baby, her friend had her hands full. "You look great."

Scarlett's eyes suddenly flooded. "I look horrible. My ankles are swelling, I'm constipated, and I have stretch marks that will never go away." Her lips wobbled. "And my clothes are as big as a circus tent."

"You look awesome." Scarlett wore an oversized black T-shirt over black leggings, with a colorful scarf cinched under her abdomen. "You're the most stylin' pregnant person I know."

"I'm the only pregnant person you know."

True, but—

"This is Lukas's T-shirt, and it almost fits me!" Scarlett's disgusted gesture was so violent that she nearly lost her balance. "I used to wear skin-tight leather! I used to wear icepick heels! I used to be kinda hot!" she wailed. "How can Lukas stand to look at me right now?"

She looked at Sasha, baffled.

Sasha mouthed "hormones" over her shoulder as she led Scarlett back to the chair. "Do you want to change into a different shirt?"

"No, of course not. This one smells like Lukas."

"Okay," Sasha said evenly, making sure Scarlett was comfortably settled in the chair. "How about something to drink?"

"I want potato chips," Scarlett stated. "I'm craving salt something fierce."

Hadn't Scarlett just complained about water retention?

Sasha simply nodded, heading for the kitchen. "Can I get anyone else a drink?"

"Nothing for me, thanks," she said.

"Please, sit." Scarlett waved a hand at the seating arrangement, and she and Bailey took seats on the furniture closest to Scarlett's chair. "How's work going? I understand you're working on a series about human trafficking."

Tia glanced at Bailey. "Yeah, I'm doing some research on how the story plays out locally." How much did Scarlett, Antonia, and Sasha know about Stephen's activities leading up to killing Scarlett's sister, Annika? Ah, hell, who was she kidding? As Council members, Scarlett and Antonia could get any information they wanted. Sasha, being related to so many Council members, certainly knew how to keep her mouth shut.

Actually, Sasha had been the person to give her the idea for the human trafficking series in the first place, when she'd mentioned her concern for some of the young people who came into Crackhouse Coffee in the winter. Wary and worn, hungry and cold, runaways faced so many risks, even if they managed to escape the grasp of pimps and opportunists who'd exploit them. Some of the stories she'd heard from hotel and motel employees made her stomach lurch. "You know how it is," she said. "Lots of interviews, lots of research." Damn, now she sounded as non-committal as Commander Lupinsky had, but she didn't want to upset Scarlett.

"Lukas told me about the break-in at your house—the snakes, feeling like you're being followed," Scarlett said. "How are you holding up?"

Their eyes met. Scarlett had had more than her

share of experience with stalkers and batshit fans. "Fine," she said. "I should be able to go home soon." To *her* home, not Wyland's. "And I don't want to talk about my problems today. Can I ask you some questions about the GPL?"

Scarlett shifted her bulky weight in the chair. "The Genetic Purity League? What about them?"

"I'm working on a project with Wyland. The subject came up."

Sasha came back from the kitchen carrying a tray laden with potato chips, Top the Tater chip dip, a glass of ice water, and a steaming mug with a spoon standing upright in the cup. Ice cubes tinkled as she set the tray on the table next to Scarlett, then sat on the couch next to Antonia. Scarlett snatched the tub of chip dip, grabbed the spoon from the mug, then started eating the chip dip like it was ice cream. "Every bit of gossip you've heard about the Genetic Purity League? The reality is probably worse—not that we have any hard evidence." Scarlett and Antonia exchanged a look. "Off the record," Scarlett stated.

"Of course." Apparently Scarlett was as careful as Wyland was about protecting information.

"We suspect the GPL is fronted and financially supported by Krispin Woolf."

Though she'd long suspected the same thing, hearing a Council member say it out loud was a sucker punch. "The werewolves deserve better representation." She looked at Bailey. "Hasn't he left a trail of some type?"

"Not that we've found," Bailey answered. "The WerePack Alpha is an avowed technophobe. The only time I've seen him touch an electronic device is to issue a Council vote."

"How convenient." And how smart, damn it.

"The GPL has had a markedly lower profile the last year or so," Scarlett added. "I think Krispin was really surprised when Jacoby voted against his proposal that we fast-track genetic sequencing of the organic materials that Lorin's crew found in that capsule, up at the Isabella dig."

Organic materials? Genetic sequencing? "What capsule?" She'd heard about the lockbox Lorin had excavated last summer—advanced technology found next to ancient wild rice kernels, and still functional despite being buried for a couple thousand years— but a capsule containing organic material was news to her.

It took long minutes for Scarlett to describe the discoveries that Lorin Schlessinger and her bondmate, Commander Lupinsky's brother Gabe, had made at the Isabella dig last summer. In addition to the lockbox and the tech unit, Lorin and Gabe had also found the doomed *Arkapaedis'* debris field, and a capsule, nearly two feet long, made of the same unknown metallic alloy as both the lockbox and the ship's wreckage. Gabe, a geologist, had been taking alloy samples at Sebastiani Labs when he'd accidentally touched a hidden mechanism that opened the capsule, revealing vials of organic material stored inside. "Thankfully Gabe was working under a bio-hazard containment hood, because several of the vials were broken."

Wreckage from the ship? Unknown metallic alloys? Organic material, stored with obvious premeditation and care? Her thoughts whirled like a prairie tornado.

"We can't yet state with certainty that the Isabella

finds are extra-planetary in origin," Bailey said, "but that's the working theory, especially given your culture's oral histories."

Every child of their culture had heard the story of how a ship carrying their ancestors had crashed to Earth, leaving the marooned survivors fighting for their lives in the dead of a Minnesota winter. "What did you find? In the vials?"

"Sperm and ova from nearly thirty individuals, representing all of our known sub-species."

Tia sagged back in the chair.

"Mind-blowing, isn't it?" Scarlett said.

"Um, yeah."

Scarlett licked dip off the spoon with a flourish. "Sebastiani Labs' Cultural Anthropology department has been in a tizzy for months."

"I can imagine." Were their ancestors explorers? Tourists? Was Earth their final destination, or was the ship en route elsewhere? Was there even…someplace else to go? The prospect, and its implications about the existence of extra-planetary life and culture, boggled the mind. "Why store egg and sperm in a capsule?"

"Survival," Bailey said flatly. "A hedge against catastrophe." She drew up her legs, crossing them. "Space is…indescribably vast. No matter how sophisticated their technology, I'd think that any travel over such long distances would have to be considered risky. If the size of the debris field is anything go by, it's amazing anyone survived the crash, but—" Bailey shrugged "—the fact that you're all here indicates that more than a few managed it."

Scarlett picked up the mug. "Even before we confirmed the capsule's contents, Krispin wanted to fast-track genetic research, with his goal being potentially reversing the genetic damage that generations of in-breeding and lack of diversity has produced in his wolves." She took a sip of the tea, wrinkled her nose, and set it back down on the tray. "Every Council member thought his proposal was far too aggressive. Even Jacoby voted with the majority to take a more measured approach." She rubbed her lower back, shifting uncomfortably in the oversized chair. "I think Krispin might have throttled back on the GPL himself, opting for a lower profile while he considers his next move."

Tia wanted to ask where and how the materials were stored, but decided not to push her luck. The new knowledge she'd acquired this evening, knowledge she couldn't share, was already unexpectedly weighty. No wonder Wyland looked so tired all the time.

"Krispin might have throttled back, but the younger contingent of the GPL still meets regularly." Antonia explained that the GPL had two major groups, with a hard age distinction. "The Hitler Youth met just last week, at The Ivy," she added.

Goose bumps pebbled her flesh. "Really?"

"The Underbelly grapevine is pretty accurate."

Yes, it was. She'd used it herself, on many occasions.

"Well," Scarlett said, digging into the dip again, "I'm glad you're staying at Valerian's house for a while."

Antonia stretched full-length on the couch, draping her legs across Sasha's lap. "That's not all she's doing at Valerian's house. You go, girl."

"What do you mean?" What the hell was she

leaching? Her muscles still ached from last night's sexual exertions—quite deliciously so—but she thought she'd done an okay job disguising it.

"Nice hickey on your collarbone."

"What?" Tia slapped at her neckline, giving the shirt a reflexive upward tug. No wonder Thane had looked at her so strangely when she'd passed through the kitchen earlier.

Sasha gave her sister a shove. "Antonia, what have we told you about violating people's privacy?"

"Dude, it's right there for everyone to see." Antonia sat up, snickering. "Valerian must really be feeling better."

"Very funny." Tia looked at Scarlett. All signs of hormonal upset were gone, replaced by avid interest. Hell. Maybe if she acknowledged it, admitted it out loud, she could kill two birds with one stone—distract her friend, and maybe get some insight.

"It's Wyland, of course," Bailey said from Lukas's big leather chair. "I thought you and Chadden had a thing?"

She and Chadden enjoyed each other's company occasionally, but… "It's not like we're dating or anything." And it had been months since she'd slept with him, or with anyone else. Maybe her long sexual dry spell was the reason she couldn't get Wyland out of her mind.

"So, are you and Wyland—" Bailey gestured vaguely with her hand "—together?" Her fire opal bonding ring flashed in the light.

"No." They'd had sex, but they certainly hadn't talked about their relationship afterward. They hadn't talked at all. She'd dozed off, blanketed by his weight, but she'd woken up in the basement alone, with a huge towel draped over her body. "We slept together." She gave what she hoped was a blasé shrug. "It was great."

Bailey opened her mouth, then closed it. Concern lines creased her forehead.

"Bailey, he's an adult. I'm an adult. We wanted to have sex, so we did." She shrugged again. "No big deal."

"That's what she said," Antonia quipped.

"Stop joking. It's a *very* big deal," Scarlett said. "Do you have any idea what a monumental occasion this is?"

"That we had sex?" Tia asked. "People— animals—have sex all the time."

Scarlett lowered her voice, as if Wyland could somehow overhear. "He hasn't slept with anyone in years."

Her stomach leaped, suddenly full of frogs. "How do you know? Maybe he has a lover that no one knows about." Deirdre d'Amour floated into her mind, but she shoved the bitch right back out again. "He's a very private man."

"Tia. It's been *over a hundred years.*"

Sasha's words sent a dark thrill through her. "How in the world do you know this?"

"The grapevine's pretty reliable, and—" Sasha tapped her nose "—so is this."

Antonia nodded, crossing her legs at the ankles. "Yeah, his sexual energy's locked down like a Supermax."

Sasha and Antonia absorbed and interpreted emotional energy as easily as they breathed, so they'd probably know. Tia couldn't help it; she started to laugh. She'd just had the most stellar sex of her life, and he'd been…rusty.

It figured.

"Was it…bad?" Antonia asked. Sasha smacked her shoulder.

"No, it was awesome." He'd rocked her like a hurricane.

She was in trouble.

Scarlett reached for the potato chips, opening the bag with a crinkle that brought Calamity running. "Well, I'm glad someone is having great sex, because I'm just not up to it at the moment." She offered Calamity a potato chip. The cat snatched it out of her hand with surprising delicacy, then disappeared behind the couch with his prey. "Poor Lukas has to make do with blow jobs."

Antonia slapped her hands over her ears. "Why must you talk about having sex with my brother in my presence?"

Tia knew Scarlett had spoken to draw attention away from her, to give her a moment to absorb what she'd just heard. As Antonia went on and on—she faux-collapsed onto the wide-planked floor and lay there twitching—she gave Scarlett a grateful smile.

But Bailey watched her with an unnerving lack of expression. Tia met her gaze squarely. "What?"

"Nothing." Bailey looked at her phone. "It's time to go downstairs for our meeting."

What the hell was her deal? Well, it was Bailey's problem, not hers. She stood, leaned over, and hugged Scarlett again. "Don't get up. I'll call you tomorrow." She'd feel more comfortable talking about what had happened with Wyland without the other women there.

"Please do."

She and Bailey left the loft. As they rode the elevator downstairs, the love bite on her collarbone burned. When they reached the first floor, Bailey turned to her. "Don't hurt him."

"I don't see how that could possibly happen." Wyland's blood ran hot as any man's, but his emotions were safely encased in ice.

They stepped off the elevator. Tia followed Bailey across the lobby to the heavy steel door, flinching as Bailey slapped her hand against the palm reader.

The slap spoke louder than words.

CHAPTER TEN

Wyland loosened his necktie just slightly, then sipped at the glass of blood Lukas had pushed into his hand soon after he'd arrived at Sebastiani Security. No doubt he looked as exhausted to Lukas as Lukas did to him.

He hadn't slept in nearly two days.

After leaving Tia sleeping on the chaise by the pool, he'd escaped to the privacy of his room, his thoughts circling the carcass of his self-control like buzzards. Unable to sleep, he'd showered, gotten fully dressed right down to his necktie and shoes, and worked at his desk for long, long hours—not that he'd gotten much work done, because his thoughts kept slipping back to how Tia had held out her arms, welcoming him. To her quim's piquant taste, and its tight, slick heat. To how her cries of pleasure had bounced off the tiles.

Several hours ago, just before sunset, he'd finally admitted defeat. Analysis—creative thought—was beyond him, but he could go to the hospital. ER work was reactive, and his training was deeply ingrained. But when he'd reached the garage, he'd discovered Tia, and her car, were gone.

And he'd gotten worried, damn it.

As a doctor, he knew driving when the sun was

low on the horizon wasn't going to cause her any lasting harm. As a man, he knew she used her VampScreen religiously, because its distinctive scent still swirled in his head. She'd gone to visit Scarlett, Thane had informed him. So instead of going to the hospital, he'd driven to Sebastiani Security instead.

"How's Scarlett doing?" he asked Lukas as Jack activated the huge, flat-panel monitor mounted on the conference room's far wall.

There was a hiss as Lukas opened a can of Coke. "Fine."

Chico looked up from his mini-comp. "When I brought Tia upstairs, it sounded like she was chilling out, listening to some music."

"That was work," Lukas said darkly. "Wyland, can't you tell her she works too much? Put her on bed rest or something?"

Pot, meet kettle. Lukas looked about ready to drop. "She's perfectly healthy." Scarlett would go into labor within a week, or he'd eat his favorite tie. "Her work gives her something to focus on rather than how physically uncomfortable she feels." Distracting Scarlett had likely been Tia's motivation in coming here. He couldn't fault her intention, but…damn, the woman was working his last remaining nerve.

Lukas scrubbed his hand against what looked like a three-day beard, muttering something about vasectomies before draining half the can of caffeinated, sugar-loaded soda. He was just about to advise Lukas to drink something else when Tia and Bailey entered the room.

They didn't look happy with each other.

Lukas, Jack, and Chico rose from their chairs, and he belatedly did the same. Bailey, ignoring them all, walked around the table and took a seat at his right. Tia exchanged kisses of greeting with Lukas, Jack, and Chico, then approached him.

"Hello."

"Hello." He took in her appearance with a big, thirsty gulp. Her eyes sparkled with life, and her hair was swingy and loose, the green tips brushing shoulders left bare by a sleeveless T-shirt that said "Type O Negative" on the front. Her shorts were just that—short—exposing too much of her sleek, curvy thighs for his comfort. Her lush lips were bare, and her shoes had so little leather they hardly deserved the name. A delicate mixture of lilacs and VampScreen reached his nose, winding diabolical tendrils around his brainstem.

His fangs throbbed with each beat of his heart.

With a light touch of hands against his chest, she leaned closer, lifted her head, and brushed her lips against his cheek. As she moved to kiss the other, she grazed his skin with the tip of her incisor.

His cock hardened in a rush. It was all he could do to keep his hands resting so lightly and politely on bare upper arms. To not grab her, yank her against his body, and crush his lips against her unpainted mouth.

She backed away. He watched as the tempting little witch took a seat between him and Chico, as if her covert caress hadn't left him hard as a spike at a business meeting. As if she hadn't shut his common sense down cold.

"Why don't we get started?" Lukas suggested.

He was the only one still standing. "Certainly." He sat, picked up the glass of blood, and drained it.

Bailey looked at him strangely.

"Tia, thanks so much for visiting Scarlett," Lukas

said. "She's so uncomfortable right now. Every distraction helps."

"My pleasure," Tia responded. "It'll be over soon."

A wisp of panic crossed Lukas's face before he schooled his expression. "Right." He turned toward Jack, who was standing near the flat-screen at the end of the table. "Jack, why don't you get us started?"

As Jack pressed a couple of buttons on his laptop, Lukas surreptitiously withdrew a sleeve of antacids from his pants pocket, and slipped two tablets into his mouth. Scarlett was as healthy as a horse, but if she didn't have this baby soon, Lukas wouldn't have any stomach lining left.

Jack dimmed the lights. "Tia, Wyland, I'm glad you were both able to meet with us in person today. We have some new information on the case."

Tia drew herself upright—just an inch or so, but the movement took her posture from comfortable slouch to hyper-alert in a millisecond.

"Today, five more people reported receiving letters similar to the one sent to Lukas and Scarlett."

Tia's eyes narrowed. "What the hell...?"

What the hell, indeed. "Civilians?" he asked.

"If you can call people who work here at Sebastiani Security civilians," Jack answered. He gestured to the screen, where a document that looked a lot like the one Lukas had shown them was displayed. "Similar paper, same font, delivered to our front door by the U.S. Postal Service. The latest letters demand that the receivers voluntarily sterilize themselves so their infirmity—being of mixed race—doesn't further weaken the species."

"Are you serious? Cross-breeding introduces robustness. Hell, look what inbreeding has done to the wolves." She glanced at Chico. "Sorry."

"No need to apologize." Chico's tone was desert-dry. "That's my letter we're looking at."

"See? See how ignorant this person is? Chico's strong, smart, steady. Why wouldn't we want these attributes represented in our cultural gene pool?"

Jealousy slithered, but he pushed it aside. Something wasn't adding up. "You have Valkyrie roots in your family tree, correct?" Wyland asked Chico.

"Many generations back."

"So where is this person—" he gestured to the letter— "getting his or her information?"

"Good question." Jack flipped the lights back on, turning off the flat-screen and taking his seat. "None of the newer letters makes an overt threat—not like the one Lukas and Scarlett received, or like the comments made at *In Like Quinn*."

Tia tapped a turquoise-tipped finger against her lower lip. "Coco is healthy, and of mixed species heritage. Jacoby Woolf is a purebred werewolf, but chronically ill." She looked at Lukas, Jack, and finally at him. "This reeks of the GPL to me. It's no secret that Krispin Woolf brought the latest GPL-backed petition before the Council—"

"And we promptly voted it down," Wyland said. The proposal to require registration of bond relationships with the Council had been unacceptable. "Why would Krispin Woolf threaten his own son?"

"It's no secret that Jacoby Woolf has been voting with the majority, against his father, much more frequently these days. The Alpha might see his son's actions as disloyal." She glanced down at her tattoo, then back at him. "Would the Alpha eliminate his own son to further the goals of the pack?"

He and Krispin Woolf didn't agree with each other, but the possibility of the father killing the son had never crossed his mind.

It should have.

"The Alpha also has a massive hard-on against everything and anything Sebastiani," Tia continued. "He holds Lukas personally responsible for letting Stephen, the man who assaulted his daughter, escape from prison."

Lukas acknowledged the point. "And we have protective measures in place, but…sending letters? Scaring you with harmless snakes?" He shook his head. "Krispin's threats are usually much more blunt."

Lukas was right. Something wasn't adding up.

"Krispin Woolf can't be our only avenue of investigation," Jack said. "We're analyzing the letters that Chico, Winnie, and others have received—"

"Winnie got a letter?" Bailey asked.

Winnie Otsego, a Sebastiani Security lieutenant, had helped apprehend the hacker who'd threatened both Bailey and Sebastiani Labs' computer systems earlier that year.

"Yeah. She's fine." Chico straightened from his relaxed slouch. "Wyland asked what I think is the key question. Where the hell is this person getting their information?"

Silence.

Jack looked at Tia. "Any more creeped-out feelings since moving to Vamp Central?"

She hesitated, glancing at him. "I had a funny feeling in my stomach the last time Wyland and I went to the Archives." She shrugged. "Or maybe it was that burrito. I didn't see anything, but—"

"Why didn't you say something?" he snapped.

"I didn't see anything, so I didn't want to bother you about it."

"It's not a bother." He hadn't seen anything, either. He'd been too busy staring at her like a cock-addled fool. "Don't you think I can protect you?"

"I had my hand on my stun gun the whole time."

And he hadn't even noticed.

"Wyland, I'm better prepared than you give me credit for," she said. "There's a lot you don't know about me."

After last night, there was a lot he *did* know—like her natural hair color, the shape of the birthmark on her left hip, and the precise shade of pink that suffused her skin when she came.

And now Lukas was watching him again, damn it.

"Change of subject." Tia shifted in her chair. "Antonia said something interesting about the Genetic Purity League when we were visiting Scarlett upstairs just now."

She wouldn't meet his eyes. He was pretty sure he wasn't going to like this.

Tia explained that the GPL's younger members met at a different venue every month, with the location being passed by word of mouth. "I want to—"

"Try to infiltrate?" he guessed. "No."

"I—"

"No." One small woman, going up against the GPL? Against Krispin Woolf? The little fool was going to get herself killed. "I forbid it."

As Tia straightened in her chair, the leather creaked a warning. "I'm certain I didn't hear you correctly."

"I'm certain you did."

"I wasn't asking for permission."

Fear clawed at him. She had no earthly clue how many heinous acts Krispin Woolf was suspected of committing, or of ordering others to commit on his behalf. He took a deep breath, holding on to his control by the skin of his teeth. "Tia, any interaction with Krispin Woolf—with the GPL—is dangerous beyond your ken."

"I 'ken' just fine. If you'd let me finish a damn sentence—"

"Tia—"

She shot to her feet. "Wyland, let's get something straight right now." Glaring down at him, hands on hips, she looked like a pissed-off royal. "We might have slept together, but you need to throw this Cro-Magnon shit out the freaking window."

Had she really just...said *that*? At a business meeting?

Yes. Yes, she had—and now everyone was looking at them, their gazes bouncing back and forth as if they were watching a tennis match at Wimbledon. Chico was trying to hide a grin. Jack looked mildly amused, and mildly sympathetic. At his other side, Bailey diplomatically cleared her throat. Lukas simply...watched.

Clearing his own throat, he slowly rose and faced her. Their gazes clashed like swords. "Tia, now is not the time to discuss our private business."

"Private? Please. Everyone in this room knows we hooked up. We didn't have to say a thing."

Hooked up? What a disgusting phrase, but she was probably right about others knowing they'd slept together. Chico, with his werewolf nose, likely smelled them. Lukas's ability to interpret emotional energy signatures was unrivaled. Bailey, with her newly-discovered smidge of succubus blood, could probably read him—them—like a book. Even Jack, the sole human, didn't seem surprised.

He felt hideously exposed.

"As I was going to say before I was so rudely interrupted—" Tia shot him a hard glance "—I'd love to attend a GPL meeting myself, but I don't think I'm anonymous enough."

"Or young enough," Bailey added.

"Bitch," Tia said without heat, taking her seat again. "But you're right."

Chico looked at Lukas. "We have a couple of young-looking operatives who might be able to make progress on that front."

Lukas nodded.

"The most recent gathering occurred last week, in one of the smaller ballrooms at The Ivy."

Chico whistled. "That doesn't come cheap."

"Money doesn't seem to be a problem. Makes one wonder who's picking up the tab." With that, Tia stood again. "Do we have anything else to discuss? Lukas needs to get upstairs, and I'm going to the Archives." She glanced at him. "And you can't stop me."

What did she expect him to do, deny her permission? Tell her she couldn't go? Turn her over his knee and give her the spanking she so dearly deserved? His pulse bumped at the thought. "I'll meet you there." He'd given her a garage door opener, but—

"I can handle it myself."

"I said, I'll meet you there."

"You know what? I've lost count of the fucks I do not give. Kiss my entire ass."

He lifted a brow. "If memory serves, I did. Twice."

Her eyes widened. With an audible growl, she grabbed her purse, whirled, then stalked from the room.

Silence in her wake. His skin prickled, as if he'd foolishly taken cover under a tall tree with lightning threatening overhead.

"Now that," Chico said, "is one pissed-off woman." His admiring tone suggested he didn't necessarily think this was a problem, but Lukas and Jack wore expressions of knowing commiseration.

"You should probably go after her," Lukas advised.

Jack nodded. "Make sure she safely reaches her destination."

Bailey looked at them like they'd all sprouted second heads. "Seriously? We're done here because Wyland wants to get laid?"

His face heated.

"I don't have anything else to discuss tonight." Lukas looked at Jack. "Do you have anything else to discuss tonight?"

"Nope. Chico?"

"Nothing that can't wait. And getting laid is very serious business."

Wyland opened his mouth—to deny he wanted to go after Tia because he wanted to get laid; to tell them to mind their own business—but then closed it again. He *did* want to get laid—he felt like an addict overdue for his next fix—but even more importantly, he needed to apologize. His sexual comment, in this setting, was inexcusable. He'd acted exactly like the Cro-Magnon she'd accused him of being.

Lukas hitched a thumb toward the door. "Go."

He rose and headed for the exit.

"Make sure you apologize," Bailey called after him.

He raised a hand in acknowledgment.

There was an odd energy in his step as he left the building and walked to the car. Yes, he definitely owed Tia an apology, but what would he say? He couldn't possibly describe his primal, clenching fear with words.

Folding his frame behind the wheel, he closed the door and strapped in. With a chirp of wheels, he pulled out of the parking lot and headed east.

He had forty miles to figure it out.

❋

Across the room, another shelving unit moved with a muffled mechanical hum—the only clue Tia had about Wyland's location, because the dratted man had disappeared the minute they'd arrived at the Archives. With white-gloved hands, she very carefully turned the manuscript's brittle page. If he could concentrate on work with this…this…tension seething between them, then so could she.

But as she looked for references to Sigurd or The Old Ways, the words blurred on the page.

The long drive to Marine on St. Croix hadn't helped matters any. After she'd left Sebastiani Security, Wyland had quickly caught up with her, his car's sexy silhouette unmistakable in her rear view mirror. When it became clear he didn't intend to pass, she'd taken perverse satisfaction in slowing to the posted speed limit, making him throttle back all that power. He'd followed at a polite distance, headlights boring into her back for miles, finally passing when they'd turned onto the remote county road leading to the Archives. He'd opened the garage door, pulling in first, and stood skimming the tree line as she entered, quickly closing the door behind them—and thank the freaking universe, because her headlights had illuminated a set of eyes peering at them through the long grass.

A deer? A dog? Her overactive imagination? "Damn." She pushed back from the table. Working with centuries-old books required a delicacy she wasn't capable of at the moment. Banging on a keyboard sounded a lot more satisfying. Pulling off the gloves and dropping them on the table, she went to the kitchenette, made a bloody Diet Dew, and carried it back to the workstation Bailey said she could use.

She sat down, logged on, pulled up Valerian's bio, and then hesitated. Maybe she should check with Bailey before updating such critical files.

Nah. If Bailey didn't like her updates, Bailey could damn well change them.

She scrolled down, down, down, skimming, assessing the material with an eye to structure. Given Valerian's near-millennia of life and service, his file was immense, spanning so many historical eras and containing so many footnotes and cross-references that her eyes nearly crossed just looking at it. Other areas of the bio were woefully incomplete, with section headers present but saying nothing but

"TBD" or "information not available" underneath. She added a new section header—*Interviews*—and went to work.

In no time at all, the transcript from her first interview with Valerian was added, and the audio file embedded. Her links worked, expand/condense functionality worked, and she hadn't screwed up Bailey's beloved HTML. Not wanting to tempt fate, she saved her changes, exited Edit mode, then kept reading.

Bailey had spoken truthfully—the rudiments of a biography were here—but someone really needed to take this material in hand. Valerian's time as a warrior-priest, and his accomplishments as a political leader and diplomat, were well-documented, but his personal life? *Bubkes.* Other Council members' bios contained up-to-the-minute information about their significant personal relationships, but Valerian's? Nothing. No mention of lovers, bondmates, or offspring. Was the data simply missing? Lying somewhere in the Archives, uncatalogued? Had Valerian, responsible for keeping their culture's written records for centuries, simply not considered his own personal information essential?

Had he never known these relationships?

Other than Valerian, who'd know?

Thane.

She issued a quick search on Thane's name. "Bingo." Not only did Thane have multiple mentions in Valerian's bio, he had his own lengthy file, complete with a fourteenth century birth date. If the data was correct, Thane had served Val for nearly five hundred years, several centuries longer than Wyland had been alive. As she read, she shook her head in amazement. Thane's bio read almost like a novel, full of heroic tales and derring-do, but...no mention of bondmates, lovers, partners or offspring. They'd been each other's family for half a millennia... "Oh." There were two toothbrushes in Valerian's bathroom.

They *were* a family.

She'd lived in the same house for nearly a week, and she hadn't noticed a thing. "Some investigative journalist I am," she mumbled. Her thoughts whirled. Why in the world wasn't such a significant, long-term relationship part of their biographies? Who else knew? Across the room, there was a whirring hum as Wyland moved yet another shelf.

Wyland surely must.

Her lips tightened. One more secret the Vampire Second kept.

She went back to her search results, then clicked on a cross-reference connecting Thane's bio to Wyland's. According to the bio, it had been Thane who'd brought the young Wyland to Valerian's attention. "No interest in being the Vampire Second yourself, Thane? I don't blame you." She quickly scrolled past Wyland's recent headshot, away from those piercing, loch-blue eyes, looking for the picture of him, Deirdre d'Amour, and Bram Stoker... Okay, where the hell was it? She paged up, paged down. Navigated to the top of the document and scrolled down, slowly and carefully. Issued a search.

Nothing. The picture was gone.

All references to Deirdre and Bram, gone.

She leaned back in the chair, tapping her index finger against her lower lip. The picture had been there a couple of days ago. Who'd deleted the information between then and now?

Why?

She was paging to modification records when she heard Wyland approach. "Crap." She minimized his file, leaving Valerian's visible on the screen.

"There you are." His voice stroked like crushed velvet.

She turned her chair to face him. Somewhere along the way, he'd taken off his tie and unbuttoned his top two shirt buttons. His sleeves were rolled up, exposing muscular forearms and his antique Piaget watch. After last night, she knew exactly what kind of bodily terrain the fine fabric of his clothing covered. She'd mapped every inch of it with her eyes, her hands, her mouth.

He stopped about an arm's length away. With her sitting and him standing, her eyes were level with his belt buckle. Yes, she knew every thick, glorious inch.

"Not working on the manuscript anymore?"

"No." Clearing her throat, she gestured toward the bloody Dew sitting on the desk. "I wanted something to drink."

"I fear for your teeth." Leaning over, he peered at the screen. "What are you working on?"

He smelled…amazing. "I've started to record some interviews with Valerian—a day in the life—and I'm adding the information in his bio." She paused. "Some Council members' biographies seem to have significant gaps."

He cleared his throat. "You're interviewing Valerian?"

"Yes." She knew damn well he'd deleted information from his own bio, but his expression gave nothing away. "Transcript, audio…I'd like to capture some video as well." She explained her interest in doing the same for all Council members. "With today's technology, there's no reason future generations can't know exactly what their representatives looked and sounded like."

He leaned closer, skimming the transcript. "You've accomplished this since you've been our guest?"

"Val and I spend a lot of time together while you're at the hospital." She gave an uncomfortable shrug. "I ask him a kickoff question, and then let the recorder roll. He's quite the raconteur."

When he straightened, the summer-weight wool covering his thigh brushed against her bare arm. "Alka Schlessinger started doing something similar before she went on sabbatical last year. She and Valerian had these long dinners together, and she'd record their conversations. I don't think she's had a chance to do anything with the materials yet. You might contact her, and tell her about your project."

"I have a project?"

He gestured to the screen, as if the answer was obvious. "Please focus on Valerian first." A wisp of sadness crossed his face, but quickly disappeared. "Recording him, and embedding the materials in the Archive, is an excellent idea. I should have thought of it myself."

"You can't think of everything. There's not enough time in the day." *And you spend too much of it working as it is.* "Are you done for the evening?"

"There's one last thing," he said.

More work? "Wyland—"

"We really have to stop interrupting each other."

She snickered; she couldn't help it.

"What's so funny?"

"You interrupted me to tell me we shouldn't

213

interrupt each other."

He took a deep breath. "You're going to drive me to the madhouse." Taking her hands, he drew her to her feet. "I must apologize for my behavior earlier this evening."

His voice was clipped and controlled, with that wisp of upper crust England, but the edgy frustration seething in his eyes made her melt. Somewhere along the way, she'd learned how to read him, noticed how precise gradations of tone conveyed his moods. Did he really think she wouldn't accept his apology? That she wouldn't offer one of her own? Because, yeah— her own behavior at the meeting had been less-than-professional. She touched his crisp shirt, resting her palm over his thumping heart. He felt so warm, so alive—and so, so tense.

His forehead was suddenly against hers, his gaze boring down. "I'm sorry."

She wrapped her arms around his waist. "Me, too."

He was hard against her stomach. As his mouth descended, his fangs flashed in the fluorescent light.

He was magnificent, and he wanted her.

She could taste his apology on his lips and tongue, could feel it in his rough, roving hands. Such edgy, pounding need—a need she shared. She tugged at the band holding his hair in its disciplined queue, then plunged her fingers through the silky drift. "Something about your loose hair makes me want to drag you to the floor."

Wyland glanced at the white tiles, as if he was actually considering it. "I'm supposed to be apologizing."

"You are." She tilted her head to the side. "Very

nicely, I might add."

He dropped his hands to her waist. "Tia, the thought of you investigating the GPL, or the house where that poor human was killed, chills my blood, but…'I forbid it'?" He shook his head. "I was out of line. I should have been more diplomatic with my phrasing. The fact that we're having a sexual relationship is now common knowledge, and I apologize for violating your privacy."

Having a sexual relationship? She hadn't dared think of last night, or of any future nights, as anything beyond a casual hook-up, but Wyland used language precisely, and wasn't a casual man. "I was the one who revealed the nature of our…relationship…to your work colleagues." The word 'relationship' tasted odd on her tongue. Maybe she'd get used to it if she said it more often. "Why did you leave me alone in the pool room last night?"

"I needed to think," he admitted. "There are political ramifications to any relationship I engage in, no matter how superficial or serious." He sighed. "And you're so damn young."

She swept a glance over his frame. "You're not exactly decrepit. As soon as word gets out that you've taken a lover, I'm going to have to watch my back."

"I want you to watch your back regardless," he said. "Why didn't you tell me you felt like you were being watched the last time we were here? The security cameras haven't picked up anything unusual, if that reassures you at all."

Were the eyes she'd seen gleaming in the grass usual or unusual? Who the hell knew?

"Shall we go home?" Wyland murmured against the corner of her mouth. "Find a more comfortable place to continue this conversation?"

Such heat, such anticipation.

"Let's go." Nothing long-term could possibly come of this, but that was okay. She'd make sure the short-term rocked.

CHAPTER ELEVEN

"How about watching a movie in bed?" Tia suggested as they walked up the stairs to the second floor bedrooms.

Agile fingers danced at the small of his back, reassuring him she was still interested in the 'bed' part of the evening's entertainment, but...a movie? Wyland didn't know if he could keep his hands off her for the twenty footsteps it would take to reach his bedroom, much less for an hour and a half. Back at the Archives, he'd almost taken her on the table, heedless of the precious books he insisted no bare fingers touch. Thankfully, they'd driven home in separate cars, because he'd needed every centimeter of the drive to put a choke-chain on his libido.

"If you wish." He wasn't an animal. He could control himself—for a while, to please her.

She laughed, low and knowing, as she slipped her fingertips under his belt. "Haven't you ever necked at the movies?"

Her suggestive tone shot to his head like top-shelf liquor. "No." He hadn't watched a movie in years, but any activity involving her luscious neck sounded intriguing. As they reached the top of the stairs and turned down the hallway, the household's window shutters engaged, shutting out the rising sun with a whoosh and a click.

"Do you have a TV and DVD player in your room, or should we use Valerian's?" she asked.

"I have them."

"Let me get something from my movie box." She gave his arse a cheeky pat before creeping across the hall to Valerian's sitting room.

Her warm touch lingered, and her scent was absolutely intoxicating. He was drunk on her, absolutely piss drunk, and he'd barely touched her yet. Hell. It didn't matter what film Tia chose, as long as she was lying on the bed beside him.

Beneath him.

On top of him.

Soon.

Entering his room, he flicked on the bedside lamp. After giving the room a quick glance—it was neat enough, except for his desk—he hurried to the bathroom. Thankfully, it was in better condition now than he'd left it, with the glass shower enclosure wiped clean of water droplets, and a new bar of soap at the sink. The damp towels he'd used earlier were gone, replaced with dry, fresh linens. On the toilet tank, a small wicker basket of pine needles and pinecones had appeared, filling the room with a subtle scent.

The utilitarian room looked like a spa. He cast a mental 'thank you' to Thane.

You're welcome. Sleep well. With that, Thane withdrew, leaving him in privacy.

"What a beautiful room," Tia said from the bathroom door, holding a slim black box. "So many shades of blue, and what a gorgeous shower." She looked at the clear panel of glass, then at him, as if visualizing what he'd look like standing behind it.

Naked.

His teeth tingled, and his cock gave a warning throb. If he didn't get her out of here, he'd take her on the hard tile floor. With a hand at the small of her back, he guided her back to the bedroom. Leaving her to explore, he bent to the chest at the foot of his bed and pressed a couple of buttons. A flat-screen television slowly rose, perfectly positioned for viewing from the bed.

"Awesome! Just like on *Cribs*."

He wanted to bask in Tia's obvious delight, but Thane had chosen the outrageous piece of furniture. "What is *Cribs*?"

"A show that used to be on MTV—you know, the music television station? Famous musicians would invite a camera crew into their homes for a day and show off their larger-than-life décor. And this—" she gave the mattress a testing push, then winked at him "—is where the magic happens."

His blood pressure spiked. "What?"

"That's what the people on *Cribs* always said when they toured the bedroom." She scanned the room, running her hand over the bluish-gray duvet. "I have to say, your bedroom looks more modern than I expected."

"What did you expect?"

"Antiques," she said with a shrug. "Something a little more traditional."

Meaning staid, of course. And if they'd had this conversation a year ago, she'd have been right. When Thane expressed an urge to redecorate last year, Wyland had given him free rein here in his private quarters. Unlike Valerian, he had no sentimental attachment to furniture; he was more concerned about functionality, utility, and a basic level of comfort. After spending gleeful weeks with color swatches, tile samples, and carpet squares, Thane had definitely met his requirements—the mattress was sinfully comfortable, and the L-shaped desk was a quantum improvement over the tiny Victorian secretary he used to use—but he'd never considered whether a lover might find the room pleasing.

Perhaps Thane had.

Tia crouched in front of the entertainment center and turned on the DVD player. Opening the black container she'd brought with her, she extracted a disc, and slid it into the machine.

"What's tonight's feature?"

"*Bram Stoker's Dracula.*"

He froze.

"Come on, don't be so stuffy." When she rose, there was a remote control in her hand. "It'll be fun."

Fun? He glanced at the plump, accordion-pleated folder sitting on his desk. If she only knew how much bloody *work* Bram's little story had created for him over the years.

"There's this really hot ménage scene…"

His pulse gave a bump. If Tia wanted to watch a movie, they'd watch a movie. Even *this* movie. He'd focus her attention elsewhere soon enough. "Would you like something to drink?"

"Sure, what do you have?"

When he opened the small refrigerator next to the desk, he blinked in surprise. In addition to the usual water, juice, and blood, there was a six-pack of Tia's favorite soda, several bottles of excellent wine, and a beautifully arranged platter of cheese, fruit, and crackers.

Tia chose the Riesling. "I'll start the movie."

As he dealt with the cork and poured, he heard a series of electronic clicks. Fabric rustled, making his body hair stand on end. His perfectly-tailored suit coat suddenly seemed two sizes too small.

Tia Quinn was finally in his bed.

He took a deep breath. Another. A third. Once he regained a modicum of control, he picked up the wine glasses, turned toward her, and nearly dropped them.

Tia Quinn was *naked* in his bed.

She was under the duvet, on the side where he usually slept, her shoulders bare against the pillows she'd propped against the headboard. Her clothes were strewn across the carpet, dropped where she'd removed them. Right next to the bed was a wisp of white lace, a garment so insubstantial it barely deserved the name.

He swallowed with an audible click.

"Wyland?"

His gaze jumped to the bed. The Tiffany lamp turned her reddish hair to flame, and the green tips glowed against the pale gray pillowcase. Her eyes sparkled, and her skin seemed lit from within. She was a kaleidoscope of color against his monochromatic sheets. He didn't know where to look first.

"Wyland? The wine?" She sounded amused, as if she knew exactly how addled he was. He walked to the bed and handed her a glass. "Thank you." Her throat shifted as she drank, her shadowy veins fluttering beneath her skin. Jerking his gaze away, he took a hasty gulp from his own glass. "Mmm, this is lovely," she said, her lips wet from the wine. "And look at you. Pure suit porn."

His suit? Pornography?

She ran her finger down his thigh, her eyes skimming his body with appreciation. "There's something so arousing about a beautiful man wearing a beautiful suit. That steely gray, with your coloring?" Her lips made an approving moue. "Gorgeous."

No woman had ever complimented his appearance quite so frankly before. The roles—the *rules*—regarding sexual congress had definitely changed since he'd last had relations, and…he liked it. How utterly refreshing that a woman could look at a man with frank sexual hunger in her eyes, and not hide her desire. That a woman could speak openly and without shame about how much he aroused her. He sat on the edge of the bed, the mattress dipping with his weight. "You're the gorgeous one." Was there anything more beautiful than seeing your own desire reflected back from the face of your lover, her anticipation written there for you to read?

Such a thing could enslave a man.

Setting her glass on the nightstand, she brushed the covers aside, rose to her knees, and pressed her nude form against his fully-clothed body. She slid her hands under the suit coat, stroking upward from his stomach to his chest. "I love the suit," she murmured, trailing her mouth along the border where his shirt collar met his neck. "But why don't you take it off?"

Each word was a maddening caress. Down at the foot of the bed, Vlad the Impaler kissed his doomed wife Elisabeta goodbye, but Wyland was too busy watching Tia crawl away from him on hands and knees to care.

She reclaimed her wine before settling back against

the pillows again, not bothering with the blankets this time. Pale skin, soft curves, firm muscles over fine bones...the multicolored Tiffany lampshade spilled color over her shoulders and breasts, highlighting her pebbled nipples. Her waist nipped in, flaring out to hips that any Renaissance master would yearn to sculpt or paint. Sleek thighs, muscular calves...her feet were crossed at the ankle, exaggerating the vee of her mons.

"Start with the jacket," she murmured.

His pulse pounded. He'd never undressed for a lover before. Deirdre had always— *No*. Deirdre had no place here. The past had no place here—not when Tia, this enchanting, exasperating woman from the here and now, watched him with a hunger she didn't hide.

Her hot gaze slowed time to honey.

When he set his wine on the table next to hers, the click of glass against wood sounded unnaturally loud. He toed off his shoes, nudging them under the bed so no one tripped on them, then shrugged off his coat. She made an inarticulate sound deep in her throat, one that made his body hair stand on end. She watched his hands, staring at them as he draped the coat over the foot board, as he reached for his belt. Leather creaked. Metal clanked. He flicked open the button at the waistband, then worked the zipper over his straining cock. Leaving the pants sagging at his hips, he yanked out his shirt tails.

Bloody hell, how was a man supposed to focus on the task at hand when she lay there, wearing nothing but skin and light, watching him so greedily?

Her gaze was a phantom, caressing him through the air. His cock throbbed; his bollocks ached. Energy snarled low in his pelvis, a long-forgotten sensation.

"God." Her throaty curse was poetry.

He made fast work of his shirt buttons, yanking it off and dropping it to the floor. Shoving his hair aside, he grasped the neck of his undershirt, hauled it over his head, and tossed it next to the dress shirt.

She chuckled.

"What's so funny?"

"Men undress so matter-of-factly. No delicacy to it whatsoever."

He refused to think about where she'd gained such knowledge. After a fortifying breath, he stepped out of his pants.

Tia's avid gaze raked him up and down. "Calvin Klein boxer briefs. Very hot."

He still thought it was a strange thing to have another man's name written on his smalls. "They're quite comfortable." Rather, they usually were, when his penis behaved itself instead of fighting with the fabric.

As she moved toward him, he didn't know where to look. At her erect nipples, standing out in little points for his tongue? At her hips, shifting so mysteriously? Arousal flushed her cheeks, flashed in her eyes, and her fangs glinted in the light. Kneeling before him, reaching for him with a graceful hand, she looked as alluring as a courtesan.

When she cupped his cock through the soft cotton, he clutched her shoulders for support, locking his knees as she explored him with keen, knowledgeable hands. Cock, bollocks, hipbones, his arse…no bit of his anatomy was spared. His breath hissed as he watched. Obviously, he'd forgotten more about foreplay than he remembered, because this was torture, sheer bloody torture.

She lifted her hand. Before he could miss her touch, she was crouching, rubbing her cheek against his hard, aching flesh.

"You're killing me," he gritted out.

She smiled against the head of his cock. Before he could recover from the diabolical caress, she opened her mouth. Hot breath blossomed through the soft cotton, twining up his pelvis and spine. She pulled at the elastic waistband, working the garment over his arse and down his thighs. Letting gravity pull the fabric to the floor, she grabbed his hips and put her mouth back on him—not on his cock, but on the crease where his leg joined his torso, right over his femoral artery.

He drove his fangs into his lower lip, tasted his own blood. How had the little witch zeroed in on his most sensitive erogenous zone? As she licked and nibbled at the sensitive skin, his lifeblood surged like a whitewater rapids. His penis throbbed with every beat of his heart.

He wanted to wallow in the suck and pull of her mouth. Wallow in her until he drowned.

But when her tongue swirled against his skin, as if preparing it for her bite, he jerked away, tipping her back against the pillows and following her down. He came to rest covering her body, her full breasts pillowing his chest, lying between her spread thighs— an equally dangerous position.

With one subtle shift of his hips, he could be inside her.

One. Subtle. Shift.

A desperate groan escaped.

She wrapped her arms around him. Whispered his

name.

Her eyes were heavy with arousal, and soft, slick heat gathered between her thighs. The lamp highlighted her collarbones, casting shadows at the juncture where her shoulder met her neck. Under her skin, blood rushed through her arteries and veins, branching out into tributaries he yearned to explore.

Deep in his lizard brain, a small voice whispered, "Drink." He could please them both, and level the playing field between them, in one fell swoop.

So, so tempting.

He reached for the lamp, but she stopped him with a hand on his forearm. "Leave it on."

Such sex-drenched words. Such a throaty demand. She'd probably packed more sexual experience into her meager thirty years than he had in three hundred.

Her strong legs came up, wrapping around his hips. "Leave it on," she murmured against the notch between his clavicles. The points of her fangs scratched his skin. "Leave it on and fuck me."

The wicked word blasted him broadside, lighting up his brain stem like a Beltane fire. He grabbed her head and kissed her—a wild, uncontrolled kiss, a clash of lips, teeth, and tongues. A kiss that drew blood—his, hers? He licked into her mouth, trying to gather more of its delectable, dark sting. His hips gave a helpless, instinctive roll.

He paused, panting, as his penis notched against the opening of her vagina. *So warm, so wet.* He gave another testing flex, hissing at the give of her resilient flesh.

"I have condoms in my purse."

Condoms. The sensible, clinical word was a lifeline. Last night, he'd noticed the birth control patch on

Tia's hip, but condoms were a necessity between lovers who hadn't yet exchanged sexual histories. His last sexual experience had literally occurred in the Victorian Age. "I'll get them." He levered his upper body off hers, then paused. Thane had provided everything else he needed for a romantic encounter; why not condoms? He reached into the bedside table's drawer, and sure enough, came out with a small black and gold cardboard box.

He peered at the label. Ten latex condoms, pre-lubricated with a reservoir tip. "Ribbed for her pleasure," he read. What the hell did *tha*t mean? The last time he'd used a condom, latex hadn't been invented yet, but...surely they worked the same way?

Tia grabbed the box and tore it open, spilling condoms onto the bed. Snatching up a strip, she tore off a single small packet, ripped it open with her teeth, and withdrew a small, flexible disk about the size of a British crown. He smelled latex, and chemicals—odd but not off-putting, especially compared to sheep intestine—but before he could take it from her, she nudged him back, rolled the condom onto his penis, and pulled him back between her legs.

He lifted a brow. "Such efficiency."

"You were taking too long." Reaching to the nape of his neck, she none-too-gently pulled at the elastic band he'd put back on in the car. His hair spilled down, curtaining their faces.

Even in the shadows, her eyes mesmerized him. The combination of green and brown reminded him of tender shoots pushing through rich, fertile soil in springtime.

Damn it, now he was waxing poetic. When had

everything gotten so bloody convoluted?

She broke their gaze, wrapping her arms and legs around him, pulling him closer. The tip of his cock skimmed her slick folds. Tia writhed against him, clawing at his back and tugging at his hair. A delicate pink flush suffused her cheeks, chest, and neck…her beautiful neck, with its enticing blue veins… He nuzzled them. Nipped.

She tipped her head back, giving him unfettered access. "Drink from me," she whispered. Her words were a dark, sultry invitation, an invitation to as much pleasure as a vampire could possibly stand.

He looked down at the fluttering vein, stared at its rhythmic throb. Imagined driving his fangs into it, and drinking her lush, rich lifeblood. Yes, having access to her thoughts and emotions would help level the playing field between them, but—

He couldn't.

Could he?

It had been so long.

No. He couldn't drink from her if he wouldn't let her drink from him in return—and thanks to Valerian, she'd already sipped more of his blood than he was comfortable with.

"Wyland." Her gaze was steady on his. "Don't mind-fuck this to death. I want you to know me. I want you to drink from me. I want to feel your fangs and your cock inside me."

"Tia…" How could she take such risks? How could she give so freely, expecting nothing in return? Once he drank from her, he'd be able to read her like a book—until she learned to protect her mental boundaries, at any rate.

Tia wrapped her arms around him, embracing him.

"Drink from me." Her eyes glowed with heat, anticipation, and welcome. Her pupils were huge, dark as the infinite night sky.

With a minute shift of his hips, the tip of his cock skimmed her slippery heat. He stilled, closing his eyes and clenching his teeth. Her heels dug into his arse, spurring him on. With a slow, steady glide, he buried himself to the hilt.

"Mmm." Her velvety groan twined around his vitals, her fingernails biting into his back with a tiny, erotic sting. Her arms and legs tightened, enveloping him in a languorous embrace.

Through the ultra-thin condom, he felt every hot clutch and ripple with a violent clarity. *Do not spend. Do not.* He would bring her pleasure first, even if it killed him.

He started to move—slowly, so slowly—trailing his hands anywhere and everywhere he could touch, delving his tongue into her sweet, tart mouth. He lost himself as their lips and hips surged together, swallowing her throaty moans whole. Lost himself in the lush cavern of her mouth, and in the tight, slick channel he forged again and again.

They strained together, harder. Faster. Her inner muscles clutched and clung. "Please," she whispered, her eyes blind and wild. "Now."

Tilting her head back, she exposed the long, white column of her neck.

He stared, mesmerized, as if he hadn't written a half-dozen textbooks detailing its anatomy. As if he hadn't examined, resected, and repaired every millimeter of every life-giving tributary, a thousand times over.

He couldn't resist.

He couldn't refuse.

This is the most selfish thing I've ever done.

"Wyland…" Her hips moved faster, her breath huffing against his ear in thin, reedy moans. Her heels dug into his buttocks, spurring him on.

He homed in on the external jugular pulsing just under her skin. He gently nuzzled it, licking and swirling with his tongue.

She suddenly tensed, her body strung tight as a bow. "Oh, god." The strong muscles of her vagina clenched around him, poised for the leap. One more hard thrust—another—and she shattered beneath him with a cry, her nails biting into his back.

He plunged his fangs into the tender vein. Her lifeblood gushed like a geyser, flooding his mouth. A searing bolt of pleasure sizzled into him, zinging between fangs, brain stem, and cock. Sunlight, shadows, sweet and tart…endlessly complex…a throb of Valerian's immense power… His sensory system was going haywire, but he didn't care. He could do nothing but swallow or drown, drink and thrust, drink and thrust until she was fully satisfied, until… Ah, there it was—that exquisite ferrous filament, a receptor his greedy DNA immediately recognized.

Reaching for him.

He reached back, and felt the delicate synaptic connection click into place.

Oh, my.

Right? She sighed, trailing a languid hand from his hair to his stinging back to his arse. The gush in his mouth had slowed to hot, silky pulses, but he didn't mistake it for weakness. She was strong, so strong— strong enough to share her blood with him and ask for nothing in return.

Guilt nudged at him. Her boundaries were non-existent—she didn't know how to protect herself yet—and now, he could read her as easily as a billboard.

She thought he was smoking hot, and didn't think him old and decrepit in the least. She was intrigued by him. Confused by him. He was the best lover she'd ever had…and she wasn't entirely happy about it.

His hips picked up the pace, his chest puffing with an absurd masculine pride. *I'll show you my best.*

Her white grin flashed. "Bring it."

His eyes narrowed, but then his orgasm was looming, rearing over him like a huge, cresting wave. He could do nothing but thrust, and let it pound him down.

Let it take him under.

CHAPTER TWELVE

Several hours later, Wyland sat at his desk, sipping his second cup of coffee. The bright midday sun streaming through the UV-filtering windows felt luxurious against his skin. *This must be what it feels like to laze on a beach in San Tropez.* He indulged himself in sensation until a soft chime announced the arrival of more email. With a sigh, he set the mug down. Opening his top desk drawer, ignoring Tia's ring lying inside, he grabbed the reading glasses he'd just put away.

Across the room, she still slept, her head and body buried in an avalanche of blankets. The covers couldn't hide her stunning curves—curves he'd explored with exacting attention to detail. When the hospital had called, waking him but not her, he'd been reluctant to answer, not wanting to extricate himself from her strong, clinging limbs. At the memory, his penis gave an enthusiastic lurch—which he ruthlessly ignored.

He had to ignore it, because he wanted to crawl back into bed with her too damn badly.

E-mail could wait. Perching the damned readers on his nose, he rolled his office chair more squarely into the knee well, and reached for the thick envelope that hadn't been there yesterday. Heavy ivory parchment sealed with red wax, and undoubtedly hand-delivered, Lyudmila's ornate handwriting rivaled that of any professional calligrapher. He broke the seal, extracted the invitation, and read. He was cordially invited to a gathering at the Lake Minnetonka home of Lyudmila and Stanton, *et cetera, et cetera*, and so forth. He squinted at the tiny letters engraved at the bottom left of the invitation. Black tie, the first week of September.

Labor Day was almost here. Where had the summer gone?

He'd have to attend; Lyudmila, Stanton, and their daughter were his. On the positive side, going to the party would give him an opportunity to observe Mila in a non-medical setting. He sorted through the layers of card stock and translucent vellum, found the RSVP card, replied Yes, and sealed his response in the envelope which was provided. Picking up his phone, he updated his calendar.

Would Tia attend? He glanced at the messy mound of clothes still lying on the floor—the thong, the shorts, the well-worn concert T-shirt she'd stripped off and so carelessly dropped—and tried to imagine her wearing a formal gown, or a dress that was in any way appropriate for the occasion. Such a dress wouldn't quite come into focus, but he could visualize removing it.

Very, very slowly.

"Damn it," he whispered. From the worn, accordion-pleated file folder that rarely left his desk, he withdrew a copy of the picture of him, Bram, and Deirdre, standing outside the Lyceum Theatre. Though the picture was black and white, Deirdre's vivid green gown was seared into his memory. That night, he'd been proud as the proverbial peacock, so proud that she was with him. Proud of the covetous looks other men cast his way. Proud of the knowledge that, no matter how much of herself she gave her audience that night, *he'd* be the one to remove the dress when the night was over. Proud that she'd chosen him.

But, as it turned out, not him alone.

Tossing the picture to the desk, he turned to his email. With Halloween on the horizon, his digital alert had routed too many ads for costumes, fangs, coffins, and capes his way. He quickly deleted them so he could better assess the remaining emails, the ones whose contents might lead people to suspect that real vampires walked the earth, and had for several millennia.

There were two new journal entries on Renfield's Syndrome, the psychiatric condition in which a patient developed an obsession with drinking blood, but it was the press release announcing a new reality show filming in Romania that drew his immediate attention. Though the Draculesti family had contributed nothing but their colorful last name to Bram's legend, the poor family hadn't been able to shake the Dracula association…an association *he* relentlessly, ruthlessly, and anonymously perpetuated whenever the opportunity arose. The fact that enterprising Romanian locals continued to make the most of the situation, turning Dracula lore and vampire myths into a thriving tourist industry, helped ease his conscience somewhat.

He went to the humans' Wikipedia, to the entries that were the most powerful magnets for Dracula buffs, crypto-zoologists, cosmetic dentists, and conspiracy theorists. No one had updated either the Dracula or Draculesti pages within the last week, but Bram's entry had been modified. He clicked through and skimmed the file he knew as well as he knew his own circulatory system. There, near the bottom, was a link to a new article on the Vlad Tepes/Dracula connection.

As he read, the oil slick in his stomach spread. Though the article had been published at a pop culture website rather than in a peer-reviewed scholarly journal, the author referenced material from Bram's own research notes discounting the Draculesti family connection. "Damn it." There was too much truth in the article for comfort, more accuracy than he could allow. He clicked on the edit button—

"What are you mumbling about?" Tia's arms wrapped around his bare shoulders from behind. "Mmm," she purred. "You're all warm from the sun."

A shiver went through him as she kissed her way from his shoulder to his neck, then up to his ear. He hadn't heard her wake up, or even get out of bed.

She gestured to the laptop with her chin. "What are you doing?"

"Working." He brought his lips to hers, as much to distract her as anything else. Maybe if he kept her occupied, she wouldn't notice what—

"Bram Stoker's Wikipedia page," she said blandly. "Isn't that interesting?"

He gave what he hoped was a casual shrug. "I like to monitor what's going on in online vampire lore."

"You're not monitoring, you're editing." She paused. "You're really good at that."

"What do you mean?"

"Oh, stop with the lawyerly dissembling already."

She gestured to the picture lying on the desk, the one he hadn't put back in the file where it belonged. "You recently made significant changes to your own biography."

He lifted a brow. "You question my right to do so?"

"Not at all." Reaching over his shoulder, she grabbed his coffee cup and took a healthy swig. Her bare breasts flattened against his upper back. "I'm more interested in why." Setting down the cup, she picked up the picture. "Deirdre d'Amour." Her tone was as neutral as he'd ever heard. "She's very beautiful."

She was right. Being on the receiving end of such dissembling *was* maddening. "How do you know her name?"

"Wyland, I'm an investigative journalist who just got access to the Archives. The first thing I did was pull your bio, all the Council Members' bios, and make local copies for my research notes."

He should have left well enough alone.

"Tell me about Bram. About her."

Her boundaries were wide open. He sensed no jealousy—she was honestly interested—but talking to his current lover about a former lover was very poor form. "Bram and I were friends for a time." Until Bram revealed he was writing a vampire story, which was too much of a coincidence.

"It's so cool that you know the man who wrote *Dracula*," she enthused. "This picture was taken at the Lyceum Theatre?"

He nodded. "Bram was the theatre's business manager. Miss d'Amour was an actress."

"And your lover, of course." Reaching over his

shoulder, Tia stroked his photographed face with her turquoise fingertip. "I can see why you'd choose her. Vampire, right? She's absolutely gorgeous."

"As are you." Actually, the two women shared distinct physical similarities. Deirdre would have coveted Tia's multi-colored eyes and Crayola-tipped hair, but they were both redheads, with near-translucent, finely grained complexions. Deirdre had been taller, but the women had killer curves in common.

Apparently he had a type.

But had he chosen Deirdre, or had she targeted him? After he and Deirdre had become lovers, he'd practically abandoned his private estate, spending too much time, distracted, in her bed. He wasn't the only man who'd done so.

"Why delete her information from your bio?" Tia asked quietly.

Because he hadn't wanted her to learn that Deirdre had cheated on him. That he'd been so easily duped, tugged around by his privates. That he'd made such stupid, costly mistakes.

How interesting that, at his age, he could still discover new sources of shame.

"You know Bailey's going to restore the file, right? After I tell her you deleted so much information? Because I'm definitely going to tell her."

Despite their unexpected enmity at the meeting last night, the two women were becoming thick as thieves.

She shivered as the air conditioning came on with a mighty wheeze. "Let's continue this discussion under the covers." Before he quite knew what was going on, she picked up the coffee cup, took him by the hand, and led him back to the tumbled bed.

So easily led—again—but damn it, in bed with Tia Quinn was exactly where he wanted to be.

They propped the pillows against the headboard and settled in under the covers. She took a sip from the mug, then companionably handed it to him. "So, tell me, straight up. What's your deal with *Dracula*?"

Her wide-open mind was a surprisingly comfortable place. He couldn't perceive a single whiff of judgment. Accepting the mug, he sipped slowly, giving himself time to think.

He was actually considering it—actually considering whether to reveal the shameful secret he'd kept hidden for so long, even from Valerian. The air felt thin, as if he was standing naked on the summit of Everest. His next step, regardless of direction, would send him tumbling down the mountain.

Better she know now, before this went any further, exactly how fallible a leader—how fallible a *man*—he could be. "My carelessness gave Bram the idea for his book."

She didn't react. Didn't say anything. Didn't seem to notice that finally saying the words aloud had sent him into an emotional free-fall. Instead, she sat there with a distinct lack of expression on her face.

How…annoying.

The wind-up clock on the bedside table ticked away the seconds, stretching his nerves to the snapping point. Finally, he set the coffee mug on the bedside table. "Say something."

She opened her mouth. Closed it, then opened it again. "You're the inspiration for Dracula?"

Why did she sound delighted rather than aghast?

Her pupils were dilated, and her fangs were— "No," he snapped. "Deirdre and I spent a lot of time with Bram. Soon after making our acquaintance, he started writing his vampire book, a book that's wildly popular to this day." He pressed his lips together. "I wasn't careful enough. He saw...something that put our people at risk."

She tipped her head to the side, as if considering his words. Her shoulders suddenly lurched under his hands. Then, she laughed—a long, belly-clutching laugh that shook the bed. "Seriously?" she gasped out. "I'm sorry, but...really? *This* is your huge, existential burden?"

He stared at her. "I'm glad the exposure of our culture's existence to humanity provides you with such amusement."

"I'm sorry." Another hiccup of laugher escaped. "Really." She laid an apologetic hand on his arm. "But...are you serious?"

And here he'd thought her an intelligent woman. "My lack of vigilance might have been responsible for Bram's book, a book whose popularity exposed our existence to the world."

Tia shifted in the bed, looking at him directly. The blanket shifted, baring her beautiful, berry-tipped breasts to his gaze. "How do I put this politely?" She tapped her index finger against her lips, considering. "Sir, you're tripping balls."

He reared back.

"Though I shouldn't be surprised," she continued. "You have an oversized habit of taking responsibility for things that are completely out of your control."

"What?"

"You heard me." She rested her hand over his

galloping heart. "It's not like Bram invented vampires. *Varney the Vampire* was published at least fifty years before *Dracula* was."

Exasperated, Wyland leaned back against the mound of pillows. Of course she was disagreeing with him; she did so for sport. But...she had a valid point—a very *small* point—about *Varney*. Bram's own notes indicated he'd researched known vampire lore quite thoroughly, delving into regional superstitions, Eastern European history, and local folklore. Bram had heartily enjoyed gothic novels, reading them until they were ragged.

Had Bram simply wanted to write a vampire story?

No. The fact that Bram's vampires so enthusiastically drank blood from their victim's necks was too much of a coincidence. How many times had Bram seen him nibbling Deirdre's neck? If he looked at that damned picture closely enough, he'd see barely-healed bite marks. His...intemperance had put his people at risk.

And by revealing so much of himself to Tia, he'd done the same thing.

He'd made a horrible mistake. Again. How many centuries would it take for him to learn his lesson?

The mattress shifted. "Wyland." Before he realized her intention, she'd straddled him—all the better to look down at him with a severe expression he found oddly arousing. "Even if what you suspect about Bram's inspiration is true—and I'm not saying it is— think about the outcome."

How was he supposed to think when her breasts were shimmying mere inches from his mouth? When his blood supply was flowing away from his brain, pooling in his cock?

"The popularity of Bram's book tipped vampires firmly into the *fictional* realm," she explained. "You might actually have *helped* us preserve the secret of our existence."

"That's a mighty charitable interpretation."

"But a potentially accurate one." She shifted her weight, squirming against his stiffening cock. "Did you see the local media coverage about the Zombie Pub Crawl?"

He shook his head.

She slipped off his reading glasses, carefully folding the bows before setting them on the nightstand, then speared her fingers into his hair. "A couple of years ago, Minneapolis earned a Guinness World Record for the largest number of zombies gathered in a single place. We could do the same thing with vampires, and no one would think anything of it." The fingers tightened. Tugged. "Wyland, vampires have saturated pop culture to such a degree that we could walk into the Mall of America with gaping bite wounds, our fangs dripping blood, and no one would look twice."

His fangs tingled as he stared at her neck. The place where he'd bitten her earlier was completely smooth, fully healed. "Mall security certainly would."

"Well, sure—but they'd think we were cos-players. Or weirdos." She lowered her head. Nibbled at his earlobe with her sharp little teeth. "The possibility that we were real vampires would never cross their minds in a million years."

"But—"

"Stop. Just stop beating yourself up. Not everything is your responsibility." She dropped a kiss on his temple, right at the border where hair met skin.

Her fingernails bit into his skull, sending delicious zings down his spine. "Not everything is your fault."

She was dead wrong about the responsibility issue, but he could tell she believed what she was saying. It was the height of self-indulgence, but he wanted to believe her, just for a little while. To be the admirable, sensual man her thoughts reflected back at him.

Deirdre was dead. Bram was dead.

And damn it, they were alive.

Spearing his fingers into her hair, he tugged her head toward his. Their lips met in a silky tangle, clinging, changing to get another angle. She tasted of bold coffee, and even bolder desire. Her hips made maddening circles against his cock, scorching him through the thin fabric of his cotton workout pants.

Rising up on her knees, she pulled the drawstring at his waist. "Take these off."

The wicked images in her mind... He'd barely worked the waistband over his hips when her lips enveloped his cock with hot, maddening suction.

"Bloody hell." He closed his eyes, clenched his jaw, and let her drag him down.

✸

"Wow." Tia stepped into Wyland's decadent shower enclosure and closed the tempered glass door behind her. Water fell in a soft rainforest patter from multiple shower heads, and down at the far end, a wide fixture spilled a tumbling foot-wide waterfall. "This isn't a shower, it's a water park." Choosing the rainforest, she stood in the center of the stall, lifted her arms, and hummed as the water streamed down her body.

This sinful playground of a shower? The high thread count bedsheets? Wyland's shiver of reaction as her hair brushed his bare abdomen, and how she'd found him luxuriating in a sunbeam, like a very satisfied cat? Wyland was a closet sensualist.

And his mental shields dropped, utterly and completely, when he had an orgasm.

Did he realize it? Deirdre d'Amour likely had, no doubt taking full advantage, the perilous, blood-sucking bitch. Tia didn't know the full story yet, but she'd gotten the gist: Deirdre had cheated on him. Wyland's sexual confidence, and his ability to trust, had taken cataclysmic hits. It was going to be her distinct pleasure to help build both back up again— not that *his* reaction to *her* wasn't a damn healthy ego boost.

Watching his eyelashes flutter as he'd fed from her was one of the most beautiful things she'd ever seen.

Her previous lovers had almost all been creative types—musicians, chefs, novelists. It was one thing to watch Chadden putter around the kitchen nude as he whipped up a decadent dessert, or to hear a song a former lover had written played on the radio, but lust slithered through her just watching Wyland *read*. Those rectangular-framed reading glasses? Utterly modern, and absurdly hot.

Now that she and Wyland had been pulled into each other's orbit, the attraction, like gravity, was undeniable. She'd explored every inch of the long, lean body he kept covered with his severely tailored clothes. She knew the salty tang of his skin. Knew the resilient give of his shoulder muscles as her fingernails dug in. She'd found a dozen places on that long, lean body that, when touched or stroked, made him squirm with pleasure.

Made him beg for more.

The water slid over her still-sensitive neck, where he'd pierced her skin with his long, sharp teeth. She'd known full well Wyland's decision to drink from her was logical and self-serving. She was a risk he needed to manage, for himself and for the species he governed, and having even superficial access to her thoughts and emotions helped. Sure, she'd yearned—burned—for his bite, but she'd also wanted to ease his mind.

Cold air suddenly gusted. "Gah!"

"Hello." Wyland stepped into the shower enclosure, surprising her. She would have bet serious cash money against him accepting the invitation to join her.

"Tia."

"Yes?"

"Your singing voice is…"

She let the silence hang for a couple of beats, then burst into laughter. "It's horrible, I know. I have the ability to assess a song for craft, and describe its merits to others, but I can't carry a tune to save my life." Reaching for the clever wall-mounted container holding body-cleaning products, she pumped shower gel into her hand. The subtle ice water scent—Wyland's scent—turned her knees to noodles. Stiffening them, she rubbed her hands together to create a mound of foam. "I'm so damn jealous of Scarlett I could spit. Honestly, it's a miracle we're even friends."

His lips quirked as he stepped under one of the

shower heads.

She stared at his mouth, mesmerized. She could count how many times she'd seen him smile using the fingers of one hand.

He tipped his head back and stood under the water. The hot spray drenched and darkened his hair, slapping against his shoulders and sluicing down his frame. Her gaze followed the water as gravity dragged it down, down.

"We'll never get out of this bathroom if you keep looking at me like that." His voice was low and rough, and despite the steamy heat, his nipples stood out in sharp little points. His cock was at half-staff, and climbing.

She grasped it with her foam-covered hands. "And that's a bad thing, why?"

A frustrated groan rumbled. "I have a meeting at Sebastiani Labs in less than two hours. It's going to take me over half that time to drive there."

The commute from Marine on St. Croix to Chanhassen was a haul and a half under the best of conditions. "Okay, I'll take a rain check." She innocently lathered her breasts.

Swearing under his breath, he reached for the shampoo. "What are your plans for the night?"

Biceps and triceps flexed as he worked the shampoo into his hair. The ice water scent sharpened, intensified. White lather drifted down the wet strands, fell to his shoulders, slipped down his chest—

"Tia? What are your plans for tonight?" he repeated.

With a blink, she dragged her gaze back to his face. "I have a story to write for *ILQ*. Then some paperwork, and some phone calls to make." She had to start researching property records—who owned the suburban home-turned-sex-dungeon where Robert Johnson had been killed?—and she needed to return a call from one of her street contacts, who'd tipped her off to possible trafficking activity out of a motel in Maplewood. Scarlett had left a voice mail saying she going stir-crazy, that she wanted some company at Underbelly that night.

And her mother had left a message, asking whether she was attending a party that Lyudmila and Stanton were having over Labor Day weekend. She hadn't seen an invitation yet, but of course she was going; the glamorous and powerful vampires were two of the foundation's most generous patrons. She'd have to dress up. Network. Work the room.

A light film of guilt settled over. She hadn't talked to her mom since she moved into Vamp Central. Her mother wouldn't need a blood bond to know she and Wyland were lovers. The woman was shock-proof, but...what would she think about her daughter sleeping with the Vampire Second? The mismatch seemed obvious, until one had the privilege of seeing beyond Wyland's austere surface.

What could she say to ease her parents' minds? "I've seen his O-face" probably wouldn't cut it.

He rinsed the last of the shampoo from his hair. "Do you have everything you need to work from here?"

Shaking off the worry, she nodded. "Your network is lightning-fast." And incredibly secure, given the highly sensitive work Wyland did from his home office. "Does Valerian use computers?" She hadn't seen one in his bedroom or sitting room.

"He used to, but no longer." A wisp of sadness,

there then gone. "If he wants to use the Internet, Thane or I help him."

Tia pumped shampoo into her hand, and started washing her own hair. "After work, I'm starting some boundary training with Valerian and Thane."

Wyland reached for the conditioner. "Thane will start off with machine training, but it shouldn't be long before you're ready to move on to advanced techniques."

Of course he knew the details; he'd probably worked with Thane on the damned lesson plan. Was there no aspect of her life he hadn't utterly invaded?

No. There wasn't. She was living under his roof. Working with him. Sleeping with him, in *his* bed, sharing her body and her mind. An overwhelming need to wrest some control back nearly knocked her sideways. She started scrubbing again, her movements sharp and jerky. "And I need to go to my house for a while."

"Why?"

Because it's my house. Because I live there. Because that's where I'll return after this is over. "Because I say so," she said flatly. "The why doesn't matter."

He looked at her, no doubt trying to navigate the minefield she'd laid with her tone. "Of course the why matters," he said. "Nick, or one of the other guards, can retrieve whatever you need."

And surf on the comfortable wave of his power? His money? *I don't think so.* "I don't want Nick, or one of the other guards, digging through my underwear drawer."

Something feral flitted through his eyes. "Thane can launder what you brought with you—"

"No. He won't." The thought of Thane, or anyone

else, doing her laundry absolutely horrified her. "It's not just the panties." She needed to pick up her mail. Lyudmila's party invitation no doubt waited, and a text message RSVP would *not* suffice. She needed to check her closet to see if she had anything to wear. She suspected not—her last donation to the prom dress place had been a sizable one. "Am I supposed to drag Nick, or a guard, dress shopping with me?"

"Yes," he replied. "Whenever you leave this house, if Thane or I aren't with you, Nick or one of his guards is."

She goggled at him. "For how long?"

"Until I know you're safe, damn it!"

She jerked as his voice ricocheted off the tiles. As his fear filled the enclosure.

He was deathly afraid. Afraid for her.

She stepped into his arms. Felt them wrap, too tightly, around her.

Water streamed over them. She rested her cheek against his chest, waiting until his heart stopped thundering against her ear. "Okay," she murmured. "I'll allow Nick or one of the other guards to accompany me when I leave the house." She could give him that much. "I'll take reasonable precautions, but Wyland? I will live my life."

"Thank you." He kissed her temple. "You still have shampoo in your hair."

His lips were skating down her cheekbone, and his penis was rock hard. Mere millimeters separated their wet, slippery bodies. "You have a meeting," she reminded him, drawing away. "Don't start something you can't finish."

"Can't finish?"

"Hurry along to work now," she teased, making a

shooing motion with her hands. "I'm going to enjoy this playground of a shower for a bit longer." She brushed away a fleck of foam clinging to her nipple. "All by my lonesome."

He kissed her, a soft, lingering kiss with barely-banked sexual heat. She'd just opened her mouth to stoke the fire when he backed away with a groan of the damned and left the shower. He grabbed a towel, slung it around his hips, and with a curse and a final backwards glance, walked out of the room.

She stared at his terry-covered ass until it disappeared from view. Giving herself a mental shake, she moved under the waterfall, planning her evening as she finished rinsing her hair. After spending some time with Scarlett at Underbelly, she'd swing by her house, if only for a while.

If only to prove that she could.

CHAPTER THIRTEEN

Gangsta rap pounded out of Underbelly's legendary sound system, but it was the scent that hit Dominic like an uppercut. Perfume and cologne, musk and sweat. Beer, wine, top-shelf liquor.

Sex.

"Thanks so much for celebrating with me," Mila said. They walked single file through the metal detector, then joined hands as they entered the club.

"Hey, it's not every day someone gets such a nice promotion. Of course we have to celebrate." Though when Mila had called him with the news, celebrating had been the very last thing on his mind.

His father had tried to shift earlier that day. It hadn't gone well.

After the doctors left his hospital room, his dad, face etched with fatigue and hair damp with sweat, had gestured him closer to the bed. "I know I can count on you to do the right thing when the time comes." What the fuck did that mean? Just as he'd been about to ask, a team of too-cheerful nurses had come in to bathe his father, and see to his bladder and bowel needs.

He'd never been so glad to leave a room in his life. His father deserved a better son.

"I love Guilty Pleasures night," Mila said.

She wasn't the only one. Once a month, Sasha Sebastiani let her freak flag fly, pleasing herself and everyone else with her eclectic music choices. The place was packed. The mass of writhing bodies overflowed the dance floor; people were dancing on the stage. Up on the second and third floors, all the tables were full, and people who couldn't find seats were wedged into spaces along the balcony rails. Every chair, table, booth, and banquette was taken, and the area around the nearest bar looked like a rugby scrum. "Back bar?" he half-hollered into her ear. "There might be fewer people back there." She nodded. Grasping her hand more firmly, he shouldered his way through the crowd.

"Hey, Dom."

He turned toward the raised voice. Over near the wall, some buddies from work sipped beer. "Hey," he called back, waving but not stopping. Their brows lifted when they saw whose hand he held. Craned even higher when they noticed what she was wearing.

Never in a million years would he have guessed that Mila Stanton owned a pair of leather pants, much less that she'd look so fucking hot wearing them. She wasn't wearing a bra, either. Her tiny breasts shifted beneath the silky, long-sleeved blouse, and her nipples jutted against the fabric. In a club where there was so much skin on display, somehow *she*, fully covered, was the one who made him want to howl and rut. Her scent, a mysterious combination of shampoo, leather, and pheromones, grabbed him by the balls.

Her fingers tightened around his.

Why was she here with *him*? Whatever the reason, he wasn't about to question his luck.

The crowd thinned as they approached the back

bar, and he soon saw the reason why. The big table located adjacent to the bar was crawling with Underworld Council members and their bondmates. Before he realized what was happening, a man and a woman who hadn't been there a second ago blocked their path. He, Mila, and the people walking alongside them found themselves redirected to a path well away from the table.

Security. Very subtle, very slick—and given the importance of the people who sat at that table, very, very smart.

How many people knew *he* was responsible for putting that fearsome expression on Lukas Sebastiani's face? With his heavily pregnant bondmate at his side, the big man positively radiated menace.

"There," Mila suddenly said, pointing at an opening that had appeared at the bar.

He bulldozed his way into the gap. "What would you like to drink?"

"Tequila shot, please."

He ordered two. As they waited, Mila tucked herself under his arm and told him about her new office. "It has a door! And bookshelves! And a leather chair!" As she spoke, he took occasional glances at the big table. Sebastiani's attention was glued to his bondmate. Seated at Scarlett Fontaine's other side, Jack Kirkland coolly eyed the crowd. Behind Jack, Antonia Sebastiani swayed to the music, her arms looped around the waist of a woman with silver lips and a punky crew cut. The rest of the table—Bailey Brown, Rafe Sebastiani, Lorin Schlessinger, and her bondmate, Gabe Lupinsky—talked, drank, and laughed up a storm. In a massive case of the randoms, Chadden, the vampire chef, sat next to Bailey Brown.

His hand rested on the hip of the curvy brunette using his thigh as a chair.

Tia Quinn, socializing and sucking up instead of speaking truth to power.

A spike of rage hammered him. Lukas Sebastiani suddenly angled his head, his nostrils flaring.

Shit.

"Dominic?" Mila pointed to their shots, now sitting on the bar.

Calm down. He paid for the drinks, handed her one of the small glasses, then lifted his in a toast. "To your well-deserved promotion."

Mila laughed. "You don't know whether it's well-deserved or not."

"Of course I know." She had beauty *and* brains, something it paid to remember. "*Skol.*" He tossed back the shot, savoring the smooth, silky burn. "That's good."

"Right?" After a tiny, testing sip, she slammed the shot. After a gasp, she flashed him a happy grin.

Looked like the woman could handle her liquor.

"Let's dance," she said.

He set the empty glasses on the bar, then led her toward the packed dance floor. As they melted into the crowd, the music slowed to the lazy, sexy grind that seemed to be Sasha Sebastiani's specialty.

Mila wound her arms around his neck, flattening her breasts against his chest. "Finally," she murmured against his ear. "An excuse to get my hands on you in public."

Excitement sizzled under his skin, and he draped his arms around her narrow waist. She was so small, but her muscles were strong and lithe. As the music played on, he pulled her closer, losing himself in sensation, in lights, in motion. In the feel and smell of her. He was an okay dancer, but she was a natural. All he had to do was hold her, and sway to the sound. Give her something to grind against. She was riding his thigh like a saddled pony.

Beneath his jeans, he was hard as a barbell. He clenched his jaw and scanned the room, looking for something—anything—to distract himself. Much more of this and he'd come in his pants, right here on the damn dance floor— "Shit." He stumbled.

There, at the edge of the dance floor, Jacoby Woolf sat in one of those electric scooter things, a statuesque blonde draped across his lap. One of the Beta's hands worked the controls so the chair moved with the music, and the other rested low on the woman's hip. Their heads were close together. Whatever she whispered made him smile.

They looked...happy.

A wave of helpless fury nearly blasted him broadside.

Mila grinned. "They look like they're having fun."

If the rumors were true, the Beta could barely walk anymore, but damned if Woolf and the sexy blonde didn't make dancing on a high-end Hoveround look pretty damn hot. Dom was tempted to whip out his phone and take a picture.

He could show his father that it was possible to have...a life.

"Hey." When Mila lifted a hand to his cheek, he realized they weren't dancing anymore. "Are you okay?"

A giant hand was squeezing his throat, and his chest was about to explode. "Could we get out of here?" There were too many incubi, succubi, and faeries here who could too easily get an emotional bead on him. On the other hand, it might be nice if someone could tell him exactly what he felt.

He was so fucking confused.

"Sure," she said. "Let's go."

Weaving through the jostling crowd, they worked their way to the perimeter of the room, giving the Beta, and the big table in the back, a very wide berth. They walked toward the exit. When the doors closed behind them, leaving them in the lobby of the Sebastiani Building, there was sudden, blessed silence.

Mila sidled close, her lips grazing his jaw. "Could I interest you in a tour of my new office? And of what I'm not wearing under these pants?"

Lust kicked high and hard. He spared a thought to the piled-up laundry at home, to the mound of dishes he told his mom he'd take care of. To the hours of research awaiting him behind his father's closed office door, and to the next set of letters he needed to write. He still had to figure out what was going on at that storage facility—

"Dom." She cupped his cock.

Hell, if Scarlett Fontaine, Jacoby Woolf, and Tia Quinn could laugh and relax and enjoy themselves despite everything happening in their lives, so could he.

Damn it, so could he.

He leaned over, clasped her head, and gave her a tongue-tangling kiss. "Lead the way." He couldn't wait to lose himself in Mila's body. Grab onto her.

Grab onto something, just for a little while.

✳

Standing just outside the door to Valerian and Thane's sitting room, Wyland watched Tia and Thane stare into each other's eyes. Valerian was nowhere in sight, and the biofeedback machine sat, abandoned, in the corner.

"Block me, Tia."

"I'm trying."

"You're trying too hard," Thane said.

It looked like it. Tia's hair was up in a sloppy bun, and the curly tendrils at her hairline were damp with sweat. If Thane had abandoned machine training already, Tia was progressing at a highly accelerated pace.

"Just relax, use your instincts. You're part faerie; you know how to do this." Thane's voice was as smooth as melted chocolate. Tia might not recognize the slight bit of thrall, but he did.

"But trying to repel you is like using my instincts in reverse. My instinct, my default, is to stay wide-open. To absorb, to perceive."

"But you'll react—protect—when you perceive people are in danger?"

"Of course. Who wouldn't?"

Plenty of people, but that was beside the point. In one training session, Thane had identified her instinctive lever, her primal trigger. He'd mined the deepest veins of her mind, and had hit pay dirt.

"Visualize the castle moat," Thane murmured. "The castle is under attack. The people inside are in danger."

The moat, the drawbridge. Thane was trying to use the same visualization technique to teach Tia as he'd used with him, hundreds of years ago. The same technique Wyland used to this day.

"The castle is mine," Thane rumbled. "You cannot succeed."

"This isn't working," Tia said, exasperated. "I keep visualizing the *Enterprise* dropping its shields."

"Okay, forget the castle," Thane said. "I'm a...Kardashian, attacking the *Enterprise*."

Tia snorted a laugh. "I think you mean a Cardassian."

"Bah, they're both toast. Protect your ship, girlie."

Her smile dissolved. "Bring it."

The fanciful cuckoo clock in the corner ticked off the seconds as they dueled with their eyes, with their thoughts. Thane kept his expression neutral, but Tia's face reflected the effort it took for her to stave off Thane's mental bludgeoning. Her eyes narrowed, then bulged. Her lips tightened. Her fangs flashed as she gritted her teeth.

When she groaned, he barely held himself back.

"Extraordinary, isn't she?" Valerian murmured from behind him. "She's really giving him a workout."

Wyland clutched the door jamb with tense fingers, ready to leap. Across the room, Thane narrowed his eyes, testing, then grinned. "Your shields are holding." He wiped a bead of perspiration from his temple. "Congratulations."

Shoving to her feet, she did a victory dance around Thane's chair, nearly losing her balance when she spiked an imaginary football. "I did it! I raised my shields and vanquished your Bird of Prey."

"Yes, you did." Thane gave her a high-five, followed by a hearty hug.

"What's a Bird of Prey?" he murmured to Val.

"Klingon warship. From *Star Trek*."

Thane saw them over by the door. "Did you guys see that?"

"Yes," Valerian said as they entered the sitting room. He hugged her. "That was beautifully done, my dear."

As Tia talked with Val and Thane, spilling her unique brand of faerie-dust charm over the men, Wyland focused on the line of sweat darkening her T-shirt along the spine. Yes, what they'd seen was a great start, but Thane had given her advance warning. Once Tia could reliably repel a surprise attack, she'd be less susceptible to being thralled by older, stronger vampires. And then the *real* work would start, with her learning how to shield her thoughts from someone with whom she shared a blood bond.

Training he could assist with, because she'd shared her blood with him.

Across the room, Thane's eyes danced.

Tia approached him. She was tired, but healthily so, exhilarated by her accomplishment. Grasping his tie, she pulled his head down and kissed him—just a light kiss, a gentle meeting of pursed lips. As if touching and kissing him in front of his family was something that happened every day.

"Hello," she said softly.

"Hello." He could still smell Chadden on her body. He hadn't known she planned to go to Underbelly, or to any of the other places Nick's report had mentioned. Instead of staying here, safely at her desk as he'd envisioned—as she'd led him to believe—Tia and Nick had crisscrossed the greater Twin Cities metro area since he'd seen her last. After spending nearly an hour at Tia's house in Stillwater, they'd gone to a convenience store in Anoka, where

Tia had met with a young female—one of the sexually exploited teenagers she worked with?—while Nick stayed in the car. Then they'd gone to Underbelly, where she'd stuck to Diet Mt. Dew, distracted a very uncomfortable Scarlett, and chatted with Bailey and Chadden, sitting close enough to the other man that his scent had transferred.

On the other hand, Chadden had no doubt smelled *him* on *her*. *All* over her.

"What's that smile for?"

Nothing he could share with her. "I watched the last of your training," he said instead. "You seem to be a natural."

Though she shrugged off his compliment, she looked pleased. "Thane thinks something about my faerie blood amplifies my abilities, though we haven't yet figured out how." She bit her lip. "Sorry again about the machine," she said to Thane.

"No worries."

"What happened to it?" he asked.

"She blew it out on the first try."

Tia blew on her fingernails, then buffed them against her T-shirt. "My work here is done." Stepping back, she pivoted. "Guys, I really need a shower. Then…" She glanced at him over her shoulder. "I'm off to bed."

The look latched on, nearly tugging him along in its wake. It was a fight, but he held steady. "Good night," he managed.

"Good night, my dear," Valerian said as he and Tia kissed each other's cheeks.

Thane did the same. "Sleep well, Tia."

She went into the hallway. After a short pause, he heard a bedroom door open and close.

His bedroom door.

Blood pounded, hard and hot, in every extremity.

Valerian and Thane stared at him. "Follow her, you stupid git," Thane said. "Do you not recognize a sexual invitation when you receive one?" He turned to Val. "And here I thought we'd raised an intelligent man."

"So much for that genius-level IQ."

He shot them both a death glare.

"I wish you'd given me some advanced warning that you'd decided to take a lover," Thane continued. "I would have baked a cake to celebrate. No candles, of course. We wouldn't want to burn the house down, would we?"

Damn it. He'd never hear the end of this.

Thane glanced at his watch, then cursed. "I have dough that needs my attention."

Val's face lit. "Are you making cinnamon rolls?"

"Just for you." Leaning closer, Thane murmured something that made rosy color climb into Val's cheeks. They kissed, and Thane left the room.

Wyland simply stood there.

"Why so indecisive?" Val asked.

He opened his mouth, and then closed it again without saying anything. How could he put such confusion into words?

"She's nothing like Deirdre."

Trust Val to zero in on the crux of the matter.

"Come sit for a moment." Val headed for the couch. "These old bones of mine need a rest."

After a glance back at the hallway, Wyland followed, ready to support Val, but the other man waved him off. Old bones or not, Val looked strong and spry, and his cheeks were still ruddy with color.

Whatever Thane had murmured was effective medicine indeed. "Are we going to talk about the birds and the bees?"

Val laughed. "It's centuries too late for that. But seriously, Wyland—though they may share some surface similarities, Tia is nothing like Deirdre. Their personalities are like sun and shadow. Day and night."

It helped to hear Val say it, but....

"If that venal harpy wasn't already dead, I'd kill her myself," Val snapped.

"Why?"

"For causing you to question your own judgment for so long."

Wyland absorbed the bracing slap of his words. Recognized the truth in them.

"Your dedication to our people, and the decisions you make on their behalf, are impeccable. The work you do to protect our culture's history, and to ensure our species' survival, is undeniable. But your personal life has been a barren wasteland for far too long."

"That's a little strong. I have—"

"Friends? Family? Work colleagues? Of course you do." Val waved them off with a flick of his wrist. "But a lover? Ah, Wyland...a lover helps fill those dark, empty spaces. Believe me, the centuries are easier to bear with a partner at your side."

A partner? "Easy for you to say," he grumbled. "You and Thane have been together for centuries. You have history. He's proven himself trustworthy time and time again."

"Because I gave him a chance when we first met!"

He couldn't remember the last time Val had raised his voice, or flashed his fangs, in anger. Val's cheeks were cherry red, and a vein throbbed in his left temple. *Calm him down.* "I'm listening."

"Stop looking at me like I'm about to keel over," Val snapped. "I'm not going to die tonight."

Silence.

"Damn it, Wyland, you've sipped from the girl. If there was a single self-serving thought in her head, you'd know it already. Don't let a long-dead woman corrupt the relationship you could have with Tia. Do not give her that power."

"I'm working on it," he finally replied.

"Well, work harder," Val advised, exasperated. "Other men aren't stupid, or blind. Did you smell—"

"Yes."

"Good. She's very easy to talk to, isn't she? And the questions she asks! She's made me remember things I haven't thought about for hundreds of years. I've quite enjoyed our conversations, though I don't know who's going to listen to all the recordings she insists upon making."

If Val only knew the plans Tia had for those recordings.

"Wyland, she's passed every possible background check. She's never published information that could put our culture at risk, never even danced close to the line. Again and again, she's complied with our culture's confidentiality imperative, and she did so before we came to know her. She takes her responsibilities very seriously—so much so that she's etched a reminder on her very skin."

He raised a questioning brow.

"You don't know the origin of her tattoo?" Val shook his head in disgust. "Why am I not surprised. It's a line of dialogue from one of the *Star Trek* movies."

"I thought *Star Trek* was a TV show?"

"It's both. Anyway, the ship's first officer, Mr. Spock, enters a radiation-filled room and makes the repair that allows the *Enterprise* to escape their enemy, knowing all the while that doing so will kill him. When Captain Kirk realizes what Spock has done, he asks his friend why he made such a sacrifice. Spock, near death, replies, 'The needs of the many outweigh the needs of the few. Or the one.'" Val paused. "It's absolutely heartbreaking."

He'd traced the tattoo's cursive letters with his tongue, but hadn't asked her about its significance.

"Wyland, be honest with yourself. You wouldn't have allowed Tia anywhere near the Archives if you didn't, deep in your gut, already know you could trust her."

He wanted to deny Val's observation, but...he couldn't. He took a shaky breath. "Working with her at the Archives has been...enlightening," he admitted. "She can argue a subject from every perspective, seemingly judging none." Tia saw the world not in black and white, but in endless shades of gray. "She might not change my mind, but she makes me think very carefully about my position."

Val smiled, nodding. "A good partner challenges you."

His pulse gave a kick. "Who said anything about partners?" He was still coming to terms with the fact that he wanted to be Tia Quinn's lover.

"We need our partners to challenge us, Wyland," Val said, as if Wyland hadn't spoken. "The right partner does so in a manner that invigorates. That makes you feel enriched by the experience rather than diminished."

He crossed his legs to disguise his current state of…invigoration.

"An extraordinary woman has entered your life," Val murmured. "The man I raised would have the testes to do something about it."

"My testes have been plenty busy."

"Don't split sexual hairs with me, boy. Where are your guts, your gonads?"

"I told her about Bram," he admitted. "And about Deirdre." A little bit about Deirdre, at any rate.

"I'm glad."

Rising to his feet, he said, "Do you need anything before I leave? According to Thane, a lady just issued me an invitation. It would be rude to keep her waiting any longer."

Val waved him toward the door. "She broke a date with me to do so."

A bump of guilt. "Did you and Tia have plans?"

"Boundary training, then a movie."

Tia and her movies.

"*Blackula*, followed by an episodic television show called *Buffy the Vampire Slayer*." Val pursed his lips. "Her media collection is really quite fascinating."

"Last night, Tia suggested to me that movies, books, and TV shows have helped disguise the reality of our existence from humanity."

"She's right—so stop beating yourself up about Bram and Deirdre. Let it go," Val advised. His gaze shifted to the door, where Thane lounged against the door jamb. "Focus on the here and now, because tomorrow is promised to none of us."

Val was right; fate had put an extraordinary woman in his path.

Now he had to figure out what to do about it.

CHAPTER FOURTEEN

Wyland would have been happy to laze in bed for a few more hours, but Tia had other plans. "Come on," she said, dragging him into the garage. "If we hurry, we might make it to the animal barns before they close for the night."

Tia wanted to go to the Minnesota State Fair, and she wanted to drive. "Come on, live dangerously. My car's already scratched."

He'd considered her untreated car windows, and the angle of the setting sun. Live dangerously, indeed. He couldn't remember the last time he'd traveled in the daylight with nothing to protect him but VampScreen and his wits. With Val's comments about his gonads still ringing in his ears, he folded himself into her passenger seat.

She was a good driver, confident behind the wheel, but once at the Fair, she'd stopped in front of a parking space that was too small for the car. He pointed down the row, to an opening that could easily accommodate a small RV. "There's a good spot." One that wouldn't scrape the car's paint even more, or put his hips in a bloody vice when he tried to get out.

"This one's closer to the entrance."

"By a hundred feet." Given the miles they'd cover

on foot tonight, the additional distance seemed negligible.

After a fair amount of back and forth, and some colorful curses, she finally wedged the car into the space. If more than a foot separated his door from the Suburban parked next to them, he'd eat his shoe.

Tia eyed the sky. "We'll have to hurry if we want to visit the animal barns."

"I can smell them from here." The ripe scents of manure, hay, and animals wafted through the air.

"You're a doctor, I'm sure you've smelled worse." Tia grabbed her purse from the back seat. "Come on."

He slowly opened the car door, pivoted on the seat, and planted his feet on the pavement. Sucking in his stomach, he stood, then squirmed through the stingy space without unmanning himself. When he took his first step, he slipped, barely catching himself on the door jamb.

Melted ice cream.

"Are you okay?" Tia circled around to his side of the car and peered down at the melted mess. She bit back a giggle. "Oops."

"Is that…bacon? In the ice cream?"

"Probably." She leaned down. "Yep."

"That is absolutely disgusting."

She shrugged. "It's the State Fair. If it's not on a stick, there's probably bacon involved."

Side-stepping to the front of the car, he used the patch of grass to scrape the gooey mess off his shoe.

"Ready?"

"As I'll ever be."

The sun was setting, and the sky was a hazy grayish-orange. As they paid at the gate, streetlights came on, illuminating paved streets carrying throngs of foot traffic. The bright lights of the Midway glowed in the distance, and across the fairgrounds, a band played at the Grandstand.

Tia sidled close, so their hips bumped together when they walked. Her arm suddenly curved around his waist, her hand sneaking into his back pocket. "Come on, you're supposed to reciprocate." Amusement danced in her eyes. "This is how lovers walk at the fair."

"Far be it from me not to conform to appropriate social norms." He slipped his hand into her pocket. Resilient flesh shifted beneath the soft denim as she walked. "I see the appeal."

"Right?" She gave his butt a squeeze. "One of the best things about coming to the fair is people-watching." A silent laugh shook her body. "I imagine we're amusing more than a few people right now."

He raised an inquiring brow.

"Look at us. You look like Gatsby minus his croquet mallet, and I look—"

"Delicious." Her denim shorts exposed a scandalous amount of skin, the frayed hems riding high on her thighs. The heavy purse she'd slung across her body pulled the neckline of her gauzy white shirt askew, exposing a bright purple bra strap. Her beat-up brown cowboy boots looked like they might have been worn to muck out a stall or two.

When a cow mooed from inside a nearby barn, she glanced at the sky again and sighed. "We probably only have time to visit one animal barn. How about the Petting Zoo?"

"Lead the way."

Several minutes later, they entered a red and white

barn filled with excited children, all up past their bedtimes. He watched as Tia patiently waited her turn to pet a baby lamb. Newborn chicks, all beaks and yellow fluff, huddled under a heat lamp. Next to where he stood, all the rabbits were asleep in wire crates. "Smart animals—ow!" Wheeling around, he glared at the SUV-sized stroller that had just clipped his heel. "Damn it."

The child in the stroller reached into the bucket of cookies sitting on his lap. Given how many crumbs rimmed the little human's mouth, it was far from his first. "Mommy, that man said a swear word."

The mom, cell phone at her ear, absently nodded. "Yes, hon. See the bunnies?" She returned to her conversation without bothering to apologize for nearly severing his Achilles tendon.

His lips flattened. Common courtesy wasn't so common after all.

"Swearing is bad," the boy solemnly advised him. "You're bad."

"So is eating so many cookies." The kid's blood sugar level had to be off the charts.

The kid's face crumpled. "Mommy!"

"Get away from my son!" the woman snapped, punching at a button on her phone. She shot him a dirty look as she wrestled with the gigantic stroller and hurried away.

Damned if the little devil didn't turn around and stick his cookie-coated tongue out at him.

Tia was suddenly at his side. "Come here. You have to feel how soft this is." Taking his hand, she drew him over to the lamb's pen. Crouching down, she held out her hand and allowed the days-old lamb to sniff her before stroking it gently under its chin.

"Feel this," she marveled.

He touched where she indicated, stroking the soft wool as she murmured to the animal. When the lamb bleated and trotted away, he pulled Tia to her feet. She was wearing the ring he'd returned to her earlier that evening. "Is this ring a family heirloom?"

She laughed, shaking her head. "It's the Gem of Amara from *Buffy the Vampire Slayer*. Thirty five bucks at Amazon.com."

"I'm almost afraid to ask, but what's the Gem of Amara?"

"According to the show's mythology, it's the Holy Grail of all vampiredom," she informed him. "It conveys complete invulnerability to whomever wears it. Stake wounds close, burns miraculously heal, you're immune to crosses and fire, yadda yadda yadda. The vamp who wears it can come and go in full daylight without regard for the sun."

He traced his finger over the gold strands encasing the green stone. The show's writers had been right about the sun susceptibility, but stake wounds? Crosses? "What complete and utter hokum."

"I know it's not real, but I like the idea of it. It's a talisman. Wearing it reminds me to live ferociously." She looked up at him. "Of course, on the show, its mere existence tempted far too many vampires into corruption. Angel destroyed it." Tia suddenly twisted. "Hey, stop that." The lamb was nibbling at the frayed threads dangling from Tia's jean shorts.

"Tastes good, doesn't she?" he said to the lamb, carefully pulling the fabric from its mouth. Pulling Tia safely out of range, he kissed the ring, her hand, then the veins of her inner wrist. As he worked his way up her forearm, he added a hint of teeth.

Dissolving into giggles, she yanked her arm away. "Let's go to the Midway."

With the animal barns closing, most fairgoers seemed to have the same idea. As they approached the Midway, the streetlights seemed to dim, like the house lights going down at the theatre just before the curtain rose. Blinking lights, clanging bells, whirling rides, joyous screams...talk about sensory overload. Everywhere he looked, lovers—yes—walked with their hands in each other's back pockets.

Tia suddenly veered toward a bright yellow structure. "Let's buy tickets."

"For what?"

"For whatever."

As they joined the short line, Tia cocked her head toward the Grandstand. "Fitz and Noelle are tearing it up tonight."

"You know the band?"

She nodded, smiling. "They played First Avenue earlier this year. Awesome show."

He'd never set foot in the venue Prince had made famous. He had no clue who Fitz and Noelle were, what band they were in, or how famous they might be.

The difference in their ages yawned wide as the English Channel.

When they reached the front of the line, Tia bought a fluttering strip of tickets, refusing his offer to pay. "See what I mean about hiding in plain sight?"

"Hmm?"

She jerked her head toward the Funhouse. "Those kids over there."

Sure enough, a pack of vampire youth lurked near the corner of the building, half of them with their fangs exposed.

It was a flagrant violation of law—*their* law.

He started toward them, but Tia held him back. "Wyland, look around. No one is paying them the least bit of attention—no more than they're paying anyone else, at any rate."

He looked around, at people from all walks of life, eating, drinking, and enjoying themselves. She was right. The humans were oblivious.

"Come on," she said, tugging at his arm.

"Where?"

"Let's go into the Funhouse." Her eyes sparkled with mischief. "We can neck in there."

One of the youths had noticed him. The teen's eyes widened. He nudged his friends, gesturing wildly. By the time he and Tia reached the entrance, they'd all straightened from their laconic slouches. Those with shot fangs hid them, as they damn well should.

"Gentlemen," he said.

"Sir. Miss." They dipped their heads respectfully— all except the teenager who stood most deeply in the shadows. He was too busy staring at Tia's legs.

Understandable. They *were* spectacular.

"Dude," someone hissed, elbowing the boy.

The movement jostled the young man's gaze up to their faces. "Sir. Miss," he blurted out, bobbing his head in greeting.

The hero worship in the boy's eyes made him feel like a groupie-nailing rock star.

He couldn't help it; he winked at the boy. "Have fun, guys. You're good for my reputation," he murmured as Tia handed tickets to the woman at the Funhouse entrance.

She rolled her eyes. "Says no one to me, ever." As

they climbed the stairs and walked inside, the lights dimmed to nearly nothing. "I thought I'd have to get tough with you about the Funhouse," she admitted. "Somewhere, deep in that straight-laced psyche of yours, a tiny sense of adventure lurks."

Straight-laced? He might have spent the last century celibate, but that hadn't always been the case. He'd seen things, done things, that would rob her of speech—and god knew his fantasies about her were absolutely debauched. Suddenly, his cock was hard as a pike, and his pulse pounded in a rhythm as old as time. "So, it's adventure you want?"

"Of course. Who doesn't?"

He whipped her around a corner, deep into the shadows, and pinned her against the plywood wall with his hips.

"What are you doing? Wyland, there are people— kids—all over the place."

He didn't need a blood bond to sense her arousal, to know she'd locked her knees to keep them from wobbling out from under her. Didn't need more light to know her pupils were ink black pools, or that her fangs had shot down. Her hitching breath, her shifting hips, enticed him. Incited him.

Jerking her arms over her head, he cuffed her wrists against the wall with his hands. He stared into her eyes, grinding the hard ridge of his erection into her soft belly. Her needy groan combined with the pre-recorded moans and shrieks. Suddenly, incendiary images filled his head: Tia, pressing *him* against the wall. Fumbling with his fly...cool air wafting over his penis...her fingers wrapping around him, stroking hard and fast.

This time, the groan was his. The little witch was

in his head.

She flexed her wrists against his fingers, glanced down at his groin, and raised a brow. "Care to release me?"

Did she have some siren in her lineage? The sultry invitation in her voice could lure a man to the rocks. She was pinned against a wall, but far from helpless. Her hands were shackled by his grip, held immobile, but he could almost feel them yank at his zipper.

Was she getting stronger, or was he simply more attuned to her needs and desires now that he'd sipped from her vein? Hell, if he ever allowed her to drink deeply from him—if they had a reciprocal blood bond—they'd never leave his bedroom.

His phone suddenly vibrated—one ring, then two, in a very familiar pattern. He backed away from Tia, releasing her arms. "I have to take this." Plucking his phone from his front pocket, he punched the Talk button. "Lukas, hello. What—"

"You have to come. Quick." Lukas sounded panicky. Frazzled.

"What's wrong?"

"Scarlett's water broke."

"When?"

"Earlier this afternoon," Lukas admitted. "She wouldn't let me call you."

But he was calling now. Scarlett had probably been in labor for hours.

In the background, he heard Scarlett call out to Lukas. The thread of panic in her voice cut like a saber. "We need you," Lukas said shakily.

"I'm on my way." He took Tia's hand and started leading her toward the entrance. "Scarlett's in labor," he murmured to her.

"Who are you talking to?" Lukas asked.

"Tia." As they pressed back against the wall to allow an incoming group to pass, a demonic wail split the air.

"Where the hell are you?"

The group passed, and they started walking again. "We're at the State Fair." He had to get Lukas focused, and fast. "We've prepared for this, right? Do you have your task list?"

"It's in my pocket." He heard a crinkle as Lukas removed the well-worn piece of paper from his back pocket. He'd carried it there for months, fondling it like a string of worry beads.

"What's item number one?"

"Make Scarlett comfortable," Lukas read. "Comfortable? Fuck, how am I supposed to do that? She feels like someone's stabbing her in the stomach." Lukas let out a gasp as Scarlett groaned again. "How do women do this?"

Bloody hell. Lukas, the strongest and most sensitive incubus on the planet, was sharing not only Scarlett's emotions, but her labor pains. Nothing about how Lukas's body responded to sensory stimuli should surprise him anymore, but...

"She wants to sit on the couch."

"Good, good. Sit down with her." The last thing he needed was for Lukas to keel over before help could arrive.

"Heads up," Tia murmured. They'd reached the Funhouse entrance.

"Hey!" The worker who'd taken their tickets didn't look happy. "You can't come out this way."

Tia jerked her thumb over her shoulder. "Medical emergency. He's a doctor." Without waiting for a response, she bullied her way down the stairs to a chorus of complaints. Once they reached the bottom, she navigated a route through the throngs of people filling the Midway, calling out apologies as she cut through the crowd.

"She's sitting on the couch now," Lukas told him.

"That's good. If she wants to walk, let her—it will help the labor advance." Though from the sound of things, her labor might already be more advanced than he'd like. A hush descended as they left the cacophony of the Midway. The crowd had thinned out considerably, so they put on a burst of speed. "What's the next item on the list?" he asked Lukas.

"Call Jack. Start the phone tree." A pause. "Jack's downstairs, in his office."

"Good." As Scarlett's pregnancy had progressed, Jack had quietly picked up whatever he could of Lukas's workload, piling it on top of his own. "Call him now, then focus on Scarlett. Get some rest if you can. Pretty soon you'll have more people at your place than you know what to do with." For some unfathomable reason, Scarlett had put almost a dozen names on her call list. "Claudette and Elliott will be there soon."

"Claudette." Lukas repeated her name like a lifeline. Scarlett's mother would preside at the birth, singing her granddaughter into the world in the ancient way of the sirens.

When they reached the parking lot, he saw that the Suburban was gone. Thank the universe for small favors; they'd need plenty of them this night. "Lukas, hang up and call Jack now."

"Okay." Silence hummed on the line. "Wyland...thank you."

"There's no need for thanks, my friend," he said softly. "It's my honor. Now—" he put some briskness back in his voice "—call Jack, then focus on Scarlett." They'd reached the car. Yanking open the passenger side door, he got in, then slammed it closed. "We'll be there soon. 'Bye." He hung up the phone with a punch of his thumb.

As soon as he buckled his seat belt, Tia put the car into motion. She backed out of the parking place, then carefully exited the lot, weaving around all the pedestrians who'd decided that *now* was the best time to leave the fair.

"Don't these people have homes?" he muttered.

As Tia joined the long line of cars waiting to turn north onto Snelling, he took mental inventory of the bag he'd transferred from his car's trunk to Tia's, and of the treatment room on Sebastiani Security's first floor. Between the two, he could perform minor surgery if he head to, but it wouldn't hurt to put an ambulance on stand-by, just in case something happened that was beyond his capabilities. He called Memorial and made the necessary arrangements. By the time he hung up, Tia was on Highway 36 westbound. "I think Lukas is in labor, right alongside Scarlett."

"What? Labor pains, the whole bit?"

He nodded.

"Ha! A female fantasy has finally come to pass. Seriously, you have no idea how many generations of women have been waiting for this moment. Not that we can tell anyone about it."

"Well, let's just hope his experience is limited to experiencing the pain." If Lukas's body tried to carry out labor to its logical conclusion, he could sustain serious internal injuries.

Yes, he had two patients tonight.

"All humor aside, that level of physical enmeshment isn't normal, is it? Not that I know anything about childbirth." Tia hit her blinker and passed a slow-moving semi. "My entire adult reproductive focus has been *avoiding* pregnancy."

Her words gave him a jolt. As her lover, he appreciated her diligence. *Trusted* it, given they'd made love at least twice without using a condom.

Without discussing the matter.

He could imagine Val's reaction— "If *that* isn't trust, what is?" —and he'd have a valid point. But…what would he do—what would *they* do—if, despite her birth control patch, Tia got pregnant? Did she want to have children?

Did *he*? It was a question he'd never considered.

"Wyland?" Tia waved a hand in front of his face. "Lukas's reaction isn't typical, is it?"

"No, it isn't." All sirens interpreted and amplified emotion with their voices, and all incubi and succubi absorbed emotional energy for sustenance, emitting pheromones in response, but… "Scarlett's voice is legendary, and Lukas's abilities are unmatched. Typical is completely off the table." And if typical was off the table, the list of potential complications was endless.

How would absorbing Lukas's pain-laced pheromones impact everyone else in the room? Shit, one more risk he hadn't considered. The people on Scarlett's list might really come to regret their invitation to Coco Fontaine's birthday party.

"Hey." Tia put her hand on his thigh. "You've got this."

He covered her hand with his own, taking comfort in its weight, its warmth. "With any luck, they won't need me at all."

"You're their friend. They need you there regardless. And when this night is over, I'll bring you your first glass of champagne." She tugged her hand from under his, putting both hands on the wheel again. The Washington Avenue exit was just ahead. "Get sloppy drunk if you want to, because I'm your designated driver."

"I'll keep your offer in mind." He'd never been sloppy drunk in his life, but there was a first time for everything. The events of the night to come might very well drive him to drink.

And by sunrise, Lukas and Scarlett's lives would have changed forever, their every future action and decision influenced by the needs and desires of a howling scrap of new life.

Something he'd never imagined wanting for himself.

Before tonight.

✺

When they reached Sebastiani Security, Tia followed Wyland through the lobby to the stairwell door, lifting a brow when he slapped his hand against the biometric pad instead of waiting for someone to buzz them up. There was a soft click, and the tiny light on the panel switched from red to green. "Come on." He opened the door and started up the stairs. "I can sense pheromones from here."

She nodded. "Pain. Pleasure. Purpose." Lukas was absorbing every nuance of Scarlett's physical and emotional experience and telegraphing it to the air—to everyone else—via the pheromones that pumped from his body as instinctively as he breathed.

Her ovaries twinged, like they did when she ovulated.

"It might be better if you went home."

"Why?"

"Lukas's pheromones will be challenging enough for bystanders to deal with, but add his family's reactions into the mix…"

Understanding came in an instant. Absorbing emotional energy and producing pheromones in response was an instinctive, autonomic behavior for all incubi and succubi. Members of the Sebastiani family would produce pheromones, too. The resulting feedback loop could be overwhelming.

It was one thing to surf the pheromone haze dancing at Underbelly. Experiencing labor, even second-hand, was another matter entirely.

"This is going to be an unpredictable experience for everyone concerned," Wyland said. "You should probably go home."

"And leave you to handle it alone? I don't think so. And that glare won't work. Save your energy for climbing the stairs." He sighed but didn't argue, confirming she'd made the right decision. "Let's get going."

By the time they reached the top floor, the air seemed thicker somehow, as if it had physical weight. Thankfully, she had some ibuprofen in her purse—

"Aaaahhereitcomesagain. Damn it damn it damn it damn it…"

Scarlett's groan speared her right between the eyes. The twinge low in her abdomen turned into an uncomfortable ache.

"Sounds like things are progressing." Wyland rang the doorbell, then opened his bag. He withdrew two plastic-wrapped packets, handed her one, and pocketed the other for himself.

Silicone earplugs. "Bless you."

The door opened. "Hello, Wyland." Scarlett's mother, Siren First Claudette Fontaine, seemed calmer than the situation merited. "Ms. Quinn." She cast a questioning glance at Wyland, but covered it quickly. "Please, come in. Don't let the cat out."

They entered the loft. Standing just inside the door, Lukas's father looked harried. Lukas's father, the president of the Underworld Council.

And here she was, looking like an extra from *Coyote Ugly*. She probably had shit on her boots from walking around at the fair. Wyland, with his khakis, loafers, and rolled-up shirtsleeves, looked elegantly casual, like he'd been sipping champagne in the Hamptons instead of necking in a sticky-floored funhouse.

Hell.

"Claudette. Elliott." Wyland kissed Claudette on both cheeks, then did the same with Elliott. "Please allow me to introduce Tia Quinn." A slight pause. "She and I were at the State Fair when Lukas called."

"Oh, what fun! I haven't been to the fair in years." Claudette extended both hands in welcome, kissing her cheeks. "I'm delighted to meet you."

She looked like she actually might be. "Please, call me Tia."

"And we're Claudette and Elliott."

Yeah, right.

"Tia." President Sebastiani leaned down to kiss her cheeks. "*In Like Quinn*, right? I've read some of your work."

"No shit?" She slapped her hand over her mouth.

He laughed. "No worries, I've heard the word before." He glanced over to the couch, where Lukas supported Scarlett, half-reclined in his arms. "Less than a minute ago, as a matter of fact." Indicating the living area with a sweep of his arm, he said, "Welcome to the madhouse. Make yourself at home."

Rafe and Bailey sat curled together on the sectional couch opposite Lukas and Scarlett, and Sasha and Antonia were squabbling in the kitchen. Jack paced by the windows, Calamity hot on his heels. It wasn't a madhouse; it was a family. In the short time it had taken her and Wyland to drive here from the fair, the entire Sebastiani family had gathered.

Wyland approached Lukas and Scarlett. "Happy Labor Day," he said, leaning down to kiss Scarlett on both cheeks.

"Seriously? You're making Labor Day jokes?" Despite her surly tone, Scarlett clutched his hands tightly. "Hi, Tia." If Scarlett was surprised to see her, it didn't show. "Where are my fucking drugs?"

Her siren's voice turned the words into weapons, but Wyland appeared unscathed. "I see things are progressing well."

"'Progressing well'? Shove that sarcasm up your aristocratic ass—ow ow ow ow!" She doubled over, clutching her stomach. "*Fuck* me, that hurts."

Did Wyland have some high-test muscle relaxants in his bag? Because *damn*.

"Breathe through the contraction," Claudette

counseled. "Breathe."

Gaze locked with her mother, Scarlett started whooshing like a steam engine. Behind her, Lukas gritted his teeth, but silently supported her bulky weight.

After the contraction was over, Wyland and Claudette exchanged a glance. "I think you'll be more comfortable in bed, honey," Claudette said, taking Scarlett's hands and helping her to her feet. "I think it's show time."

Wyland, Claudette, Scarlett, and Lukas disappeared behind the large, rolling partition that separated the bedroom from the rest of the living space. Though the sprawling loft was cleverly separated into purpose areas by rugs, furniture groupings, shelving units, and movable wall partitions, only the bathroom had solid walls. Sheets rustled as Claudette helped Scarlett into bed. Male voices murmured.

She couldn't imagine having so little privacy on a day-to-day basis, much less while in labor.

Suddenly, a ferocious wail came from behind the partition. The windows rattled in their frames.

"Do you have earplugs?" Jack asked. He was already wearing his own.

"I'm set." Opening the package Wyland had given her, she quickly fit the little silicone blobs in her ears. "Are those windows going to be okay?"

"Bullet-proof glass," Jack said matter-of-factly. "They might crack, but they won't break."

"That's reassuring." *Not.*

Jack looked over to the kitchen, where Sasha and Antonia still squabbled. "They're supposed to be mixing drinks. The last time I went in, Sasha about snapped my head off."

On the other side of the exposed brick half-wall, Sasha swigged from a bottle of Jack Daniel's while Antonia, holding a nearly-empty wine cooler, pointed at her accusingly. "They must be…uncomfortable." If *she* felt pounded by a vicious wave of PMS, she could only imagine how the two succubi must feel.

"I get that," Jack said, rubbing the bridge of his nose with his thumb and forefinger. "Liquor helps takes the edge off for the incubi and succubi, but—" he raised his voice slightly "—they're so busy fighting with each other that they've forgotten about everyone else."

"We have not," Sasha called back, dropping ice cubes into the lowball glass she'd just filled with the Tennessee whiskey. "Don't get your panties in a wad."

Before he could reply, Sasha turned from the kitchen counter carrying a beverage-laden tray, weaving slightly. "Oops!" She quickly regained her balance, then made a circuit of the room, handing the lowball glass to her father, then delivering beer bottles to Rafe and Bailey. When Sasha sauntered toward them, Jack took a deep breath and straightened to his full height, as if steeling himself—and understandably so. With all the estrogen-laced pheromones floating about the place, Sasha was sexuality personified.

"Here's your Coke," Sasha murmured to him.

"Thank you." Rather than waiting for Sasha to hand him the red and gray can, Jack took it from the tray himself. "The other beer's for Tia?" At Sasha's nod, he handed her the bottle of Angry Orchard Ale.

"And the Jack is mine." Setting the tray down on a nearby end table, Sasha picked up the bottle. Eyeing him, she took a slow, deliberate sip.

The wave of sexual energy nearly knocked her sideways.

"Sasha!" Elliott snapped from across the room. "That's enough."

Over on the couch, Bailey pulled a small pillbox out of her purse. Opening it, she extracted two white tablets. After tossing one in her mouth, she offered the other to Jack. He quickly took the pill, chasing it with a gulp of soda.

Wyland popped his head around the bedroom partition. "Does anyone need muscle relaxants?"

She almost dropped to the floor so she could kiss his feet. "Me me me," she chanted, waving her hand. "Me."

"Just a moment." He disappeared for a couple of seconds, then walked into the living room carrying his big, black satchel. She followed him to the kitchen, where he set the bag on the counter, found a water glass, filled it from the tap, and drained it.

"How are things going in there?" she asked.

"Better than I expected. Scarlett's doing well."

"And Lukas?"

"He's in pain, but not in active labor."

"That's a relief." Up close, she could see the toll Scarlett's labor was taking on Wyland. His temples were damp with sweat, and his ponytail was slightly askew. There were stress lines bracketing the sides of his mouth, and his cheekbones were too prominent. She wheeled to the refrigerator, took out a bag of blood, and set it on the counter.

He skimmed her up and down. "How are things going out here?"

"The Sebastianis are getting drunk." She rubbed her fist low on her abdomen. "I prefer the muscle relaxants."

Opening the bag with a practiced flick, he rooted around and withdrew a sheet of blister-packed tablets. "How much have you had to drink?"

She held her nearly full beer bottle up to the light. "First bottle. Just a sip or two."

"Any chronic health conditions? Prescription medications?"

"Nothing but birth control," she answered cheerfully. "I'm healthy as a horse."

"Apparently so." He eyed her again, then removed two tablets from the blister pack. "Take one now, and the other if you need it." He dropped a kiss on her forehead, then picked up the bag of blood and the satchel. "Go easy on the beer," he advised. "And have some blood yourself."

"Will do."

The hours passed with a steady rotation of booze, beer, sodas, and snacks. Calamity jumped on the table and helped himself to some of the spinach dip, but no one scolded him. Chico came upstairs to check in, but left very quickly. Time became fluid as Scarlett labored, cursing like a sailor. Singing, yelling, grunting... words and phrases dissolved into a swirl of tones and sound. At times, the room seemed to pulse around them. She didn't see Wyland again, but she could hear him—hear his calm voice, his confident instructions.

Suddenly, her uterus wrenched.

"Here she comes, honey," Claudette said from the other side of the partition. "Here she comes. Push! Oh, look at all that red hair..." When she added her powerful voice to her daughter's, the floor seemed to undulate.

The windows cracked.

With a final, dissonant shriek, little Coco Annika Fontaine was sung into the world. After a pause, her angry, newborn squalls joined her mother and grandmother in a trio as old as time.

And then, blessed silence. As she removed her earplugs, she blinked back tears.

"The kid's already got us wrapped around her little finger," Sasha muttered, dabbing her eyes with a tissue. "I'll get the champagne."

Jack followed to help.

Suddenly she yearned for her camera—the good one, down in her car. She'd take some candid shots, develop the pictures herself, and make a scrapbook as a baby gift. Walking over to the window, she nudged the curtain aside. Through the fractured glass, dawn pinkened the sky, but she had more than enough time to run down to the parking lot, retrieve her camera, and get back to the safety of the building before the sun broke over the horizon.

She dropped the curtain and found Bailey, once again curled up with Rafe on the couch. "I'm going down to the car to get my camera. I'll be right back."

At Bailey's nod, Tia slipped away from the celebration, closing the door as champagne corks popped.

CHAPTER FIFTEEN

From his parking spot on Washington Avenue, Dominic had a clear sightline on the beige brick building that housed Sebastiani Security. On the other side of Hennepin, the Guthrie Theatre stood with its chest proudly out-thrust, but here, a mere five or six blocks down the street, drug dealers were plying their trade, and Sex World did brisk business.

In a back-handed way, Lukas Sebastiani had been smart to build his business here, because the security cameras glaring down from every light pole in the parking lot seemed prudent rather than pathological. Right now, the lot was full, but no one had come in or out of the building for hours. Tia Quinn's Civic was parked closer to the building than he liked, with the driver's door facing the entrance.

Now was the time. Fate wouldn't give him a better chance to steal the garage door opener he'd seen her use to enter the mysterious storage facility down the road from Vamp Central.

He tied the bandanna around his head, covering his face, then pulled on the stocking cap and leather work gloves. Sliding the crowbar into the side pocket of his baggy jeans, he got out of the car and shrank into the shadows.

It didn't take long to reach Tia's car. He dropped

to a crouch at the Civic's passenger side, using the car's body to hide from the view of anyone who might pass through Sebastiani Security's well-lit lobby. *There.* The garage door openers—there were two—were clipped to the driver's side visor, but they'd be easy enough to reach. He pulled the crowbar out of his pocket, gripped it like a baseball bat, and swung for the fence.

The window's safety glass fractured but didn't break. After a second, shorter swing, the glass finally shattered, sending small shards crumbling onto the passenger seat. He snaked an arm through the broken window, found the interior car door handle, and yanked.

After brushing most of the glass onto the floor, he edged his way inside, keeping his body low until he lay with his upper body resting on the passenger seat. Carefully avoiding everything in the console—a half-empty bottle of water, a small notebook, a couple of cheap pens, and an open bag of Skittles—he slid one of the garage door openers off the driver's visor, then stuffed it in his pocket. As he reached for the other, he heard—felt—an ominous *ka-thunk.*

The automatic door locks.

"Hey!" Tia Quinn wrenched open the driver's side door. "Don't you *dare* take that camera."

He hadn't even noticed a fucking camera, but to disguise what he was *really* there to steal, he grabbed the strap.

She was stronger than she looked. As they played a vicious game of tug-of-war, a mighty tug jerked him into the driver's seat. She swiped at the bandanna covering his face.

No. He threw up his arm to block her, clipping her

face with his elbow. He heard a sickening crack.

"Shit," she gasped, clapping both hands over her nose. The momentum knocked her backward, her head hitting the open car door with a hollow thunk. She fell, hitting the pavement hard, the camera bag still looped around her arm.

The blood flowing from her nose and temple was all that moved.

"Shit." This wasn't what he'd planned. Panicking, he scrambled out of the car. There was still no activity in Sebastiani Security's lobby. Over at the Washington Avenue stoplight, a semi downshifted, then glided to a stop. Down the street, a food truck opened its awning, ready to serve breakfast.

The city was waking up. She…wasn't.

He had no choice; he had to get out of here.

Quickly walking away, he abandoned Tia Quinn to the sun.

＊

Leaving Scarlett and Coco snuggling, and an exhausted Lukas sleeping like the dead, Wyland escaped to the blessedly empty bathroom. He desperately needed a couple of minutes to himself—some silence—and this room had the only solid walls and door in the place. Leaning against the sink, he rolled his head, trying to loosen stiff neck muscles, then turned on the water faucet. There were two hand-sized bruises developing on his forearm. With Claudette handling the business end of the birth—Scarlett had come through labor like a champ—caring for Lukas had fallen to him.

The big man had a hell of a grip.

He took off his shirt, grabbed a washcloth from the stack, and turned on the hot water. Using some liquid soap he found in the shower enclosure, he freshened up, running the cloth over his face, neck, chest and underarms, then he put the shirt back on again. The abbreviated bath would have to do until he and Tia got back home.

He could really use some blood.

When he came out of the bathroom, Bailey handed him a glass.

"Thank you." He sipped the rich, red nectar. Where was Tia? She'd promised to hand him his first glass of champagne. Jack and Rafe chatted in the kitchen. Sasha and Antonia were stretched out on the couch, either sleeping or passed out. Elliott and Claudette were in the bedroom, holding their granddaughter. "How is everyone doing?" Had Tia gone downstairs? Gone home? Maybe the second-hand pain had gotten to be too much for her to handle after all.

Shit, he should have checked on her.

"The Sebastianis drowned themselves in liquor, but the pheromone intoxication meds Jack and I took worked like a charm." She smirked. "Once again, the supposedly weak, puny humans are in better shape than the paranormals are."

Sebastiani Labs had developed the experimental medication so Jack Kirkland, the first human they'd told about their existence, could keep a clear head working with so many incubi and succubi. "How's your stomach?" Barely six months ago, trying to control her attraction to Rafe, Bailey had taken so much of the medication that she'd needed surgery for a perforated ulcer.

"It's fine." Bailey gave him a sharp nudge with her elbow. "Hey, watch out."

"Hmm?"

"The window."

The curtains were closed, but bright sunlight framed the window. Where was his brain?

Elliott, bleary-eyed but sober, came out of the bedroom and kissed him on both cheeks. "Thank you," he said. "Thank you for being here, for—" his voice cracked "—taking care of my family."

"Scarlett and Claudette did all the work."

Bailey passed out flutes of Dom Perignon. Jack and Rafe came out of the kitchen, joining them.

"I'd like to make a toast." Elliott raised his glass. "To the Ladies Fontaine. To Claudette, to Scarlett, and to Coco, my precious first grandchild." He paused, blinking away tears. "And to our beloved Annika, ever with us in name and spirit."

Wyland's throat tightened. Annika's senseless death still stung.

"And to Wyland, the rock upon which we stand. *Salut*, my friend."

Jack and Rafe raised their glasses. "To Wyland."

"*Salut*," Bailey echoed.

When he managed to speak, his voice sounded like a rough gravel road. "To the Fontaines." He took a quick sip of champagne, more for form's sake than anything else. "When did Tia leave?" He should call Thane to make sure she'd arrived safely home. Even with muscle relaxants on board, she probably felt as physically beat up as he did.

"She didn't," Bailey said. "Leave, that is. She went

downstairs to get her camera from her car."

He glanced at the window, at the bright light framing the borders. Warning bells started clanging. "How long ago?"

Bailey looked puzzled. "She should be back by now."

"How long ago?" he snapped.

"About an hour?"

He strode to the door, trying to stay calm. Tia was probably downstairs, in the building, talking with Chico or another Sebastiani Security worker. Perfectly safe.

But maybe not.

As he twisted the doorknob, Bailey caught his shirt from behind. "Wait. The sun—"

He jerked out of her grasp.

"Damn it, wait for some help."

"Get it. I'm heading down." He raced to the stairwell, taking the stairs two at a time. When he reached the first floor lobby door, he hit the crash bar on the run. "Oh god."

She was outside, crumpled on the pavement next to her car.

Covered with blood.

And the sun…oh god, the sun…

He started for the door, but someone stronger than Bailey grabbed him from behind.

"You'll fry," Jack snapped. "Wait here. Get ready to treat her."

Wyland wrenched his arms away. Jack was right; he knew Jack was right, but—

The stairwell door crashed open again, and Bailey and Rafe hurried into the lobby. Rafe carried a colorful quilt.

"Wyland, we've got this." Jack was already half out the door. "Rafe, follow me."

Standing safe and worthless behind the lobby's UV-treated windows, he watched Jack and Rafe cover the ten or so yards separating the building from Tia's parked car. Rafe held up the quilt, blocking the worst of the sun's burning rays, while Jack performed a quick head, neck, and back assessment. "Hurry, hurry…" he muttered. Jack's actions were absolutely necessary—moving her prematurely could result in permanent injuries—but the sun…

So much blood…

"We're taking her to the treatment room, right?" Bailey asked, propping the heavy steel door leading to Sebastiani Security's working area with her body.

He nodded. "How's your break room's blood supply?" Until he could assess her injuries, he had no idea how much blood Tia would need to jump-start her recovery.

Bailey winced. "You just drank the last bag in the building. Blood bank is delivering later this morning."

No blood?

The door alarm suddenly shrieked. Red lights flashed. After a couple of seconds, heavy boots pounded down the hall. "Finally," Bailey muttered.

"What the hell, Bailey," Chico complained as he reached the door. "You know better than to prop the security door—"

"Tia's hurt. Get the gurney from the treatment room—"

"We won't need it," Wyland told them, watching Jack scoop Tia off the pavement and run toward the building.

He held the door open, ignoring the sting of the

sun. Tia's body sagged in Jack's arms; she appeared to be unconscious. Head wound, left temple. Stitches, possible concussion. Nasal fracture. Between the head wound and the broken nose, her face was so covered with blood he couldn't assess her burns.

"Unconscious," Jack confirmed, carrying Tia into the shadowed safety of the lobby and through the propped security door. "Broken nose, gash on her temple, a knot on the back of her skull. Looks like first and second degree burns." Jack strode into the treatment room, gently laying Tia on the exam table as Bailey flicked on the overhead lights. "There's blood on her driver's door, and the passenger window's broken. Looks like she interrupted a burglary in progress."

Everything in his body clenched up tight—jaw, diaphragm, fists—but he shoved back the rage, swallowed the helplessness down. Pulled chilly professionalism around him like a protective cape.

"I'll get your bag from upstairs." Rafe was already half out the door.

There wasn't much in the bag that wasn't available here in the treatment room, but having it here wouldn't hurt. As soon as he was certain Tia was stable, they were high-tailing it to Memorial. Thankfully, the door alarm went silent.

"Need me here?" Chico asked, hovering outside the treatment room door. "I can process the scene, pull the security tapes from the parking lot."

Jack gave a curt nod. "Go ahead."

Wyland stared at the smear of red blood on Jack's white dress shirt. "Do you have a phone to assist with evidence collection?" he asked.

"Yeah." Jack pulled it from his pants pocket.

Wyland fumbled with his own phone, flipped on the voice recorder, and set it on the counter. His physical exam would be taken into evidence, as well. He went to the sink and washed his hands. "Speaking of security cameras...how could someone lying unconscious in the parking lot in broad daylight *possibly* escape someone's notice?"

Jack looked grim. "We'll find out."

"Damn right you will." He turned toward his patient, toward all the blood. The lilac perfume she'd applied last night was barely noticeable anymore, but the scent of VampScreen lingered, thank the universe. Pulling the telescoping examination lamp closer, he turned it on, gloved up, and did a thorough exam, narrating for the record. No apparent spinal injury. Hematoma on the back of her skull, probably from hitting the pavement. The nasal fracture was a simple break, with no significant deformity, but the swelling and bruising would get worse before it got better. A dozen or so stitches should be sufficient to close the gash on her temple. Jack had accurately pegged the burns—mainly first degree, with some blistering along her left ear, neck, and collarbone. They'd be painful, but they'd heal. Reaching for a small penlight, he carefully lifted her swollen eyelid, shining the light at her pupil before flicking it away. "Normal contraction," he noted.

As he checked the other eye, she tensed, then jerked her head away. "Stop that."

Relief coursed through him. She was conscious again—and if she could move her neck like that, it probably didn't hurt very much. "Can you hear me?"

"Of course I can hear you. You're standing right next to me." She pushed his arm away. "Get that light out of my eyes, damn it."

"Let me finish examining you."

"My head hurts." Wincing, she reached for her nose. "Where are we? What happened?"

"We're in the treatment room at Sebastiani Security," Jack said. "What do you remember?"

She shoved up onto her elbows. "That little prick! Did he get my camera?"

"What little prick?" Jack asked.

His blood pressure started to climb, like the rollercoaster he'd seen at the fair.

"I went out to my car to get my camera. When I got there, I found this...this...masked dude lying across my front seat. He'd broken my passenger side window, and was taking my camera. We...scuffled."

"You risked your safety for a bloody camera?" he snapped.

"It's a very nice camera. And I wanted the pictures I had on the disk." She looked at Jack. "Did he get it?"

"No," Jack said. "I found it on the pavement. I put it in the back seat."

"I hope it didn't break," she fretted.

"We'll check."

The rollercoaster crested. Started barreling down. "Fuck the bloody camera! Tia, you could have burned to death!"

She recoiled.

"Wyland." Bailey jerked him away from the exam table and into the farthest corner. "You need to calm down and let Jack do his job,"

He hissed at her—a full-on vampire hiss, with fangs flashing. "When is he going to start doing it?"

"She's hurt, she's scared. She's the victim, and

right now, he's talking about what she wants to talk about." She took both gloved hands and squeezed them. "Give him time. Now, settle down. Breathe with me."

He obeyed, filling his lungs with air. In and out. One more time. And another. When his fangs retracted, Bailey released her death grip on his hands. Jack *was* doing his job, comforting an assault victim and obtaining important information at the same time.

Now he had to do his.

Over on the table, Tia was describing what happened. "We fought for the camera, pulling the strap back and forth between us. The bandanna covering his face started to slip. When I made a grab for it, he threw up his arm and hit my nose with his elbow."

Of course she'd grabbed for the bandanna.

"It hurt like hell. I remember falling back, but—" she shrugged "—nothing after that."

"There's a smear of blood along the top edge of your driver's door," Jack told her. "I think you hit your temple coming down."

"I don't remember anything after that." She shot him a sullen glance. "Nothing until Wyland's damn flashlight."

As Jack took pictures of Tia's injuries, Wyland gathered the equipment he'd need to clean and stitch her wound. Though the pre-assembled suture packs contained the basics, he set out extra sterile water, gauze pads, a small-gauge syringe and some Lidocaine. No matter how careful he was, the sutures would probably leave a scar.

"Are you okay staying here?" Jack asked Bailey.

"I'd like to check in with Chico."

"Go ahead."

Bailey chatted with Tia, keeping her occupied while he stripped off his soiled gloves, washed and dried his hands, then gloved up again. As he approached the examining table, Tia stared at the tray he carried. "Bailey just told me there's no blood here in the building."

"No."

"How about painkillers?" she asked hopefully.

He gestured to the Lidocaine. "You won't feel a thing." When he unwrapped the syringe, she went pale. *Shit.* "Tia, are you afraid of needles?"

"I wouldn't say afraid. Exactly." Squaring her shoulders, she gave him a wobbly, determined smile. "I've been hurt worse than this playing hockey."

Where? If she had a single suture mark on her body, he hadn't found it yet. "You didn't answer my question."

"Go ahead," she said, patting him on the arm. "You're the most experienced doctor on the planet."

Who was she trying to reassure, him or herself? Bloody hell. "Let's get you cleaned up first."

"Okay," she squeaked through chattering teeth.

He gently wiped the blood from her face, but her breathing changed as he approached the wound. Too fast, too shallow. She was dangerously pale, and using energy she couldn't spare to block her thoughts. "We're going to Memorial." If he could get some blood into her first, she'd feel less anxious, and start healing more quickly. She didn't have any symptoms of a brain bleed, but it wouldn't hurt to get a head CT just to make sure. He removed his gloves and grabbed his phone. If he called ahead, a machine would be available as soon as they arrived.

Less than two minutes later, he grimly hung up. The ER was treating four patients right now, two of them vampires in critical condition. "I'll have to treat you here," he said.

"It's okay, Wyland."

The trust in her eyes just gutted him, slicing him open and spilling his entrails onto the ground. He was already dreading causing her a moment's more pain, but it couldn't be helped—

Yes, it could.

He had everything he needed, right here.

Time slowed as he removed his watch. He cradled her cheek with his right hand, and lifted his bare left wrist to her mouth.

She jerked her head back. "No."

"Drink."

"No. You don't want this." She looked at Bailey, still standing next to the wall. "You've got some drugs here, right? Some Valium or Xanax?"

"Sorry, no."

Damn it, he should have known she'd refuse. She'd noticed his reluctance to share his blood when they'd slept together. She'd agreed with his reasons.

But she'd heal more quickly if she drank his blood. And…everything had changed. "Tia. Tia, look at me."

The trust in her eyes…

He shoved the guilt aside, and gave her a mental push. *Drink. Drink from me.*

Her brow wrinkled. There was a pause, as if she was wondering whether to obey the voice slithering into her head. "Ow," she said.

"You have a concussion." He gave her a harder push: *Damn it, drink.*

She obeyed, plunging her tiny, sharp fangs into his wrist. Fleeting pain lanced through him, quickly becoming pleasure as she suckled his lifeblood with strong, rhythmic draws. He drowned in sensation as she drank, each swallow pulling them closer, until... There. There it was, that delicate, mental tendril.

So...close...

He reached for it. Made the connection. Felt the indescribable mental click as their neural pathways joined.

Wyland, damn you...

Sleep.

She fought him, but her eyes finally closed. *Damn it...*

He waited several seconds, then lifted her eyelid to make sure she was out.

"You're going to pay for that," Bailey warned.

"I know." No doubt they'd have words when Tia woke up. No doubt he'd have second, third, and fourth thoughts about what he'd just done, and why. Pulling the lamp closer, he stroked her hair out of the way, thoroughly irrigated the wound, and reached for the syringe.

But right now, he had work to do.

CHAPTER SIXTEEN

Voices, nearby.

Tia tried to open her eyes, but they wouldn't obey. Were they sealed with Super Glue?

"Wyland, let her sleep. Go to work." Thane sounded exasperated. "You've examined her over and over again, all through the day. She has a mild concussion. No facial fractures other than the nose. Her stitches are fine. It's okay to go to work."

"That bump on the head worries me," Wyland said. "I'd like to get a head CT, to rule out—"

"Wyland, you're the most experienced doctor on the planet. You've examined her with eyes and hands. If you saw someone with Tia's injuries on the battlefield, you'd patch them up and send them back to the front line."

Seriously? Right now, she doubted whether she could stand upright without help.

"Drink some blood and go to work," Thane urged. "Or better yet, forget about work and get some sleep yourself."

How long *had* she been asleep, anyway? She had a vague recollection of pain, of fitful sleep, of Wyland's long, lean body spooning hers, warm and reassuring. Of his wrist, pressed against her lips. Of him murmuring, "Drink from me…" and the pain floating away.

She could feel his powerful blood surging inside, helping her heal. Worry, exasperation, guilt, exhaustion…his thoughts were loud enough to raise the dead. If he had any reservations about allowing her to drink from him, she couldn't tell. But why had he done it?

"Wyland, if she needs more blood, I can feed—"

"No."

Wyland's response was polite enough, but his inner possessive snarl sent a shiver through her.

"What I meant to say," Thane said carefully, "is that there's plenty of blood in the refrigerator. But I don't think she needs any right now."

True. Right now, she felt like Violet Beauregarde, the girl who'd turned into a blueberry in *Willy Wonka and the Chocolate Factory*. One more sip of blood and she'd burst.

Lifting a hand to her temple, she felt the gauze, the surgical tape, the slight soreness of the stitches underneath…stitches that she didn't remember receiving, thank the sweet baby Cthulhu. But she remembered scuffling with the guy who'd tried to steal her camera. Remembered the bright spear of pain as his elbow hit her nose.

I feel like I've gone ten rounds in the cage with Lukas.

She tried to open her eyes again—tried and failed. Panic lashed like a whip. "What's wrong with my eyes?"

Wyland grabbed her hand. "They're fine. They're just a little swollen, and there's some dried fluid… Thane, could you get a warm, damp cloth?"

She heard water run from the left side of the room instead of the right. Why was she in the guest room instead of Wyland's room?

She tried to sit up, but the pain stabbing in her temple convinced her lying down was fine for the moment.

"You took quite a knock, but you're recovering well." The mattress dipped as Wyland sat on the side of the bed. "Let me wipe your eyes."

The soft touch of the warm, damp cloth felt heavenly, but his voice was so remote. She tried to get a sense of his feelings, but he'd battened down the hatches.

"You should be able to open them now."

She could, and she was definitely in the guest room. Thane took the washcloth and disappeared into the bathroom, leaving her and Wyland alone. "Thanks," she croaked. Her vocal cords felt rusty. "How long have I been sleeping?" The window shutters were closed; she couldn't tell whether it was day or night.

"You've been asleep for sixteen hours. It's just after nine p.m." He reached over to the bedside table and held a glass of water to her lips.

Though she was perfectly capable of holding the glass herself, she allowed him to help. "Thank you."

"Any blurriness in your vision?"

"No."

"I'd like to check your eyes." Wyland was dressed for work, wearing one of his dark business suits, a white dress shirt, and a tie that swirled with all the colors of the ocean. His hair was lashed back. His jaw was clenched tight, and his eyes were distant, professional.

Yes, the ice was back.

Even after sharing his blood with her, after lying

with her for hours, skin to skin, he was going to freeze her out? Two could play . *that* game. Pushing past the headache, she lifted her mental shields. "Is that absolutely necessary?"

"Yes."

Over by the bathroom, Thane shook his head.

She pushed herself upright, sitting silently and stoically as Wyland did a quick exam, taking her pulse, gently checking her nose and the bump on the back of her head, and peeling the gauze pad off her temple to check her stitches. And then he pulled out that damned flashlight. He was quick about it, lifting her swollen eyelids just enough to flick the light into her eyes, then quickly away. "Your pupils are reacting normally," he said. "Are you sure there's no blurriness?"

"Yes, I'm sure," she said. "What's your deal?"

"My deal?"

Could his tone be any more condescending? "I get it—your drawbridge is up, none shall trespass. But *you* thralled *me*, dude. You thralled me into drinking from you, so don't you *dare* treat me like I crept into your head like some thief in the night."

Wyland just looked at her, his expression stony.

"Would you, for once, just speak your mind? I'd rather see you flip your shit than freeze me out."

His eyes sparked with...something. "You want me to yell at you?"

"Yes! If you want to! Express some anger, some genuine emotion! Out here in the world, instead of hiding in your head."

His face remained placid, but his fangs shoved down. The ruthless display of self-control stroked something deep inside. "You want to know how I feel?" he whispered.

His eyes…burned. The air felt unstable. The ground beneath their feet was about to crack.

She held her breath…

…but then the tension receded, as quickly as it had formed. The fire in his gaze? Doused. And she just didn't have the strength to deal with him anymore. "You know what? Go. Just go to work."

"Tia—"

"I want to take a bath."

"I'll help you."

"No, you have things to do. Thane, can you help me?" Pushing the blankets aside, she swung her legs to the side of the bed and rose to her feet.

She was naked.

Wyland scrambled to cover her with the comforter, but she shoved him aside. "Like you haven't seen me naked before."

"Well, Thane hasn't."

"As if he cares." If she didn't get to the bathroom soon, she'd crumple to the floor. "Go, Wyland. Just…go."

Thane was suddenly there, wrapping her in the comforter. She sensed a heated debate taking place between the two men—a debate that, given Wyland's annoyed sigh, Thane apparently won. "I've got her, Wyland," he said. "We'll be fine."

Wyland reached for her, but the death glare she shot him stopped his hand dead. "We'll speak later, Tia." With an abrupt turn, he left.

She sagged against Thane. "Why does he have to be such an epic butthole?"

"Because he's a man, and you scared him shitless." Thane's arm steadied her as they slowly walked to the bathroom. "Would you like to take a bath or a shower?"

Finally, a man who asked her opinion. "I think a shower would be pushing it," she admitted. "A bath sounds—whoa." She caught a glimpse of herself in the medicine cabinet mirror. No wonder she hadn't been able to open her eyes. If *this* was minor swelling, what did Wyland consider major? She gaped at the constellation of bruises smudging her face, at the black half-moons underneath each eye, and the blood obscuring the white of her left eye. "Holy hell."

"You'll heal," Thane said briskly, turning her away from the mirror. "Now, let's run that bath."

Wrapped in the comforter, she sat on the closed toilet seat, watching Thane putter as water slowly filled the claw-footed soaking tub. Once it was full, he reached for her arm. "Ready?" He guided her to the tub, supporting her weight when it became clear her knees weren't quite up to the job. She dropped the comforter and stepped in. Once she was seated, he left the bathroom.

They hadn't shared blood, but somehow, Thane knew exactly what she needed—to be left alone.

She shut off her brain and soaked.

✳

Thane finally came into the hall.

Wyland pushed away from the wall that had provided such necessary, silent support. "Took you long enough," he muttered. "One more minute and I would have come back in."

"And dug an even deeper hole for yourself, laddie? I'm glad you didn't."

"How is she?"

"Shaky as a newborn foal, but she gutted it out. I didn't have to talk her into taking a bath rather than a shower." Thane suddenly grinned. "She called you an epic butthole."

"I'm not sure whether to be relieved or concerned."

"Let her cool off," Thane advised. "Go to work, gather your thoughts. Because she's right—she doesn't deserve to be treated like a criminal because you thralled her into drinking from you." After a pause, he asked, "Why *did* you thrall her into drinking from you?"

He closed his mental drawbridge with a clang. *Because seeing her crumpled on the pavement, bloody, burned and unconscious, scared me more than anything in my life. Because I love her.* "Needle phobia," he said. "I had to stitch her, and she was scared shitless. And she had a concussion. With a blood exchange, I could—"

"Bah. Memorial Hospital was less than a mile away. You had other options, and you know it."

"I—"

"You know it." Thane's hand on his shoulder was a comforting weight. "You don't have to justify your actions to me, but for god's sake be honest with yourself, and with Tia."

Be honest with himself? He loved her, and it felt like someone was yanking his entrails out through his throat.

"Go to work, Wyland. She'll be here, and feeling better, when you get home. I'll be sure of it."

"Thank you." He kissed Thane on both cheeks,

then went next door to his bedroom to get his briefcase. Thane was right; he needed time to think this through. How could it be, now that he had access to Tia's emotions, that he understood her more poorly than ever?

When he got home, he and Tia would talk.

Using spoken words.

＊

When Wyland walked into the kitchen some eight hours later, he still hadn't figured out what to say to Tia, much less when, where, and how. Setting the scene seemed a good first step, but a romantic meal, or a glass of wine in bed, seemed stereotypical. Trite. And not medically advised.

Thane could help. He had a feel for things like this. "Thane?" he called.

No response.

How odd. At this time of the day, Thane was usually puttering in the kitchen. He'd clearly been here recently. The handle of a pan jutted from a sink full of soapy dishwater, and an unopened bottle of Ensure sat on the counter top.

Voices in the living room.

Dropping his briefcase onto one of the kitchen chairs, he quietly went through the swinging door into the dining room, pausing just out of sight. "Bloody hell." They had company—Diana and Alexander Quinn.

Tia's parents.

Thane was making small talk as he served them

coffee. Behind the bar, Tia poured coffee for Valerian, using a larger mug he could more easily hold. Val sat in his throne-like chair, looking hale, hearty, and pleased to receive visitors.

From the sleep creases on her cheek, and her messy tumble of hair, it was safe to conclude Tia had just woken up. The stretchy exercise clothes covered most of her skin, but clung too faithfully for his comfort. But her face...her poor face. No amount of blood could heal bruises so soon after an injury, and today, her black eyes were at their most spectacular degree of coloration. In the unlikely event her parents had missed the bruising, black sutures marched across her temple like railroad tracks.

She tucked her hair behind an ear, exposing more of her gorgeous, sunburned neck. Despite the burn, his fangs throbbed, and guilt crept up on silent feet. Tia's father was part faerie, and highly empathic. If mild-mannered Alexander Quinn had the slightest inkling of Wyland's lascivious thoughts, the man would probably string him up.

And he'd deserve it.

He suddenly felt like a pimple-spotted suitor.

By any measure, the Quinns were an impressive pair. Like most vampires who'd reached over century of longevity, Tia's parents were wealthy. Though their first fortune had been built upon timber and logging, Diana Quinn, a financial whiz, had increased the family's net worth dozens of times over by investing in some of the twentieth century's most successful technologies: mass-produced automobiles, plastics, and computers. She and Alex had formed The Quinn Family Foundation, funneling most of what Alexander called their "first world spoils" to the developing world, providing food, clean water, sanitation, and medicine to those who lived in poverty.

Tia handed Valerian his coffee, her hand lingering until she was certain he had a firm grasp on the oversized mug. "So, how was Ethiopia?" she asked her parents, sitting on the overstuffed chair. She tucked her feet under her seat, curling up comfortably before reaching to the side table for a tall glass of lime green soda.

As they talked about distributing anti-diarrheal medication, Tia's parents exchanged a glance Wyland had no trouble interpreting. Helping serve beverages? Touching Valerian so familiarly? Curling up, barefooted, on a chair in her leaders' home? Her parents didn't know Tia had been living here for weeks, and had made their home her own.

She'd made *his bed* her own.

Bloody hell.

Why had he agreed with Tia's decision not to tell her parents about the break-in at her house? She'd been in danger for weeks—months—and her parents were completely in the dark.

"Wyland, there you are," Thane said.

The too-hearty voice was a tip-off that he needed to step carefully. "Hello."

"Diana and Alexander have come to see Tia."

"So I see." How much information had Tia shared with her parents? How many secrets remained? "Diana, Alexander, how nice to see you."

"Wyland!" Setting her saucer on the coffee table, Diana rose, walking toward him with her hands extended in welcome. "It's been too long."

Wearing distressed jeans and a turquoise silk

blouse, and with her hair dyed an unrepentantly unnatural burgundy, Diana looked more like Tia's sister than her mother. He met her halfway, taking her hands. "Diana." As he bent to kiss Diana's cheeks, he saw Tia mouth "sorry" at him from behind her mother's back. "Hello, Alexander."

"Wyland."

After kissing Alexander's cheeks, he urged them to sit, to relax. To reveal why they were here.

As if Tia's bruised face wasn't reason enough.

"Tia?"

Tia looked at her mother. "Hmm?"

Diana exchanged an exasperated glance with her bondmate, then looked back at her daughter. "Please rise and greet your Second."

Diana Quinn's voice brooked no argument, and Tia rose to obey.

Only he could see her expression, see her lips quirk and her eyes sparkle with mischief as they flicked over his frame. Only he heard her murmur "suit porn" as she kissed his cheek. Only he felt her tongue scrape against his beard as she kissed the other.

"Hello, Wyland."

"Hello." He was as hard as a henge beneath his tailored suit, and the little witch knew it. "How are you?"

"Horny," she whispered. She cleared her throat. "And I'm sorry."

"For what?" All signs of her earlier anger were gone, as if a quick thunderstorm had washed away all the dirt and grime, leaving fresh, clean air in its wake. When Deirdre had been displeased, the whole world knew it. Her dark moods had been tempests, violent storms that took days to pass.

Tia gave a vague, one-shouldered shrug. "For being a brat earlier. For not thanking you for taking care of me. For my parents showing up without notice." She glanced over her shoulder. "They stopped by my house earlier, and then FaceTimed me when I didn't answer the door. I answered, Dad saw the bruises, and he—they—insisted on seeing me for themselves."

He nodded. "Understandable."

"But I'm fine."

She probably felt better, but her face looked like a father's worst nightmare. Black eyes, bruising on her left cheek and nose, and rather than its usual white, the sclera of her left eye was suffused with blood. He was lifting his hand to her bruised cheek when Thane spoke.

"Wyland? Would you like a beverage?"

Shit. He dropped his hand. "How much have you told your parents?" he murmured.

"Let me do the talking."

"That's not the least bit helpful."

He chose a chair as far away from Tia as possible. Thane handed him a bloody Perrier.

"I understand you treated Tia after her mishap in Sebastiani Security's parking lot," Alexander said. "Thank you so much."

"I was glad to help." If he'd only prevented her from getting hurt in the first place. "Her recovery is progressing nicely."

"And I wouldn't have missed Coco's birth for the world," Tia added. "Scarlett is fine, and Coco is absolutely adorable, of course. She has a full head of bright red hair."

"Of course she does," Diana said wryly.

There were a disproportionate number of redheads in their culture, with three—Tia, Diana, and Thane—sitting right here in this room.

Tia suddenly straightened in her chair. "What's the date today?"

"September first."

"Crap." Tia gestured to her face. "I think I'm going to have to reschedule my meeting with the Senator."

Alexander nodded, wincing. "That might be best."

Why would Tia be meeting with a human senator? He was glad when Valerian asked.

"Apparently the senior senator from Minnesota is reading my human trafficking series. She'd like to talk about Jane, a young human woman I interviewed who recently escaped her pimp. He had her working at the man camps near North Dakota's Bakken oil fields."

Tia's work had come to the attention of a United States senator?

"Minnesota recently passed a law that protects sex trafficking victims from being prosecuted as criminals," Tia said. "The Senator's pushing a similar bill at the federal level. The fact that Jane's exploitation took place across state lines shouldn't matter. "

North Dakota's recent oil boom had attracted laborers from all over the country, creating an imbalance in the ratio of men to women in the areas surrounding the oil fields. It didn't surprise him that pimps, seeing a business opportunity, had moved to fill the gap. He'd seen similar boom and bust cycles happen time and time again.

"Jane's story is, unfortunately, a familiar one," Tia

said. "Her parents kicked her out, something about a boyfriend. She couch-surfed with friends for a while, but finally ended up on the streets." Her lips tightened. "A guy offered her food, a place to stay, and then brought her to North Dakota, where she and two other women worked out of a trailer. They each had a daily quota, and they were beaten and starved if they didn't meet it."

"How horrible," Thane said.

"Well, Jane escaped, and made it back to Minneapolis. The Foundation helped her find safe shelter, and I have a line on a possible job, but she's not ready to go to the police yet."

"Baby steps," Alexander said. "She's safe, and right now that's the most important thing."

"I know, but…" Tia gave a frustrated sigh. "I just wish I could do more to help."

More than offering a young crime victim food, shelter, safety, and possible employment? She'd already performed miracles.

"Give her a chance to make her own decisions," Diana advised. "She'll contact you when she's ready." A trio of silver bracelets jingled when she reached for Alexander's hand. "So, does the Senator realize you'll be interviewing her as much as she'll be interviewing you?"

Tia's only answer was a canny smile.

Even dressed in exercise gear, sitting cross-legged in an oversized chair, with two black eyes, sleep creases marring her face, and drinking noxious green soda, Tia looked capable. Formidable. Businesslike.

Tia's blog was no trust fund baby's attempt to fill the time. *In Like Quinn* had a much wider reach, and a more significant impact, than he'd ever realized.

Why hadn't he ever asked her about her work?

She was starting to tire, to wilt a little in her chair. *That* was something he could do something about. As Valerian talked to Diana and Alexander about their trip to Ethiopia, he went behind the bar and warmed a bag of blood. After pouring it in a tall tumbler, he went to Tia's chair and swapped it for the half-empty glass of soda.

"Hey." She made a grab for the glass, but missed. "Give me that."

"You need blood, not sugar and chemicals."

Tia slowly rose. Despite her bare feet, she looked haughty as a queen. "Wyland, we talked about this. My teeth, my body, my nutrition, my decision. You're not the boss of me."

"Tia!" Diana gasped.

"Well, he's not."

He shouldn't find her display of temper so bloody arousing, but he did. He could almost see steam shooting from her ears. *So alive.* "Actually, I *am*..." Her eyes narrowed to slits. "Your doctor," he finished. "And your doctor—" *your lover* "—advises you to drink this blood to aid in your healing." Under her half-zipped jacket, a white lace camisole teased him. He smelled lilacs mixed with Thane's liniment, the minty homemade balm that made painful muscles sing *The Hallelujah Chorus*.

Heat brewed in the space between them, mere inches now instead of several safe feet. "Please," he murmured, stroking her bruised cheek with a touch that was nowhere near professional. "Drink it for me."

Her lips compressed into an annoyed, adorable pout. He'd backed her into a corner, and she knew it.

The snap in her eyes told him he'd pay for it later.

Any price you wish.

When her gaze dropped to his neck, lust coiled like a spring.

Diana looked confused. Alexander's eyebrows climbed his forehead.

He didn't care. "Please."

With a put-upon sigh, Tia drank the blood, then set the glass on the table with a snap. "There." She wiped her mouth with the back of her wrist. "Happy now?"

"Yes." *For the time being.* "Thank you."

"Tia Tèodora Quinn." Alexander's voice snapped like a whip. "What in the world is wrong with you?"

"Sorry," she said.

Her answer didn't seem to satisfy her father, who eyed him with a dawning knowledge, and a father's understandable concern. "Wyland, may we speak with Tia privately?" Though Alexander's request was respectfully phrased, the demand was clear.

"Certainly." Did he think Tia was a prisoner here?

"My room is lovely," Tia suggested. "How about there?"

The room *was* lovely, but if not for her injuries, it would show no sign of recent use.

Across the room, Thane was working hard to keep a straight face. Unholy amusement was about ready to bend him double.

Tia brushed a soft kiss against his lips, then turned to her parents. "Come on." She indicated the stairs. "Mom, you're going to die when you see this bathroom."

Shock shackled him in place. Did she realize what she'd done? Given the glances bouncing between

Diana and Alexander as they followed their chattering daughter upstairs, her parents certainly did. "Bloody, bloody hell." He stalked to the bar, poured two fingers of scotch, and tossed it back. The liquor burned down his throat, leaving warm embers in its wake.

Thane snatched the bottle from his hands. "Laddie, that's no way to treat thirty-year Lagavulin. If you're looking to get stinking drunk, choose a lesser beverage."

"I'm not going to get drunk." Truth be told, Tia's surprise kiss made him feel a little tipsy all on its own. Whatever had possessed her to kiss him like that—kiss him like a lover—in front of her parents?

"That's good to hear. If you drink too much, you'll be limp as a noodle later, after her parents leave." Thane winked. "If you know what I mean."

"I'm ignoring you."

"So, meeting the girlfriend's parents." Thane leaned against the bar, nudging him with an elbow. "Alexander's a pacifist, but he looked ready to call you out for trifling with his little girl."

"I'm not trifling with her—"

"For god's sake, Thane, stop teasing him," Valerian said from his chair. "Tia's not a little girl. She's not a casual lover."

Valerian was right, but...so was Thane. Tia's parents had *not* looked happy. "How am I going to explain this to them?"

"You tell them that you love their daughter."

He looked upstairs, to where Tia was no doubt being interrogated by her parents. "It's not that simple."

Val shrugged, exchanging a private glance with

Thane. "Nothing worth doing ever is."

Shame crawled through him. The two men had limited time remaining together, and yet they dared to love.

They dared to love.

And speaking of daring… Tia had claimed him, publicly, in front of her parents. What had he done? Stood there like a dolt.

Tia was right. He *was* a chickenshit.

"Bloody hell." Wyland glanced upstairs again. He wasn't so daft that he'd interrupt Tia's conversation with her parents, but if he had anything to say about it, she wouldn't spend one more night in that lovely guest room.

He'd take her to bed—to *his* bed, where she belonged.

And she'd know he loved her before they left it again.

CHAPTER SEVENTEEN

Tia set her laptop on the floral Marimekko duvet, then scowled at the guest room door. Where was Wyland? She'd expected to see him the minute her parents left, but here she was, an hour later, propped against the headboard. Alone, and working.

However, the work time *had* been productive. Searching through Hennepin County property records, she'd discovered that the house where Robert Johnson died had recently changed hands. Did the new owners realize that the quiet, four bedroom home they'd just bought used to be a sex dungeon? That someone had been killed there? The seller, T.S.D.C. LLC, probably hadn't revealed those pesky little facts to the broker, much less the buyer.

A limited liability corporation; it just figured. It would take time, and serious effort, to find the sentient being hiding behind the acronym, but it could be done. It *would* be done, by her. But not today, because her concentration was crap.

Where was Wyland? And what had possessed her to kiss him—like *that*—in front of her parents?

"What the hell am I doing?" she mumbled. She reached for the pile of mail at the foot of the bed, mindlessly separating the bills from the solicitations, sorting them into stacks. The conversation she'd had with her parents—her revelation that, yes, she was sexually involved with Wyland, the Vampire Second—had been difficult, primarily because she hadn't been able to define the relationship beyond that. Though she hadn't shared blood with her parents in years and wasn't privy to their mental conversation, their facial expressions had been easy to read. Her mother, usually the more excitable parent, had studied her for long, long seconds, finally giving her a subtle, woman-to-woman nod that conveyed approval, confidence, and an appreciation of her daughter's taste in men. "Back off, Alex," she'd said. "Tia's affairs are her business."

"Sweet bleeding universe, Diana, we're not talking about a chef, or a novelist, or some random guitar player. She's sleeping with the Vampire Second."

"And the problem is…?"

Her father stared at her. "It's a huge freaking deal."

"Alexander, will you listen to yourself?" her mother scoffed. "You sound like a tool of the patriarchy."

Her father recoiled, then took a deep breath—a conscious technique he used to process strong emotions. He experienced them, acknowledged them, and then watched them pass by, freeing him to think critically. "Diana, this isn't about Tia having a sex life. It's about who she's having that sex life *with*."

Her own temper spiked. "What's wrong with Wyland?"

"Nothing. Absolutely nothing. He's a fine leader—probably one for the history books—and from what I've seen, he's a fine man. But Tia, he's so…constrained, so controlled."

"He has to be."

"Yes, he has to be. But you don't. You...aren't."

"I'm not what?" It wasn't very often her parents talked about her in terms of what she *wasn't*.

Reassurance and love—her father's faerie empathy—wrapped around her like a soft cashmere blanket. "You're not constrained and controlled. He's older, colder, and very powerful. He's so...*different* from the men you've been involved with in the past."

"Once you get to know him, he's anything but cold."

"Okay." Her father nodded. "But given his commitments and responsibilities, how can you possibly get what you need out of this relationship?"

What *did* she need out of this relationship? It was a question worth asking, and an uncomfortable one at that. Somewhere along the way, her involvement with Wyland had morphed into something more than simple physical attraction, or scratching a sexual itch.

She was falling in love with him.

"Tia, I'd hate to see your passion, your spark, extinguished in any way. Stifled by protocol."

If her father only knew how many f-bombs she'd heard some of their Council members drop.

"Wyland's a fine leader, but...as my daughter's lover?" He looked at her mother again. "Diana, I can't believe you're not concerned about this."

"Tia has a good head on her shoulders. She doesn't need our permission to share her body, mind, or heart with whomever she pleases."

"But can he share his heart in return?"

And that was the crux of the matter. Tia sighed, continuing to sort the mail on auto-pilot. In bed, she and Wyland were a perfect match, but...what was the phrase her father had used? A leader for the history books? Did she have it in her to be the partner, to be the mate, of a historic man? "Talk about putting the cart before the— Whoa." She drew herself upright, studying the envelope at the top of the pile. White, business-sized, no return address, and mailed from a busy downtown Minneapolis zip code, it was utterly generic, right down to the vaguely patriotic red, white, and blue adhesive stamp. "I suppose it was my turn." Steeling herself, she carefully opened the envelope, withdrew the sheet of paper, and read. "Yep." Such ugly words, about how her father should never have been born. About how *she* should never have been born. About how her mother should be punished for tainting her family's pristine bloodline. "Misogynist pig with a eugenics fixation, check and check." She looked at the envelope again, then froze.

It was addressed to her, using Vamp Central's mailing address.

The letter-writer knew she was here.

Dread galloped into her system. She closed her eyes and waited as her father had taught her, letting the panic run wild and free, watching it buck and whinny and neigh until it finally tired itself out.

After a deep breath in and out, she focused on the letter again, analyzing the language. The letter-writer seemed to know a great deal about her 'rotted' family tree, but also claimed to have seen her and Wyland in 'a compromising position.' Compromising position or not, who'd even *seen* them together?

Soft footsteps outside her door. A weighty pause, then a knock. *Finally.* As she set the letter aside, anticipation crackled like heat lightning. "Come in."

The door swung open on silent hinges. Though

Wyland's hair was still lashed back in that unforgiving ponytail, he'd removed his suit coat, loosened his tie, rolled up his shirtsleeves, and taken off his shoes. The fact that he'd come to her with his armor half-removed made her soften. Simmer.

Her father was right about one thing. After years of drooling over lovers wearing jeans, chef's whites, and stage leathers, finding a tailored suit sexy was definitely a change. "Hey."

"Hello." Wyland didn't come into the room, or close the door behind him. Instead, he leaned against the door jamb, looking at her with carefully banked heat. A crack in the window shade cast a filtered, safe sunbeam across his legs.

Sunlight and shadows. The calm before the storm.

"How did it go with your parents?" he asked.

"Well enough. Mom called Dad a tool of the patriarchy, and that doesn't happen every day."

His lips twitched. "I imagine not. Why did she call him that?"

"Because he's worried about us sleeping together."

He stared at her. "You described our relationship using those words?"

"Yeah."

"Your parents think this—" he gestured to the air between them "—is merely a sexual relationship?" He stalked into the room, stopping when he reached the bed. "No wonder Alexander looked like he wanted to gut me when they left."

Her sexual circuits zapped to life. Annoyance looked...really, really good on him. "Of course it's not merely sexual," she said, shrugging. "We...enjoy each other's company."

"What?"

His single, snapped word sent a frisson of excitement up her spine. Awareness crackled and popped between them like a downed electrical wire. "We enjoy each other's company," she repeated mildly. "Don't we?"

Tell me it's more. I dare you to tell me it's more.

His expression was positively thunderous. The air felt heavy and charged, like she'd get a shock if she touched it.

"Tia."

"Hmm?"

"This isn't just about sex." He whipped the bed covers back, exposing her camisole, panties, and the gooseflesh sheeting her skin. "And you're in the wrong bed."

When he extended his hand, she saw fresh punctures on his wrist. He'd been feeding Valerian—another reminder that Wyland had responsibilities beyond her petty need for validation.

She stared up at him, into his seething gaze. Yesterday, she'd accused him of revealing nothing, of being locked down tight. Today, something had changed. He was a maelstrom, letting her feel every unfiltered emotion as it battered him. Fear, confusion, and anger were all tangled up with want, need, desire, lust. Joy and light, dark and dread...and there, hidden in the center, something soft and precious pulsed.

And she wanted it.

She clasped his hand and stood, bringing her body against his. Blessed warmth leached into her; his familiar scent wafted into her nostrils.

He reached for her hip with his free hand, but hesitated. "What doesn't hurt? I'm afraid to touch you."

Her muscles were screaming despite Thane's magic liniment, but need was screaming even louder. She needed him, needed his touch. "I won't break," she whispered.

He lifted their clasped hands to his mouth, softly kissing her knuckles, then skimmed his palm against her cheek—lightly, so lightly. "Tia..." So much need, so much desperation, embedded in one word. So much helpless anger—anger at himself, that he hadn't prevented her from being injured in the first place.

That, she couldn't allow. "Touch me," she invited, pressing a kiss to his palm. Wrapping her arms around his waist, she lifted her lips to his. "Please touch me."

He groaned against her mouth, then obeyed, claiming her lips in a kiss so soft and succulent, a tasting so careful and reverent, that her throat tightened. Clasping his head, she pulled harder, tilting her head to get deeper, to sample more of his decadent, elemental flavor—

She hissed in pain as their noses bumped together.

"Damn. Are you okay?"

She nodded, eyes watering. "Yeah. Just smarts a little." Okay, it smarted a *lot*, but she didn't want Wyland see her as a patient, not right now. Taking his hand, she started walking toward the door. "And you're right, this is the wrong bed." She slanted him a look he couldn't possibly misinterpret. "I want to be in yours."

The floor suddenly tilted as he scooped her up in his arms. Cradling her against his chest, he strode into the hallway, past Valerian and Thane's closed sitting room door, and into his room, closing the door behind them with a nudge of his shoulder. His blinds were closed, casting the room in shadow, but the Tiffany lamp on his bedside table threw colorful shards of light across his turned-down sheets.

He set her down on the bed, bundling her under the blankets. A muscle jumped at his jawline, but his expression was too controlled for comfort.

Not for long.

She shamelessly watched as he undressed, draping his clothes over the footboard. Tie, belt, then socks. Shirt, pants, then T-shirt. Still wearing his boxer briefs, he slipped between the sheets, absently reaching for the elastic band holding his ponytail in place. With a tug and a shake, his hair tumbled loose.

It was all she could do to keep her tongue in her mouth. "Why are you still wearing your underwear?"

"To remind myself that you're in no condition to make love right now." His voice was rough, but the touch of his fingers against her cheek was soft and reverent.

Make love. His choice of words was just that—a choice, not a slip of the tongue. Something inside her melted, heated. She wanted to make love, too—right now. She wanted to connect with him, in the most primal possible way. When he levered himself up, reaching across her body to turn off the lamp, she strummed her hands over the hard planes of his chest, down his sensitive sides. Clutched a handful of his cotton-covered butt, then shifted so he lay between her legs.

"Tia…" he groaned, dropping his arm and gazing down at her. "I don't want to hurt you.."

"I'm fine, Wyland. And I want you so much."

Soft fingers stroked her cheekbone. "You're so bruised."

Damn it, she should have let him turn off the light. "I wouldn't want to look at me, either."

Discipline and self-denial carved his expression into stark, taut planes, but his gaze was wild and turbulent, and his erection pulsed against her hot, slick core. "How you look isn't the problem."

Where was the man who'd frozen her out yesterday? Today, he'd opened the spigot full-bore, and emotions gushed from him like water from a fire hose. She wanted to wallow in them, in him. Swallow them up. "Wyland, you're an anatomy expert." Relaxing back against the pillow, she didn't hide her hunger. "Surely you can find a place to kiss me—" she dragged his hand to her panties "—where I'm not bruised."

Before she quite realized what was happening, he pushed himself upright, removed her camisole and panties, and laid her back against the pillow again. Resting on his haunches between her legs, he stripped off his T-shirt, then his underwear.

His fangs, his flexing muscles, the hungry jut of his penis...the position was pure alpha masculinity, and his eyes gleamed with diabolical sexual intent. Her skin felt too tight. She was going to explode if she didn't get some relief. She reached for him, but he pressed her back against the pillows. "Lie back," he murmured. "Let me kiss you."

She spread her legs wider.

A knowing, dark chuckle. "So much for romance."

"I don't need romance, not tonight."

"What do you need?"

Dratted man. Wasn't it perfectly obvious? Locking gazes with him, she flooded his mind with images: his shoulders, between her thighs. His hair, brushing her breasts and stomach. His fingers, spreading her wide. His tongue, flicking at her folds until she—

"You're killing me," he gritted.

"Same goes." What in the world was he waiting for? Lifting her hand, she trailed her fingertips over her breasts and torso, meandering down the curve of her stomach, down, down…

She touched herself.

Fangs flashing, he stared at her pussy as if cataloging her anatomy for future reference. As if analyzing which touch made her shiver versus shake versus shudder. Finally, with a tortured groan, he shouldered between her legs, nudging her hand aside.

She waited expectantly, but the touch of his tongue didn't come. Instead, he inhaled, deeply and luxuriantly, pulling her scent into his lungs. Blunt, primal lust. Utterly transcendent pleasure. Both danced into her mind, swirling with her bliss. He exhaled, bathing her flesh in warm, moist air. Her core gave a violent clench, and her nipples drew painfully tight.

From his breath.

At this rate, she was going to come before he even touched her— "Aah!" The unexpected touch of his tongue, right where she needed it most, almost made her levitate. She lifted her hips, pressing against him, seeking, writhing against his mouth. "More…" she gasped, clutching his hair.

He lifted his head, searing her with his hot, blue gaze. One side of his mouth kicked up in a wicked grin. Then, he peeled her outer lips back with his thumbs and gave her the most erotic kiss she'd ever experienced, licking, sucking, and laving her flesh with hungry swipes of his tongue. She clutched at his hair, pushing it aside so she could watch him explore her body. Watch him learn, over long, delicious minutes, exactly which touches made her sigh, made her squeal.

"Wyland…"

His pulse galloped in response.

Aah, he liked it when she said his name. "This sexual mind meld thing is…fun." His answering hum vibrated against her violently aroused flesh. "Holy shit," she gasped.

He smiled against her folds, a diabolical caress.

When her nails bit into his shoulders, he grunted with pleasure. So she did it again.

A groan this time. "Harder," he whispered against her.

When she complied, his fingertips dug into her thighs. She'd have new bruises tomorrow, but she gloried in it. All signs of the courtly, careful gentleman were gone.

He rimmed her opening with the tip of his tongue, then made a teasing push inside. The knot between her legs twisted, tightened. She held her breath, held herself poised, but the plunge she craved didn't come. "Wyland…" she strangled out.

Propping himself up on an elbow, he looked at her.

Her stomach gave a lazy flip. His face was drawn into stark planes, his eyes slumberous with need. His hair was a messy tumble, and his mouth glistened from her pussy. No, this was no effete gentleman. This man could fulfill every fantasy, every filthy desire, and inspire her to think of more. "Why are you—"

"Drink from me," he murmured. Extending his

free arm, he brought his wrist to her lips. "Drink from me while I make you come."

Her pulse beat a furious tattoo. This was no sexual power play; his silent yearning for a more intimate connection sang between them. Yes, something had changed with him, and she liked it. "If you drink from me, too."

"We need to wait until you're stronger."

"Seriously? I feel great."

"You need your blood to heal." Self-disgust flicked over his face. "Bloody hell, I should be shot for even starting this."

"You didn't. I did." Grasping his arm, she kissed his inner wrist. Did she dare ask? "I want to drink from your neck." He didn't respond. Instead, he stared at her pussy, as if considering how he'd make her come once he moved his head out from between her thighs. *Jesus.* "You have hands—very talented ones, at that. Come up here where I can reach you."

"Demands, demands." Rising onto his hands and knees, he crawled to the head of the bed like a slinky panther, sliding one arm under her neck and draping the other over her breast as he lay beside her. "Nothing's ever easy with you, is it?"

The teasing was unexpected. Turning toward him, she curled up against his warmth like a cat in a sunbeam. "I think that's the nicest thing you've ever said to me." The position gave her easy access to his neck, and inches from her hand, his hard cock stirred under the soft, white cotton. Yes, this position would do nicely. "Admit it—you'd be bored out your gourd with easy." She cupped his cock. His hips arched against her hand, and he gave a groan that was music to her ears. "Hard can be very, very nice."

"Tia…" He looked as if he was being tortured, stretched out on a rack, but he didn't move her hand. Instead, he shifted his hair aside.

Offering her his neck.

"Mmm." She dipped her nose into the shallow canyon behind his collarbone, where his scent pooled and deepened, then nuzzled her way up the taut neck tendon, pausing at his throbbing, pulsing vein. As she suckled against his skin, preparing it for her bite, a purring groan rumbled in his chest, vibrating into her body. He slid his hand between her legs, combing through her curls, giving her clit a glancing caress as he stroked through her slick folds. He teased her opening.

Nudged inside.

She plunged, driving her fangs deep into his flesh.

The first surge of power made her eyes roll back in her head, made bloodlust surge to the fore. With a greedy groan, she adjusted the seal of her lips against his skin, clutching at his hair to pull him closer. His pure blood was delicious, a dark metallic sting, but his emotions…oh, gawd, his frenzied need crashed and churned, tossing her like a white water rapids. She sucked and swallowed, sucked and swallowed, caressing his cock as she frantically gulped him down.

His clever fingers delved and plundered, stroked and swirled. All too soon, her orgasm loomed. She gasped as she felt its glittering, inexorable approach.

"Tia." His voice sounded dragged from the depths. His hips were moving in urgent, spasmodic jerks. "Come with me."

Ecstasy, carnality, eroticism…an urgent, helpless yearning…pulses of promise, of possibility…eddying and swirling, tugging her along.

"Tia…" he strangled out, shuddering.

A warm flood of release against her hand.

She broke apart in his arms. Flew over the edge.

Let the undertow pull her under.

*

When Wyland woke up, she was gone.

He glanced over to the bedside table, where the digital clock mocked him with a steady red glare. "Damn." He'd been asleep for over twelve hours, the deepest and longest stretch of sleep he'd gotten in recent memory.

Napping like an old man. No doubt Tia had been awake for hours.

A peal of laugher from across the hall let him know Tia's whereabouts. He threw the blankets back, sat up, and swung his legs over the side of the mattress. Thane had probably fed Valerian already, but he should check.

A throb of reassurance from Valerian: *I'm fine.*

Is Tia with you?

Yes. We're watching TV. Take your time.

Apparently he wasn't needed right now.

There was a vague, scolding throb from Tia. Valerian's amusement immediately followed. *She's annoyed that she can't hear our conversation.*

But having shared blood with both of them, she could *feel* it. This triangulation between him, Val, and Tia could become damn uncomfortable.

I apologized on your behalf.

Thank you. He stared at his discarded underwear,

lying on the carpet. Her body's plush clutch, its hungry rhythmic clench against his fingers as she climaxed, was seared into his brain. Never had spending outside a woman's body satisfied him so much.

A pulse of naughty amusement slid into his mind from across the hall.

He sent her the mental equivalent of a wink, then gently but firmly severed the bond. Tia might be comfortable with the always-on, wide-open-to-everyone connection Thane had warned him she favored, but he was not—and even if he wasn't by nature a very private man, his position as the Second precluded such rash behavior. If he and Tia were to share any sort of future together, she needed to learn how to block—effectively, ruthlessly, and often. If anyone could train Tia how to do so, it was Thane, the Vampire First's bondmate.

He pushed to his feet, dropped the underwear in the hamper, and headed for the shower, mentally sorting through his workday as he washed. He didn't have office hours tonight, and the resident could handle rounds. Legal paperwork, phone calls to return, a Council meeting for which he should prepare...all of which he could do here at home. After showering and dressing, he headed across the hall to check in on Val and Tia.

Never before had crossing the hall to Val's sitting room caused his stomach to turn such lazy, erotic backflips—and never before had such a strong chemical scent assaulted him. "Bloody hell." He picked up speed, entered the room where Tia and Val were watching TV, and quickly discovered the odor's source: Tia held a small, red bottle in one hand, and a tiny brush in the other, painting her toenails. On the table closest to her was an open bottle of remover or solvent, several sharp little tools, three turquoise-stained cotton balls, and a big mug of coffee. Her phone lay out of spilling range, but still within reach.

As he stared at the exotic feminine mess, one of the three contestants on the television screen leaned over to spin a colorful horizontal wheel, yelling, "Come on, big money!" while everyone else clapped. A slim blonde woman wearing an evening gown stood next to a wall of white, illuminated rectangles.

"Big money!" Val called.

Tia grinned down at her toes.

Val looked hale and hearty, his skin a ruddy pink against the collar of his burgundy velvet smoking jacket. If Wyland was a gambling man, he'd bet everything that he and Tia hadn't been the only lovers to share body and blood since they'd all seen each other last.

"Hi, there." Tia had noticed him. Somehow, her casual greeting sounded significant, intimate—or maybe it was the way she skimmed his body, like she could see right through his clothes.

"Hello." For some reason, Val was sitting in the club chair instead of his favorite place on the couch. Tia was curled up on the couch's far right cushion, leaving Val's seat open.

For him.

"Wyland, hello!" Val waved toward the couch. "Please. Join us."

After a pause, he sat in Val's place, his gaze snagging on Tia's legs. She wore a pair of those clingy black workout pants she seemed to live in, and seven of her ten toenails were painted a shiny, carnal red.

His pulse gave a kick, but he ignored it. He could keep his hands to himself in front of Val—not that Val, who'd led centuries of pagan rites, would be the least bit shocked by anything he might imagine.

Or anything he might do.

Val's silent laughter echoed in his head.

Tia and Val chatted, watching the game and discussing the simple word puzzles. Val, much to his relief, solved many of the puzzles more quickly than the contestants did, though he suspected Tia purposely let Val shout the answers out first. "What's this show called?" As a cognitive exercise, it was simple but effective.

"*Wheel of Fortune.*" Tia closed the bottle with quick twists of her wrist, set it on the table, and, after a slight hesitation, took his hand.

Lifting their joined hands to his lips, he kissed her knuckles. Her sunny pleasure slipped into him, but a tiny shadow remained. Apparently he still had some making up to do.

Ya think? Val thought.

Val, these things take time.

So says the man who hasn't taken a lover in a century, Val scoffed. *Don't assume you have all the time in the world, son.* "Tia, were you able to reschedule your appointment with the Senator?" Val asked. "Your face looks much better today."

Val was right; the dark half-moons under her eyes had definitely faded.

"We're meeting next month," Tia said, "and when we do, I'd really like Jane to join us." She fiddled with her thumbnail. "I'm going to mention it tomorrow when I give her a ride to a job interview. Give her some time to mull it over. She's…twitchy."

"Understandably so," Val said. "I'm sure you'll think of something."

Tia, behind the wheel? No bloody way. "I'd prefer you wait a bit before you drive," he said as mildly as he could manage.

"Why?"

"Tia, you were knocked unconscious." Not that her possibly concussed state had prevented her from making him come harder than he ever had in his life. "And your car's in the shop." Instead of simply replacing the broken passenger window, he'd asked the mechanic to replace every window with those providing UV protection.

"I'd planned to ask if I could use one of the SUVs."

"Of course you may, but—" *neutral, neutral* "—in my medical opinion, driving at this early point in your recovery puts your safety, and the safety of others, at risk. How about using a driver along with the SUV?" A driver who was also a trained bodyguard, because she damn well wasn't going to leave the house without one.

"Bubonic Plague!" Val suddenly exclaimed.

"What?"

Val pointed at the television. "The answer to the puzzle. It's Bubonic Plague."

Tia studied the puzzle. "So it is."

Val folded his hands over his stomach. "Speaking of which, have you moved Sigurd's trunk to the Archives yet?"

Apparently Val's thoughts were skipping rocks again.

"What do you mean, Val?" Tia asked.

"Sigurd's trunk. It's down in the catacombs."

Tia straightened from her comfortable slump. She reached for the phone sitting next to the nail polish bottle, then turned on the voice recorder.

Bloody hell, he knew exactly which trunk Val was talking about. Over a century ago, when they'd moved into the house, he and Thane had carried the simple wooden box deep into the caverns, with Val nipping at their heels, urging, "Take care, take great care…" They'd set the trunk against the far back wall, then had gone upstairs to retrieve the next item.

Thinking nothing of it, because there were so many items to move.

"What catacombs?" Tia asked.

"When we built the house in the early 1900s, we had to consider requirements beyond mere shelter," Val explained. "We needed a place to store our collected history, and the property next door—the Archives—wasn't yet ours. The cave system we dug under the house was the solution."

"Caves under the house? How cool."

Cool? Moving the artifacts had taken countless hours of hot, sweaty effort.

"Sigurd had been dead for months when I found him."

Wyland reeled at the abrupt change of subject, at the pain in Val's voice.

"I'd been in Italy on business, and while traveling home I saw a brutal scourge ravaging the land, infecting the old and young, the hale and hearty, the rich and the poor," Val said. "The Black Death—and being blood drinkers, vampires were particularly hard hit. Those who drank from the sick died themselves. As healthy donors became fewer and farther between, many vampires starved, or succumbed to bloodlust."

"How did you survive?" Tia asked.

"I drank from uninfected animals, mainly from deer. By avoiding the main traveling routes, I managed to find a meager supply of untainted donor blood. But when I arrived home..." Val paused, swallowing hard. "When I arrived home, our village was empty. Silent. Everyone was...gone. Sigurd had dug a pit and burned all the bodies."

"And Sigurd?" Tia asked softly. Empathy poured from her like water over a wound.

"I found him in our hut, lying on his pallet. Dead, of course. Black boils were still visible on his skin, and his journal lay open next to him." A tear spilled, rolling down his cheek. "The...the knife he'd used to slit his own throat was still in his hand."

Wyland wasn't surprised that Sigurd, ill and in extremis, had committed suicide rather than succumb to bloodlust. It was a vampire's final act of control over his own destiny.

Tia rose from the couch, knelt on the floor in front of Val, and took his gnarled hands. "I'm so sorry."

Val wiped his wet cheek. "It happened a long time ago, but thank you, my dear." Val looked down at her, then over to him. "I've forgotten more than I remember, but his journals might provide some of the answers you seek."

Wyland blinked. "You have his journals?"

"Of course I do. His journals, his pens and tools, and more. Everything the horse and I could carry."

Sigurd's journals, written in his own hand, downstairs all this time. Energy buzzed through him. After being stored in a battered trunk for nearly seven hundred years, were the pages still intact? Was the writing still legible? What had Sigurd used as paper and ink?

Had there been other Firsts before him?

Bloody hell.

"Could you and Tia bring the trunk upstairs for me?" Val asked.

"Up here? Why?" The trunk contained precious historical artifacts. Wyland wanted to assess their condition, and start necessary preservation work immediately.

"I'd like…" Val cleared his throat. "I'd like to see his things again." *One last time.*

His stomach lurched. *Val, you have plenty of time—*

"Of course we will." Tia scrambled to her feet, squeezing Val's hands. "We'll bring the trunk upstairs for you, right now."

He rose more slowly. "Will we?"

"Oh, stop with the eyebrow already. Of course we will." Turning off the voice recording, she looked down at Val. "Would you like to come with us?"

Val patted the arms of his chair. "These old bones are happy right here." Thane suddenly appeared at the sitting room door, carrying Val's breakfast tray. They held a silent conversation and shared a private, bittersweet smile. "Thane will keep me company while the two of you go to the caverns."

He hesitated. How would Val react to seeing Sigurd's belongings again?

"Go," Thane urged, shooing them toward the door as he set the tray on the table closest to Val. *Val's fine, and look how excited Tia is.*

She was practically dancing, shifting from foot to foot.

Three against one; he was on the losing end of this

argument. "You'll want to put some shoes on," he told Tia. "And maybe a jacket."

Grinning, she bent down to kiss Val's papery cheek. "We'll be back soon." As she rose, she snitched a piece of bacon from Val's plate, then walked toward the door, glancing at him. "I'll meet you in the hallway."

He followed her out. While Tia was in the guest room retrieving footwear, he went to his bedroom and found the flashlight he kept for emergencies. When he went back out to the hall, Tia was waiting, wearing a zip-up sweatshirt and those horrid black flip-flops with the sparkles on them. "Do you not own real shoes?"

"My toenails are wet."

"Heaven forbid you ruin a pedicure."

"Hey, I'd ruin the shoes, too." She started walking toward the stairway with an annoying snap-snap-snap, leaving him to follow. At the bottom of the stairs, she paused. "Where, exactly, are we going?"

"The basement."

"Oh, down by the pool?"

Nodding, he led the way to the basement door. "The entrance to the catacombs is down here." She followed him down the stairs, her noisy shoes telegraphing every footfall. At the bottom of the stairwell, he went to the south wall, to the shelving unit holding stacks of fluffy, folded towels. "Stand back." Reaching behind it, he pressed the hidden latch.

The shelving unit swung away from the wall on silent hinges, revealing a shadowy opening.

"Oh, awesome!"

"Indeed." Reaching into the stale air, he tugged the

pull chain of the nearest of many light bulbs hanging suspended from the ceiling. Flicking on his flashlight, he shone it ahead, past the built-in wine racks to the next bulb, a hundred feet ahead. "Follow me."

She obeyed, but not for long. What he'd envisioned as a brisk walk to the end of the cavern didn't happen, because Tia had questions, so many questions: About the initial excavation process. About the 'quaint' 1930s-era electrical system. About Valerian's wine collection, and about Wyland's work to transfer items stored in the catacombs to the Archives next door. And she touched everything— the walls, the light bulb chains, the floor—sniffing with her eyes closed, as if imprinting herself with scent.

"This is amazing," she said, stroking the wall's rough surface with her fingertips. "I wish I hadn't left my phone upstairs."

If she kept stopping to explore, they'd never get to the end of the passage. He took her hand. "Come on."

Finally, twelve light bulbs later, they reached the last storage room dug from the rock. Several pieces of furniture rested under protective sheets, and boxes sat neatly stacked, their contents waiting to be rediscovered. The battered wooden trunk sat right where he remembered, against the back wall, out of the light bulb's weak reach. He shone the flashlight's tight halogen beam against the trunk. "There it is."

"We walked south, right?" Instead of rushing to the trunk, she trailed her fingertips over the slats of a rough wooden box. "Toward the Archives?"

He nodded.

"We must be almost halfway there," she mused.

"Have you ever thought about connecting the two buildings?"

"Yes, but it's not a priority right now." He watched her walk toward the back wall, into the shadows. "Thane and I will revisit the idea when we update the electrical system." Which, given its Edison-era vintage, should probably be done sooner rather than later, unless they wanted a damn fire on their hands. "I haven't been down here in about a year," he said, following her.

"When Val came down with pneumonia?"

"Yes."

Tia shook her head in wonder. "Imagine living during the Black Death. Imagine surviving it." She suddenly grinned, her teeth flashing in the dim light. "Imagine you, having to record for posterity that the Vampire First remembered where Sigurd's trunk was while watching *Wheel of Fortune*."

Bloody hell, she was right.

Tia crouched beside the trunk, touched the worn wood. Tested its size by stretching her arms out to the side. When she lowered her head to sniff the wood, he almost yanked her back. There was no possible way that active *Yersinia pestis* remained, but who knew what kinds of dusts and bacteria lurked in the— "Tia, don't!"

Too late. She'd already opened the trunk. Peering inside, she covered her mouth with her hand. "Oh my stars."

"Back away," he ordered, pulling at her shoulders. "Don't breathe. Don't touch anything."

She shrugged him off. "I won't touch anything without wearing gloves."

"I'm more concerned about how your immune

system might react to ancient spores and bacteria."

She paused, then gave a fatalistic shrug. "If there's damage, it's already done, so let's take a look at what's in this trunk." She smiled winningly. "If I get sick, I know a really kick-ass doctor."

"I'm glad you're so confident of my abilities."

"Oh, you thought I meant you?" she teased, winking before peering into the trunk again. "Oh, Wyland. Look at this…."

He leaned over her shoulder, noting the heavy robes, the coarsely-woven linens…and there, toward the back, were three thick, bound journals.

A treasure beyond price.

Adrenaline surged. If anything might provide some information about Sigurd and the Old Ways, it would be these manuscripts, written in the man's own hand.

"Wyland?"

"Hmm?"

She pointed toward the back. "Is that…is that a bone?"

He saw a pale sliver of color. "Perhaps." He aimed the flashlight into the shadowy corner, then used it to nudge the swaddling fabric aside.

Shock speared through him.

It was a skull.

CHAPTER EIGHTEEN

With one eye on her screen and the other on the clock, Mila scrolled through the output of her latest test—or tried to. Dominic had his arms wrapped around her from behind, nuzzling her neck. "Dom, I really have to get this done." She gave him a half-hearted nudge with her elbow. "When you said you had a fetish about watching me work, you weren't kidding, were you?"

"Mmm hmm." His answer vibrated against her skin.

She leaned into his touch for a moment, then shrugged her shoulder to dislodge him, gesturing to the framed print leaning against the wall. "Would you mind hanging up that picture while I finish up? Five more minutes, then I can take a short break." A short one, because she was swamped, and his visits had become a near-daily habit. In hindsight, extending that open invitation for Dom to swing by whenever he was in the building had been a mistake. Being his dad was a patient, Dom was in the building a lot.

Sometimes he stayed for a few minutes, sometimes for an hour, just hanging out in her visitor's chair, but admittedly, she'd come to anticipate the moment when he'd rise from the chair, walk behind her, lean down, and wrap his arms around her. "Don't mind me," he'd invariably murmur. "Just keep working." It had become a game between them, an unspoken challenge: How long could she concentrate, keep her fingers flying over the keyboard, with him kissing her shoulder? Licking her earlobe? Nibbling his way up her neck? How long before she gasped or groaned, before she turned her back on her work and kissed the bejeezus out of him?

She cut a quick glance to her door. Necking in the office was so, so wrong. "Dom. The print?"

He reluctantly straightened. "Do you have a hammer? Some nails?"

"Right here." She opened her lower desk drawer and retrieved the hammer and the box of small hooks and nails Hansen had given her last night.

Taking them, he eyed the wall. "Any place in particular?"

"Eye level, vaguely centered. Thanks."

Leaving Dom to his task, she turned back to her screen, spot-checking the output from the extraction program she was testing. Unique identifiers, patient names, birthdates, contact information, medical records...it was a fast-flowing stream of green characters against a black background, of binary and hex, upper case and lower case, of data blocks and field demarcations...and at a quick glance, the output appeared to be correct. She double-checked the program's runtime. The enhanced program was running ten percent faster than the current production version—no small thing when data files approached a terabyte in size.

She leaned back, satisfied. Next up? Creating the corrupted data files they'd use for the next phase of testing. She loved working with data in the raw, designing corrupted files that would trigger every known failure scenario, hopefully producing the appropriate error message at the expected time, but…she'd consider it a personal failure if she couldn't plunge at least one unexpected stake into the program's heart sometime during the test cycle. "Fail gracefully, my ass." The smile turned evil at the edges. The developers didn't call her The Wicked Witch of the West for nothing—

Something unexpected caught her eye. Bailey Brown, a patient at Memorial? No way. They didn't treat human patients here; humans weren't supposed to know this hospital even existed.

She leaned closer, peering at the data dump. Yes, there was Bailey's name in all caps. Presented at the ER last winter…perforated ulcer…Drs. Melvin, Penn, and Wyland…laparoscopic surgery, and a three-day hospital stay.

"Hmm." Apparently they *did* treat humans at Memorial—extremely well-connected humans, that is.

She skimmed the file—temperature, blood pressure, blood work, labs—a full genetic panel? Why would someone with a perforated ulcer need a… Her eyes widened.

Bailey Brown had succubus DNA?

"Who's this?" Dom asked.

Blinking, she focused on Dom instead of the screen. He was standing in front of the chest-high bookshelf, holding the small, framed picture she'd set there just yesterday. Her, holding Katarina. The sight punched her in the gut.

"The little girl is obviously you—look at that dark hair—but who's the baby?"

She released a shaky breath. "My sister."

346

"You don't have a sister."

"She...died not long after that picture was taken." It was the only picture of Katarina she'd ever found in her parents' house, and she'd discovered it snooping through her mother's desk drawers. Furtively photocopied and quickly returned, the picture was her most prized possession.

Dom skimmed a fingertip over Katarina's face. "Was her death related to her Down's Syndrome?"

A wild laugh almost escaped. *You might say that.* "SIDS. She was two months old." Sudden Infant Death Syndrome was accurate enough, because Katarina had died suddenly, all right. One night, her parents put them both down for naps, but only Mila woke up—and in the horrible, chaotic aftermath, no one had thought to ask a little girl about the odd noises she'd heard coming from her parents' room next door. About the violent, emotional battering that a vampire child who shared blood with both parents hadn't been able to escape. Loud voices. Mommy and Daddy fighting. Daddy, terribly sad but terribly resolute. Mommy, wailing like a wounded animal.

Then, a brittle, frightening silence.

Hansen had finally found her, hiding in the closet. His arms had become the only safe place in her world.

Dom set the picture back on the bookshelf, then came over to her desk. This time, when he hugged her from behind, there was nothing but comfort in his touch. "I'm so sorry."

She leaned against him, twining her arms with his. "Thanks," she whispered. "It happened a long time ago." But she still remembered Katarina's big, gummy smile, and her sweet baby scent. To this day, catching an unexpected whiff of baby powder, or disposable diapers, made her throat clog with tears.

Dom's phone chirped. "A reminder I set about Hannah's soccer game," he sighed against her hair. "I'll leave her a message that I'll be late."

"No. I'm fine." She squeezed his hand. "Really, go to your sister's game." *Leave, so I can pull myself together and get some work done.* "We'll see each other again in a couple of days."

"Your parents' party." He pressed a sweet kiss to her cheek, straightened, then twirled her desk chair so she faced him. "Are you getting excited?"

"Mother is excited enough for both of us." Her mother was positively manic, consulting her checklists, and working the party planner's very last nerve. In a familiar act of self-preservation, her father had left the planning entirely to his bondmate; his only responsibility would be to show up wearing appropriate clothing. "I *am* excited about my new dress." The burgundy tea-length ball gown, long-sleeved with a portrait neckline and a nipped-in waist, was the most beautiful dress she'd ever seen, much less worn. At yesterday's final fitting, she hadn't been able to hide her delighted smile. The dress softened her angular lines, showcased her meager curves— subtle and classy enough to please her mother, but unmistakably sexy. Somehow, the designer had accomplished the impossible: pleasing them both.

Dom's wolfish grin made pleasure curl around her spine. "I can't wait to see it—or should I say, I can't wait to see how you look wearing it." His expression turned slightly uncomfortable. "Mom's taking me shopping tomorrow."

She grinned. "That should be fun."

"Not," he said, deadpan. "I hate shopping. But Mom insists I need a new suit, and going to the mall will get her away from the hospital for a while." He paused. "You're positive I don't need a tux?"

She shook her head. "Some of the older guests will wear tuxedos, but a dark suit will do very nicely."

His cell phone bleeped again. Plucking it out of his back pocket, he looked at the screen. "It's Hannah, wondering where I am. I'd better get going. Traffic's going to suck."

She rose, nodding in commiseration as they walked to her office door. It was almost 6:00 p.m., still the thick of rush hour. "Thanks so much for hanging up my print." Up on the south wall, the daytime shot of The Minneapolis Sculpture Garden's iconic *Spoonbridge and Cherry* spilled a rectangle of sunlight into the windowless room.

"You're welcome." But Dom wasn't looking at the print anymore; he was looking at the shelf again, at the picture of her and Katarina.

"I'll walk you out." Curiosity about Katarina, about her short life and sudden death, was the last thing she needed. No, strike that—the *actual* last thing she needed was for him to find out about her illness. Sure, Dom was hot, fun, and he kissed like a dream, but he'd guzzled an entire pitcher of the GPL's toxic, batshit Kool-Aid. His personality had some dark corners she wasn't sure she had the energy to explore—but on the other hand, maybe she could expose him to other points of view.

Do I really want to take that on? The more time she and Dom spent together, the greater the risk that he'd discover she had some dark secrets of her own.

They left her office and walked down the long

hallway, past empty cubicles and workspaces. "Where is everyone?" Dom asked.

"At happy hour." She'd been invited to go, but declined. Her new position came with more administrative work than she'd anticipated, and she'd let too much of it pile up. When they reached the end of the hallway, she opened the heavy security door. "Have fun at Hannah's game. Say hello to your family for me."

"I will."

Lifting onto her toes, she gave him a quick peck on each cheek. "And have a good time shopping."

Dom's eye roll was interrupted by his ringing phone. "Hannah." Reaching for the phone, he dropped a kiss onto her upturned lips. "If I don't take this, she'll never stop calling."

She made a shooing motion with her hands. "Go. Talk to your sister. I'll see you Saturday."

"'Bye." After another quick peck—and another— he pivoted and started walking away, punching a button on his phone and lifting it to his ear. "Hey, Hannah."

The affection in his voice positively melted her.

She watched him walk down the hall, waiting for him to give his usual jaunty wave as he turned the corner and disappeared from sight. When it came, she waved back, then trudged back to her office. Sitting at her desk once again, she looked at her screen. Nope, she hadn't been hallucinating. There was Bailey Brown's name, screaming at her in all caps, followed by her species: HUMAN-SUCCUBUS.

Though the humans' HIPAA law didn't apply at Memorial, the mere existence of this intermediate file made her skin prickle. She clobbered the file and kicked off a new run of the program, one that would extract the records of patients whose names started later in the alphabet. Doing so put her even further behind schedule, but it had to be done—and while the program ran, she could go to the break room and get some blood.

She touched her tingling lips. Did she have the time, or the emotional energy, to deal with Dom's complex life and mercurial moods? A burst of self-mocking laugher escaped. What made her think *she* could pull him into the light, when her own secrets were so deeply buried?

✳

Dom walked to the parking ramp with Hannah still yammering in his ear. Any security guard watching from the ceiling-mounted cameras would think the phone conversation was responsible for his gob-smacked expression, but...nope.

Mila had a dead sister who'd had Down's Syndrome? Bailey Brown was part succubus?

Holy shit.

"Dom, are you listening to me?"

"Yeah." Bypassing the elevator, he entered the stairwell and started climbing, reining in his impatience as his sister told a convoluted story about a dude at the soccer field who could be Harry Styles' twin, "if he had, like, a buzz cut, and only one tattoo."

Ever since their father's accident, Hannah called and texted him several times a day, just to touch base. He understood why she did it, but... "Hannah?" he interrupted, opening the fourth floor door. The Pathfinder was parked halfway down the nearest row. "I'm in the parking ramp. I'm going to lose signal soon." Thank the universe, because *damn*. "I should be at the field in half an hour or so."

"You and Mom are driving separately?"

"Yeah." Dom had crossed paths with his mother about an hour ago, outside his dad's hospital room. She'd been arriving for her daily visit, and he'd been leaving, on his way up to Mila's office. "If Mom's not on the road already, she will be soon."

"And then we're going to the Mall of America?"

"Yeah."

"Awesome!"

At least one of them was excited.

"Gotta go," she said. "Coach is starting warm-ups."

"Okay. See you soon."

As he hung up the phone and got in the car, a huge yawn escaped. Scrubbing his hands over his face, he glanced at his glove box, where he'd stashed the garage opener he'd swiped from Tia Quinn's car. Which garage did it open? The one at her house in Stillwater? The storage facility up the road from Vamp Central? Hell, Vamp Central itself? He'd planned on driving to Marine on St. Croix later tonight, but maybe it would be smarter to test the garage door opener during the morning hours, when the vampires were more likely to be asleep.

No need to take stupid risks.

Yeah, a night at home sounded good. He'd chill for a while with Mom and Hannah, maybe make some popcorn and watch a movie. And after they were both asleep, he'd sneak into his father's office, and explore the database some more.

On its face, the database was a collection of genealogy records—including species information, which helped him a lot—but digging a little deeper had yielded so much more. Family gossip, legal trouble, drug problems, secret affairs, kinks and exotic sexual habits...the database was a treasure trove of blackmail-caliber information.

But he'd save blackmail for later. Tonight's research? The Stanton family. As Mila had spoken about her sister, her stale, clammy fear had filled the room. Something about the situation didn't pass the sniff test. Surely the database would contain a record of Katarina Stanton's death. He also had more letters to write.

Had Tia Quinn received hers?

He backed the Pathfinder out of the parking spot, then headed for the exit. Tia hadn't posted anything new at *In Like Quinn* for days, and she'd completely dropped off social media. If she'd gotten seriously hurt during their altercation—hell, if she'd *died*— surely the news would be splattered all over the grapevine? He'd almost asked Mila to check whether Tia Quinn had been admitted to the hospital recently, but given he'd already seen admissions data he wasn't supposed to see, he hadn't pressed his luck.

Imagine, Bailey Brown, a human-succubus cross.

He navigated the parking ramp's tight, downward exit spiral. Yes, he'd stay home tonight—do some research, and write more letters—and check the garage door opener early tomorrow morning. And in a couple of days, Bailey Brown would receive a letter of her own.

❋

"Sigurd was a very erratic correspondent," Tia said to Wyland. Tugging off the white cotton gloves, she jotted the date of the volume's last entry in the wire-bound notebook sitting at her elbow, then stretched her arms overhead. "He'd write every day for three weeks in a row, then months would go by without a single word."

Wyland glanced at her over the upper rims of those ridiculously sexy reading glasses. "He *was* rather busy."

"I imagine." She hadn't actually read any of the journal entries yet. Instead, she'd offered to take a high-level view of the journals, noting dates and frequency of entries, leaving Wyland to focus on the contents of Sigurd's last journal. Over the last two days, he'd made copious notes on a yellow legal pad, wearing the white cotton gloves she found so annoying like he'd been born to them—which, given his age and his profession, he…had. As a Regency gentleman, and as a modern doctor, wearing gloves had to be second nature.

Leather riding gloves, cotton gloves, latex gloves…his gloved hands, stroking lazily over her skin…

Wyland cleared his throat. "Sigurd's final journal spans a period of approximately five months. The first half of the volume contains priceless information about ordinary village life in the Middle Ages…neighborhood squabbles, a missing horse, plans for the spring planting. Here—" he tapped a gloved finger against a specific entry "—is the first mention of illness, and within a week, dozens of villagers had fevers and chills, headaches, muscle pains, and swollen lymph nodes in the armpits and groin. Sigurd started out recording the name and age of each villager who died, but—" Wyland flipped to an entry near the center of the journal "—starting here, the entries get shorter and shorter, until, near the end, all I see are hash marks indicating what must be the death count since the last entry."

"And his last entries? Any information about why Sigurd committed suicide?" she asked gently.

A cheek muscle ticked as he turned to the last written page of the journal. "Unfortunately, no."

She looked at the yellowed page and recoiled. Sigurd's last journal entry consisted of a single, autobiographical hash mark, and a rusty spray of dried blood.

Wyland removed the gloves and then his glasses. Setting both on the legal pad, he rubbed his eyes.

"Let's take a break," she said, rising from her chair with a stretch. His cheekbones were too prominent for her liking. "I need some blood, and if I sit here any longer, my ass is going to sprout roots."

He glanced at her backside, bemused. "We wouldn't want that." As he stood, he tipped his head from side to side, trying to loosen stiff muscles. Who knew that reading for hours on end could be so hard on the body? As they walked to the kitchen, she glanced at the wall clock. Maybe she could talk him into going home, taking a long, hot shower together, and crawling into bed for a while. Lyudmila and Stanton's party started at midnight, and if she didn't take a nap first, she'd fall asleep in the canapes. Earlier, Wyland had asked if she'd be ready to leave by 11:00 p.m., giving them an hour to drive to Lyudmila and Stanton's Lake Minnetonka home.

Did he realize the conclusions the other guests would draw when they arrived at the party together? Did he care?

When they got to the kitchen, Wyland headed to the sink to wash his hands. That, too, was probably second nature. "Anna Mae called today," he said over the sound of running water. "She's finally done with Sigurd's trunk."

She joined him at the sink. "You're the one who insisted we bring it to Sebastiani Labs in the first place." After she'd discovered the skull, Wyland had quickly closed the trunk, and in what he'd described to Val and Thane as an abundance of caution, he'd asked Dr. Anna Mae Whitman to meet him at Sebastiani Labs' bio-hazard facility. During the long drive to the Sebastiani Labs campus in Chanhassen, Wyland had glanced at her far too frequently, as if reassuring himself that she hadn't dropped dead in the passenger seat.

Sebastiani Labs had been a revelation—what she'd seen of it, at any rate. Instead of using the main entrance, Wyland had driven around to the back of the building, pausing to speak at a machine that looked like one you'd find at a fast food drive-thru. After a short conversation, the loading dock door opened its giant maw. They'd pulled in, waited for the door to close behind them, and then driven down, down, finally stopping in a loading dock adjacent to a high-tech lab that reminded her of Iron Man's subterranean lair. And there, Dr. Whitman, a tiny, terrifying woman with more than a hint of bayou in her voice, had matter-of-factly unpacked Sigurd's trunk under a bio-hazard containment hood, a process Tia had recorded for posterity. In addition to Sigurd's journals and skull, the young, grieving Valerian had also packed Sigurd's robes, some linens, an ancient set of tools, and some writing implements. After declaring the items free of airborne toxins, Wyland and Dr. Whitman had debated about what should happen next. Wyland wanted to take the trunk and its contents back to Val, but Dr. Whitman had urged further tests.

Dr. Whitman had won. They'd left Sebastiani Labs with only the journals in their possession.

"She took a sample from the skull, and some blood off the knife," Wyland said, stepping back from the sink to dry his hands. "She'll sequence Sigurd's DNA for the Archives, and assess the chemical composition of the blood."

Chemical composition? Sigurd hadn't been poisoned; he'd committed suicide. "Why do that?"

"Anna Mae is an expert on anthropocentric environmental impact."

"Anthropo what?"

"Anthropocentric." He walked over to the refrigerator. "The study of humans' impact on the planet during the time they've been the dominant species. Some scientists theorize that modern humans' impact on Earth's natural systems is so visible, and so significant, that the planet has entered a sixth geological epoch called the Anthropocentric."

"Hmm."

He paused at the refrigerator door. "Within my own lifetime, we've gone from four-legged horsepower to nuclear energy, from mud huts to steel high-rises, from villages to megacities. There were fewer than a billion people on the planet when I was born, and now there are over seven billion."

"We're an industrious species, that's for sure."

"It leaves a mark."

She blinked at his vehemence.

"New research indicates that today's babies are born already carrying traces of hundreds of industrial chemicals and pollutants." Opening the refrigerator, he retrieved two bags of blood. "Sorry about the soapbox, but humanity has the dubious distinction of being the first Earth species 'evolved' enough to engineer its own bloody extinction."

"You, Val, and Thane—older vampires—definitely have a unique perspective on what's short term versus long term."

"And given we can't reveal our existence to humanity, we can't share our first-hand observations with anyone who isn't part of our culture." Wyland handed her one of the bags. "Sometimes I think we should reconsider. We live here, too. We have a vested interest in keeping the planet habitable…at least until we find a way to leave it again." He tightened his lips. "But that's a discussion for another day. I was willing to give Anna Mae time to get her samples, but I really want to get that skull back for Val."

As far as she was concerned, Dr. Whitman could keep the creepy, yellowed skull that had stared up at her with its empty eye sockets, but Wyland was right—Val's desire to see and touch Sigurd's things was the thing that had started this whole extravaganza. "We could pick the trunk up on our way home from the party tonight."

"We'll be on the right side of town." Wyland lifted

the bag of blood to his mouth, then hesitated. "You're right, you know. I'm *am* old."

"What? I didn't say—"

"You said 'older vampires', lumping me in with Val and Thane. I'm too old for you, Tia."

A merry laugh escaped as she skimmed his frame. "Yeah, right." The man was in his prime, sexually and otherwise. But...he wasn't laughing. He wasn't joking. "Are you serious? Sure, you're a little tired right now, we both are, but—"

"You can't deny the three hundred years between us."

"I don't deny them in the slightest, but I see them as a positive, not a negative. And for the record, Val's pretty damn hot."

He smiled, but then dropped his gaze to the bag of blood he held, studying the label as if it fascinated him. "Sometimes I feel..." His eyes were unfathomable, with an expression she'd seen only once before: on Valerian's face as he mentally detached from the here and now, and traveled back into memory.

Alone.

She took the blood from his hand and set it on the countertop. "Tell me. How do you feel?"

"Like a man in a place out of time."

She wrapped her arms around his waist, tethering him. "All I know is that you're the man I need, in the here and now." She pressed a gentle kiss to his beard-roughened jawline. "Let's go home."

When he looked down at her, the immortal ennui in his eyes was gone. "Are you tired?"

"Yes. Despite your so-called advanced years, *I'm* the one who needs a nap." But before falling asleep, she'd drag him into bed and let him rock her world. He'd never question her attraction, or his potency, again.

He looped an arm around her waist, examining her face in the harsh fluorescent light. "Your bruises are nearly healed."

Frequent infusions of his blood had faded them to nearly nothing, but no amount of makeup on Earth would hide the scar at her temple. "I'll have to figure out how to explain this at the party tonight."

"The truth won't suffice?" They left the kitchen, turning off lights as they went. "You tripped and fell getting out of your car. There's no need to discuss the circumstances."

She considered. "That'll work."

Wyland closed the journals so the weight of the pages wouldn't pull at the ancient bindings. "I wish we could stay home tonight," he muttered, pocketing his reading glasses. "I'd rather treat virulent pneumonic plague than go to this party."

"Why?" Did he not want to be seen with her in public after all?

"Dealing with Lyudmila can be rather...labor-intensive."

"That's an understatement." She flicked off the lights next to the door, then wound her arm through the crook of his elbow as he opened the door to the stairwell. "As our leader, you have to be diplomatic. But she has to be nice to me."

"Why?"

She grinned. "Lyudmila wants a nice write-up about the party. *ILQ*'s gossip page is its most-read feature."

"Aren't *you* the political mover and shaker?"

"Of a sort."

They entered the garage, got into Wyland's sexy car, and opened the garage door. As they backed out into the morning sun, something caught her eye.

"What?"

She stared toward the woods. "I thought I saw something."

"Nick mentioned a stray dog hanging around recently."

Or maybe she was just being paranoid. She took a second look, but saw nothing but swaying grass. As she consigned irresponsible pet owners to the seventh circle of hell, they headed home.

CHAPTER NINETEEN

Wyland accepted a flute of straw-colored champagne from his host. "Thank you." He took a sip, his eyes narrowing as tiny, tart bubbles exploded on his tongue. "Very nice. Valerian will regret not sampling this vintage."

"I'll send a bottle home with you," Stanton said magnanimously. "How is Valerian's health?"

"Much improved."

"That's good to hear." Despite their long business relationship, Stanton knew better than to ask for details. "Please send him my regards."

Across the room, Tia worked the room like a pro, floating from group to group like a modern Cinderella in her exquisite purple gown and heels. As she laughed and touched Jack's tuxedo-clad forearm, he tried not to stare at her exposed back, at the subtle flex of muscle. Her spine was a plumb line that his eyes helplessly followed, until it disappeared behind fabric that draped well below her waistline.

What undergarment could she possibly be wearing?

"Wyland?"

He fought his attention back to Stanton. "Fine turnout tonight."

Stanton skimmed the crowd, no doubt counting

social currency. The absence of three Council members—Valerian, Lukas, and Scarlett—no doubt rankled, but if anything was certain in Lyudmila and Stanton's world, it was that there would always be another party. They entertained frequently enough, and on a large enough scale, that their home had its own ballroom. Parquet floors gleamed, chandeliers threw warm, flattering light, and the liquor and champagne flowed. A string quartet played in the corner, softly accompanying the murmur of dozens of intimate conversations. Tuxedo-clad servers circulated with hot and cold *hors d'oeuvres*, and black-suited security guards nearly outnumbered the wait staff. Krispin Woolf had arrived with his own security team, as had Elliott Sebastiani. Despite the guards, Jack hadn't moved from the President's side since they'd arrived.

"Lyudmila is the consummate hostess, and my Mila is certainly following in her footsteps," Stanton said. "It's a fine quality to have in one's mate."

Wyland could think of two dozen qualities he'd desire in a mate more than the ability to plan a party, but he lifted his glass in a toast. "To Lyudmila."

"To Lyudmila."

As they sipped champagne, Tia moved on, greeting her parents. Standing behind the Quinns, Lyudmila, resplendent in a floor-skimming gown and dripping with diamonds, spoke with her daughter. Mila looked healthy enough, but having watched Tia wield a makeup brush like a magician's wand earlier that evening, he knew looks could be deceiving. Tia's bruises were now invisible, and the tiny bump on her nose noticeable only if you knew it hadn't previously been there, but there was no disguising the stitches at her temple.

Tia turned her head toward him and smiled. Then, while talking with her parents, she filled his head with torrid mental images. Sexual images, incendiary images. Images that answered his question about her undergarments.

She wasn't wearing a damn thing under that gown.

He shifted uncomfortably. How many years had it been since he'd tried to control an erection while wearing formalwear?

Tia's sensual, knowing laughter echoed in his head.

"I noticed you and Tia Quinn arrived together tonight," Stanton said, letting the statement hang—a conversational technique Wyland recognized because he frequently used it himself.

"Yes." Where was Stanton going with this? And why was Chadden, who now stood next to Tia, touching her bare back with such easy familiarity?

You know why. They'd been lovers, you dolt.

His fangs gave a warning tingle. Tia glanced over her shoulder, eyebrows raised.

He managed a tight smile, and turned his attention back to the conversation at hand.

"I'd heard Ms. Quinn recently moved to your side of town," Stanton continued. "How nice that you arranged transportation for tonight."

Did Stanton really think he and Tia had arrived together because of a polite carpooling arrangement? Did the man not have eyes in his head? "Ms. Quinn and I are romantically involved."

"Ah." Somehow, Stanton managed to stretch the word out to several suggestive syllables. "I can't say I blame you. She's a delicious morsel." A knowing expression crossed his face. "The young ones can be so…creative."

His hands formed fists. "Take care with your words, Stanton." The man had no clue how close he was to being laid out flat, right on his own ballroom floor.

Or maybe he did, because Stanton took a hasty step back, bowing his head. "My apologies, Second. We're both men of the world, and…" He swallowed, glancing at the fangs Wyland didn't bother to hide. "I must be honest. I'd hoped to suggest a match between you and my daughter."

"Mila?" Surprise made him recoil.

Stanton shrugged. "Her physique may not be to your liking, but she's healthy, and her bloodline is impeccable. After giving you an heir and a spare, you'd each be free to—" he glanced at Tia "—seek your own amusements." Stanton's gaze lingered on Tia's sweet, rounded bottom, as if assessing what her curves would feel like under his hands.

Lingered too long.

An inarticulate growl leaped from his throat. Party sounds receded, and his pulse pounded like a war drum.

He tasted blood.

Across the room, Tia's head turned. She separated herself from the group and started toward him.

Toward them.

Wyland took a deliberate step backward. Stanton would not get an opportunity to speak to her, much less shake her hand, kiss her cheeks, or breathe the same bloody air. "Hear me, Stanton. You'll not barter your daughter like a breeding sow." He held up his hand when it appeared the man might dare interrupt. "If I get the slightest wind that Mila has less than full agency in her choice of dates, partners, or mates, we will have...words."

Stanton paled, and extended a placating hand. "Wyland—"

Turning on his heel, he walked away.

Walked toward Tia.

They met in the middle of the floor. Though her face was carefully neutral, concern and comfort warmed him like sunlight, an analgesic seeping into all his jagged cracks. He smelled lilacs, her personal flower garden.

"How about some fresh air?" Taking him by the elbow, she led him to the French doors at the far end of the ballroom, onto the wide balcony overlooking the lake. She took a quick look around. "Looks like we have the place to ourselves."

Lake Minnetonka was an inky black pool, and moonlight gilded the birch trees with delicate silver filigree. Frogs croaked, crickets chirped, and fireflies danced near the cattails. Across the bay, the neighbors enjoyed a blazing fire. Tia led him to the railing, took the champagne flute from his hand, and sipped.

For long minutes, they simply stood there, leaning against the rail, drinking in the humid night air. And gradually, eventually, his fangs receded and the tension leached away. Tia must have interpreted his sigh as some sort of sign, because she slipped her arm around his waist. He turned, pulling her into an embrace. Despite the gown's distinct lack of coverage, she was warm. Yards of silk skirt whispered against his legs. "Thank you," he murmured against her lips. She hadn't tried to soothe him, hadn't murmured platitudes. Instead, she'd let him settle in his own time, and on his own terms.

Her perception was an exquisite gift, one he wanted to give in return.

"I knew you were agitated, but I didn't know why." Her kittenish tongue lapped at the corner of his mouth. "You're bleeding."

He reached up. Damn it, blood had dripped down to his chin. "Stanton…angered me."

"I guess so. Your poor inner lip." She swirled her tongue against the bite, sighed, then pulled away. "I thought you two went way back. Didn't he and Lyudmila move here from England about the same time you did?"

"Soon after." Which, now that she mentioned it, probably explained Stanton's 'heir and a spare' comment. Stanton had lived the life of an English aristocrat for centuries, but now, after earning untold riches here in America, it seemed his ambitions had taken a political turn. To suggest that Mila become his bondmate was preposterous.

"You're tightening up again."

He made a conscious effort to relax. "Stanton and I are business colleagues, not friends."

"I'm glad to hear it, because the way he treats his wife and daughter makes me want to smack that cheesy Rhett Butler mustache right off his face."

Yes, she had excellent instincts.

"But—" her clever fingers gave a subtle twist, unbuttoning his tuxedo jacket "—let's not talk about our esteemed host." With a glance over to the French doors, she pulled him to the far end of the shadowy balcony, slipping her clever hands under his jacket. "Have I told you how ridiculously hot you look tonight?"

Heat crept up his neck. "I believe you might have

mentioned it." Right in front of Nick, as Wyland had handed her into the limo.

"It bears repeating," she murmured against his neck. Her forefinger took a meandering journey over his black bow tie, down one of his shirt pleats, down, down, until she reached the juncture where their bodies met, where crisp cotton kissed her delightful décolletage.

Wyland wrapped his arms around her, tugging her closer. Her red-soled shoes added inches to her height, changing the alignment of their bodies in very intriguing ways. She made the most of it, exploring his neck and jawline with lips, tongue, and teeth. It was all he could do to not grind his cock against her soft, sweet heat. His hand drifted south, caressing the back that so enthralled him, until he reached the drape of silk just below her waist.

He paused. "Are you really not wearing anything under this gown?"

Teasing laughter vibrated against his neck.

He glanced at the French doors. He could find out in seconds, could simply slide his hand beneath the concealing drape of fabric. Then he'd know for sure—not that he could do anything with the information except be taunted by it. Tormented by it.

"You're considering it, aren't you? Considering groping my bare ass at this fancy party, with other people standing not twenty feet away." Her voice was an incantation, inflaming nerves already scraped raw. When she looked up at him, her eyes seemed to glow.

"Witch." He pressed her against his erection. "You think I won't?"

A delicate shiver shook her frame. "I think you will."

She was right, damn her eyes, because his hand was already sliding under the filmy fabric, skimming the slope of her sweet, rounded bottom.

Nothing but skin. "Bloody hell." His fingers flexed, squeezing her resilient flesh. An image suddenly popped into his head, of her standing at the balcony railing, looking at the lake, and of him, embracing her from behind. Of her, surreptitiously shifting her skirt. Of him, unzipping his pants. Of a fast, furtive fuck, right here, right now.

Christ, his cock was going to burst right out of his pants, and from the sultry expression on her face, she damn well knew it. He gave her butt cheek a smart little tap. "I wish I could turn you over my knee and give you the spanking you so dearly deserve—"

"Someone's coming," she hissed. She tried to back away, but his hand was caught in her dress.

The French doors opened. Mila Stanton strode onto the balcony, followed by the young man he'd seen her with earlier. "Dom, what the hell did you think would happen? Didn't you notice the guards?" She threw her hands in the air, exasperated. "You don't just…just casually approach Krispin Woolf and start a conversation."

Wyland backed Tia into the darkest corner of the balcony.

"He's my Alpha," the boy said. "I just wanted to thank him for everything he's doing for my father."

Ah, Perry Reese's son Dominic. Wyland had been in the ER when Reese had arrived, barely clinging to life after a horrific car accident. Now a quadriplegic, one of Krispin Woolf's closest advisors cursed the doctors who'd saved his life.

"The guards didn't have to get so rough." The

young man scowled, rubbing his upper arms through his suit coat. "What did they think I was going to do, pull a knife on him or something?"

"It wouldn't be the first time," Tia whispered.

He brought his finger up to his lips. Mila and Dominic were on the other side of the balcony and hadn't noticed them yet—which was good, because he was still hard as a pike. Given the young couple's body language, and their easy annoyance with each other, Wyland guessed they were lovers.

"Dom, you have to be careful around Krispin Woolf."

"Tell me something I don't already know."

"Then why—"

"Mila, what did you think I was going to do? Tell him how worthless last month's GPL meeting was over *hors d'oeuvres*? Please. I just wanted to thank the man."

"But you can't just...there's a protocol...damn it, there's no talking to you." Mila shot her young suitor a scathing glance. "I'm leaving."

"Mila..." Dominic tried to take Mila's hand as she passed, but she stepped out of reach, her heels tapping an annoyed staccato toward the door. The young man followed, catching her by the wrist, whirling her around.

Time to nip this in the bud. "Hello, Mila," he said, stepping out from the shadows.

Mila's gaze flicked from him to Tia. "Wyland. Ms. Quinn. We didn't mean to disturb you."

"You did no such thing," he said. "It's a beautiful evening." As they joined the young people, Mila took Dominic's hand, the hand she'd tried so hard to avoid not five seconds ago. Apparently Mila didn't need rescuing after all. "Allow me to introduce my companion, Tia Quinn."

Mila shook Tia's hand. "How nice to meet you. I read *In Like Quinn* all the time." She gestured to the young man. "And this is Dominic Reese."

"Ms. Quinn." Dominic nodded, then quickly met his gaze. "Sir, I understand you treated my father after his accident," he said. "Thank you."

"You're welcome." Did Dominic realize his father still asked every doctor who examined him to let him die?

After several uncomfortable seconds of silence, Dominic cleared his throat. "Mila, are you ready for another glass of champagne?"

Sweat had popped at his hairline. For some reason, Mila's young man was very nervous.

"I'd love one," Mila said. "May I bring you two a refreshment?"

"We're fine, thanks," Tia answered with a kind smile.

They watched the two youngsters go back to the ballroom. As soon as the French doors closed behind them, Tia grabbed his hand. "Did you hear that? The comment Dominic made about the GPL?"

"I was paying more attention to how he touched Mila."

"The grabby-hands? Yeah, that was a total dick move." Even though they were alone, she lowered her voice. "Remember what Sasha and Antonia said about the younger contingent of the GPL meeting at hotels around the city?"

A puzzle piece clicked into place. "Ah."

"Perry Reese is one of Krispin Woolf's closest advisors. Like father, like son?"

Did Tia have proof that Perry Reese was a member of the Genetic Purity League? Before he could ask, she started walking toward the French doors. "Where are you going?"

"Back to the party. I think I'd like some champagne after all."

He recognized that expression. She was a foxhound, hot on the trail. "Tia…"

"Just some champagne, and maybe a little girl talk." As she opened the door, she gave him a cheeky wink. "I'll hook up with you later. And yes, I mean 'hook up' as defined in the Urban Dictionary."

Before he could ask her to be careful, or what the hell the Urban Dictionary was, she was gone.

✹

Tia found Mila standing alone at one of the bars, ordering a Long Island Iced Tea. Despite its innocuous name, the beverage had a serious kick. "That sounds awesome," she said, joining her. "Make that two." She glanced at Mila and smiled. "I decided I wanted a drink after all."

"Tell me about it."

Mila sounded really annoyed, which both sucked and rocked. She didn't wish the younger woman pain or ill will, but emotionally compromised people often spoke without thinking, revealing information they later wished they hadn't. As the bartender poured shots of top shelf vodka, tequila, rum, triple sec, and gin into highball glasses, Tia pushed aside a spurt of guilt. Mila had ordered the drink before she'd even arrived. She was simply going to…be there when all that liquor hit. "Where's the delectable Dominic?" The young man was nowhere in sight.

Mila waved a hand toward a hallway. "That way. Bathroom, I think."

"Trouble in paradise?"

Mila gave an exasperated sigh. "Have you ever heard that saying, 'If it has tires or testicles, it's going to give you trouble'?"

Tia laughed. "Oh, that's perfect. My car's in the shop as we speak." Wyland's testicles, on the other hand, were in perfect working order.

The bartender finished mixing their drinks. Mila thanked him, took both highball glasses, offered one to Tia, and lifted her own in an ironic toast. "To tires and testicles."

"I'll drink to that. Them. Whatever." The fumes rising from the glass were enough to give her a contact buzz, but she took a first testing sip. "Whoa," she strangled out. Alcohol tap-danced on her tongue, paralyzing her vocal cords.

Mila took a sip. "Good, right?"

"Mmm." She tilted her head toward the sitting room Mila had indicated. "Do you mind if I sit for a minute? My feet are killing me." She started walking toward the red-walled Victorian parlor without waiting for an answer. The younger woman would certainly follow. Hospitality was bred into Mila's blood and bone.

And she did, inviting Tia to sit on one of a pair of delicate, curvy-backed chairs she suspected had crossed the Atlantic with the family over a century ago. As soon as she settled onto the seat, she slipped off her shoes with a sigh of pleasure.

Mila companionably did the same.

As they made small talk—the party guests, the weather, their work—Tia bided her time, waiting for the right moment to nudge the conversation toward the meeting Dominic had mentioned out on the deck. She took a tiny sip of her drink, then leaned closer to Mila. "So, you and Dominic." Her tone, a carefully calibrated blend of sensual appreciation, knowing feminine humor, and faerie empathy, invited confidences. "Are you dating?"

"I don't know if I'd call it dating."

She lifted a droll brow. "Just taking him for a test drive, then?"

Mila snickered. "You might say that." Lifting her glass, she downed a good quarter of the beverage. "Speaking of which, are you and Wyland, you know, together? I got the feeling we interrupted something out on the deck."

Together? What an interesting word. She and Wyland were lovers, yes, but …their relationship was more than just physical. She wasn't just taking him for a test drive. She drove her cars until they died.

Somewhere along the line, she'd fallen in love with him.

"Tia? I beg your pardon." Mila looked down at the sweating glass. "It was an intrusive question."

"No worries." The smile she gave Mila was a little shaky around the edges. "I was just thinking that 'together' is a word I rather like. I've never liked the word 'girlfriend'; it seems childish to me. 'Lover' feels too intimate for day-to-day use, but 'partner' isn't intimate enough." How had Wyland introduced her to Mila and Dominic out on the deck? As his companion. Yes, that worked, too. "Yes, we're together."

"I could tell. His mouth was all swollen from kissing." Her lips tipped mischievously. "And the way he looks at you? Rawr."

How could Mila tell Wyland's lips were swollen? "You seem to know him quite well."

An odd expression flashed across Mila's face. "He and my father do a lot of business together. He's also my doctor. Speaking of which, what happened to your head?"

"I tripped getting out of my car," she said. "Clumsy me, I bumped my head against the door as I fell—"

"Mila, there you are." Dominic Reese strode into the sitting room, looking harried. He stutter-stepped when he saw her. "Oh, Ms. Quinn," he said. "I'm sorry for interrupting."

Damn it. Her opportunity to talk to Mila alone was gone.

Mila reached for his hand. "Is something wrong?"

"Hannah had a nightmare." He shrugged helplessly. "She didn't want to wake up Mom, so she called me instead."

"Of course you had to take the call," Mila soothed. "Is she okay now?"

Tia sat quietly as they talked about Dominic's young sister, who, in her opinion, might very much benefit from seeing a counselor. He clearly cared about his sister, and despite Mila's earlier annoyance, she was offering him comfort now.

In his beautiful suit and tie, the young werewolf looked perfectly respectable, but something about him made her body hair stand on end.

Suddenly, two of Krispin Woolf's oversized

bodyguards entered the room. "Mr. Reese? Would you come with us, please?"

"Why?" Dominic asked.

It was a reasonable enough question.

"The Alpha would like to speak with you."

Dominic tensed. "Of course." He quickly buttoned his suit coat. "Ladies, please excuse me. Mila, I'll find you later."

Mila nodded.

They watched as the bodyguards escorted Dominic from the room. "What's that all about?" Mila muttered.

"I have no idea." Earlier, on the deck, the young couple had been arguing about how Dominic had introduced himself to the Alpha. Maybe Krispin Woolf was rewarding his chutzpah.

Or maybe not.

Mila rose from her chair, casting a worried glance after Dominic. "I should really get back to the party." She reached for her shoes.

Girl talk was definitely over. "I should circulate, too." Suddenly, the prospect exhausted her. Tia reluctantly stood, stepping into her discarded Louboutins as Mila fastened her ankle straps. "Thank you for the drink, and the conversation."

"Any time."

When? She and Mila didn't run in the same circles; Mila was simply being polite. Asking for another meeting, another conversation, so soon after the party would presume upon a relationship that simply didn't exist.

Hold off. Bide your time.

Patience was not her strong suit.

She and Mila parted ways at the sitting room

entrance. Instead of following Mila back to the party, she escaped to the ladies' room, which had a pretty— and blessedly empty—sitting room of its own. She sat on the delicate upholstered chaise, kicked off her shoes again, and pulled a small notebook out of her clutch. After scribbling down notes and impressions for her column about the party, she set the notebook aside and thought about subjects that *wouldn't* find their way into her column: How could she engineer a casual conversation with Mila Stanton about the Genetic Purity League? What had Dominic Reese's mysterious conversation with Krispin Woolf been about?

And how the hell had she managed to fall in love with the Vampire Second?

CHAPTER TWENTY

The sounds of the party receded as the bodyguards led Dominic down a maze of hallways off the north side of the ballroom. It was all he could do to control the bounce in his step. The Alpha wanted to speak with him. Tia Quinn wasn't dead.

Maybe things were finally going his way.

Why had he been nervous about coming to this party tonight? Yeah, Mila's family's mansion was pretty damn intimidating, with its acres of shining floors, the sparkling chandeliers, museum-quality art, the servants... Mila's family had a damn *ballroom* in their *house*. But no one had treated him like he didn't belong—no one except the intimidating Lyudmila, that is—but Mila had told him not to take it personally; her mother looked down her nose at everybody. Mila's father had given him a polite, firm handshake when he'd arrived, but he was pretty sure it had been Stanton's gaze boring into his back most of the night.

He surreptitiously tugged at the hem of his suit jacket. Mila had been right about the suit—all the tux-wearing guests were older—but their age and power hadn't stopped anyone from shaking his hand when Mila made introductions. President Sebastiani had even asked after his father's health.

And speaking of health…Tia Quinn looked pretty damn fine for a vampire who'd been left for the sun. Yeah, she had some visible stitches, but if the sun had damaged her in any way, he couldn't tell. Earlier that morning, he'd discovered the garage door opener he'd stolen from her car opened the big, double garage door at River City Storage.

He was getting pretty damn good at this surveillance stuff.

When the hallway came to a T, one of the linebacker-sized guards jerked his head to the left. "This way." The rich red carpet gave way to polished hardwood, and their footfalls clicked as they walked to the end of the hall. Each step brought them closer to a portrait of a younger Lyudmila, wearing a pearl-encrusted gown with a stiff, white ruff that hid her neck. Same disapproving gaze, though. It judged them as they approached.

"Stop here." The guards gave him a thorough pat-down, taking his phone from his pants pocket before gesturing to the door.

The windowless interior room looked like an old-fashioned library, the walls covered with shelves and the shelves filled with books, and it smelled pleasantly of furniture polish. An antique globe stood in the corner, glinting with what looked like real gold. To the right of the fireplace was a towering grandfather clock, and exotic-looking objects from Stanton's many travels were displayed under lights throughout the room.

And there, sitting at a glossy wooden table with a guard at his back, was the WerePack Alpha, casually paging through an atlas.

Talk about looks being deceiving. He had salt-and-pepper hair and an average-sized frame, but Krispin Woolf could take care of himself in a fight. His nose was crooked, his left earlobe was gone, and his closely cropped beard couldn't disguise the scar that sliced across his left cheek. The previous WerePack Alpha had inflicted the grievous wound during an unusually bloody leadership challenge—a fight Krispin Woolf had won.

Among the werewolves, leadership challenges were to the death.

"Mr. Reese." Krispin Woolf rose, then walked around the table with his hand extended. "Your father has spoken of you many times. How nice to finally meet you in person."

Even at ease, power eddied around him in near-visible waves. "Sir." Dom shook his hand, then kissed both cheeks. "Please, call me Dominic." He cringed as the words left his mouth. The Alpha didn't need his permission for a single fucking thing.

"And how is your father doing today?"

How do you think he's doing? He slammed the door on his thoughts. "As well as can be expected." The Alpha had a fine nose, and would pick up any stink of fear or resentment—

"You have something you wish to say to me?"

Shit, too late. His balls shriveled into tiny peas as he eyed the Alpha's black tuxedo. Rumor had it that despite the bodyguards, he carried at least three weapons on his person at all times—

"Dominic." The Alpha rounded the table and sat back down. "Please, speak freely."

He glanced at the Alpha's right hand. No blade, no garrote, just a big, chunky ring he'd never noticed before. Did he dare take the Alpha at his word? Hell, what choice did he have? This was his opportunity to ask questions, questions only the Alpha could answer. Looking through the genealogy database, he'd found dozens of asterisks, which he was able to correlate to people of their culture who'd been allowed to die with dignity. Katarina Stanton's record had reflected that same, telling tag.

He swallowed the softball-sized lump in his throat. "Alpha, why won't you ..." He eyed the corners of the room. Was this a safe place to speak? "Why can't my father's final wish be granted?"

"I see you're considering the security of this room. Fine instincts." An expression of mild annoyance clouded the Alpha's face, then passed. "All surveillance devices have been...temporarily disabled."

"Listening devices? Bugs?"

"I can't blame Stanton." The Alpha shrugged a shoulder. "Knowledge is power, and there are many powerful people here tonight."

Dom looked around, aghast. Was the whole house bugged? Who could live like that?

Did Mila live like that?

"Allow me to answer your question about your father in what might seem a roundabout way," Woolf said. "First, let's discuss your unauthorized use of the secure computer in your father's office."

His diaphragm clenched.

"Using your father's login credentials, you've spent dozens of hours searching my confidential ancestry database." The Alpha lifted an imperious brow. "Explain."

The guard standing behind the Alpha unbuttoned his suit coat.

A wave of panic nearly dropped him to his knees. Of course the Alpha knew; he knew everything. What explanation could he possibly give? How could he explain the pride he'd felt when his father had shared such sensitive information with him? Entrusted him with it? Dom had let himself dream of a day when he and his father might work together, with him serving as his father's arms, legs, feet, and hands. But he couldn't expect the Alpha to care about his feelings. Actions were what mattered. And he'd repeatedly accessed the database before he'd been given permission to do so.

He made himself meet the Alpha's hard gaze. "It's true, Alpha."

"What's true?"

"I accessed the database without permission."

The grandfather clock ticked away the time. Finally, the Alpha spoke. "Excellent."

"What?" Relief made his voice wobble.

"You didn't deny your actions, but you didn't supply extraneous information. You also didn't try to protect yourself by revealing that your father *told* you about the database. That he shared his login credentials with you."

"Sir, I don't understand."

"That's a fine thing to be able to admit, under the right circumstances." The Alpha shifted in the chair, crossing his legs. "I value both curiosity and initiative. Given the hours you've spent logged onto the system, you appear to have plenty of both."

A hope he didn't dare acknowledge started to stir.

"We also haven't found any evidence that you've used the information inappropriately."

It took a couple of seconds for him to read

between the lines. "You're monitoring my…" Emails? Texts? Phone calls? Heat climbed up his neck. Some of the phone conversations he'd had with Mila had been…pretty graphic.

The Alpha gave him a knowing look. "There's nothing I—we—haven't seen or heard before. Indeed, I admire your initiative with Mila Stanton."

Mila. The database. Surveillance. This conversation was bouncing all over the place. "About my father's request that his suffering be ended…"

The Alpha's lips flattened into a thin line. "Unfortunately your father has requested a solution I cannot sanction."

"But you can," Dom protested, clenching his fists. "You have, on many occasions."

Woolf didn't confirm or deny his statement. "I cannot sanction his request," he repeated.

Dom's vision started going bloody around the edges. His mouth throbbed and pulsed, and sheathed claws gave a warning itch under his skin. "My father has served you well," he growled.

The nearest guard quickly closed in, grasping him by the upper arms. "Pup, you'd best control yourself."

The Alpha and his guards watched as he shoved back his wolf, as he fought to regain control of his body and his emotions. As he fought himself. Finally, his vision cleared, and his nose and jaw stopped their infernal throbbing. Bowing his head, he blinked away tears of anger and shame.

He'd fucking blown it.

"Dominic." The Alpha waited until Dom met his gaze again. "I owe you no explanations, but I will enlighten you in this instance. Because, yes—your father has served me well."

Dom tried to pull his arm away from the guard. No go.

"Have you ever heard the saying, 'May you live in interesting times?' We live in very interesting times, and it's both a blessing and a curse. Technological advances have impacted every field of endeavor—medicine, law, forensics—and it's those very advances that now make it impossible to give your father the merciful ending he deserves." Woolf's sigh seemed to carry the weight of the world. "Perry's situation is…unfortunate. He doesn't have the physical ability to take matters into his own hands, and I cannot allow you to sacrifice your future so he may end his. As a leader, I cannot allow that to happen."

He wouldn't have to go to prison. Relief rained down, followed by a huge guilt chaser.

He was a bad, bad son.

But… "No more Old Ways? Ever?" What did that mean for the GPL? He'd spent so much time being pissed off that no one at GPL meetings seemed to care about the group's work. Now it seemed the Alpha didn't care, either.

What the hell was going on?

When the guard released him, Dom rubbed his smarting upper arms. His suit coat was wrinkled to hell and back.

"Dominic, are you interested in continuing your father's work?

His pulse leapt. "Of course, Sir."

"I'm glad to hear it. Family is important, Dominic—a fact I think you realize, given how much time you've spent at your father's bedside, and researching prominent families." A heavy pause. "Including my own."

His mouth went dry. "Your family tree is very interesting, Sir." The database had confirmed Mila's statement about the Beta's health. Jacoby Woolf's neurological problems had been diagnosed quite recently, well after he'd taken his Council seat—one more thing Mila had been right about. And speaking of Mila… He ignored the twinge of conscience. *You knew you were going to use her.* "My relationship with Mila Stanton has been enjoyable, and unexpectedly useful."

The Alpha's dark brow lifted a mere millimeter.

"She works at Memorial Hospital, in their IT department, and at least some of her work requires that she access people's medical data." Dom looked down at his nails, mimicking the gesture he'd seen the Alpha make a few moments ago. "Such data might be a valuable addition to your database."

Woolf's gaze sharpened. "Go on."

He explained that he'd seen Bailey Brown's hospital records while visiting Mila in her office, that Bailey had been brought into Memorial's ER last year for a perforated ulcer. "Follow-on genetic tests revealed that she has succubus heritage."

"How very interesting." The Alpha sat silently, as if lost in thought. The guard standing behind him approached, then murmured something in his ear. The Alpha nodded. "Dominic, I'd like to discuss your idea in greater detail." He glanced up at the guard, who pulled out a phone, tapped and swiped, then bent again. The Alpha nodded once. "Come to my office at 10:00 a.m. next Tuesday."

He worked the day shift next Tuesday. "I'll find someone to cover my morning hours at the health club."

"You work at Woolf Den, correct?"

"I'm one of the assistant managers. Your daughter Andi is my boss."

"And I am hers. Give Andi two weeks' notice, and we'll start your transfer paperwork Tuesday."

Transfer to where? Doing what? The Alpha named a starting salary that made his eyes pop. Hell, for that kind of coin, the details didn't matter. "I appreciate the opportunity, Alpha."

"Sir?" The guard who'd taken Dom's phone earlier now held it in his hand. "A text from Mila Stanton, wondering how much longer Dominic will be."

And three men hovered outside the door, waiting.

The Alpha stood. "Carry on, Dominic—and welcome to Woolf Enterprises."

Should he mention his letter writing campaign? The one that had half the members of the Underworld Council shitting their pants? *No.* That information would keep until they met on Tuesday. "Thank you, Sir." After kissing the Alpha's cheeks, he strode to the door, nodding at the men who entered as he exited.

The guard returned his phone. "Do you need help finding your way back to the ballroom?"

Something in the bodyguard's voice, something in his eyes, made Dom's stomach churn. "No, thank you."

"Take care, son."

He managed to find his way back to the ballroom, but instead of finding Mila, he went to the bathroom instead. Once inside, he glanced around, searching the ceilings and corners, as if a hidden surveillance device might overhear his private thoughts.

What have I gotten myself into?

A sick, clammy sweat suddenly filmed his

forehead. Saliva spurted, and his stomach gave a warning clench. It lurched again as he dove into the nearest stall.

Sagging to his knees, he puked all over the pristine white toilet seat.

❋

As they pulled away from Sebastiani Labs with Sigurd's chest in the trunk, Tia noticed Nick had closed the privacy window separating the front seat of the limo from the rear. Smart man—but on the other hand, he probably hadn't needed his keen observational skills to realize that she wanted to jump his boss's bones. But first... "I hear Scarlett and Coco are doing well," she said to Wyland. She'd gotten the information second-hand, from Sasha and Antonia. Wyland had apparently visited them twice since Coco's birth, and he hadn't mentioned it to her.

"Mmm." He sounded distracted, lost in thought as he looked out the window at the dawn sky. When she slipped off her shoes, her sigh of relief got his attention. "Sore?" Wyland shifted closer, lifting her bare feet onto his lap. The fine fabric of his tuxedo pants felt decadent against her skin, and when his strong thumbs started rubbing her aching arches, she almost moaned.

"I wish you'd told me you were going to see Scarlett," she said. "I haven't seen them since the night Coco was born."

"I wasn't making a social call. And you were rather indisposed."

"True." Sasha and Antonia had shared plenty of information Wyland couldn't, and what information they hadn't, Scarlett's mother had. In most of the pictures Claudette had proudly shown her, little Coco Annika seemed to be screaming her head off, her red face nearly matching her sprout of red hair—but the picture Claudette had snapped of an exhausted-looking Elliott cradling his napping granddaughter made her ovaries twinge. Claudette confided that she'd asked Rafe to create a sculpture of the moment as a gift for Elliott's next birthday, "If only to memorialize that the child once had a silent moment." Pride eclipsed the exasperation; it was clear that Coco was already exhibiting signs of her powerful siren lineage.

Wyland's thumb pressed into a particularly sore muscle. "That feels fantastic," she groaned. "If you ever feel the need to take up yet another career, you can add masseur to the list."

His lips twitched at the corners. "Flex and point for me." She obeyed, brushing her toes against his half-hard penis. "Brat," he murmured. "Did you learn anything from your conversation with Mila Stanton?"

"Not much," she admitted. "Unfortunately, we weren't alone very long before Dominic joined us. But get this. Right after Dominic arrived, two of Krispin Woolf's bodyguards showed up, saying the Alpha wanted to speak with him." She leaned back against the seat. "Why would Krispin Woolf want to speak to a young werewolf?"

"I spoke with every vampire at the party tonight. Woolf likely did the same with his people."

She'd done plenty of circulating herself. High-powered parties were always both work and play—

she was always networking on behalf of the foundation—and as a journalist, she'd learned to keep her eyes and ears open. Whether hosted in the human world or in theirs, parties were places where information and influence were sought, exchanged, bartered, and sold. "Be careful," she teased. "I think you just suggested Krispin Woolf was behaving as a good leader might."

"He *is* a member of the Underworld Council."

A pregnant pause. In the silence, she could almost hear the 'for now' he didn't say. "You're investigating him, aren't you?"

Another pause. "No."

She bit back a hiss of frustration. He hadn't lied; he'd answered precisely the question she'd asked. He might not *personally* be investigating Krispin Woolf, but Lukas and Jack probably were. "You're such a…a…lawyer," she complained.

"Have I told you how beautiful you look tonight?" He nibbled her wrist. "That dress could incite a riot."

"You're trying to distract me." And succeeding.

"I wasn't the only one who noticed."

His sulky tone was…really hot. "Whatever do you mean?"

"Does Chadden always touch you so much?"

"Yes." Two could play the one-word answer game. Chadden touched everyone.

"Someone needs to speak with him about that."

She leveled a gaze at him. "I'm perfectly capable of letting a man know when I don't want to be touched."

"You were lovers."

"Yes, lovers and friends. And my friend is worried about me." She let some steel enter her voice.

"Apparently he showed up at Vamp Central a couple of days ago. Thane told him I wasn't receiving visitors."

"You needed sleep."

"Oh, come on," she said, exasperated. "You were so rude to him tonight."

"He understands why," he grumbled.

And now his fangs were dropping. *Men.* If the jealous dolt would drink from her, as she had from him, he'd realize the only lover she wanted was him.

She glanced at the window Nick had so intelligently closed. At the butter-soft leather seats, at the dim, rosy light. At Wyland's fangs, and at the hard-on he couldn't hide. Knowing she pleased him was a gift—one she yearned to share with him through the blood.

What better time than now?

She sat up, then tugged at the end of his black bow tie. The knot slowly loosened, leaving two strips of fabric trailing down the sharp pleats of his shirt.

He shot a warning glance at the window shielding them from Nick's view. "What are you doing?"

"He can't see us," she whispered, working at his top shirt button.

After a slight hesitation, he leaned back against the leather seat, watching as she unfastened three more buttons.

Fangs tingling, she watched right back—because damn, who wouldn't? With his tie hanging loose and his open shirt revealing a slice of bare chest, lounging against the seat and sitting with his legs slightly spread, he looked deliciously disheveled. She stroked the warm skin she'd just uncovered, pausing over his pectoral.

His heart thundered against her knuckles. He was anything but relaxed.

"I have a fantasy," she murmured, reaching behind his head to tug at his hair band. When the blond weight spilled over his tuxedo-clad shoulders, her core gave a greedy clench.

A muscle jumped at his jawline. "Tell me."

Gathering her skirts, she straddled him. "I've never made out in the back seat of a limo before. Have you?"

"No." His hands, now on her hips, were heavy and warm. "Given how many musicians you've dated, I would think limousines would be old hat."

She laughed. "Limos are few and far between for most working musicians." She reached for his thin leather belt, unbuckling it and unzipping his pants with deft movements. "No, this is a new experience for me."

As her hand curled around his cock, he slipped his hand under her skirt. His fingertips ghosted up her thighs, up and up... "Bare," he whispered, half-groaning. "I've been dreaming of getting under this dress again all night long."

She gasped as his nimble fingers skimmed her slick folds. Squirmed as he circled her opening, then went no further. "Wyland." Her voice cracked. "Stop teasing me."

"Like you teased me?" His voice was a soft, gravelly rumble. "I was walking around half hard all night long."

He was fully hard now, and in the proverbial palm of her hand. She gently twisted her wrist, giving his glans a diabolical caress. "I liked knowing I made you that way," she whispered. "I liked knowing that, under this custom-made, perfectly tailored tuxedo, you were aching. Burning for me the same way I burn for you." She opened her thoughts to him, incendiary thoughts about their mouths on each other...licking, sucking...

Biting...

His hips jerked beneath her. "You want me to drink from you."

"Yes."

"Here, in the back seat of a limo."

"Yes."

"You're so wet for me," he whispered.

"Always." She couldn't imagine a time when it wouldn't be true.

Suddenly his fingers were gone. She lost her grip on his penis as he lifted her, slid off the seat to kneel on the thickly carpeted floor, and then set her back down. Pressing gently against her shoulders, he urged her to stretch out, to lie back.

Cool leather kissed her hot, hot skin. Excitement lashed like a whip.

"When I imagined drinking from you for the first time, I pictured doing so slowly, and romantically, in a big, soft bed."

She almost melted into a puddle, right there on the seat. "Am I ruining your plans?"

His fangs flashed in a wolfish grin. "Plans can be changed, especially when I can fulfill a fantasy." Leaning over, he captured her lips in a fiery, succulent kiss, opening his mental floodgates: He wanted her. Needed her. Desired her, and wanted to please her.

Repeatedly. Endlessly.

Irrevocably.

When her breath caught, he pulled back slightly.

"Are you okay?"

His hair was awry, his fangs were elongated, and his eyes gleamed in the rosy light. His jacket was gone, his shirt half stripped off, and his cock jutted from his open fly. He was looking at her like a starving man bellying up to an all-you-can-eat buffet, his everyday sophistication gone, ripped away.

That she could tear away his outer layers, expose his essence like this…that they could do this to each other… She reached for his hand, lifting it to her mouth. "Drink from me," she whispered against the veins throbbing in his wrist.

He dragged their joined hands on a tour down her body—cheek to throat, throat to breasts, breasts to abdomen, abdomen to hip. "Where shall I bite?"

A smile threatened. Even with his penis bobbing in the breeze, trust Wyland to ask such a heated question using utterly proper grammar. "Do you have a preference?" As a doctor, he'd know the location of every vein and artery, every obscure location from which pleasure could be wrung. Her blood sizzled just thinking about it.

"Your neck? Your breasts? Hips?" His fingertips tickled her mons through the fabric of her skirt. "Here?"

Her hips lurched against his hand.

"You like that idea." His voice stroked like dark velvet.

She liked the idea a lot, but Wyland would be mortified if Nick suddenly opened the window and found his head under her skirts. She'd save that particular pleasure for their big, soft bed, where they'd have privacy and all the time in the world. Right now, she wanted him to mark her, to possess her, in the most primal way a vampire could. "Neck, please," she replied. "But keep your hand right where it is."

A carnal smile flashed. "As you wish."

He leaned over, his hot breath puffing against her neck, then…the touch of his lips. His tongue swirled, softening the skin over the vein he'd chosen—her left carotid. The scratch of his fang was a dark, erotic sting, one that made her gasp in silent pleasure. She tipped her head to the side, giving him room. Waited, tense and poised.

Waited.

"Tia."

She almost punched him. "What?"

"This will change things between us."

By inviting him to drink, she was giving him the most intimate possible access to her thoughts. How like him to ensure she understood the ramifications of what they were about to do.

"You will be mine."

The blatant possessiveness rocked her to her core. She stroked his cheek, then tucked his disheveled hair behind his ear. "You silly man," she whispered. "I already am."

He closed his eyes, then opened them again. "Hang on," he murmured, adjusting his hold.

"Always."

When his strong fangs pierced her, she hissed with pain-laced ecstasy. Clutching at his head, she sagged back against the leather seat, eyes rolling back as she gave herself over to the hot suction of his mouth. To her lifeblood, mingling with his.

Surely. Sweetly. Irrevocably.

✳

Her blood was a shot of adrenaline straight to the heart—immediately addictive, a taste he'd forever crave. Hot, piquant, coppery...absolute bloody bliss. Her pulse fluttered like hummingbird wings against his tongue. Her head was tipped back, her neck exposed, but she was in no way submissive. She held his head in place, demanding he press closer, suck harder. When he slipped his hand under her skirt, slipped his fingers inside her, she cried out in ecstasy, nearly levitating from the seat.

Faster...oh my god, faster...

During the time they'd been lovers, he'd learned how to read her body language, but having intimate access to her thoughts while he touched her was...indescribable. She couldn't hide what she wanted, or how much pleasure she felt. How much pleasure *he* brought her.

She didn't even try.

Her hips jerked. "Wyland..." And then she was coming, breaking apart in his arms, her hot, tight channel spasming against his fingers. Her thoughts dissolved, forming a speedball of pure heat, pure feeling. Pure pleasure that he gladly took broadside.

"Wyland." She grabbed his free hand. Yanking his wrist to her mouth, she bit. And then she was drinking from him, a drugging suckle he felt to his very last corpuscle.

Oh, sweet universe...

She loved him, and she wanted him to know it. Feel it.

I love you...

Was it his thought, or hers? He didn't know, and he didn't care. He sank his fangs into her neck ever more deeply, submerging, suckling for all he was worth.

He took instinctive gulps, knowing he'd retrieve liquid, not air.

Drowning, in her.

CHAPTER TWENTY-ONE

Two days later, Wyland used the Underworld Council meeting's last scheduled break to return some phone calls. He'd just left his last message when Bailey gestured to him from the conference room adjacent to Elliott's office, where she sat with Jack. He glanced across the lobby to Sebastiani Labs' open boardroom doors. The catering staff was still refreshing the beverages, and Elliott's executive assistant, Willem Lund, was nowhere in sight.

They had time.

When he entered the room, Bailey, looking simultaneously annoyed, resigned, and excited, handed him an evidence bag. "Look what I received at work today."

Mental alarm bells clanged. Peering through the clear plastic, he studied the familiar-looking business envelope, with its generic Times New Roman font, lack of return address, and downtown Minneapolis postmark. "Where's the stamp?" he asked Jack.

"We're testing it for trace."

Flipping the packet over, he read the letter from beginning to end. His eyes narrowed. "The fact that you have succubus blood is closely-guarded information."

"*Very* closely guarded," she agreed.

A puzzle piece clicked into place. "You suspect a confidentiality breach at the hospital."

Bailey nodded curtly. "And if I'm right, we just caught a huge break."

Pissed off that her private data had been compromised, she was a sniper on the hunt. "Who else knows about your test results in the…" What was that disgusting phrase he'd heard her use? "In the meat world?"

"Rafe, of course. You and Jack." She ticked names off on her fingers. "Lukas, Scarlett, Elliott, Claudette. Dr. Melvin and Dr. Penn."

Too many people, but every person except Rafe was either a Council member or a doctor, and well-versed in confidentiality. "How about Sasha or Antonia?"

"No." Bailey tapped her index finger against her lip. "No, we need to look at the hospital. Every person who treated me had access to my records."

"With a valid reason, and within specific parameters," he said. "I have to log on and log off every time I examine a patient. I have to log off if I leave a patient alone in an exam room for any reason. There are access limitations, and policies and procedures, governing who can access which data, when, why, and how."

The cynical look she shot him called him naïve. "And who slaps your hand when you forget to log off? Who even realizes it happens?" she asked. "Policies and procedures are only as good as the programming and oversight which enforces them. All programs have bugs. All processes have loopholes. People are the weakest link."

Jack pulled a notebook from his briefcase. "We

need a list of everyone who treated you, everyone who accessed your records, when you were in the hospital."

"And since," Bailey muttered. "We need help from the technology staff. We need to suspect the technology staff. And depending on the security architecture..." Bailey rattled off a series of technical questions. Jack, scribbling in his notebook, tried to keep pace.

"I'll get you the names of people who can answer your questions," Wyland reassured her. The hospital's CTO would answer to him, tonight. It was bad enough that Bailey had received a threatening letter from an unhinged species purist, but if that unhinged purist exposed her private medical data to humanity, they'd have a much bigger problem on their hands. He turned toward the door. "I'll roust the CTO out of bed as soon as the Council meeting is over—"

"Hold on." Jack reached into his briefcase again. "A couple more things before you leave. First, I have some information about the man who assaulted Tia in SebSec's parking lot—not a lot of information, but some."

His hands formed fists.

"We finished analyzing the security tapes," Jack continued. "The assailant is male, about 5'10",wearing a long-sleeved black shirt and jeans. Black knit hat covering his hair, a dark bandanna tied around his face. No hair color, no eye color. There was a crowbar left at the scene, but there were no prints." Frustrated, he tossed the file folder onto the table. "Someone's been watching *CSI*."

"Approximate age?"

Jack shook his head. "Adult male muscle mass,

and he moved smoothly, with purpose."

"Until Tia showed up," Bailey broke in. "Her arrival threw him."

"Given where she parked, and the angle of the security cameras, we can't see what happened in the front seat of the car," Jack said. "He was already inside when Tia opened the driver's door. There's a struggle; Tia said he was trying to steal her camera. She falls backward, hits her head on the edge of the driver's door, then falls, unconscious, to the pavement. He runs westbound from the parking lot."

Leaving Tia for the sun.

"We're canvassing the neighborhood, pulling security tapes from other businesses. It's taking some time." Jack's lips tightened. "We also discovered why she lay undiscovered in the parking lot for so long. The person monitoring the cameras here at SebSec stepped away for a glass of champagne when news of Coco's birth made it down to the first floor. That person is no longer employed by Sebastiani Security."

Wyland nodded, satisfied. The worker's lapse had almost cost Tia her life. "And the other thing?"

Jack pulled another evidence bag from his briefcase.

"Another letter? Whose is it?"

Jack looked at him oddly. "Tia's, of course."

His heart skipped a beat. "What?"

Jack and Bailey exchanged a glance, then Jack handed him the bag. "Tia gave it to me at Stanton and Lyudmila's party."

Fear was cold, like a polar vortex. "When did she receive this?" And why hadn't she told him about it?

"She said she found it in her mail the day of the party," Jack answered. "Honestly, she didn't seem very worried about it. When she handed it to me, she rolled her eyes and said it was probably her turn."

But why hadn't she told him about the letter? She'd had plenty of opportunity: When he'd gone to the guest room. When he'd carried her to his bedroom. After they'd made love, while they'd showered together. They'd had nothing but time during the long ride to the party, or on the way back, when they'd finally joined in the most elemental way two vampires could.

Several days had passed. He'd sensed nothing amiss.

The emotional sting, for that's what it was, receded slightly. Jack was right. He hadn't sensed even the slightest throb of concern from Tia because she hadn't been worried about it. "She *should* be. Worried, that is."

"Damn right she should." Jack's expression was grim. "Look at the mailing address on the envelope."

Marine on St. Croix, not Stillwater. His address, not hers. Damn it. "He knows where she is." And he hadn't had heard from her today. He made a clumsy grab for his phone. The evidence bag fell, unheeded, to the floor.

Jack was suddenly at his side, holding onto his arm. "Wyland, she's okay. She's okay. Nick's with her. He dropped her off at the Archives not fifteen minutes ago."

"He dropped her off?"

Jack's grip tightened. "A figure of speech. He pulled the SUV into the garage, closed the door behind them, then escorted her downstairs. He made sure the security doors were engaged on every level before he went back to Vamp Central. She promised

Nick she'd call him when she was ready to leave."

The ventilation system seemed unnaturally loud…or maybe that was him, struggling to draw a single, stingy breath. *Okay. Okay.* She'd promised to call Nick. *She'd promised.* "Sorry." When he cleared his throat, he tasted bile. "You can let me go now." Because Jack still held him by one arm, and Bailey by the other. Supporting him. "Thank you."

After an embarrassingly long hesitation, they backed away. Jack had just picked up the fallen evidence bag when Willem appeared at the door. "Sorry to interrupt, but we're ready to resume."

Time to get back to business.

They followed Willem back to the boardroom, where the Underworld Council's representatives, two for each species, gathered around the long, glossy table. Except for Lukas and Scarlett, they had a full house today, with Val attending the beginning of the meeting via holo but then departing. He and Bailey were next on the agenda, with an update on their archiving project, followed by Jack, who'd provide a Security and Technology update. In one more hour, two at the most, he'd be able to go home. Once there, he'd chew Tia out personally, then tie her to the bed for a whole goddamn day.

While Bailey connected her laptop to the display device, he made a detour to the beverage station. While he prepared his drink, Willem took a quick walk around the boardroom, ensuring the windows' security filters were still activated before closing the big double doors and taking his seat at Elliott's right. "Are we ready to resume?"

At his nod, Willem resumed the meeting recording. Picking up the ceramic coffee mug,

Wyland sipped, then nearly stumbled. Instead of warm coffee, chilly carbonated bubbles danced on his tongue.

He'd made himself a blood-spiked Mountain Dew.

"Wyland?" Bailey's voice dragged his attention to the oversized flat screen monitor mounted on the far wall. Their presentation was displayed, ready to go, and around the table, a dozen colleagues looked at him expectantly.

Waiting.

He drained the mug as fast as the carbonation allowed. The blood zinged into his system, giving him the boost he needed, and as Bailey advanced the slides, he quickly and succinctly provided their update, focusing on document preservation and digitization work. Unfortunately, Tia's priceless contributions—her interviews with Valerian—were condensed to a single anonymous bullet point. "We're embedding audio and video materials as time and resources allow," he concluded. It was better all the way around if Krispin Woolf assumed Bailey was doing the work. "Are there any questions?"

As Krispin opened his mouth, the air around Lukas's empty chair flickered. When he shimmered into the seat, he wasn't alone. Scarlett sat at his side, cradling Coco. With the holograph optimized for one large person, not two people sitting hip to hip, their slightly translucent bodies exceeded the width of Lukas's boardroom chair. They looked tired but ecstatic.

Elliott's grin nearly split his face in two. "There's my little Coco Bean—"

"Shhh!" Scarlett whispered, frantically waving her hand. "She's finally asleep."

"We just wanted to say hello," Lukas said quietly, "and to thank everyone for their gifts and good wishes."

Though the holo wasn't the best diagnostic tool, Scarlett seemed to be moving well, and her cheeks were washed with healthy color. Lukas clearly hadn't touched a razor in days, but the stress lines around his eyes had smoothed out.

His patients were on the mend.

After a couple of minutes that found half of the Underworld Council lapsing into baby talk—an audio file Tia would probably kill to get her hands on—Lukas and Scarlett dropped off the conference call.

"Well." Elliott leaned back in his chair, every inch the proud grandpa. "Where were we?"

Willem consulted the record. "Wyland had just opened up the floor for questions about the archiving project."

"I have a question for Wyland," Krispin said. "More of a comment, actually."

Danger suddenly stained the air, and his fangs dropped to meet it. Jack and Lorin glanced at each other and straightened in their chairs.

"Congratulations." Despite his jocular voice, Woolf eyed him like prey. Their gazes clashed across the table, both of them wielding silence like swords. Finally, Krispin spoke again. "I understand you have a new lover. A very...young lover."

"Wyland's private life is not a subject for discussion," Elliott snapped.

"Maybe it should be."

The other man's words twisted like a dirty knife, but he'd be damned if he let Woolf know he'd hit his target. His blood was boiling, his vision bleeding red at the edges, but this was the Underworld Council boardroom, a neutral space. Violence was verboten.

A vein throbbed at his temple. Bloodlust pounded a savage beat.

He wanted to tear Woolf's throat out.

"Wyland, I know it's been a long time since you dipped your wick," Woolf said, "but...fucking an investigative journalist?"

He burst to his feet. Papers flew and the mug tipped over, spilling what was left of his drink. Jack and Lorin shoved out of their chairs, sending them rolling toward the wall. Before he knew it, Lorin had his wrist clamped in a vice-like grip, and Jack stood behind Krispin Woolf, who hadn't moved a muscle.

He might not have moved, but his eyes positively danced.

Wyland hissed, exposing every fang in his mouth. He tried to jerk away from Lorin, but she simply clamped down harder.

Woolf started rising to his feet.

Jack reached for his shoulders.

"Stop!" Claudette's powerful siren's voice rolled through the room. His muscles obeyed, locking him—locking everyone—in place. Across the table, Jack's arms hung suspended, parallel to the floor; he'd been reaching for Woolf, who was frozen in a half-stand. Seated next to his father, Jacoby Woolf looked horrified. Lorin's grip was painfully tight. His spilled drink dripped over the edge of the table and onto his shoe.

"Don't panic," Claudette said. "I've primarily targeted large muscle groups. The effects will wear off in approximately thirty seconds."

Bloody hell, what if they didn't? He couldn't move,

couldn't speak. Best he could tell, his brain, lungs, and circulatory system were working, but everything else was immobile.

Any Council member stupid enough to think Claudette Fontaine had bonded with Elliott Sebastiani primarily to share his power had just been reminded that she had plenty of her own.

As Claudette walked towards Willem, whose hands hovered, suspended, over his keyboard, she rattled off the date and time. "Meeting adjourned." Reaching around his fingers, she poked a key with her manicured nail. "Recording off." She looked at Krispin, then at him. "Gentlemen, here's how this is going to go down. Once you regain normal muscle function, Bailey will escort Wyland from the room. Krispin, Jack will accompany you to your car, and you will leave the premises. Do you understand?"

Clearly she didn't expect an answer, but he tried to show his agreement with his eyes. Tried to apologize, for all the good it did. Her voice had frozen him with his fangs flashing—proof positive that he'd violated the Council's most fundamental principle.

Krispin Woolf had played him like a grand piano.

Across the room, there was movement; Jack's arm suddenly dropped. A couple of seconds later, Wyland felt his own muscles come back on-line, quickly and painlessly, with none of the neural tingling he'd expected. Lorin relaxed her grip on his wrist.

"Relax, everyone." Claudette's voice was a soothing balm, removing all tension from the room.

Everyone took a deep breath. His fangs receded. Lorin gave his hand a quick squeeze.

"Bailey, please escort Wyland from the room," Claudette said.

He and Bailey both took an involuntary step toward the door. It felt like someone had nudged him from behind.

"Damn," Bailey whispered.

Damn was right. At least Claudette hadn't marched him from the room like a marionette on strings. Like he deserved. "I—" His vocal cords felt rusty. Clearing his throat, he tried again. "I apologize for the disruption." After a pause, he bowed his head, then strode from the room. Bailey followed closely behind, grabbing his elbow as they crossed the executive suite's carpeted lobby. She led him to the small conference room they'd so recently left.

Bailey pointed at a chair. "Sit."

He sat.

"I'll be right back." She closed the door, leaving him alone.

But not for long. They, along with most of the people in the room they'd just left, were supposed to attend a follow-on meeting in Elliott's office after the Council meeting ended.

If he still had a job, which was by no means a safe assumption. "Bloody hell," he breathed, rubbing his temples. He had to inform Val, tell him—

"Here." Bailey plunked a tall glass of warm blood onto the table, then sat down. "You know Woolf's talking out of his ass, right?"

"Is he?" Woolf hadn't said anything at the Council meeting that he hadn't privately said to himself, more than once.

"Wyland, don't let him in your head."

Too late. "Maybe he's just the first person to have the guts to say what everyone else is thinking—that I'm a middle-aged man besotted by his

407

inappropriately young lover." A bleak bark of laughter escaped. "What a fucking cliché."

"No—"

"Never mind her age, she's a bloody *journalist*. Woolf's right—what the hell am I thinking?"

"That you love her! That you love her, and that she loves you. Now shut up and listen to me for a minute. Christ on a cracker, what is it with lawyers?" she muttered. "Between you and Jack, it's a miracle I get a word in edgewise."

He lifted a brow. "You appear to be doing just fine."

She took his hands in a none-too-gentle grip. "Listen. Yes, she's younger. Yes, she's a journalist. But she's a journalist from your culture, and she knows the goddamn rules. I know, because I've checked." The grip tightened. "I've *checked*, Wyland. Exhaustively. Thoroughly. I can't find even one time where she's leaked information, or fed the grapevine. She's never published anything that could put your culture at risk. She hasn't violated your trust." She paused. "Unlike Deirdre d'Amour."

Shock rocked him back in his seat. "How do you know about—"

"Dude, who do you think wrote your bio for the Archives? A bio I notice you modified recently, but I'll save that lecture for another time." She leaned forward in her chair. "Wyland, I get that you've been burned. We all have. But Tia makes you happy. You've been happy."

"Do I look happy to you?"

"No, you look miserable," she said cheerfully. "You're in love. Welcome to the club."

He opened his mouth to deny it, but then closed it

again, thinking back to the limo ride home, to the snarl of emotions they'd exchanged along with their blood. To the way their heartbeats had combined, thundering together. "Does everyone else really walk around feeling so...out of sorts? So off-balance? How in the world do you get any work done?"

She laughed. "The 'oh shit' feeling passes. It does," she reassured him.

"I just want my life back."

"No, you don't."

He arched an eyebrow.

"Wyland, you weren't living. You were existing."

She was right. He'd been living in black and white for over a century. Tia lived in Technicolor, leaving vivid splashes in her wake. Tia was laughter and light, the sunlight to his shade, bringing him pleasure after centuries of duty. But...the yoke of duty satisfied him, too, and brought him a true sense of purpose and accomplishment. He said as much, adding, "Other people rely upon me, but...she doesn't."

"An independent woman bothers you?"

Her facial expression told him he'd better consider his answer very, very carefully. "No, of course not, but—"

"Wyland, she's with you because she *wants* to be, not because she *needs* to be. You mentioned the yoke of responsibility?" Bailey gave a half-shrug. "Let her share the load. Be happy, and enjoy the journey."

"How can I be happy if I have to resign from Council to keep her?" The decision would cleave him in two.

"Oh, please," Bailey scoffed. "No one's going to ask you to resign."

"I broke the rules. No violence in the boardroom."

"You didn't touch him."

"I would have," he admitted. "Claudette stopped me before I could."

"Yes, she stopped you. Nothing happened."

"Your interpretation of events is far too charitable. If I hadn't exhibited clear, violent intent, Claudette wouldn't have found it necessary to act." The fact that she had would go down as one of the most mortifying moments in his very long life.

"I think you'll find everyone else agrees with me." Bailey gestured behind him. "Look."

He peered through the narrow slice of window, where everyone except Krispin and Jacoby milled in the lobby, waiting for them. "We're late for the meeting." If he still had a job five minutes from now. Well, he'd find out soon enough.

"Dude, they don't give a damn about the meeting. They're worried about you."

He pushed to his feet, then straightened his suit jacket and tie. "Ready?" Without waiting for her answer, he opened the door, then walked directly to Elliott and Claudette.

"Wyland." Claudette clasped his hands. "I'm so sorry."

"For what? I'm the one who—"

"Scared the crap out of Krispin Woolf?" Antonia sidled up with a delighted grin. "That was *so* freaking awesome."

He shot her a quelling glance. "It was completely inappropriate."

"He was inappropriate first."

"Yes, he was," Claudette seconded. She gave his hands a squeeze. "How are you doing?"

Everyone crowded around, too many bodies

standing too close. He didn't deserve their comfort. Couldn't accept it. His throat tightened up. If he didn't speak soon, he'd never be able to get the words out. "Elliott, please accept my resignation from the Underworld Council."

Silence descended. Elliott finally spoke. "No."

"What?"

"No," Elliott repeated. "Your offer is declined."

"But, surely you can't allow—"

"Wyland." Elliott looked tired. "If you want to argue as an intellectual exercise, you and Jack can have at it, but Krispin instigated the situation. His comments were inexcusable." He glanced at his bondmate. "Thankfully, Claudette was there to prevent the situation from escalating."

"He…blind-sided me," Wyland admitted. Relief coursed through him. "It won't happen a second time."

Claudette's nod seemed reluctant. Hell, he wouldn't find his words very convincing, either.

"We are fractured," Claudette said softly. "The Council is fractured." She waved a hand at the room. "Look at us. Look at this. It's 2:00 a.m. We just finished a nine-hour Council meeting. We're about to go into Elliott's office to discuss these threatening letters, but without the wolves. We're having a de facto Council meeting, without the wolves, because there's a fair chance that—that—"

"That the Alpha, or someone in his employ, might be responsible for sending them," Bailey said.

Claudette took a deep breath, then released it. "Yes."

Elliott gestured to his office. "Let's take this conversation behind closed doors."

It didn't take long for everyone to settle. Jack and Bailey set up laptops at the four-person conference table next to the wall-mounted monitor. Antonia sat, cross-legged, on top of her father's massive mahogany desk. Lorin and her mother, Valkyrie First Alka Schlessinger, joined Elliott and Claudette on love seats in the sleek furniture grouping, leaving the chair next to Elliott for him. Lukas and Scarlett usually shared the other chair.

The smaller group met here frequently enough that they basically had assigned seats. Claudette was right; the Council was fractured.

Elliott picked up the conversation. "We suspect Krispin Woolf of being responsible for a great many things, but there's never been any evidence to connect him to a crime. Has that changed?"

Jack looked up from his laptop. "No."

"It's there," Antonia muttered. "Keep looking."

Elliott didn't censure his daughter for saying what everyone was thinking. "Any evidence, should it be discovered, must be incontrovertible. No loopholes, no mistakes." Elliott turned to him. "Please continue your research."

Six months ago, Elliott had privately asked him to prepare a legal brief listing all possible scenarios under which a Council member could be removed from their seat. Though Wyland hadn't asked, he'd known *exactly* which Council member was in the president's crosshairs. What a relief to know Elliott still trusted him—

Jack's phone pealed with a Code Red. "Excuse me," he said, quickly silencing the device.

While Jack read, Bailey closed his laptop, collected his notebook and pen, and slipped them into his briefcase, a dance they'd performed countless times before. Their covert police force tagged Sebastiani Security when serious crimes occurred. A Code Red meant Jack had to leave.

"How about we adjourn?" Elliott suggested with a tired-sounding sigh. "Let's go home, get some sleep. This isn't a problem we're going to solve tonight."

"Seconded," Antonia said through a yawn. "Let's stick a fork in it."

Wyland rose. He had rounds at the hospital, so the comfort of his own bed was at least half a day away— and once he dressed Tia down for not telling him about that letter, there was a good chance he'd be sleeping there alone.

"There's been a break-in at the Archives," Jack said.

His heart punched him in the ribs.

"Tia's fine," Jack reassured him. "She's a little rattled, but she's fine."

The woman was going to be the death of him. "What happened?" He joined Jack and Bailey at the table.

"According to Nick, someone accessed the garage, then tried to force the security door at the top of the stairs. The alarm had barely gone off at the house when Tia called Nick, and dead-bolted herself in the lower-level bathroom. When he and the team got there, the perp was gone."

Tia would never work at the Archives alone again.

"How the hell did someone get in the garage?" Bailey asked.

Jack's expression was grim. "Good question."

When Wyland's phone vibrated, he grabbed it. A text from Tia: *Attempted break-in at the Archives. I'm* *fine. Artifacts fine. Nick is here. Talk to you soon. <3.*

In five simple sentences, she'd covered the basics—enough to ratchet his tension down a notch, at any rate—but... He showed the message to Bailey. "What does that symbol at the end mean?"

She grinned at him. "Aww, Tia sent you a heart. Or testicles. Depends on the context."

Heat crept up his neck, but he ignored it. During the time frame the break-in must have occurred, he hadn't felt even a blip of second-hand fear or fright from Tia. They hadn't exchanged enough blood to have a reliable long-distance connection yet, but even if they had, he'd been too busy snarling at Krispin Woolf to notice. "We're an hour away," he said to Jack.

"Nick's there," Jack reminded him. "And the sooner we leave, the sooner we arrive."

Jack's logic was impeccable. Annoying, but impeccable. "Let's go."

They left Elliott's office and took the elevator down to the underground parking garage. Wyland's Porsche was in the row closest to the door. "Keep that thing to the posted speed limit," Jack advised. "You're no good to her dead."

"You're just full of pithy platitudes tonight."

"But I'm right." Jack started walking toward his Volvo sedan. "See you there."

As Wyland climbed behind the wheel, he sat for a couple of heartbeats, then glazed his emotions with a sheet of ice. Jack was right. He'd concentrate on the drive, and he'd arrive alive. He'd hold it together, for a time.

But sooner or later, the ice would crack beneath his feet.

It inevitably did.

CHAPTER TWENTY-TWO

Tia tried to focus as Jack and Nick examined the damaged doorknob—close enough to observe, yet well out of range of the fingerprint dust—but Wyland kept stealing her attention. Standing in the middle of the open garage, wearing a gorgeous gunmetal gray suit and looking calm, cool and collected, he watched Chico, in werewolf form, search the perimeter of the parking lot.

She brushed up against his mind.

No reaction.

She nudged a little harder.

He didn't budge.

She poked.

Nothing. Nada. It was like trying to chip a glacier with an ice pick.

"County sheriff coming up the road," Chico called from outside.

His human voice, not a growl or bark. When had he shifted back to human form?

"There are too many cars in the lot," Nick muttered. "She'll pull in, check things out."

They did *not* want to draw human law enforcement's attention, and with the door handle broken and fingerprint powder all over the place, there was plenty to look at. Hopefully Chico wasn't standing in the parking lot naked.

"I'll take care of it." Wyland walked toward the entrance.

Toward the rising morning sun.

Be careful! As soon as she issued the mental warning, she wanted to snatch it back. The man was over three hundred years old; he'd been managing his exposure to the sun a lot longer than she'd been alive— "Whoa." Wyland was thralling the sheriff. She could sense the immense power and precision second-hand. Behind it, an emotional maelstrom raged.

Had something happened at the Council meeting? What the hell was going on?

Wyland and Chico returned—and yes, Chico was dressed. "That was…" Chico shook his head admiringly. "She just drove by. Didn't even slow down."

Wyland didn't acknowledge the praise. His face a smooth mask, he joined them by the security door and considered the broken handle. "Chico didn't find anything amiss outside."

Chico nodded. "The windows are intact, and the other locks are undisturbed. There are a lot of animal scents around the building and in the parking lot."

"We have a couple of scratches and pry marks here, but no prints," Jack said. "Looks like a knife of some sort."

"So, someone tried to force open the security door, setting off the alarm both here and at the house," Nick said. "No fingerprints, no broken windows, no obvious signs of a break-in. How did someone get in the garage in the first place?"

Chico half-shrugged. "It's easy enough to do if you

know how."

The discussion that followed, dissecting all the ways an automatic garage door could be breached, made Tia very happy she hadn't installed hers yet. There were two garage door openers weighing down her sun visor as it was; pretty soon the thing would be so heavy it wouldn't stay up.

Wait a minute. The garage door opener.

The hair on her arms stood on end. "What if the guy who broke into my car wasn't after my camera after all?"

She felt a subtle, inner click as Wyland connected the dots. "Bloody hell." Fire in his eyes, ice in his voice. Steam wisped from the tiniest of cracks.

"When I moved into Vamp Central, Wyland gave me two garage door openers: one for the house, and one for the Archives," she explained to the men. "We need to verify whether they're both still there."

After a beat of silence came a volley of curses. "Where's the car now?" Jack asked.

"At the mechanic's, having windows installed." Nick's phone already was in his hand. His thumbs were flying, no doubt informing the security team at Vamp Central of a potential threat to the house. "Shit, I didn't even think of garage door openers."

"No one did," Wyland said. "Don't blame yourself. There's plenty to go around." Such bleakness and self-loathing in his voice. "Thankfully, unless the person has the security code for the door connecting the garage to the house, they'll run into the same issue there as they did here."

Nick's jaw was clenched tight. "I'll call the mechanic." He strode to the far corner of the garage to make the call.

"Wyland, if Tia's car break-in wasn't simply a crime of opportunity, we have even bigger problems," Jack said grimly.

"Someone's still following you." Wyland's voice was as cold as liquid nitrogen. "Still watching you."

She wrapped her arms around her torso. With on-site bodyguards and drivers on demand, she'd gotten lazy, ceding responsibility for her safety to others. She'd led her stalker right to Vamp Central. "And now both the house and the Archives are at risk."

Wyland whirled to face her. "Do you really think that's what I'm concerned about? You're in danger!"

His eyes were wild. He looked ready to explode.

"Well, I have good news and bad news," Nick said, rejoining the group. "The mechanic says there's only one garage door opener on Tia's sun visor. Given that the break-in occurred here, it's safe to assume which one was stolen."

"So the house is safe. That *is* good news." She gave Wyland's hand a reassuring squeeze. He didn't squeeze back.

The fissures were widening, cracking apart. She had to get him out of here.

"I'll pick up the car later today," Nick said. "The manager said he'd store the other garage door opener in his office until then."

Chico's nostrils flared. "Does anyone else smell that?"

"Smell what?"

Chico didn't answer Jack, because he was already on the move. Nose in the air, he sniffed, wandering around in what seemed like a random pattern, until he abruptly veered toward some wooden pallets stacked near the security door. Dropping to his haunches, he sniffed at the wood, working from the floor upward. He paused at about waist height, then peered at the wood more closely. "Jack, I need an evidence bag."

"What did you find?"

"A couple of hairs, caught in the grain. Scent's fresh."

Jack grabbed latex gloves, a pair of tweezers, and a clear plastic evidence bag from his kit, then joined Chico. When they turned back around, there were three very short, nearly invisible reddish hairs in the bag. "Body hair. Someone brushed up against the wood," Chico said. "I smell Pack."

"A werewolf?" Hope leaped. "Do you know who it is?"

"No." Chico looked at Wyland, then Nick. "Do any werewolves have access to this building?"

Wyland and Nick exchanged a glance. "No," Wyland answered. "To my knowledge, you're the first werewolf who's ever been here."

"That stray," Nick blurted. "There's been a stray dog hanging around the neighborhood the last couple of weeks. Red brindle coat. Damn, I never considered that it might be a werewolf."

"We don't know that it is, but we have something to go on." Jack sealed the evidence bag, scribbled something on the label, put the bag in his kit, then closed the box with a clank. "I'll get this over to the lab."

Something about the hair tickled the back of her mind, but Wyland was almost vibrating with tension. "Does anyone need us for anything else?" She had to get him out of here before he shattered apart.

Nick waved a hand toward the house. "I'll change the garage codes here, then secure the building."

Chico eyed the stand of tall trees separating the parking lot from the river. "I'm going to take one more pass while I have the scent." He reached for his belt. "Jack, I'll meet you back at the office."

A jagged shard of possessiveness from Wyland. "Let's go," he muttered, tugging her toward the open garage door without saying goodbye to anyone.

She trotted to keep up. In any other situation, she'd find his jealousy and lack of etiquette oddly reassuring, but right now he seemed...fragile, as if *any* burst of emotion would be too much.

Their feet crunched against gravel as they walked to the car. The rising sun was merciless, highlighting every line on his face. "Are you okay to drive?" she asked softly.

"Yes."

She studied him, then climbed into the passenger seat. The drive home was so short that he wouldn't get the Porsche out of third gear. "Let's go home."

They were silent during the drive, his hands clutching the steering wheel at precisely ten and two. When they approached the driveway, he reached up to the sun visor, where his own garage door openers hung. Tightening his lips, he pressed a button, pulled into the driveway, and braked to a stop. As they waited for the door to lift, he yanked the opener from the visor and threw it into a storage alcove in the dash.

It bounced out, clattering to the floor by her feet.

She looked at it, then at him.

"Leave it."

Her seatbelt pulled against her chest as she scooped the gadget up and matter-of-factly set it in the storage alcove. "You'll need it to close the door behind us."

A muscle ticked near his cheekbone, but he didn't respond.

She sat still as Wyland pulled the car into the garage and pressed the button to close the door behind them. It descended with a mechanical hum, a dimmer switch on the sun. When the big double door met the floor, leaving them in shadow, Wyland took the car out of gear, set the parking brake, and turned off the ignition with careful, deliberate movements.

Neither moved. Neither spoke.

The air felt breakable. Combustible.

She had to get him into the house, up the stairs. What she'd do with him once they reached the bedroom was anyone's guess, but anything was better than sitting here in the car, waiting for him to quake apart. Moving slowly, she unbuckled her seat belt, then reached over and unbuckled his, guiding the retractable strap back into its holder. "Let's get out of the car," she murmured.

He reached for the door handle, obeying as if on autopilot. She quickly got out of the car, meeting him near the door connecting the garage to the house. He stood there, staring at the security keypad as if wondering what to do with it. "How can I help you?" she asked softly. "What do you need?"

"What do I need?"

She felt something give, felt a mighty mental crack, as if a glacier had calved, breaking away from the shore. He straightened then blinked, as if trying to compose himself. To bind his own wounds.

"Wyland, look at me. Look at me."

Their gazes crashed together, but he jerked away. He was drifting away from her, trying to shore up the damage all by himself.

"Oh, no, you don't." She grabbed him, then shoved into his mind. He tried to push her out, but she pushed back harder, searching for something—anything—she could do to ease him, to bring him comfort.

But...the pain. Snapping, crackling lights. A murderous red and black rage, and a yawning pit of guilt that threatened to swallow him whole. His essence was volcanic, tectonic, tearing her breath away and shattering the ground beneath their feet.

"Tia..." he gasped.

He tried to push her away, but she shoved harder. God, it hurt. She tasted blood, but bullied on, seeking blindly, searching the seething ether for something solid, something familiar, but ice was cracking, rocks were falling, the fissures were multiplying and dividing, carrying him away to a place she couldn't...she couldn't... *There*. Back there, nearly hidden...a reddish-pink orb glowed. Throbbed like a beating heart, beating in time with hers. So warm and soft—encapsulated, yet vulnerable, so dangerously exposed...

Come to me. Come on...

She reached for him. Grasped at nothing. Saw rocks starting to crumble overhead, and under his feet.

Terror was a ripsaw, slicing clean through.

Grab on, damn it.

NOW.

His weightless leap almost yanked her off her feet. She clutched at him, scrabbling for a toehold, then wrenched him back, away from the crumbling ledge, with a mighty mental heave.

Together, they tumbled backwards.

Breath heaved in and out of her lungs, and a bead of sweat rolled down her temple. The hood of the Porsche was warm against her ass—somehow, they'd ended up at the car—but Wyland, standing between her spread legs and reaching for her, was so much warmer. Though his designer suit and tie still hung perfectly, and his hair was tame and smooth, his face was flushed. His fangs flashed. His eyes spilled blue sparks.

Pure geothermal heat.

Arousal slammed into her, but she shoved it aside, patting and clutching at his body, then lifting shaky hands to his cheeks. "Are you okay?" She reached out with her mind, and this time he met her halfway. The dangerous maelstrom had subsided, but…he still seethed and burned—burned for her, with the heat of a thousand suns. She grabbed on tightly, braving the staggering heat.

He closed his eyes. When he opened them again, there was no escaping his gaze. "I love you," he whispered.

"I know."

The corner of his mouth quirked. Thankfully he'd recognized the Han Solo joke she hadn't been able to resist. "You're such a brat." He grabbed a hank of her hair, giving it a gentle, admonishing tug she felt right between her legs. "What am I going to do with you?"

"Whatever you want, because I love you, too."

A pause. "I know."

She grinned, delighted with him.

He returned her smile, but not for long. Clouds formed in his eyes.

"What's wrong?"

His thumb brushed the corner of her mouth. "You're bleeding."

She shrugged. "I bit my tongue. It's nothing." When he popped the thumb in his mouth, sucking away the red smudge, a tiny moan escaped. She was so wet she was about to slide off the damn car. "Wyland?"

"Hmm?"

She removed the thumb from his mouth, leaned in, and licked his upper lip. "Kiss me."

Their mouths crashed together, and they gulped each other's air, tongues and limbs frantically twining. Their hands were rough, clutching and pulling. Her T-shirt flew away. He picked her up like she weighed nothing, stripped off her shorts and underwear while she took care of her bra, then set her, bare-assed, back on the hood of the car. Their hands bumped and fumbled when they both reached for his belt buckle, so she dealt with his shirt and tie while he worked on the suit jacket and pants. Once he was unbuckled and unzipped, she shoved his pants and boxers over the curve of his ass, letting gravity pull them down.

She grabbed him again, hard enough to bruise, and poured everything she had into a soul-searing kiss—heat and fear, blood and tears, love and a driving, pounding need—a need to be in his arms. In his head. In his heart.

Skin to skin, joining in this most elemental way.

She lay back on the hood, arms and legs spread. Sun-warmed metal kissed her skin. A remote part of her laughed at how she was writhing over his sports car like an '80s video vixen.

She...liked it.

"You look like a virgin sacrifice." His voice was soft and deep. His pupils were bottomless black pools.

She reached for his cock, stroking it from tip to base with a slinky twist. "I'm no virgin."

"Thank the universe."

She caressed him, exploiting every intimate, sensory secret. Hard and soft, warm and pulsing, with a tiny liquid pearl at the tip...so many tastes, so many textures. She cupped his balls, savoring their weight, their heavy heat.

His heartbeat was in the palm of her hand, pounding in time with hers.

"Wyland." Sliding closer, she twined her legs around him, wrapping him in the tightest embrace she could manage. They both hissed when his hard, blunt flesh notched against her slick opening. "Love me."

Gathering her in his arms, he pulled her upright, bringing her breasts against the hard, hair-roughened planes of his chest. They were skin to skin, face to face, heart to heart. "Always," he whispered against her lips.

He entered her, simply and directly. Filled her, anchored her, hot and thick and hard. Gazed at her with eons in his eyes. When he kissed her, she tasted the zing of her own blood on his tongue.

The overhead garage light snapped off with a quiet click, plunging them into darkness as they moved together, as they rolled and surged, in an invisible rhythm that only they could hear. She felt the scrape of his teeth against her neck, then a white-hot pain that immediately turned to pleasure. When the tremors started, when the ground shifted and shook, they clasped hands. Lost themselves, and made the leap.

Tethered together. Forever found.

✳

Dom ignored the slap of branches as he crashed through the woods. Ignored the itchy burrs clinging to his fur, ignored the animals scurrying out of his way. Chico Perez was a good distance back, but he was gaining.

Pursuing.

How stupid he'd been to just sit there, watching from the tree line.

His muscles burned, his lungs were screaming, and the plastic grocery bag he carried between his teeth swung back and forth as he ran. *Don't drop the bag. Don't drop the bag.* Dropped clothes and shoes would be easy enough to explain, but latex gloves, a switchblade, and a garage door opener? Not so much.

Destroying that door handle had been really fucking stupid. He should have known it would set off an alarm, that it would bring the security guard he'd been dodging for a couple of weeks running. He'd barely managed to shift back to wolf form, pick up the bag, and dive into the grass surrounding the parking lot before the guard arrived, swearing up a storm at the open garage door. After a quick, professional-looking search, the guard made a couple of phone calls, then went back into the building. He and Tia Quinn reappeared a short time later, when Chico Perez's beat-up Jeep Wrangler pulled into the lot. Then Jack Kirkland had showed up, then Wyland.

Why was Sebastiani Security responding to a break-in at a business on the Minnesota/Wisconsin border? A *failed* break-in, at that?

What the hell was going on in that building?

Crouching low, he veered sharply left. The Pathfinder was over there, just through those trees. His peripheral vision blurred, his lungs burned, as he put on a final burst of speed. He'd planned ahead, parking behind a dilapidated barn a good five miles away from Vamp Central, but why had he driven his own damn car? And hell, he was leading Perez right to it.

Too late for second guesses. He'd gotten a good head start. By the time Perez tracked him here, he'd be gone.

When he reached the car, he dropped the bag, collapsed onto his belly by the driver's door, and called his wolf. Time whirled like a tornado. When he came back to awareness, he scrambled to two feet, stumbling over the bag. It split open, spilling the garage door opener, one glove, and the switchblade onto the grass. "Shit." He glanced over his shoulder. No sign of Perez, not yet, but dressing would have to wait. Moving quickly, he opened the driver's door, scooped up his belongings, then tossed them onto the passenger seat.

He climbed behind the wheel. "Damn," he hissed, jerking his hips away from the sun-baked seat. Holy parboiled balls, why hadn't he parked in the shade? Grimacing, he lowered himself back down to the seat. He had to get out of here, fast.

He started the car, threw it into gear, and hit the gas. As the Pathfinder bounced down the rutted farming road, he glanced in his rear view mirror. Still no sign of Perez, but it was too soon to relax. He had to make sure Perez lost his trail.

So he drove. Drove for miles. Drove until the adrenaline shakes stopped, and the upholstery cooled. When he finally pulled over, he was on a remote dirt road, surrounded by trees. No houses in sight.

Perfect.

He grabbed the bag, opened the door, then stepped out onto the gravel. The rocks bit into his feet, and the wind found every crack and crevice. The sky looked ominous to the west; storms were moving in. Hannah's soccer game would probably get rained out, but he needed to get home just in case it wasn't. *Once I figure out where the hell I am.* His cell phone was sitting on the dash. After a couple of taps and swipes, he had his answer: just east of Eau Claire, Wisconsin.

He'd driven nearly eighty miles, bare-ass naked.

"Shit." He did some quick traffic math. Rush hour wasn't a factor, and if 94 Westbound was moving at the posted speed, he'd reach Minneapolis in an hour and a half, easy. Plenty of time to ditch the gloves, stash the garage door opener someplace safe, then get Hannah to her soccer game.

It was a solid plan. "Better late than never," he muttered. Today could easily have turned into an epic clusterfuck.

He took another look around. Remote, rural, lots of trees...this was as good a place as any. *I should probably get dressed first.*

After pulling on clothes and shoes, he grabbed one of the latex gloves off the passenger seat. He trotted about forty yards into the woods, jammed it under a rotted tree stump, then ran back to the car. He'd ditch the other glove once he crossed the state line back into Minnesota.

He picked up the switchblade from the passenger seat. He'd keep the knife, a beautiful antique he'd found in his father's top desk drawer. It would be too easy to trace, and he'd gotten used to its reassuring weight.

He slipped it back into his front pants pocket, then headed home, toward the darkening sky.

CHAPTER TWENTY-THREE

As Mila sent yet another document to the print queue, she tried not to stare at Jack Kirkland, who her boss had escorted to her office not ten minutes ago. On the credenza behind her, the printer hummed, spitting out confidential documents Kirkland would take with him when he left.

Why the interest in the hospital's data management policies, processes, and procedures? What was he looking for?

She glanced at her second screen, at the work his arrival had interrupted. Unencrypted data scrolled by, faster than the eye could read. She bit back a sigh. So much work was piling up, and now Kirkland was here, asking such odd questions. "What's this in relation to?" she asked again. Just before leaving them, Kate had murmured that this request for information had come from the top. "The *very* top." They were to give Jack Kirkland their full, complete cooperation.

"I'm gathering some background information."

Was he here as an Underworld Council member or as the managing partner of Sebastiani Security?

"Next on the list is the hospital's data protection policy," he said.

He had a list? She glanced at the screen. Damn it,

how long was this going to take?

She retrieved the document and sent it to the printer, trying not to look at Kirkland. Tall, blond, and handsome, wearing an impeccably tailored navy business suit that would send her mother into paroxysms of designer delight, he dwarfed her visitor chair, yet didn't look the least bit uncomfortable. Nope, *she* was the one who felt uncomfortable, as if she was being audited or deposed.

Well, he *was* a lawyer. Maybe it was just his way.

Long minutes passed as Kirkland asked questions about data security, backups, offsite storage procedures…all topics with which she was intimately familiar. Relaxing slightly, she answered, happy to see that Kate no longer paced the hallway outside her office. But the sense of relaxation didn't last long, because he then segued into perplexing questions about paper, printers, and postal procedures. Snail mail? She couldn't remember the last time she'd actually mailed something, either at work or at home. And now he needed a handwriting sample? Her lips started to tingle. "Do I need a lawyer?"

"It's just procedure." His voice was as smooth as buttercream frosting.

"Whose procedure?"

He didn't respond. Crinkles fanned from the corners of his eyes—evidence that he smiled, at least occasionally—but he wasn't smiling now. No, right now he looked as serious as a server crash.

Okay, a handwriting sample. She reached for a small notepad and pen. "Are these okay?"

"Perfect."

Trying to ignore the tingle spreading to the skin around her mouth, she thought for a moment, then wrote, "I, Lyudmila Stanton, provide this handwriting sample at Jack Kirkland's request, in the spirit of cooperation, and without benefit of legal representation." She scrawled her signature, added the date and time, then handed him the paper.

As he read, a ghost of a smile appeared. "You are your father's daughter." He dropped the paper in the cardboard box sitting beside the chair. The box could hold a lot of documents, a lot of paper. That was its job, to hold reams and reams of paper.

"Mr. Kirkland, I'm very confused," she blurted. The tingling was creeping up to her cheekbones, a progression she recognized all too well. Dread rose like water in a leaky boat. "If you could tell me more about your case, your area of concern, I might be able to provide more helpful information." *And I can get you out of here before I faint.* The full glass of blood, sitting next to her monitor, mocked her. She'd poured it, then forgotten all about it.

Big mistake.

"You've been very helpful, thank you." He crossed his legs, settling more comfortably into her guest chair. "As I'm sure you can understand, our case files are confidential."

A couple of black pinpricks wandered into her peripheral vision. She reached for the glass of blood, taking a stingy sip. When she set the glass down, he was looking at her second screen, at the river of characters streaming against the black background.

Her pulse jumped.

"Your boss mentioned that you have an affinity for data, Ms. Stanton."

It was a generous description, and only partially accurate. She loved to *manipulate* data. To control it, to impose a sense of order and structure. To mold, massage, and manage, twisting and tweaking, until the data complied, and became information—information someone could actually use. She gave a self-deprecating shrug. "In this job, an affinity definitely helps."

"Yes. About your job." He pulled a small, wire-bound notebook and pen from his suit pocket. "Could you describe, at a high level, what your job responsibilities entail?"

As she talked, he took quick, sparing notes, and asked very few questions. "Am I correct that your job duties require you to access patient data?"

She took a breath, trying to slow her jack-hammering pulse. "Yes, but I'm bound by the hospital's confidentiality procedures, and by the terms of a non-disclosure agreement. I take those commitments very seriously."

"I'll need a copy of your NDA."

Of course you do. She found it, fired it off to the printer, and turned back to him. "In addition to our confidential data handling procedures, access to this floor—to this office—is badge-controlled." She indicated the badge hanging from a lanyard around her neck. "And there are security cameras at the entrances, at the end of the hallway." Heat rushed to her cheeks. If anyone pulled the video files, they'd see her kissing Dom—and not just a goodbye peck on the cheek, either.

Was *that* what all this was about? Annoyance spurted. Okay, public displays of affection at work might be less-than-professional, but sending Jack Kirkland to question her about an ill-advised smooch in the hallway was a *serious* case of overkill. She'd kissed Dom at the end of the hall, when no one else was there, and well away from her work—

The scrolling on her screen stopped. No crash; the cursor blinked serenely at the command line prompt. "Huh," she said, pleasantly surprised.

"What's that?"

"What's what?"

Kirkland gestured to the monitor, where the tail end of the program's run was still visible on the screen.

Where unencrypted patient data was still visible on the screen.

With a couple of quick keyboard taps, she cleared the screen, wiping the tiny characters away. "Test results," she chirped. Under her desk, her foot started shaking.

Kirkland didn't seem to notice. He nodded, then continued with his questions.

Her stomach lurched at the narrow miss. He either hadn't recognized what he'd seen, or hadn't been able to read her screen.

"Next, I need a blank piece of your printer paper."

"What?"

"Just a sample for our records."

In her world, there was no 'just' about it—samples were statistically significant, and records were sacrosanct. Tightening her numb lips, she swung her desk chair around. As she reached for the printer, a sudden wave of déjà vu struck: Dom, interrupting her at work. Dom, swinging her away from the monitor so she faced him. Nibbling on her neck for long, delicious minutes…while Bailey Brown's unencrypted patient data burned into the screen behind her.

This was about Bailey Brown.

Dom, what have you done?

Her hands shook as she handed Kirkland the piece of paper.

What have you done, and how long have you been using me? More black dots filled her peripheral vision.

"Are you okay, Ms. Stanton?"

"Just a little lightheaded." Blinking, she glanced at the glass of blood. "I think I waited too long to feed."

"And I've taken up quite enough of your time." Rising, he shook her hand, then picked up the box. "Thank you so much for your assistance. Bailey Brown may contact you with more detailed technical questions."

And would probably uncover evidence that her own patient data had been breached. Awesome. Just fantastic. She made herself stand. Made herself nod.

"There's no need to walk me out."

Yeah, right. She was going to follow company policy to the letter.

After escorting him to the security door, she returned to her office and collapsed into her desk chair. She grabbed the glass of blood and gulped it half down, shaking with weakness. With hunger. With an anger that threatened to… "Damn you, Dom." She set the glass down. Picked up her cell phone.

Dialed Dom.

Waited.

Crap, voice mail. "Dominic." A long pause. "We need to talk. Call me as soon as you can." She hung up without saying goodbye. She'd say goodbye to his face, when she ended this…this…whatever this was.

Or wasn't.

Her desk blurred, then came back into focus again. The blackness encroached, the numb, familiar chill.

"Ah, shit," she whispered.

She'd waited too long. The blood wasn't enough.

What to do?

Wyland. Wyland had office hours today. If he was in the building, he'd be able to help—quickly and discreetly, without half the damn ER storming in with gurney wheels rattling.

Her desk phone was miles away, and her hand weighed a hundred pounds, but she finally managed to punch the speaker phone button, then hit Wyland's autodial number. As the phone rang, she lowered herself to the thin, rough carpet. If she fainted again, it was better that she already be sitting on the floor. This time, there'd be no falling, no hitting her head on the desk as she went down. No staples, no blood to clean off the floor... Damn it, his voice mail. "Wyland?" she said, squinting against the dimming light. The dark, narrow tunnel was collapsing, dirt crumbling in around the edges. "Wyland..."

She tipped. Fell in.

The hole swallowed her up, and then there was nothing.

✳

Wyland turned away from his office window, with its stingy view of the setting sun, and glanced at his watch for the third time in as many minutes. Tia was two floors down, in Neurology. She'd agreed to a consult to ease his mind, but he'd expected her back half an hour ago. "So much for easing my mind," he muttered, ignoring his ringing desk phone. She was supposed to call his cell when her appointment was over so he could escort her back to his office. The phone in his pants pocket was stubbornly silent.

Worry took root. Had Rothenberger found something after all?

No. Tia was fine; he'd feel it if she wasn't, but... When she'd told him she loved him, she'd given him the right to feel anxious about her. They'd given those rights to each other, in a dark garage, on the hood of his Porsche.

On the hood of his Porsche.

So much for romance.

But Tia hadn't seemed to need romance, or courtly manners. After giggling at the impression her sweaty arse had left on his car, she'd hurried them back into their clothes, and they'd run, hand in hand, to his bedroom. Thankfully Thane had left them a fruit and cheese platter, because they hadn't come up for air until sunrise this morning, when he'd had to leave her, sleeping and fragrant and rumpled, to meet with Elliott. After that, he'd come to the hospital.

Thank the universe he'd finished rounds before Tia had started dreaming, filling his head with dark, erotic images.

Focus had been impossible.

He paced his office like a caged lion. Since what had happened in the garage—since she'd nearly thralled him—their mental bond had grown immeasurably stronger. Since they'd admitted their love for each other, he felt...alive, like a creature of flesh and blood and testosterone, for the first time in over a century. But this feral possessiveness, this raw, urgent need, was damned inconvenient.

Where the hell are you? he asked her.

I'm right down the hall.

You said you'd call first. Not only had she not called, she'd somehow gotten past Aleta at the front desk.

I'm perfectly safe. No one followed me.

"Bloody hell." When he yanked his office door open, she was standing there. In her bright pink cigarette pants and black sleeveless blouse, carrying a sweater, that heavy purse, and wearing a wildly patterned scarf as a headband, she reminded him of a young Sophia Loren. Lust coiled, raw and inappropriate. He pulled her inside and closed the door. "You were supposed to call me." Her mind was an open book—she was relaxed, comfortable, happy to see him—but that didn't stop him from raking her up and down with his gaze. "Are you okay?"

"Perfectly fine. Sorry it took so long." Rising on tiptoes, she kissed him—a quick, artless kiss meant to reassure, not arouse—then stepped into his embrace. "Dr. Rothenberger was running late. Why are doctors' schedules always so backed up?"

He wrapped his arms around her, drawing in the scent of spring lilacs. "Sometimes a patient needs more time than we allocate." Her bruises were completely gone, her burns were healed, and the scar on her temple was healing well. The bump on the bridge of her nose was permanent, a reminder of how quickly something so precious could change forever.

"Having a doctor in the household has obviously spoiled me rotten."

"I live to serve," he said lightly, running a fingertip over her silver hoop earring. If he had anything to say about it, she'd stay spoiled for the rest of her days. "Did Rothenberger find anything?"

"Nope." Drawing back slightly, she threw the

sweater toward the couch. The purse followed, landing somewhere with a thunk. "I am, in her words, 'disgustingly healthy.'" Sliding her arms around his waist again, she pressed her lush frame against his. "I listed you as my primary care physician on the intake form," she said. "That means you'll get a copy of her report, right?"

Something inside him softened to putty. As the referring physician, he'd get a copy anyway, but… "You listed a hematologist as your primary?"

"I listed *you* as my primary. You just happen to be a hematologist."

It was…another declaration of love.

"Yes. It is," she whispered against his lips.

He glanced at the closed door, then back at her. "What you do to me," he muttered. "I'm all hormones and gonads."

Her gust of laughter jiggled into him. "Join the club."

Concern, laughter, edgy desire, love… yes, it swirled from her, into him, and back again. Swirled between them, a beguiling, sultry whirl he wanted to ride all the way down.

She captured his mouth in a silky kiss, then backed away, leaning against the door. Across the room, his desk phone rang again, but its soft, insistent chirp was drowned out by the scrape of metal against metal.

Tia had locked the office door.

"Wyland." Her voice, her glittering gaze, could lure ships to the bloody rocks.

"Yes?"

"Have you ever made love in this office? On that chair, or on that table?" Her whispered words slammed into him. "Or over there, on that uncomfortable-looking couch?"

"Of course not." And now, thanks to her, he'd never get the idea out of his mind.

"Or maybe right here? Up against this door?"

Forget the furniture; he'd never be able to reach for the bloody doorknob again without seeing her, leaning against the door, calling to him like a siren from the shore—

"Wyland? Are you in there?" The doorknob rattled. "Why is your door locked?"

"Bloody hell." If he didn't answer the door, Aleta would call Security. "One moment," he called, hustling Tia to the couch.

"Who's that?" she asked, taking a seat.

He straightened his crooked tie. "Our office manager."

"That formidable woman guarding the front desk? Faerie, right?"

"Yes." And whether due to her age or her personality, Aleta didn't kowtow to his title—a fact he usually appreciated, but tonight would no doubt regret. What would she think about finding him and Tia behind a locked door?

What would she think of Tia?

"Wyland? You might want to put on your suit coat."

He followed her gaze to the front of his pants. "Shit." Aleta had seen it all, but she didn't need to see...*that*. On his way to the door, he grabbed his suit coat from the clothes tree, then jammed his arms into the sleeves. After a quick glance down, he opened the door.

"Finally," Aleta said, exasperated. He was glad for the suit coat, because she gave him a careful look up and down as she walked into his office—some feat, being she barely cleared five feet tall. "I thought you were going to make me stand there all night long— Oh." She stopped short when she saw Tia sitting on the black leather couch, looking like an exotic hothouse bloom that had somehow been transplanted into their sterile midst. Her gaze flicked to floor, to Tia's sweater and purse, then back to him. "Please introduce us."

"Of course. This is my…" He reached for the right words, but came up empty. "This is Tia."

Tia rose from the couch, her green-nailed hand extended. "Tia Quinn. Nice to meet you."

Aleta didn't respond, but took Tia's hand in hers. Held it. Gazing at each other, the women took each other's measure using some form of alchemic feminine communion he didn't understand. "Nice to meet you, too," Aleta finally said. "Very nice indeed."

He released a breath he wasn't aware he'd been holding.

"But if you're quite through distracting the doctor—" Aleta handed him half a dozen slips of yellow paper "—he has some phone calls to return."

"I guess that's my cue to leave." Tia scooped her sweater and purse up from the floor, slung the purse strap over her shoulder, then gave him a sweet peck on the lips. "See you at home," she murmured. "Very nice to meet you, Aleta."

Aleta didn't respond. She seemed distracted, deep in thought.

"Aleta?"

"Oh, sorry." She turned toward Tia. "Ms. Quinn, it's been a pleasure."

No comment at all about the 'see you at home'

comment Tia had just made? "Aleta, what's wrong?"

Aleta hesitated, then said, "Check the most recent message first, if you would. Mila Stanton left you a very odd voice mail."

He looked down at the slip of paper on top of the pile. "She called from her office?"

"Just a few minutes ago," Aleta confirmed. "I missed picking up the call, but I listened to the voice mail. Very strange."

He hurried to his desk phone, hit the speaker button, and retrieved Mila's voice email. Mila said his name, in a very weak voice, then...nothing. The silence was haunting.

"Are you sure she didn't call you by mistake? Forget to hang up?" Tia asked.

He and Aleta exchanged a worried glance. "Not likely." But he dialed Mila's desk number anyway, hoping he was wrong. The call rolled to voice mail. "I'm going to go check on her." As he headed for the door, he patted his suit coat pocket to make sure he had his employee badge. He'd need it to get through the security door.

Tia was right behind him as he strode down the hall into the empty reception area. "Mila's a patient?"

"Yes." He punched the elevator button.

"Can I help?"

He hesitated. The last time Mila fainted at work, she'd sliced her scalp open going down. It never hurt to have a second pair of hands, but he didn't need a second patient. "How are you around cuts? Blood?"

"Don't come at me with a needle and I'll be fine."

And even when he *had* come at her with a needle, he'd had to thrall her to put her down. Yes, she'd be fine.

The elevator doors finally swept open. As they stepped on, she took his hand. Her grasp was warm and reassuring, her thoughts an oasis of calm.

Good. If Mila had fainted again, there was no telling what they'd find.

CHAPTER TWENTY-FOUR

Jamming his hands in his pockets, Dom hurried away from his father's hospital room. He stalked down the hallway, huffing air laden with too many man-made chemicals. The switchblade was a worthless weight, mocking him.

He...hadn't been able to do it.

He'd tried, he really had. He'd let his dad see the weapon, see his intent. Hope had lit his father's face—hope that had withered and died when he hadn't been able to follow through.

"You're no son of mine."

The whispered words sliced, deeper than any knife. His loyalty, a wishbone yanked between the two men, had finally cracked, leaving the Alpha holding the larger piece. When push had come to shove, he'd obeyed the Alpha rather than his father.

He'd chosen self-preservation over principle.

The hallway blurred, and his jaw and fingernails gave a warning throb. If only he could shift. Escape. Lose himself, for days, in a full-out run. Howl at the moon. But...now wasn't the time, and downtown wasn't the place.

Shove it back, shove it down. He took a stingy sip of breath. *Concentrate.* Shifting here would be too stupid for words. No one inside the hospital would be surprised, but once he went outside? Too many people, too many cars...

Just step off the curb.

It would be so damn easy...

No. Damn it, the Alpha was right: New days meant new ways. Their culture had to change, had to evolve, in order to survive. It would serve no useful purpose for Dom to go to prison for...for...ending his father's suffering.

He suffers.

A ragged sob escaped. Why the hell wouldn't Dad listen to reason? He still had eyes, still had a voice. Still had normal brain function, something half the patients on this floor would kill for.

Kill for. How fucking ironic.

When he'd yelled at his dad that he could still be useful, could still work—they could work *together*—his father had rejected the idea out of hand. Rejected *him* out of hand.

If Dad could move *his* hands, Dom could leave the blade in his hospital room and let Dad take care of things himself.

But he hadn't. Because Dad couldn't.

The fist at his throat tightened, squeezing tears from his eyes. Ducking into an empty family room, he made a beeline for the one chair the moonlight didn't reach. Finally safe in the dark, he let weeks of misery boil over. He sat in the silent shadows and cried, waiting out his wolf, ignoring the angry red stare of the coffee maker's perpetually-lit ON button. Once the tears dried up, he watched the colorful fish, swimming lazily in their aquarium.

What was he going to tell his mom? That Dad was suicidal? That he and Dad had fought? Both were old news. That he was the Alpha's bitch? "Yeah, that's new," he muttered.

So was the fact that Dad had told him to never come back.

Picking up his cell, he glanced at the screen. Mila had called, and left voice mail. "At least one thing's going right." But as he listened to the message, his stomach fell to the floor.

Hearing "we need to talk' from any woman's mouth rarely boded well.

"Damn."

Did it really matter who broke up with whom, as long as the deed was done? Ever since discovering Mila's sister had had Down's Syndrome, he'd known they couldn't last. And on the positive side, Mila sounded mad enough to do the dirty work for him.

Exhaling, he reached for his backbone. He hadn't been able to put his father out of his misery, but he *could* fulfill his responsibility to his bloodline. He and Mila couldn't afford a birth control mistake, and the longer they slept together, the higher the risk became.

Might as well get this over with.

Pushing wearily to his feet, he trudged from the family room. Once he reached IT, luck was with him: a dude with a badge had just walked through the security door without a backwards glance. Dom put on a burst of speed and caught the door before it closed. After a slight hesitation, he slipped inside, and headed down the hall. Bright fluorescent lights burned overhead, but thankfully the place was empty. Privacy was a good thing. Did Mila yell when she got upset? Did she cry?

Her door was slightly ajar, with lights on inside. *Working, of course.* He took a deep breath, and let it out again. "Mila?" When he tapped on the wood with his knuckle, the door swung open.

Mila was on the floor, crawling shakily toward her desk chair.

Shit. "Are you hurt?" There was no blood, nothing looked broken... Her face was white as snow, but she seemed more disgusted than anything else. "Mila, are you hurt?"

"Not this time."

"Huh?"

"I got light-headed," she said, reaching for the chair.

He slipped his hands under her armpits, lifted, and set her on the chair. "What do you need?"

She reached for a half-empty glass of blood sitting on her desk, drinking deeply, thirstily. When she lowered the glass, she looked wobbly as a newborn fawn, but her eyes glinted with anger.

He moved out of range, leaning against the wall next to the print he'd hung. There was an awkward silence. "Your message said we needed to talk?"

Some version of "it's not you, it's me" shouldn't take very long.

"I had an unexpected visitor today."

Damn it, he wasn't in the mood for chit-chat. *Just get on with it. Break up with me, and let me leave. Let me leave, before I—*

"Jack Kirkland was here."

"Kirkland?" He'd met the Security and Technology Second for the first time at Mila's parents' party. Nice enough guy, but Dom's self-esteem had withered just shaking the man's hand. An ugly jealousy rose, jealousy he had no right to feel. His fingernails started to tingle. "Why was *he* here?"

"I wondered the very same thing." There was no mistaking the sarcasm. "With everything else he has going on, why would the Underworld Council's Security and Technology Second ask *me* questions about Memorial Hospital's patient data management procedures?" A tiny fang flashed. "About how I do my fucking job?"

He shifted uneasily, shoving his hands in his pockets. "Did he say?"

"Of course not, but it didn't take long to figure out he was investigating a data breach."

His stomach clutched. "Um…wow." This…wasn't good.

"Yeah." She looked him dead in the eye. "Wow."

Yeah, she knew.

"He took a metric buttload of documentation with him, as well as paper samples and an example of my handwriting. He also asked a lot of questions about how we managed outgoing mail." A baffled expression crossed her face. "I have no clue what *that* was about."

I do. Sweat popped all over his body, and foreboding descended like a hangman's noose. The letters. Somehow, Kirkland had connected Mila—or Mila's workplace—to the letter he'd sent Bailey Brown.

"I can tell from your expression that you know something."

Shit, this whole thing was spiraling out of control. "Mila, I never meant—"

"Mila?" Wyland hurried into the office, followed by Tia Quinn. "Are you okay?"

Tia Fucking Quinn.

"Oh." Tia stopped short, smiling. "Hi, Dominic. I

didn't see you back there."

If only she'd done her job. If only she'd listened to him.

This was all her fault.

Wyland ignored him, focusing on Mila. "You called me? Do you feel faint?"

Mila called the Vampire Second because she didn't feel well? Talk about privilege. He was surrounded by privilege, but there'd be none for him. If Kirkland had him in his crosshairs, Dom had no expectation that the Alpha would swoop in and save him.

Blood rushed to his face, pounded at his temples, as the noose slowly tightened. His nose and mouth pulsed, and his vision bled red around the edges. The switchblade was suddenly in his hand, warm from his body heat. With a flick of his thumb, the blade silently snicked into place.

"Did you have fun at Lyudmila and Stanton's party?" Tia asked, approaching him.

"Yes." If only she'd done as he'd asked. If only she hadn't ignored his messages. If only she'd done her job, he wouldn't have to…

He grabbed her, whirled her around in front of his body, and whipped the blade up against her neck.

If he was going down, he was damn well taking her with him.

＊

"Red brindle fur," Tia gasped as Dominic dragged her toward the door. His hair was a visual match for the hair Chico had found in the garage at the

Archives.

The blade bit in. "Quiet," Dom ordered, closing the door.

"Just calm down," Wyland said. *Are you okay?*

Her neck stung, and wetness dripped down her neck. *You tell me.*

Shallow cut. Hang on.

"Dom, what in the world are you doing?" Mila asked.

His hand jerked. Tia winced and rose to her toes as the blade dug in again. "I said be quiet," Dominic snapped. "Everybody be quiet. Let me think."

Too late for that. Though she was bleeding like a stuck pig, she felt oddly calm and steady. Standing across the room in his suit and tie, Wyland radiated control, but his fangs were exposed. His blue eyes burned with unleashed power.

No way was Dominic getting away with this.

No sudden moves.

Roger that.

"Let's all calm down," Wyland said. "What's going on here?"

"Jack Kirkland was here earlier, investigating a data breach," Mila explained, rising from her chair. "I think the breach is my fault. Dom was visiting me here in my office and I think he saw Bailey Brown's hospital records, revealing that she has succubus heritage—but I don't know what in the world he did with the information."

"He sent her a letter saying she had to die," Wyland said.

Bailey has succubus blood?

Yes.

Mila stared. "Dom, what have you done?"

Mila apparently didn't know the worst of it—that Dom had also threatened Coco Fontaine, the child of two sitting Council members, while she was still in the womb.

Dominic yanked her back against his body. "Everyone, shut up." The blade skimmed her skin, but the pressure eased almost immediately. He yanked again, his breath gusting hot against her ear, but this time she didn't feel the kiss of the blade.

Stand perfectly still…

Wyland was thralling Dom. Thralling him, and holding a conversation with her at the same time.

Something's…very wrong with this boy.

This is no time for faerie empathy. This 'boy' is a full-grown man, and he's holding a switchblade to your neck. "Bailey's succubus heritage is closely guarded information," Wyland said aloud. "Very few people know. Once Bailey ruled those people out as sources of the leak, she immediately suspected a data breach at the hospital." He studied Dom, looking every bit the Vampire Second. "This information has no possible value to you. How much did Krispin Woolf pay you to—"

"He didn't," Dom blurted. "It was all my idea."

"To use me?" Mila snapped.

"To stalk me?" Tia lifted a brow. "To leave snakes in my bedroom?"

He jerked.

Bullseye.

"What?" Mila looked at Tia, aghast. "Dom, have you've lost your bloody mind?"

"Mixed blood pollutes our bloodlines." Dom's arm tightened into a hard band. "Pure blood ensures our survival."

It was classic batshit GPL, right from their manifesto.

"Look at the makeup of the Council," Dom continued. The tip of the blade skated under her chin, and she hissed in a breath.

A surge of rage from Wyland, quickly throttled. *Stay as still as you can...*

"The Sebastianis, the Fontaines, the Schlessingers? You and Valerian? All purebreds. It's no secret that in our culture, power—real power, physical and political power—runs along purebred lines."

"Dom, do you actually believe what you're saying?" Mila asked, aghast. "Or are you just repeating what you've heard your father or other GPL members say since you were a child?" She paused, making a visible effort to calm herself. "Dominic, you're an educated man. Think. Think for yourself."

"Shut up!" His voice and hand wobbled as he turned toward Wyland. "You—stay right there."

The knife tip gouged under her chin, lifting her onto her toes. "Aah!" Behind her, Dominic sucked in a ragged, sobbing breath.

"Dom," Mila said quietly, "there's no reason to hurt anyone."

Dominic was so upset right now, he probably wouldn't recognize reason if it smacked him upside the head. His emotions were roiling like a springtime river, a vicious inner conflict banging him against the rocks and tearing him to pieces. How long until he realized he had very little to lose no matter what he did? "Dominic." With the weight of her head balanced on the tip of the knife, every syllable stung, but she drenched her voice with empathy. "I know how it feels to be torn between two cultures, two schools of thought."

"Faerie! Faerie witch!" Dom pulled the knife away and slapped his hand against his temple. "Get of my head!"

"I'm not in your head," she reassured him. But Wyland was. She had to distract him. "I'm just saying, I know how you feel, Dominic. You're not alone."

Careful, Wyland cautioned.

"As a member of the press, you have a responsibility to ordinary citizens, not to the Council." Dominic's voice sing-songed, as if his words were a mantra he'd repeated to himself over and over again. "I sent you tip after tip. You ignored my comments. Modded them so others couldn't see. You made them invisible." His voice wobbled. "Made *me* invisible. You didn't listen."

"Dominic…" How could she explain this without setting him off? "In our culture, freedom of the press has some…constraints. Once I investigated the Council's 'misdeeds,' what was I supposed to do, publish them on a freaking website for all of humanity to see? Break our most important law?" Silence as he digested her words. "Dominic, which misdeeds are you talking about?"

Careful, he's starting to disassociate…

"The Alpha won't let me put my father out of his misery, as honor dictates," he whispered. "He said it was too risky, would draw too much attention."

The Old Ways. She was no fan of Krispin Woolf, but in this case the Alpha had made the right goddamn call. But…this poor young man. Torn between two cultures. Two men. Two times.

How many other similarly damaged souls walked invisibly among them?

"Would you have killed me?" Mila suddenly asked.

"What?" When Dom jerked, her purse bumped against her hip.

The purse.

"What do you mean?" Dom asked. "Why would I…"

"If this relationship had become something long-term, would you, at some point, have put me out of my misery, like you want to do for your father?"

The arm holding her around the shoulders tightened. Dom's breath hitched. "You…you don't have Down's Syndrome."

Tia surreptitiously slipped her hand into her purse, feeling about, subtly searching for… There, down at the bottom. Moving carefully, she gripped the smooth, hard plastic.

Careful… Wyland urged.

"Dom, you just found me collapsed on the floor. I have Wyland, the foremost hematologist on the planet, on speed-dial. Connect the damn dots."

"You're sick?"

"Yes."

Dom recoiled. Gulped. "Mila, I—"

Jerking her hand from her purse, Tia jammed the stun gun against Dominic's thigh.

Bzzzzzzzzzzzzzzt.

He spasmed, convulsed, and dropped like a stone, but he dragged her down with him. Pain exploded when they hit the ground, when the knife gouged in, but she rolled, rolled away…and suddenly Wyland was in the mix, twisting Dom's knife hand. When the switchblade fell, he kicked it out of range, sending it skittering under Mila's desk. The knife was still moving when Wyland's fist lashed out with a cartilage-cracking punch that knocked Dom out cold.

Wyland kicked the stun gun out of Dominic's reach, then speed-crawled to where she lay on the carpet. "Call Security, then the ER," he ordered Mila. "Tell them we need three gurneys."

Tia struggled to a sitting position, leaning back against the wall. "Not for me," she gasped. "I'm going to walk out of here under my own goddamn steam."

His fingers were at her wrist, taking her pulse. "Do you feel faint? Weak?"

"No. My ear really hurts, and I...can't stop shaking."

"Just stay here for a moment. Let me check you out." His eyes and hands roved her body. "Any cuts I can't see?"

"No, just my neck and ear. The ear hurts more." Her T-shirt looked like a blood-soaked sponge. "How bad is it?" she asked. Wyland had his thoughts locked down tight.

"Superficial lacerations on your neck, but I'm afraid you're going to need a few stitches in that earlobe."

She reached for it. "It's still attached?"

"Don't touch it." He grasped her wrist. "No need to risk infection."

"It...burns."

"I think the tip of his blade caught your earring when you fell."

"He ripped my ear piercing? Seriously?" She glanced over toward Dom, who was still out cold. Sure enough, her sterling silver hoop lay next to his elbow, all bent all to hell. "Bastard."

His lips flattened to a white line. "It could have

been worse. You could have been killed."

"Nah." She smiled at him. "I could feel you thralling him. Between that and the stun gun, I was pretty sure we had him."

"Indeed."

The smile died when she noticed his right ring finger had a noticeable crook. "Your finger's broken."

He examined his own hand, palpating the area around the break. "Transverse fracture at the neck of the fourth metacarpal," he concluded. "A quick set and splint should do it."

It had to hurt like the dickens. "The ER's going to be busy tonight." So would the hospital's security team. It wasn't every day someone pulled a switchblade in the same room as an Underworld Council member. The hospital's security chief was going to have a very long night.

Over at her desk, Mila hung up the phone. "Security's on the way." She made her way over to Dom. She looked down at him, hands on hips. Then she pulled back her foot and kicked him in the balls.

Dom groaned, clutched his groin, and curled into a self-protective ball.

Wyland sprang to his feet.

Mila pulled back her foot to kick him again, but she tripped and stumbled. Wyland caught her, and led her back to her desk chair. "Bastard." Tears started to fall.

"Where are you hurt?" he asked.

"I'm not," she sniffed, pushing him away.

Oh, she was hurt, all right—but neither of them could help heal the kick Mila had just taken to the heart.

Wyland hesitated at the side of the desk. *How can I*

help her?

Just give her a tissue.

He did, murmuring words of comfort and patting Mila's shoulder so awkwardly that she fell in love with him all over again. After several minutes, Mila sat up straight, blew her nose, and gave a decisive nod.

"Steady?" Wyland asked.

Mila glanced at Dominic, still curled up like a shrimp on the floor, then looked away with a sniff that had nothing to do with tears. "I'll be fine."

Take her at her word, she advised, pushing slowly to her feet.

"I'd rather you stay seated."

She pointed to the visitor's chair across the desk from Mila. "How about there?"

After a slight hesitation, he agreed. Once seated, she helped keep an eye on Dominic, who lay on the floor, still cupping his balls.

Wyland strode to Mila's office door, peered down the hallway, then looked back at Dominic. "Where the hell is Security?"

"Calm down," she soothed. "He's not going anywhere." Dominic seemed too quiet, too quiescent—or maybe he was just scared to death of Mila's pointy-toed shoe, which had proven to be the most effective weapon in the room. "Poor kid. Between the GPL crap, his father's accident, and Krispin Woolf, he's really messed up."

"Let the jailhouse psychologists figure it out." With little regard for his broken finger, he reached into his jacket pocket for his phone. "I'm calling Gideon." He swept a gaze over her ear, neck and shirt. "You're pressing charges, right?"

She hesitated.

"Tia."

"Yes." Whatever was wrong with Dominic, assault with a deadly weapon wasn't the way to fix it.

"Everyone, hands where I can see them."

Commander Gideon Lupinsky stood at the door, his flat cop gaze taking in the details of the room: Her, bloody from the ears down. Dominic, lying on the floor clutching his balls. The stun gun, lying next to the bookshelf. His gaze went back to her neck. "Where's the blade?"

Wyland set his phone down, then held his hands clear. "I kicked it under the desk."

Lupinsky quickly patted everyone down, indicating that one of the uniforms should do the same with Dominic. He asked another officer to recover the knife. "Took care of this situation all by yourself, did you?" he said to Wyland, gesturing to his broken hand.

"By no means."

"The stun gun's mine," she blurted. "It's perfectly legal to use in self-defense."

Lupinsky lifted a brow. "We're clear here," he called to the security team.

"Clear," said the officer crouching beside Dominic.

"Ms. Quinn, why don't you take a seat and tell me how you got those wounds?"

"Gideon, can't the questions wait?" Wyland asked. "She needs medical treatment."

Lupinsky's gaze pinned her in place. "Ms. Quinn, who cut you?"

"Him." She pointed at Dominic, still lying on the floor. "Dominic Reese."

Lupinsky gestured to the uniform, who rolled

Dominic onto his stomach and cuffed him. "Do you know why he pulled the knife?"

She glanced at the security guards, then lowered her voice. "I'll need to make my statement in a confidential venue."

Lupinsky's gaze sharpened. "Certainly."

"Medical treatment first," Wyland said, scooping her into his arms.

"Hey, I can walk."

"I know, but humor me." He carried her from Mila's office to the hallway, where three white-sheeted gurneys waited. "Let's get you downstairs."

Where she'd have to get her ear stitched up.

Needles.

A shiver wracked her frame. "Will you…" *Thrall me? Take me away, take me out of my head when I start freaking out?*

"Whatever you need."

When he wrapped his arms around her, she burrowed into his embrace, allowing the strong thump of his heart to steady her. "Ah, crap." She pulled away, ignoring the curious glances. "I'm getting blood all over your shirt."

"Don't worry about it. We'll go downstairs, get fixed up, and then go home."

She eyed his crooked finger. He needed treatment, too. "Home sounds great." Exhaustion overwhelmed her, and suddenly she was glad for the gurney. As she lay back, she heard Wyland issuing orders for Mila and Dominic, and then their little caravan was on the move. The gurney's bum wheel rattled as the orderly pushed it down the hall, but Wyland walked by her side, holding her hand.

When they paused by the elevator, her teeth

started chattering.

Wyland stroked her hair. "Just relax…"

"Damn it," she muttered. "Cut by a man holding a switchblade to my throat, but the thought of a tiny needle gives me the vapors."

"Relax…" *Sleep now…*

His voice was a featherbed—soft and safe, promising the sweetest of dreams. Closing her eyes, she snuggled into the gurney's hard mattress. The elevator chimed, and then she knew nothing.

CHAPTER TWENTY-FIVE

Several days later, sitting in Sebastiani Security's corner conference room with Lukas, Jack, Bailey, Chico, and Gideon Lupinsky, Wyland tried to focus on Gideon's report, but he wasn't having much luck. His thoughts kept drifting back to Tia's cheery wave, and to the soft, clinging kiss she'd given him as they'd parted ways in the garage earlier that evening. She'd asked if she could take one of the SUVs to Stillwater, but she hadn't mentioned why she needed to go, or how long she'd be gone.

Dread sludged through his system. Was she moving back home?

He shifted in the chair once again. The damned thing felt like it had sprouted tacks.

"Something to add, Wyland?" Gideon inquired.

"No. Please continue." Now that Dominic Reese was in custody, how could he keep Tia from moving back to Stillwater? How could he keep her, period? Bloody hell, her independence—one of the traits he'd come to most appreciate—was about to circle around and bite him on the ass.

Gideon flipped to the next page of his report. In the last hour, the Commander had covered the high points of the case, going over Tia's interview transcript, Mila's, and his own. With each moment that passed, his role in this meeting became more complex. Doctor, lawyer, eyewitness, yes—but victim? No. His fractured finger was a self-inflicted injury. Regardless of what their law might say, Dominic pulling a weapon in a Council member's presence shouldn't carry a heavier penalty than actually *using* the weapon on Tia. *She* was the one who'd been assaulted, whose throat looked like a crazy quilt.

She was the victim here.

"After being examined at the ER, Mr. Reese was transported to Central Holding, where he was processed and once again read his rights," Gideon said. "He declined legal representation. I was about fifteen minutes into our interview when a lawyer showed up and asked to speak privately with her client."

"Isn't that convenient," Lukas muttered.

And it's the law. "Who's representing him?"

"Penelope Winton Miller."

"Krispin Woolf's personal lawyer?" Jack's eyebrow climbed. "That's overkill for a case like this."

"Not if the Alpha thought Dominic might be charged with assaulting a Council member," Wyland said. Perry Reese had worked for Krispin Woolf for years. Maybe Woolf was stepping in because Dominic's father couldn't. He said as much, adding that while they'd been in Mila's office, Dominic had said that the Alpha had rejected Dominic's plea that he be allowed to end his father's life. "Apparently Woolf told him using The Old Ways would be too visible, too risky."

Bailey looked horrified. "Does that mean that if Perry Reese wasn't so high-profile, Woolf would have signed off on the idea?"

"I don't think so." Chico levered himself away from the brick wall, then dropped into the open chair next to Jack. "Say what you will about the Alpha's business practices, but I think he finally realizes times are changing."

Gideon snorted. "More likely he realizes *forensics* is changing."

"That, too," Chico acknowledged. "But I have to tell you that, among the wolves, Lorin Schlessinger bonding with your brother—one of those quote/unquote 'damaged Lupinskys'—was a game-changer." He cast a sheepish glance at Gideon. "No offense meant."

"None taken."

His response made sense. Of all his immediate family, only Gideon was healthy.

Or...was he?

Gideon had literally been the first responder the night Tia was assaulted, arriving at the same time as the hospital security team.

Gideon had already been in the building.

Why?

"During our interview, Mr. Reese seemed fixated on the issue of pure bloodlines, genetic purity, and how the Underworld Council had devolved into...what was the phrase he used?" Gideon swiped at his tablet. "Ah, here it is. A 'nest of nepotism.' One minute he was spouting the old-school GPL line, next he was apologizing to the Alpha, and then he was railing about Ms. Quinn. Before the lawyer arrived, Mr. Reese admitted he'd been following Ms. Quinn for months, since before she moved to Stillwater. He also admitted to breaking into her home, and leaving the garter snakes in her bedroom."

Wyland barely quelled a full-body shudder.

"Well, whether the violence against a Council member charges stick or not—" Gideon gave him a careful glance "—assault with a deadly, with multiple witnesses? No way he'll walk."

Not if he had anything to say about it—and thankfully, Mila was cooperating with the prosecution.

"He probably thought the snakes would give Tia a damn good scare, but why do that? To what end?" Lukas asked. "I don't get it."

"I don't, either." Gideon set his tablet on the table. "The only thing he accomplished with that stunt was to give Ms. Quinn reason to move to the most heavily guarded private home between the Twin Cities and the Wisconsin border."

"Which might have caused him to escalate." Wyland looked down at his splinted finger. "Going from scaring someone with garter snakes to cutting them with a switchblade is a significant leap."

"No shit," Chico muttered. "And why contact Tia in the first place? Did he really think she'd help him bring down the Council? Expose our existence to humanity? The dude is delusional."

Did the delusion go beyond Dominic? How much indoctrination, or radicalization, might the Genetic Purity League be responsible for inflicting upon its members? The Council must find out.

"Reese will be psychologically assessed before I can question him again—" Gideon's phone blipped. "Hang on a second. Might be the lab." As Gideon read, a satisfied smile grew. He glanced at Jack. "Looks like your hunch was right."

"What hunch?" Wyland asked.

"Mila Stanton was running a test during our interview," Jack explained. "When the test finished, I caught a momentary glimpse of unencrypted patient data, which she quickly blocked from view. I figured if I could see the data, other visitors might, too." Jack tapped his pen against the table. "Given how frequently Dominic visited Mila at work, it made me wonder whether he might have seen Bailey's data, then sent her a letter."

And what of Mila Stanton? Her punishment was his to decide—her work lapse had a confidential Council impact—but nothing he'd considered could possibly be as effective as the punishment she'd already inflicted upon herself.

Maybe Mila would be willing to provide some helpful information about the GPL. Yes, he'd give her a chance to help.

"We have confirmation that Perry Reese's home office printer was the one used to produce the threatening letters," Gideon said, setting down his phone. "We're still combing through the computers, and have yet to interview other family members about their use of the office."

"That poor family," Chico murmured.

"We'll also test the switchblade against the nick pattern you discovered on the door at the Archives," Gideon said. "All in all, I think we have our man."

Thank the universe.

"How is Tia doing?" Lukas asked him.

What was Tia doing? "She's healing well. She's already back at work." She'd bounced back quickly, having slept through the short procedure to repair her lacerated earlobe. The plastic surgeon he'd called in hadn't been pleased about Wyland's *very* close supervision.

"And Mila Stanton?"

"Fine." After examining her at the ER, Mila's mulish expression told him not to bother with his usual lecture about telling her parents about her health problems. This time, he'd listened. Mila's comments to Dominic about her little sister Katarina had burrowed into his brain, a tiny sliver he couldn't quite dislodge. As Tia would say, something felt...off.

Lukas gestured to his hand. "And how are you?"

"Fine." The splint didn't hinder his work, and he was burying himself in it. After all, if he and Tia didn't have a spare minute to talk, she couldn't tell him she was leaving.

Leaving *him*.

What the hell was she doing in Stillwater?

Lukas turned towards Gideon. "What do you need from Sebastiani Security? As always, our resources are at your disposal."

Wyland's phone vibrated. Fumbling it from his jacket pocket, he quickly read: *I'm back home. Meet me at the Archives?*

She was back. Back *home*.

Bailey leaned over. "No sexting during meetings."

"Why not? It's most invigorating."

She blinked.

Pocketing the phone, he started packing his briefcase. "Does anyone need anything more from me?" When he pushed his chair back from the table, no one looked surprised. All those times he'd left meetings to respond to emergency calls were paying off.

"Hope it's nothing serious," Lukas said.

"Quite serious, actually." His urge to see Tia was as serious as a heart attack.

"This patient requires his personal touch," Bailey said blandly.

"Indeed."

Lukas's gaze ping-ponged between them. It was time to leave.

"Hey," Bailey whispered. She caught his uninjured hand and gave it a reassuring squeeze. "Go get her."

He kissed her cheek as he rose. "I'll do my best."

As he walked toward the lobby, the idea burst from his subconscious like a submarine surfacing at sea. He knew exactly what he had to do.

What was that phrase Chico always used before a difficult job? 'Go big or go home?' He had to go big or go home. Take the home run swing.

Nothing less would do.

✻

Yet another mechanical hum behind her.

Tia stopped typing, swung away from the computer screen, and shot the shifting shelving unit a death glare. What the hell was Wyland doing back there, playing Tetris with the furniture?

What was his deal?

Yes, when he arrived, he'd kissed her hello—a very *nice* kiss hello—but as soon as he laid it on her, he'd disappeared into the stacks, processing the latest batch of books and manuscripts as if the centuries-old paper would burst into flame if he moved too quickly. He seemed withdrawn, remote, and his thoughts were on lockdown.

She nibbled on her thumbnail. Had something happened at work? Was there a problem with a patient? Should she ask him what was going on? If something *was* going on, could he even tell her?

Exasperated, she turned back to the screen, where Sigurd's biography glowed. If this was an indication of what living with the Vampire Second would be like—him, all mentally constipated, and her, trying to figure out whether it was okay to ask a freaking question? She'd tap out. It was no way to live.

Maybe moving her home office to Vamp Central had been a *wee* bit premature.

She glanced at her now-ragged nail, then plucked a flake of purple polish off her tongue. "And now he's ruining my damn manicure." She settled back to work, her fingers clacking against the keys a little more loudly than was strictly necessary.

"Tia?" Wyland walked toward her, down the center aisle, looking nervous but determined. He'd shed his suit coat, loosened his beautiful tie, and popped the top two buttons of his dress shirt. The sleeves were rolled up, exposing his muscular forearms and that gorgeous vintage watch.

A wave of sensual craving rippled through her. "Are you ready to go?"

"Not quite yet." Clearing his throat, he looked at the screen where she was working. "Working on Sigurd's bio?"

She nodded, gesturing to the open instant messaging window. "With Bailey's help, I just finished formatting the document. It's almost ready to upload to the Archives."

"Good." His Adam's apple bobbed. "I need to

update my bio."

"Tonight?" *Seriously?* "Can't it wait?"

"Just a quick update."

"Whatever." While he made his precious update, she could send Thane a text message, telling him it might be best if he put his plans to transform the second floor guest bedroom into her office on hold.

Rather than sitting down at the other workstation, Wyland reached over her shoulder for her computer mouse. She couldn't move, couldn't reach for her phone, without bumping into him. His subtle ocean scent permeated the space, scrambling her thoughts. Though the splint hindered his movements somewhat, he pulled up his own bio, and went into edit mode.

Her eyes widened as the mouse hovered over "Relationship Status." Suddenly, his mental drawbridges dropped, leaving him wide open.

Such fierce, unruly emotions, all of them for her.

"Tia Tèodora Quinn..." She heard him swallow. "Would you do me the honor of being my bondmate?"

Her eyes widened to saucers. "Oh my." She hadn't expected...this.

"I know it's fast," he blurted. "I know I'm no prize. Your life will have constraints you can't possibly imagine, political ramifications you don't yet understand—"

"Shh."

"Tia—"

"You asked me a question. Give me a chance to respond." Thankfully his left hand rested on her shoulder, because without it, she'd probably float out of her seat. Taking control of the mouse, she selected

'Bonded' from the drop-down menu, typed her own name in the 'To Whom' field, and saved the change with a surprisingly steady hand.

When he wrapped his arms around her from behind, she cuddled into his scent, his heat. "I love you so much," he murmured.

Hearing him say the words aloud was sublime. "I love you, too."

Relief flooded from him, along with a giddy happiness that twined with her own. He moved in to kiss her, but she held up her hand. "Hold on a sec." Retrieving her own bio, she changed her relationship status from 'Single' to 'Bonded,' then typed his name with a flourish. "There," she whispered. "It's official."

They were bondmates.

And then his lips were on hers, sealing the deal with a kiss that told her…everything. He loved her. Wanted her. Needed her, desperately and always.

ping

His fingers plunged through her hair, pulling their mouths more tightly together.

ping

She reached for his ponytail holder and yanked. When his hair spilled loose, she buried her face in it, inhaling as if the scent was essential to life. "We're not going to make it home," she panted.

"Fine with me."

ping

ping

ping

Wyland lifted his head with a scowl.

"Instant messages." She glanced over to the screen, where images of celebration—confetti, champagne bottles, fireworks, kazoos—filled the small instant message box. "Bailey must have noticed the status change." She grinned up at Wyland. "How many other IM chats do you think she just started?"

"Who'd be online at this time of night?"

ping

[ASebastiani:] Dudes! Congratulations! So happy for you.

ping

[SFontaine:] OMG seriously? Congratulations!

ping

[CPerez:] <high five>

She logged off without responding.

"You're ruthless. I like that in a woman." Wyland took her by the hand, nibbling her knuckles. "How about we celebrate at home?"

She grabbed her purse. "Great idea." Because that wisp of an English accent was melting her panties, and she wanted them...off. "So, about the guest bedroom..."

He turned off the overhead lights, plunging the room into darkness. "You'll never sleep there again."

No one would, but tomorrow was soon enough to

tell him.

His fangs flashed. "Tonight, you're all mine."

"Same goes," she murmured, flashing her own. She'd just drawn him into a wet, teasing kiss when Axl Rose wailed from inside her purse.

"Turn that damn thing off."

As she set her phone to Vibrate, Wyland's phone chirped. "Looks like the word's getting around," she said with a sigh.

Wyland glanced at his phone. "Elliott offers us his congratulations." When it chirped again, he flicked a button and put the device back in its holder without looking. "Let's get out of here."

"Let's." As they started up the stairs, she ignored the vibrations coming from inside her purse, snuggling closer to Wyland. Tomorrow would be was soon enough to respond, and tell others their news.

Because tonight, and always, were theirs.

ABOUT THE AUTHOR

Tamara Hogan is the award-winning author of The Underbelly Chronicles paranormal romance series. An English major by education and a technologist by trade, she recently stopped telecommuting to Silicon Valley to teach, edit, and write full-time. Tamara loathes cold and snow, but nonetheless lives near Minneapolis with her husband and two naughty cats.